Amelia's Story

C.P. Murphy

Everett Moore Books

ISBN: 978-1482762686
PUBLISHED BY EVERETT MOORE BOOKS
Printed and bound in the United States of America

Dedication

This book is dedicated to Sally, whose fate is still unsolved, my father, James Everett Poole Sr., who taught me who Sally was, and for all the cold case victims whose cases had been forgotten in time.

Does youth, does beauty read this line?
Do sympathetic tears breast their alarm?
Speak, Heavenly Spirit! breathe a strain
devine,
E'en from the grave thou shalt have power to
charm;
Tell them that tho' it is an awful thing to die,
' Twas e'en in thee,- yet the dread path once
trod,
Heaven lifts its everlasting portals high,
And bids the pure in heart behold their God."
Sally Hamilton August 25 A.D., 1813, in the
20th year of her age.
(Written on the tombstone of Sally Hamilton)

Part One
Chapter One

Summer, 1813

Dust flew up and dirtied the bottom of Amelia Samuels' dress as she made her way through the village of Millersport, New York. Her aching feet couldn't get her home fast enough. If she hadn't frolicked the day away with her friend, Emma, she'd have plenty of time to prepare the evening meal. Judging from the descending sun; she knew it must have been after 4 o'clock. As luck would have her, the sign on her father's apothecary store read, *'open for business.'* Amelia lowed her pace.

"Good afternoon, Amelia," a villager greeted her as she passed.

She nodded her head and smiled at the gentleman in return. Millersport was a pleasant community. She couldn't help but think about it as she passed the constable's station. She saw him through the opened door; his crossed legs upon the desk and his hat lowered over his face. Amelia laughed and wondered why the village, a safe place to raise a family, had a law enforcer.

A breeze came along as she neared the river. Amelia raised her arm and sheltered her face from the blowing dirt until the moving air stopped. Though the breeze brought the Earth to her, she was thankful because it was a relief from the steaming sun. As she walked along the street closest to the Hudson, a sudden quietness happened around her and a chill went up her spine. She felt a cold hand grab her arm. Amelia turned her head and hissed at the man. "Thomas Van Martin, what do you want?"

Standing in front of Amelia with his hands in his pockets, Thomas grinned. She was the only girl he ever wanted, but she rejected his every offer. "Be kind, Amelia.

1

We have to spend more time with each other," he told her, while he blocked her from advancing passed him.

"No thank you," she replied. He was the last person she would ever spend time with. The Van Martins' were the wealthiest family in Millersport. Thomas was the most highfalutin of them all, rubbing his fortune in everyone's face. He nauseated Amelia. She was just the opposite of him and didn't mind working hard for the material things she possessed. There was no reason good enough to make her agree to spend time with him.

Thomas' grin grew to laughter. She was the object of his affection and he would stop at nothing to have her. His parents, Daniel and Catherine, gave Thomas everything wanted. They couldn't buy Amelia and that made things difficult in the Van Martin home. Thomas would throw his temper around and tell his parents they weren't trying hard enough to woo the girl of his dreams.

"Won't you walk with me and hold my hand," he asked as he moved closer to her. She pulled away, and he continued, "After all; you will be my wife!"

Amelia laughed at his joke. "Thomas," she stated, "You are becoming bothersome. Now please leave me alone."

He circled around her as she walked, kicking the dirt to continue to annoy her. She didn't understand what her fate. Her father already gave him her hand. It was just a matter of time before she found out for herself. He promised not to say anything to her when he talked to Henry Samuels, but he kept his fingers crossed behind his back. Thomas glanced at her scowling face and toyed with her a little. "Oh, forgive me. I thought you knew," he put his arm over her shoulder and walked in step with her.

She pulled herself away from him and wondered why he was acting stranger than normal. "Knew what?" She quizzed.

"That you and I will get married after your twenty-first birthday," he said with confidence.

Amelia's stomach tightened. She thought for sure she would bring up her breakfast. She got herself together and continued to walk away from him. He was wrong and didn't know what he was talking about. Marriage was the last thing on her mind. "Look," she snapped as she picked up her pace to free herself from his presence. "I don't have time for your jokes."

He loved every minute of her torture. "Wait up," he shouted as he raced to catch up with her. She placed her hands on her hips and was about to say something, but he wouldn't allow it. Before she had the chance, he cupped her face and placed his mouth upon her lips. The kiss lasted for a brief second before he felt her hand slap him hard across his face.

"Don't you ever touch me again," she demanded. She had dreamed of her first kiss and never was Thomas part it. Amelia wiped her mouth, to rid herself of his drool, and turned to walk even faster than she already was.

For most men, a reaction such as hers would scare a fellow. It triggered more desire from Thomas. He was proud of how upset he made her. He knew that she didn't believe him and wished that he could be there when she discovered that his words were true. "Have it your way, my love," he called out to her. "Go home and ask your father all about our union. You'll see I'm telling you the truth. The next time you see me, you will acknowledge me as your betrothed."

Amelia ran the rest of the way to the house and slipped inside. She turned and placed her forehead on the closed door and caught her breath. It was just a bad dream, she told herself. She regained her posture and went straight to the kitchen to cook. No matter what she had done, she couldn't get the image of Thomas out of her head. His person was so unattractive. He was tall and thin, almost too thin. His head looked too big for his skinny body. His high cheekbones made him look as if his eyes sunk in his skull. The worst part about his face was the smirk he held with his lips. She couldn't tell if that was his smile or a birth defect.

Amelia could look passed someone's appearance but in this case, looking passed Thomas' appearance was even worse than looking at him. He was ornery, meaner than anyone could be towards other people. He treated his family and friends atrocious; his workers and other people of their class like dirt. Amelia shook her head. She couldn't wait until her father came home to put her mind at ease.

Henry walked in the house and could smell the meal prepared by Amelia. It was a wonderful aroma, he thought to himself. He would often stop, close his eyes, and take a deep breath to take in the scents. She was a good daughter and a loving companion. The bond between him and her had begun years before when he taught her how to help the sick. They grew closer as she helped him nurse her mother before she died and even more since she took on the responsibility of taking care of the household. Amelia didn't deserve the news he had for her. Henry paused again on that thought before he entered the kitchen where he knew his family was waiting for him.

It was his wrong doing and stupidity that put him in the hands of the Van Martin men. They pressured him to make a decision that would affect her future. He knew that she wouldn't be happy but if things would turn out for the best, he would have to pretend that he was. It was a falseness he knew but sometimes mistakes had to be covered up with even bigger mistakes.

"Good evening, father," he heard her say as he entered the kitchen. "I sent the boys to wash up then we will eat." Anxiety was grabbing her throat, but she remained silent hoping Thomas was lying to her.

"Good evening to you, Amelia," he replied. "And good evening to you, dear Anna." His youngest daughter already sat at the table, ready to feast.

"Hello, father. You'll be proud to know, I set the table tonight." Anna joined the conversation. "How does it look?"

"Beautiful." Henry felt a sense of guilt as he looked at two of his daughters before him. Though his decision affected Amelia the most, he knew it would also affect Anna. He had another, Minnie, who was younger than Amelia, out of the home and married. The rumors he had heard from gossiping ladies in his store about how Amelia should have wed first had helped him to agree to the Van Martins' demand.

He returned his attention to the girls in front of him. They were as different as night and day yet they both desired his approval. As he took his seat at the table, he reflected on their differences. Amelia was taller and curvier than Anna who was bone thin from running all the time. She was the most tomboyish girl in the village. Both girls had dark brown hair but yet Anna's was straight with short bangs while Amelia's had more of a natural curl to it. Amelia's eyes were as blue as the sky on a clear summer's day but Anna's were black. His eyes, he realized. Anna looked like a young female version of him.

Their appearances weren't the only thing that made them different; their personalities were just the opposite too. Amelia would do anything to make life easy and her younger sister was the one who always made things difficult. Though they both knew respect, Anna had mouthed off from time to time. And for taking care of the house, Anna wouldn't have a clue what to do. That thought made him stop and wonder what he would do with her. The announcement he planned on making over the meal would affect her too and she would have to learn the ins and outs of a household, fast.

Within minutes the two youngest children, Henry Jr. and Charles, ran into the kitchen and sat at the table. Charles grabbed a slice of bread and halfway shoved it into his mouth when Amelia grabbed his arm and reminded him that they have not said the evening prayer. Henry said the prayer and everyone said, "Amen."

Everyone was quiet while they ate. Henry knew that he couldn't put off telling his family the news he had. "Amelia, I talked to Thomas Van Martin today."

She swallowed her last bite of food hard when her father spoke to her. Fear rose deep inside knowing he would bring up the horrid conversation she had with Thomas. "May I ask, what about?" Amelia hoped that Thomas had just been fooling her.

"You," Henry told her in front of her siblings who were watching like hawks.

Amelia felt a lump in her throat she couldn't swallow. The news was true, and she almost choked. She could never be Thomas' wife and felt the need to protest. "Oh Father, no. He has told me I would be his wife, and I hoped that it wasn't so. I would sooner be sold into slavery than to be with the likes of him."

Henry's face had matched the burning coals in the brick oven. The rotten scoundrel promised not to say anything to her, he mumbled to himself. He should have known not to trust the young lad. There was no point in confronting Daniel about his son's behavior. The Van Martins had him where they wanted him. "I'm sorry about that," he replied, "He was told not to say anything." His words confirmed what Thomas had told her.

"Oh father, you didn't?" Amelia's stomach felt like it did the first time she'd heard the news. "How could you? Prearranged marriages don't take place around here. Isn't that one reason our ancestors moved to America to begin with?"

"Don't take that tone with me young lady." Henry hated to holler at her. But, if he would convince the community he was behind this union, he had to convince her first. "You are my daughter and it's my responsibility to make sure you are well provided for. Mr. Van Martin will be a wonderful husband to you."

"Father, don't say that. There will be nothing wonderful about Thomas."

The other children were silent as their older sister tried to argue with their father. "Don't argue with me, girl, it will do you no good."

"Who will take care of you and the children?" Amelia had been the only one to take care of them since her mother's death.

Henry glanced over at Anna who was getting squirmy in her seat. "It's about time that our dear Anna takes on the duties around here." As far as he was concerned, at fifteen years of age, Anna should know how to cook and clean.

Anna didn't like housework and this sudden announcement brought, "I swan," out of her mouth. The entire family hushed as they looked at the girl who used such dirty language.

Henry slammed his fist on the table and jerked his head toward Anna. He had a good mind to box her ears for talking the way she did; out of line again. "Watch your mouth, girl, and mind your own funeral," he was strict when he told her to keep her opinions to herself. Lowering her head, Anna paid close attention as the conversation continued.

"Oh father, isn't love important?" Amelia pleaded. She often dreamt of falling in love but knew that once her father sets his mind to something he kept it that way.

"Love," Henry quizzed. "Amelia, I understand that you want someone to love. We all do in our lives. But, you have been busy taking care of others. You took over when your mother died. You gave your time when your Uncle John was sick until he too passed away, and now you're helping Beth to prepare for the birth of the baby." Beth married his oldest son, David, and they were expecting their first born. Henry continued, "You've had no time for yourself. Let me help you with this. I promise you will learn to love Thomas."

Amelia felt stumped. There wasn't a thing she could think of to wiggle her way out of this mess now. "You can't learn to love someone. When you find someone to love, you know."

"What do you know about love? Have you ever had a beau, Amelia? Is there something you have hid from me?"

Amelia cried. Did her father think that she would ever court a boy without his permission? "No Father. I've never but I believe that someday I will."

Henry smiled. She would come to her senses. "Yes dear, someday you will love Thomas Van Martin." He paused as he looked at her distraught face. It was better to keep talking than to look into her watery eyes, he decided. "I told him I wanted you to wait until after your twenty- first birthday. That is a few months from now and Amelia, by then you will love him."

Determined to try one more time, Amelia begged, "Father, please change your mind. I promise to spend more time searching for the right man. If you want to marry me off, I will court but please don't make me marry Thomas Van Martin. You know that he is everything I'm against in a man."

Henry had to stay strong. Her hand was promised to the Van Martins and, for reasons he couldn't reveal, he intended on keeping that promise. He would not sit there and let her try to talk him out of it. Henry stood up to leave the kitchen and said, "You are my daughter and will do as I say. I told him that outside of the immediate family, nobody is to know. When you see him next, you will tell him how happy you are to be his fiancée."

He left the room as Amelia put her head on the table and cried in defeat.

Chapter Two

Weekdays, Mondays more than ever, brought commerce up and down the Hudson. The river was traveled more than most roads in the entire county. Millersport was right in the middle of Albany to the north and Manhattan to the south. Merchants would berth their ships and sell products received from the two cities. The general store sent employees down to the loading docks to pick up goods they ordered to stock their shelves. Most of the hustle of shoppers came from villagers who made their own purchases. Amelia was just one of many.

"You're fooling me right," Emma Cooper said to Amelia as they began their journey to the docks. It was almost a ritual for them to travel together down to the ships although Emma just observed. When she saw Amelia's face for the first time that morning, she knew something was wrong. Amelia confided in her, careless of what her father had told her about people knowing. Emma was her closest friend and Amelia knew she could be trusted. Emma felt horrible but was close enough to the Samuels family to know that Henry wouldn't be changing his mind about the situation. As they stepped away from the house Amelia had another plan in mind to get out of her engagement. "What kind of design is that?" Emma saw the devious look in her friend's face and wanted to know more.

Holding her head up high and not looking Emma in the eyes on purpose, Amelia answered. "If I find someone else to marry, then my father would have to release me from Thomas' hand."

"That's absurd," Emma hated to be the one to remind Amelia of the truth but there was nobody in Millersport that Amelia could wed. She placed her fingers on her chin as she thought for a moment; the available men were too old, too young, or just not worthy of Amelia's devotion. She was the most beautiful girl in the village, everyone including Emma knew that. Many whispered that there wasn't a man good enough for Amelia. There were plenty of men who would love to have had their chance but that wasn't Amelia's style and Emma knew her friend couldn't change now. "You have just a little over two months before your birthday and you think you can find someone to marry by then? Amelia, you and I both know that will not happen and it won't change your father's mind."

Amelia's steps were slow and her head hung low. Emma was right; her future looked bleak. The hopes of having a happy marriage have all gone away. "It's not fair, just not fair at all. My idea won't work, I know."

Emma whistled and looked up into the sky as she moved towards Amelia and bumped her friend with her hip. Amelia almost fell over, but it was Emma's way of cheering her. She was about to do it again but Amelia was wise and jumped over to the side and laughed. Emma knew that her friend would be okay. Amelia needed to take her mind off of her problems. "Well I know one good thing about Thomas," Emma said. "Jacob Miller is one of his closest friends."

Amelia looked over to Emma. She turned her face away but not enough to hide her rosy cheeks and quirky smile. Amelia wondered why she never knew that Emma had an interest in Jacob. "Emma Cooper," she exclaimed. "Are you sparkling with him?"

Emma's hands covered her face as she peered out of one gap. "Promise you won't say anything."

"Promise."

"What are you purchasing today," Emma asked to return their thoughts to the task in front of them.

Amelia shook her caba that carried the coins that her father gave her and replied, "Coffee, if they have it, some spices, and I would like to see what cloth the merchants will have." Since the Tariff Act, some items were becoming hard to buy and Amelia hoped that it would soon end.

"Perhaps you can buy fabric for a wedding dress?" Emma stopped herself from saying any more. She did not understand why she would say such a thing and hoped that Amelia would just ignore it.

Amelia did just that and left her friends comment unanswered for a while. She knew it would be difficult but still hoped that her father would change his mind about the situation. For a while as they walked down the road, things were back to normal. They held hands and swung their arms like school-aged children and sang *Hey, Betty Martin.* The song had become a popular marching song for the war but the girls still stumbled over the words and laughed at their mistakes.

Amelia had turned and walked backwards and was too busy frolicking that she didn't realize that she was about to walk right into someone.

Just then Emma's face looked troubled as Amelia stepped on top of a pair of black boots and could hear a man's voice groan. She turned around in an instant and said, "Oh, pardon me, Sir."

The stranger smiled as he wiped the dirt placed on his boot by the girl's shoe. "That's all right," he said as he smiled at the two girls. They were both charming in appearance but the one who had stepped on his foot caught his eye. She had dark brown hair that curled over her shoulders and the loveliest blue eyes he had ever seen. She stood tall; he estimated almost five foot six, just a few inches shorter than he. Her figure looked soft and inviting, but he erased such thoughts from his head. He didn't know who she was and never imagined thinking of a lady like that ever again.

Not recognizing the man, Emma became alarmed put her guard up. He must have been a stranger. Her friend didn't seem bothered by walking into someone they didn't know.

Amelia felt foolish, like she was a young child who wasn't paying attention. "Are you okay?" Her eyes fell to the foot she could have injured but then took their time making their way back up his body. She could see the muscles underneath the man's tight sit-down-upons that shielded his limbs. His arms were an abundance of strength and covered with bronzed flesh. Amelia then looked at his face and the mouth that smiled at her. She couldn't help but to notice how attractive he was, but she ignored those thoughts and returned her eyes to his foot.

Again he said that he was fine. He was new in town and wasn't sure where he was going. "I must not have been watching myself," he said to the girls. "I'm looking for a mercantile, does this village have one?"

Amelia spoke even though she could see Emma's look of disapproval. "Yes Sir, we have a general store. If you go in the direction you are headed, you will see it, just a few rods away."

That was about all that Emma could stand from her fearless friend. "We are not supposed to talk to strangers," she said to Amelia but kept her eyes on him.

"Oh Emma, I'm only trying to help," Amelia protested. She didn't see the harm in that. Keeping her thoughts to herself, Amelia felt like she had known him forever.

The stranger looked at Emma and spoke, "I understand. Emma? Is it?"

Amelia's friend looked at her as if she was crazy for saying her name in front of the stranger but Amelia wasn't afraid. "Yes, her name is Emma Cooper. And, I'm Amelia Samuels." She introduced as she noticed Emma's chin drop.

The man extended his hand for Amelia to shake it. "My name is Patrick Buchanan. See, Emma, now we're no longer strangers."

He stuck out his hand to her but Emma refused the shake it, offended how Amelia was open with him. She ignored him and turned to Amelia and said, "Come along Amelia, maybe your betrothed is waiting for you by the docks."

Thomas sat with Jacob Miller near the docks. He couldn't keep quiet about his engagement to Amelia and didn't care that her father said they must. She was a prize to him and nothing more. He couldn't wait to walk down the

12

street with her in his arm. "I have a secret but I won't tell you unless you promise you won't speak a word of it to anyone."

Jacob had been Thomas' closest friend all of his born years and these days it seemed he was his only friend. He knew Thomas' arrogant behavior, thinking only of himself and never of others. "You have my word. What is it?"

He looked to Jacob with a crooked smile as he felt accomplished. "Amelia Samuels has agreed to marry me."

"No. It's no secret she dislikes you." Jacob shook his head thinking that Thomas' news was just a prank of some sort. For mind games, nobody was better than Thomas.

Thomas couldn't care less that she didn't like him. All he cared about was having his way. "Yes," he explained. "She doesn't like me very much; in fact I dare say she hates me." Seeing Jacob tilt his head and studying Thomas' face, he continued. "I asked her father first, and he thinks we are the perfect match."

Jacob rubbed his chin. "She wouldn't disobey her father." He knew the Samuels family well and knew that all the children had a great deal of respect and obedience for their father, Henry.

Thomas' laughter grew strong. He wanted to tell Jacob that Henry couldn't ignore Daniel's threats but knew that talk of the blackmail would destroy his future life with Amelia. He always got what he wanted and didn't care at whose expense. "That is why she agreed to be my wife. Her father made her."

"Don't you care she doesn't love you?" Jacob questioned.

"Jacob, Jacob, what is there not to love?" Thomas stated, running his fingers through his hair and flexing his muscles. He opened his arms and said, "I'm every girl's dream."

If Thomas was anything, he was full of himself. There wasn't a girl for miles that dreamt of him. Jacob realized that his friend was too conceited and rude for any girl to consider, not even with all the money his family had. "I'm serious."

He was always serious, Thomas thought. He didn't care she might never love him because he wasn't even sure if he would ever love her. All he knew was that she made him look even better than he already was. "That doesn't matter my friend. All that matters is that she'll be mine and she must obey me."

Jacob shrugged his head. "You're terrible. So when is the big announcement?"

"That is the reason you can't say a word," Thomas warned.

Now Jacob was the one laughing. "Oh, I see," he said. "This whole thing is just in your head. Amelia would no sooner marry you than anyone else around here." He knew that Thomas couldn't be serious.

"Not a joke, Jacob," Thomas explained. "That was her father's idea. He thinks it's natural for a couple to court before marrying. Though we are engaged, he says we must 'court' until her next birthday before we announce our marriage."

Though he was skeptical, Jacob had no reason not to believe Thomas. "Well then, I'm the first to congratulate you." Jacob said as he thought of his own interest in Emma Cooper. The two had always got along well, and he looked forward to seeing her. "Thomas?"

Still wrapped up in his own thoughts, he almost didn't hear his friend. "What?"

"You reminded me what I've wanted to do. I will ask Emma if she would have me for a beau." Jacob informed Thomas.

Thomas grinned. He didn't stop to think that Jacob could have real feelings for Emma. He assumed that his friend was as devious as him. "Now you are thinking, my friend, now you are thinking."

Amelia's faced flushed with heat as she caught up to Emma. She had been polite to Patrick and told her farewells to him before continuing on with her friend. As she quickened her steps,, she wondered why Emma would refer to her engagement when she knew it was the last thing on her mind. "How dare you, Emma Cooper," she snapped as she stepped in rhythm with her. "You know that I don't want to marry Thomas, and to say it in front of a stranger. What were you thinking?"

Emma lowered her head and wiped away her tears in secret. Her fear of strangers put her on the defense but she hadn't meant to hurt Amelia's feelings. Her best friend was going through a hard time and now she was making things worse for her. She felt horrible about what she had said. "I'm sorry." She didn't know what Amelia was thinking because she had remained quiet. Lifting her head, Emma turned to Amelia in hopes to stop her from making any terrible mistakes. "I know you don't care for Thomas but it won't be as bad as it seems."

"So now you want me to marry him?"

"It's what your father wants, and what Thomas wants," Emma said. She glanced ahead and saw they were several feet away from Thomas and Jacob. "I won't tell him you were talking to a stranger."

"But," was all that Amelia could say before Emma rushed off towards the men. She followed.

Emma hurried over to Thomas and Jacob and exclaimed, "I'm so glad we found you, we saw a stranger."

Amelia couldn't get over the way Emma was behaving. "He meant no harm."

Thomas looked concerned. It wasn't often that there was a strange man in the village. He had heard nothing from the land agent about someone purchasing property. "What was he doing?"

Emma started, "Oh, he was," but Amelia stopped her.

"Emma, you are over reacting. He was looking for the general store and I told him where he could find it." She said to the group.

Thomas didn't like knowing she spoke to the man. He couldn't wait until she was his wife following his rules. "Jacob, will you take Miss Cooper home? I would like to be alone with Amelia."

Jacob had no problem walking Emma home. He looked at her, she had light brown hair that was French braided to the back of her head. Several strands had fallen out and was now blowing in her face from the slight breeze coming from the river. Her long lashes batted at him when she realized that he was watching her and then lowered in a bashful way, hiding her bright green eyes. Jacob held his arm out to Emma and she took hold of it without hesitation.

As they walked away, Amelia objected, "No, Thomas. I'm here to make purchases from the merchants."

Thomas admired the stubbornness in her. "Then I will stay with you until you are finished then I will carry your packages back to your father's house." He knew that she would try to get away from him but he wouldn't allow it. Amelia was his and he would let everyone know.

Amelia dealt with the merchants while Thomas stood close behind her. It made her very uncomfortable, but he appeared to like the attention. She wondered if this was the start of their so- called courtship.

After Amelia purchased several items, Thomas asked, "Are you ready to return home now?" Hanging around the mudsill wasn't his style.

Amelia slapped her fist against the side of her dress in anger. She hated being near Thomas and hearing him act like he cared, upset her more. "Thomas please," she started. "I can walk myself."

Thomas didn't care she objected. She was his fiancée and had a right to spend as much time as he wanted with her. He leaned over and whispered so that the surrounding boodle couldn't hear, "We are to be married. Don't you think it's about time we get to know each other better?"

"No," she whispered back. If she had her way, the wedding would never take place. "Thomas, why do you want to marry me?"

As they walked further away from the loading docks and the crowd of shoppers, he thought about her question. Amelia was an exquisite girl. She was groomed, she kept her body cleaned and her clothes washed and ironed. She was strong and knew her way around the house, having experience with hard household chores, and with raising a family. Thomas needed special attention. He needed someone who would fulfill his every desire, wait on him hand and foot. He wanted someone who was strong enough to labor in his home during the day but yet soft enough to pamper to his needs every night in bed. Amelia was perfect for both. He lied, "Amelia, I'm getting older and so are you. It's time that both of us consider marriage. I know how finicky you are and I don't wish for people to consider you an old maid. I'm doing you a favor by making you my wife."

Other people thought that Thomas Van Martin was a respectable young man but Amelia saw right through him. He was up to no good and she knew it. "I don't care about what others think. I have to know one thing, and it's very important for me to know the truth. If we will be man and wife, I insist that you be honest. Tell me, Mr. Van Martin, do you love me?"

Again he laughed. "Love you?" The one person he would ever love was himself and he needed no one to tell him that. To Thomas, love was for fairy tales but marriage was reality. "No, Amelia. I don't love you," he started but she wouldn't give him the time to finish. She walked faster to get away. He picked up his pace, caught up to her, swung her towards him and then right in the middle of the street placed a kiss upon her lips. She reacted just like she had the day before and tried to get away. "Amelia let me finish talking to you." She turned and walked again but this time not so fast so he could explain. "We will love each other. By the time we wed we will be in love, you'll see."

17

Amelia looked at him with disgust. She couldn't believe that he had the nerve to kiss her without her permission. She had half of mind to run and tell her father but then again, her father might congratulate the young man. "You sound like my father. He said the same thing."

"Well, because it's true. You are not the first girl to get married against her will." Then he told her how he felt. "You are the perfect bride for me, you're beautiful, smart, physical, and you would be socially acceptable to marry into my family. Besides, your father wants you to marry me. He doesn't even care I don't love you. He wants to see you married." It was another lie, he knew, but he loved to aggravate her.

His words stung her heart, and she wondered if he was telling the truth. Perhaps he was, she thought to herself, because her father wouldn't even hear her pleas. Amelia filled with hope once more than she thought maybe she could get him to back out of the engagement. "Thomas," she started. "This isn't the way things are meant to be. Don't you have dreams of someday finding the perfect girl for you? We can stop this right now and in time we'll both be happy."

Thomas grinned and put his arm around her shoulder. She was miserable, and that made him blissful. It didn't matter how she felt, she was his for the taken. "No, no, don't think you can talk me out of this marriage. You're mine now and nothing you can say to make me change my mind."

"But," she protested. "I will never love you. Don't you care?"

"Love is for girls," he stated. "It's fine you don't love me because I will never love you."

Amelia spoke no more but ran off ahead of him. His words were like ice being thrown at her; cold and painful. She fought the urge to cry as she advanced towards her father's house. He called out for her to return to him but Amelia denied him. "Go away, Thomas. You're making me sick." Her shoulder struck the door as she turned the knob and just about fell into the house. Tears fell once she knew that he

18

couldn't see her. She could hear him calling out to her and when she didn't answer, she heard him say he would be back to call on her at another time. Amelia groaned; things were not going her way.

Chapter Three

Amelia sat on the edge of the sofa in the sitting-room as she waited for her father to join her. He had sent a message telling her he would like a word and she hoped that he would tell her that the horrible nightmare was over. The front door squeaked as it opened and Amelia jumped to her feet. Henry walked into the room and right away reached to embrace her but she stood with her arms crossed. She was still angry at him for what he was putting her through, but glancing at his concerned eyes made her wonder how long she could stay upset with him. "What is it you want to talk about?" She questioned as her arms dropped and played with the trim on her apron.

"You've been quiet," Henry stated. He knew that she was upset about his decision but figured that she was over it. "Is there something wrong?"

She cocked her head and looked at him while he took a seat in the arm chair. He was a man who healed the ill but perhaps he was maddening himself, she thought. He couldn't have forgotten the torture he was putting her through. "Yes, this whole engagement is wrong. I can't believe I have to tell you that."

Henry placed his forehead in his hand. He could feel the heat from inside his body rush to the surface of his face. It was foolish to think that she wasn't going to continue fighting for her freedom. He was desperate to give it to her but it would cost him his if he did. Again he made himself act as if he was behind the Samuels and Van Martin union. "Amelia, we aren't going to get into that again. Are we? Don't you realize that I'm trying to do what is best for you?"

Appalled, Amelia answered, "Best for me? You can't think that Thomas is best for me."

Henry stood and faced the window. "The Van Martins are the wealthiest family in the village. You will never have to go without the things you desire, ever again."

"Except love, Father," Amelia snapped. Recalling her conversation with Thomas, she knew that it wasn't in her future. "You forgot love."

Henry could never forget about love. It didn't seem too long before when he fought for the love of his life. Henry thought he would put none of his children through a forced marriage but his mistakes had changed all of that. "Why don't you believe me when I say you will love him?"

"Why won't you allow me to marry someone I love?" It was an endless battle, she knew, but Amelia had to keep trying.

Henry looked shocked at what she said. He wondered if it were possible for her to love someone without him knowing about it. "Do you have feelings for someone?"

Amelia shook her head. "Oh but Father, there are new people moving here all the time. Perhaps I will meet someone."

Henry thought of the rumors he's heard floating around Millersport about a stranger walking the streets. Realizing that he was changing the topic, he felt an importance to tell her about it. "That reminds me," he started. "I heard there was a stranger around and want you to be aware."

Amelia laughed which caused her father to turn around to face her again. Emma mustn't have been the only one alarmed by Patrick's presence. "His name is Patrick Buchanan," she announced to him.

Surprise came over Henry. His face gave away his concern and he could hear her telling him how she met the man. "You shouldn't have talked to him."

"He isn't bad, I'm the one who bumped into him," Amelia responded. Then she wondered why he had changed the subject and thought that maybe he was coming around. "Father, does this mean you'll allow me to find my mate?"

Henry stared at her for a moment as he tried to get back on track. She was a wild fire that couldn't be put out without trouble, a trait she inherited from her mother. He remembered how feisty his wife had been at Amelia's age. "I've given my word to the Van Martins, Amelia." He wished that she could have the opportunity, but it was too late to back down now.

She stood and huffed as she straightened her apron. It was just another battle lost with him but she would still not give up. "You asked what was bothering me and I've told you," Amelia growled. "If you don't mind, I have laundry to do." She stormed out of the room and began her chores. It was the first time in her life she walked away from him without his permission but it didn't matter. There could be no consequences harsher than what he already done to her.

After finishing all of her duties, she went for a walk to clear her mind. Amelia left her house and started north and then turned towards the west. The outskirts of the village contained miles of farming areas and she knew that Thomas or anyone else that would ask her about her courtship wouldn't find her out there.

There was a slight wind blowing from the trees and onto her face as she walked but it felt delightful to her. Between the cool air and many things on her mind, she hadn't realized how far she had traveled. When she looked around to determine where she was, she knew she was over two miles from home. The land she stood on had been vacant for five years since the owner moved away. Amelia saw the back of someone's head and thought that the owner had returned. Her instincts told her to welcome him back to Millersport and continued to walk in his direction.

Patrick was busy preparing his new gained land to plant trees on it. He glanced around and knew that he paid a decent lay for the property he hadn't even seen before purchasing. Kneeling down, he dug his hand into the soil and was happy to feel the moisture in the ground. As he stood and dusted his hands off, he turned and saw the girl he had met in the village coming his way.

"Amelia," he greeted her. "What brings you so far from the village?"

Amelia didn't expect to see Patrick there but wasn't surprised. She should have known that the land's owner had not returned. Then she realized that he must have purchased the land from the previous owner which would explain why the land agent in the village had never spoken about the stranger. "I'm sorry if I'm disturbing you," she explained her presence. "I was out for a stroll and didn't realize how far I've walked."

Patrick thought she looked elegant in her soft pink dress that clung tight to her hips and then dropped to the ground. The dress tied right below her bust line and Patrick looked away so he wouldn't offend her. The capote on her head shaded her face from the midday sun. He peered in and looked at her blue eyes but they seemed to be glazed and glossy. Patrick wondered if it was him; maybe she feared him the way he sensed the other people in the village had. "Listen," he began, "I know that you don't know me but I promise I'm harmless. You need not be afraid."

"Oh, I'm not," Amelia assured him. She could tell that he was an intelligent man and must've noticed how the residents of Millersport behave around unknown men.

"I thought," Patrick started but didn't finish. If she wasn't afraid of him, he wondered what was troubling her. He didn't want her to think he was interfering, so he didn't ask. Instead, seeing her remove her bonnet, he changed the subject and offered her a rest. "You've come a long way," he said. "Why don't you sit awhile?" Patrick sat down under a tree, expecting her to lean against the oak so not to dirty her dress but she flopped down beside him. His thoughts of her confused him; she seemed so refined but yet also carefree.

He offered his canteen and Amelia accepted without hesitation. The water felt refreshing going down her dry throat. "Thank you," she said as she handed it back.

Patrick looked at her. There was no doubt in his mind she was beautiful. Engaged or not, he saw no harm in talking to her. "I know little about the people of this area but where I came from engaged couples spend a lot of time together. I'm surprised to see you alone."

Just then she cried; a cry she had wanted to get out for days. She felt so helpless and couldn't help crying in front of him. "Oh, I apologize for my behavior." Amelia just wanted to let all of her emotions out and hoped it would make her feel better.

Stiffing up a little, Patrick was feeling uncomfortable with the way she sobbed but wanted her to know that it was all right. "Now, now," he started. "It's fine. It can't be that bad. What is troubling you?" He didn't think that she would open and tell him but couldn't hold off asking anymore.

Amelia wiped her eyes and looked at the man who was being so kind to her, kind like how her father used to be before he turned her life upside down. She didn't give it much thought; she blurted it out. "You see; my father is forcing me to marry Thomas Van Martin. I'll never love him and worse yet, I'll never be able to find someone I can love."

Patrick listened with intent as she went on about how she had tried to get out of the marriage but was unsuccessful every time. "I'm sorry to hear that. Does this man, Thomas, love you?" He was feeling that the girl was tugging at his heart- strings but he forced himself to be rid those ideas.

Amelia broke down more, "No, which makes it even worse. How can I grow to love someone who doesn't even love me?"

Patrick was bold and put his arm around her shoulders and let her lean against him as she sobbed. He meant no harm in it and hoped that she would understand. It didn't seem to bother her; she differed from anyone he had ever met before. He didn't want her to be afraid of him but also couldn't figure out why she was so comfortable around someone she just met. This arranged marriage of hers was interfering with her sanity. She leaned over and rested her head against his chest and soon after his shirt became wet from her tears. "I'm not sure I'm the person you should talk to about this, it's not of my funeral but, I want you to know that we can talk anytime you would like."

Amelia sat up and wiped the tears from her eyes. Patrick reached behind him and pulled a hanky out of his back pocket and she used it to clean up her face. "There is no one to talk to. Emma seems to be on my father's side and she was the one person who I could ever talk to." She realized what she was doing, crying in front of someone who had no right to know such things about her. "Oh, Patrick, I'm so sorry. Look at me, I'm very inappropriate."

Patrick grinned. He wondered how long it would take her to realize that she had been spilling her personal life onto him. "As I told you, it's fine. I don't mind as long as you are all right with it."

She felt foolish though she had to admit to herself that she felt much better talking to someone who didn't have a say. "I'm fine as long as I have not bothered you." Then for the first time she inspected him. He had dark brown eyes and thick wavy hair that matched. His hair wasn't like other men's; it was longer and came together to form a small pigtail in the back. Amelia stared at his upper body in the same way that her brothers have stared at candy sticks in the general store. Just as they would long to touch the confectionary treats, she longed to touch Patrick's skin. She moistened her lips and batted her eyes as she avoided making eye contact with him. Then the thought of him realizing what she was thinking, caused her to blush. She had to regain her control before she made a complete fool of herself. She didn't want to get caught staring at him so she jumped up and prepared to walk back home.

"No, no. I wouldn't do that. I told you it was fine. You are not a bother at all; in fact I dare say I enjoy the company." Patrick told her she could stop by and visit him anytime she wanted as she stood up and dusted herself off. "I would offer you a ride home on my horse but am afraid it wouldn't be proper."

Amelia understood, though a ride would be nice considering she had never meant to walk so far. "Oh, thank you but you are right. I don't think my father would understand."

He wanted to see her again but yet didn't want to push himself onto her. He knew it was wrong to speak in a relaxed way to a lady already spoken for but he said, "You know, Amelia, that if you ever feel you want to get away again, you can come here anytime you want." The thought of her leaving put an emptiness inside of him that was as unexplainable as the longing he felt for her. Amelia nodded her head and thanked him as she started her journey back home.

Her entire body overheated from her extra-long journey. The ascending stairs seemed never ending but Amelia was hopeful for an afternoon nap. She entered the bedroom she shared with Anna, removed her shoes, and then fell back onto her bed. Her eyelids grew heavy and were just about to shut when she heard her sister Minnie calling her name from the hallway below. "I'm up here," she whimpered. She sat up but not before Minnie had seen her lying down.

"I'm sorry," Minnie told her. "I didn't realize that you were resting."

Wiping her eyes and yawning, Amelia replied, "It's fine. I was just a little tired from a long walk. You're not interrupting." Minnie was most like herself, Amelia thought, always kind to others feelings. "What brings you by?"

"Father," was her one-word answer.

Amelia sighed. She should have known that Minnie wouldn't call upon her on her own will. Ever since she married, the younger girl spent most of her time running her own household and when she wasn't with her husband Philip, she had her own circle of friends. She didn't visit unless there was a family get-together. Her thoughts returned to Minnie's answer. Amelia wasn't surprised that her father would have someone else try to talk sense into her and Minnie would do whatever he asked. "I already told Father what was bothering me and to be quite honest, you will not change my mind either."

Minnie sat on the bed and thought about what to say. She had heard the news of Amelia's engagement but unlike their brother David, she saw nothing wrong with the situation. "You should be happy that someone like Thomas wants you for a wife," she informed.

"Happy? Don't fool me," Amelia snapped. "He doesn't love me and I'm not his object to want." She felt bad for snipping the way she had but Amelia could tell that Minnie had called on her because their father asked her to. Other than that, she had nothing else to say. They were both quiet for a while, confirming Amelia's thoughts about Minnie's visit. "I will never forgive him for what he is putting me through."

Minnie's mouth gaped as she jumped and faced Amelia. "Take that back, Amelia Samuels, right now!" Her father couldn't do any wrong, Minnie thought, and didn't deserve Amelia's harsh words.

"No," she laid her head back on the pillow and felt the tears build up in her eyes again. It hurt her to say such things though she wasn't willing to admit that to her sister.

"You are not the only person who has ever been forced into marriage," Minnie pleaded with Amelia to understand. "You'd be surprised to know who was."

Amelia sat up again, curiosity held her. "Who was?"

Minnie faced Amelia and sat down on Anna's bed. She bit her lip, lowered her head, and wished that she had said nothing. Millersport was full of gossip and what she had overheard herself was a little more than Amelia should know. Looking anywhere except at Amelia, she answered, "That doesn't matter and you know it. You shouldn't blame Father for trying to do what is best for your welfare."

Amelia knew better than to believe Minnie. If there was someone they both knew with a prearranged marriage, she would have given a direct answer. There was no doubt in Amelia's mind that her sister was trying to make their father out to be a perfect man. "Well Minnie, since this isn't a social visit, I walked far today and wanted to get rest."

Minnie felt bad for letting her sister believe that she didn't care about her but Amelia's harsh words against their father had made Minnie keep her feelings to herself. "Fine. Good day." She didn't wait to allow Amelia to wish her farewell.

"You too," Amelia called out as she heard Minnie run down the stairs. She rolled to her side and let her eyes close the way they've been wanting to.

Chapter Four

From the moment Amelia entered the general store she felt dozens of eyes staring at her. Knowing they all wanted to know about her relationship with Thomas, she focused on the fabric displayed on the shelf. A hand touched her shoulder and she about touched the ceiling. "Emma," she said between her shortness of breath, "You scared me."

Emma covered her mouth and giggled. It wasn't her intention to scare Amelia. Her friend looked distant. "Sorry," she said. "What are you looking at?"

Amelia continued browsing by running her hands over the cloths and feeling them between her finger and thumb. "I didn't have time to pick any fabric out from the merchants since Thomas was pestering me. Anna needs a new dress," she added just in case Emma had any presumptions about wedding clothes.

Emma watched Amelia and gave her opinions. Amelia paid for the material she picked out and Emma suggested, "Want to share a bench outside?"

They sat for a while in silence. Amelia was still a little sore with Emma for her behavior at the loading docks and Emma sensed it. Emma pondered the thought of trying to make Amelia laugh but knew that she had too much on her mind. "I'm sorry for the way I acted the other day. I hope you forgive me."

Amelia's arm stretched out and her hand reached for Emma's. It wasn't her fault she was going through such a hard time and Amelia knew that. "I forgive you," she said and then, in a childish manner, stuck her tongue out. Their laughter could be heard over all the other commotion going on at the store. The sun beat down and Amelia noticed her friend fanning herself. "Do you want to come to the house with me? I made lemonade this morning." Without answering, Emma stood up and bent her elbow towards

Amelia. She leaned her head toward the Samuels house and Amelia knew she wanted to go. Intertwining her arm into Emma's, they walked.

"Jacob has asked to escort me to the social and I've said yes," Emma announced not thinking that her friend did not understand what she was talking about.

Confused and curious, Amelia gasped, "What?"

"You haven't heard about the social dance?" Amelia shook her head and Emma continued to update her on the event.

"I suppose I've been too deep into my own thoughts I have heard little at all." It upset her to feel left out of the social circle but realized that it wasn't on purpose. "What's this about Jacob too?"

Emma's cheeks blushed, and she turned her head to hide her emotions. She told Amelia about her walk home with him the day they met the young men down at the loading docks. It was a walk that changed her life and made her dreams come true. Jacob had been so kind and caring. They continued their stroll instead of returning to her house and Emma was ever so glad they did. It gave Jacob the time he needed to get out the words he stumbled over. He had asked her if he could be her beau and she was glad to accept. "I'm so happy," she finished but felt bad knowing that Amelia's case was the exact opposite.

Amelia pulled Emma closer and then put her head on her shoulder as they walked. She saw the look on Emma's face and read her like a book. "Don't worry; I'm jubilant for you." She would get used to other people being happy even though she knew she would never be. Soon they were swinging on Amelia's porch with the cool drink glasses in their hands. Amelia decided not to mention the social anymore because she knew she would have to attend with Thomas. She wasn't looking forward to him putting her on display and wondered what she could do to avoid the dance all together.

Henry was in his private office, in the back of his store, over- looking his paperwork. He had his head lowered towards the desk when he heard someone knock on the door. Without moving, he told his visitor to enter and didn't straighten until he heard the door re-shut. Glancing up, he acknowledged his guest, "Daniel Van Martin, I wasn't expecting you today."

Thomas' father reached over and shook Henry's hand before sitting in the chair that faced the desk. Though he knew he was the most prominent man in the village, he also knew that Henry ranked high among the more common folk. Daniel was determined to let the other know that he had the upper hand. His arrogant attitude wouldn't let Henry forget the mistake he was holding over his head. "Just came by to tell you I'm glad Amelia has accepted Thomas' hand."

Henry knew that this visit wouldn't be friendly for long. Daniel was the reason he was torturing his daughter the way he was. "You know that she didn't have a choice," he snapped.

"Oh yes, yes," Daniel stated as he blew on his finger nails and rubbed them against his vest. Amelia Samuels was an obedient daughter and would have to listen to her father in the same way that Henry had to listen to him. Daniel had a choice to make; either turn Henry in or give his son the one thing he wanted more than anything. Thomas admired her more than any other girl and wanted to make her his. Henry's mistake made it easy once Daniel blackmailed him. "So be it; if that's what it takes to make my son happy."

Henry was disgusted in both the Van Martin men but more disgusted with himself for allowing such behavior. He recalled the last visit he had from them. They were together and Thomas claimed that he loved Amelia though Henry knew better. Then Daniel blackmailed him and Henry had no choice but to accept the proposed offer. It was his life or hers. At least Amelia would heal. Still the thought angered him. "I wish we could have discussed this without bringing our children into it."

Daniel chuckled at the thought. As far as he was concerned, Henry could have left Thomas and Amelia out of it. He had nobody to blame but himself so Daniel thought Henry should stop belly-aching it. "You made your own bed, Samuels. Before you lie in it, tell me why you would commit treason against our country in the first place?"

With his elbows on the desk, Henry threw his head into his hands. He could feel the sweat rolling off of his forehead as he thought of the seriousness of his crimes. Without looking up he replied, "Business, it all comes down to my business." An apothecary made and sold ointments to heal the sick. It was the next best thing to being a doctor and in a small community like Millersport, it was better because most people couldn't afford to see a doctor but they could afford to see him. He also performed surgeries and to be a male midwife.

"I don't understand," Daniel responded.

"You wouldn't, now would you?" Henry shouted as he pulled his head up to look his adversary in the eyes. His blood was boiling and he could feel the redness on his face. Softening his voice so his employee didn't overhear, he continued, "The tariffs for one. Some of my supplies are from overseas. But my biggest reason is because the Indians are on the British side." He could tell that Daniel would interrupt with another question but his scowling face kept Daniel from speaking a word. "You're rich and when your family is sick, you travel to find a doctor. Most people around here can't do that. They come to me. They know they can pay me with money, make payments instead of paying outright, and some even offer their swine and chickens for payment. And I, I get my ailments from the red man. That's getting harder to do and it won't get better until the war is over."

At last, Daniel could get a word in. Before he said anything, he thought about what he heard. He didn't know that Madison's War was causing so much heartache for Henry; not that he cared. "Let me get this straight. The bottom line is that you don't care who wins the war. You just want it over."

"That's right," Henry answered before lowering his head again. He was quiet for a moment as his thoughts returned to Amelia. "Tell me, does Thomas love her?" Henry asked hoping Amelia's marriage would have happiness to it.

Daniel laughed. He knew his son well and anyone who had the chance to know Thomas as much as he did, knew Thomas could only love himself and his image. His son would never marry for love; only greed. Amelia fulfilled his greed for a picture perfect wife. "Now, I realize that she doesn't love him and no, he doesn't love her. But, my son isn't that bad and he'll make her happy in other ways. He can offer her more than any other man in New York."

Henry wasn't convinced but there wasn't a thing he could do about it. He had to pretend that he wanted her to marry Thomas. He knew that Daniel could see right through him. "Don't fret," he said. "You know that I'm not happy with this arrangement but there won't be a soul in Millersport who doesn't believe that I'm behind it one hundred percent."

"That is what I wanted to hear." Daniel stood to leave. He had done what he set out to do, and that was to reassure Henry that he couldn't back out of the deal. Daniel had information on Henry that would put him in an early grave and he planned to take complete advantage of it. He grinned again, shook Henry's hand and left.

Henry sat there and thought about what he was putting his family through. His thoughts turned to his deceased brother's wife, Ruth and how she was the only one, besides Daniel, who knew what he was up to. She didn't approve of his actions nor did she approve of him forcing Amelia into marriage. She had told him time and again that his secret could lead to serious trouble if the authorities ever found out but still he didn't listen. She told him he would lose Amelia's love forever if she found out about it. It was his mistakes that were changing her life forever. Guilt overcame him and he closed the store early and take a visit to see Ruth.

She was the only one he trusted enough to talk to; even his relationship with her was a secret. They lovers but nobody knew that. She wanted to let others know but Henry wasn't ready to reveal such emotions. He grabbed the only key to his office, told his employee he could go home, and then he was off to find comfort in the only place he knew of.

Chapter Five

There was less tension around the breakfast table the following morning. Amelia smiled across the table at Anna who had helped her prepare the meal. The companionship in the kitchen had cleared her mind for a while. Her smile grew wider as she held back laughter building up inside of her. Anna had made a mess of things trying to cook and the thoughts of flour on her face and egg in her hair had made Amelia chuckle. Anna sensed this and blushed with embarrassment.

Henry rubbed the side of his coffee cup as he studied the face of his eldest daughter. She appeared to be in better spirits and the thought of her being happy overjoyed him. He hoped that things would get back to normal. "Amelia," he started, "I was wondering if you could do me a favor today?" She had often helped him by doing small errands. Leaving the store early the day before had put him behind on a few things but he didn't regret a moment of time he'd spent with Ruth.

Relieved to have something to do other than sulk, she answered, "Sure Father. What would you like me to do?"

"Well, I meant to get medicine out to the widow Hewlett yesterday but I forgot about it." He wasn't ready to tell his children about his true relationship with Ruth. "Do you think you can stop by the store and take it out to her farm for me?"

The widow Hewlett lived on a farm south of the village and Amelia knew it would be quite a walk to the farm and back but she looked forward to it. It would get her away for a while and Thomas wouldn't find her. "I would be glad to. It's such a nice day; I look forward to the walk."

Henry leaned back in his chair and glanced out the window. The lack of sunshine and the sway of a nearby tree was evidence she wasn't correct. "Why don't you go to the stable and pick up the carriage? It looks like it might rain."

"I'll be fine. I care little for taking the carriage," she told him. Henry shrugged; there was no point in arguing with her. He stood and excused himself then left for work. Anna helped clean up and an hour later Amelia head out to the apothecary store.

When she arrived, Amelia noticed her father's employee sitting on the steps and leaning against a rail. "Where is my father?" She asked.

The young man gave her a puzzled look. "I don't know, Miss Samuels."

She was alarmed and wondered why Henry hadn't made it to his destination. "When he left the house he came straight here," she started but then caught of glimpse of her father walking down the street, rushing towards them. As he got closer she exclaimed, "Oh Father, I was worrying. What happened?"

It surprised Henry to see his daughter standing outside his building. He didn't think that she would be there that soon. "I'm sorry for the delay," he said intended more for his employee than for Amelia. He could give an excuse to his worker but coming up with something that Amelia would believe would be a challenge. As if she wasn't standing there, he said to the employee, "I will pay you your full wage of course."

Amelia was growing very impatient. "You left well before me and I still beat you here. Can't you at least tell me what happened?"

He unlocked the door and his employee worked right away. Not satisfied with his lack of an answer, Amelia followed the men into the building. "Won't you answer me Father?"

He could not delay answering her question. Henry appreciated that she was concerned, but he knew that there was no reason to be. The truth was he had forgotten his keys at Ruth's the day before when he went to visit her and this morning he needed to go retrieve them. He knew she wouldn't understand so he stretched the truth, "I ran an errand yesterday afternoon before coming home and somewhere along the way misplaced my keys."

"This is about your keys?" She asked, letting out a sigh of relief.

"Yes," Henry wondered if she believed him. "I spent the last hour traveling to all the places I was at yesterday trying to find them and I was thankful when I did." Jiggling his keys in his hand for confirmation, he looked at her and could tell that she believed his story.

Amelia shook her head as she followed him into his office. Sometimes, she told herself, she forgot who the parent was and who the child. She left but first turned to say, "I'm glad you are all right." Henry hugged her and assured her he was fine.

Though she was glad to feel his arms around her, she could sense the growing tension between them.

Amelia dropped off her father's remedy to the widow Hewlett and was on her way back home. Not wanting the thought of Thomas to bother her, she picked flowers to take her mind off of her troubles. She had walked a good mile or more away from the farm before she realized that she had other troubles coming her way. Thunder had started and was getting closer and closer. Amelia walked faster and glanced back at the farm but it was out of sight. There was no point in going back; she wouldn't make it on time. Another loud crack of thunder sounded and she knew she would get caught in a downpour.

The bit of sun that appeared throughout the morning seemed to have disappeared and darkness took over. One hand squeezed the flowers she had picked and her other hand grabbed her dress and pulled it off the ground, giving her limbs room to walk faster. The thunder lasted for what seemed like forever and when it finished, a flash of lightning lit the darkened sky. "Oh no," she said to herself and then ran. She searched for shelter but there was nothing in sight. She couldn't find a tree to stand under either for she was on part of the road that ran along the meadow. Then the rain came down.

Amelia was wet in an instant. The drops felt like ice on the back of her neck. She ran to get to shelter but the weight of her wet clothes were keeping her from advancing far.

Chills came over her and she knew that she had to dry off but the rain wasn't letting up. She let go of her dress, lowered her head so that the wind and rain were not hitting her straight in the face, and then ran forward. At last she saw a house with smoke coming out of the chimney. She felt relieved to see that someone was home and prayed that whoever lived there would let her come in until the rain let up.

By the time she arrived at the house she was wet from head to toe. She could feel water gushing in her shoes from the puddles. The bottom of her dress was full of mud. Yet, somehow she held onto the flowers she had picked before the sky had turned on her. Her body was shivering by the time she reached the door. Amelia reached out to knock with her free hand but it was shaking from the cold. She formed a fist and pounded on the wooden door.

When the door opened she was surprised to see Patrick standing before her. "Thank you for the flowers, Amelia, but you shouldn't have in the rain." He laughed and reached for her hand to bring her in out of the nasty weather. He shut the door behind her and pointed towards the fireplace, "Go warm up. I'll go get a blanket for you."

Right away Amelia thought she should continue on her way home. Her father wouldn't approve of her visiting with a man, a strange man to top it. Glancing out the window, she saw the rain she ran through just moments before and suddenly it didn't matter to her how inappropriate she was being; there was no way she would head back out into the rain. She stepped closer to the fire and rubbed her hands together. She looked around the small house that had no decorations at all. It was a simple home, unlike the houses in the village. She spotted a hound lying in the corner. His body stretched out and his stomach move up and down as he panted. He didn't seem alarmed by her presence and he moved his head once to look in her direction before nodding back off to sleep.

Patrick stepped inside his bedroom to find a spare blanket to throw over Amelia's shoulders to keep her warm. He reached for the spare hanging over the back of a rocking chair but knew that it wouldn't be enough. She would need to get out of those wet clothes or she would catch a cold. He thought for a moment on what to do. Then he bent over and pulled a chest out from underneath the bed. He hesitated before opening the latch. It had been a long time since he has seen the insides of the chest. It pained him to take anything out of it but yet he knew that in doing so he could prevent an illness for Amelia. From the inside of the chest, he pulled out a dress and laid it on the bed. Then, with the blanket in his hand, he went back to the main room. He noticed Amelia looking around the room and realized how awkward the situation must have been for her. "Get out of those wet clothes. We can hang them by the fire to dry. There is a dress on the bed. Put it on until yours is dry again."

Amelia didn't stop to wonder where he got a dress. She walked into his bedroom and shut the door behind her. The room was similar to the main room, colorless. She saw the dress lying over the bed and undressed right away. The dress was too big for her but she welcomed its dry material. Something caught her eye as she pondered who the dress belonged to. A picture frame stood on Patrick's night stand, the only picture she'd seen in his entire house. She picked the picture up out of curiosity and inspected the portrait. She saw a woman in the picture and Patrick standing with his arm around her. It all made sense to her; he was married, this was his wife's dress. She opened the door and went out to hang her clothes by the fire before sitting down next to Patrick.

"I'm glad to see that the dress fits you," Patrick told her. He never thought he would see someone wear his wife's clothing ever again.

Amelia smiled. He was a very generous man. "It's a little too big, but it's dry," then she continued to thank him for his kindness.

Patrick hung his head so that the girl couldn't see him wipe his eyes. He had not seen that dress for several years and now it was out of the chest, it seemed to have brought out bad memories. "I'm sorry that it's on the large side," he started. "My wife made that when she was pregnant with our son."

Amelia was confused. There were only two rooms in this small house; she wondered where the son slept? Amelia beat around the bush to figure her questions out. "Patrick, may I ask how old you are?"

He grinned. Amelia wasn't shy; he could tell that already by the brief encounters they had together. "I'll be thirty-two in February. Why do you ask?"

"Oh, I'm sorry if I'm being rude. Please accept my apologies," she began. "It's just that this house seems so small and I was wondering where your son slept. I thought maybe if I knew your age than I could guess his and try to figure it out for myself. I should've just asked."

He admired the curiosity in her. In fact, he realized that he was admiring everything about her. It hurt him to think about what happened to his wife and son but recalling how she blurted out her personal life to him earlier in the week, he decided that she would understand his story. He stood up and leaned his forearm against the mantle and then laid his head on his arm. He could feel his throat harden and his eyes water as he told her, "I lost them three years ago. My wife suffered a hard labor, and I lost them both that night." He looked over at her but she had lowered her head. He explained the matter more, "I wanted to go fetch a doctor,

40

but she insisted that I stay. I kept telling her it was many miles to the nearest doctor and that I had to go. She cried and cried and begged me not to leave her. She gave in and let me go but by the time I returned with the doctor, our son was already stillborn. The doctor told me we had to make my wife comfortable. I tried everything I could do, but she was still in pain. She passed on just before dawn."

Amelia had tears rolling down her face. She didn't mean to bring up so many painful memories for Patrick and prayed that he would forgive her. "I'm so sorry, Patrick. I feel I brought back heartache for you."

He wiped his eyes and sat back down. Patrick couldn't let her go on thinking that any of this was her fault. He was the one who opened the chest to give her something dry to wear. "It's not your fault. I couldn't let you sit in wet clothes. It was my decision to let you wear that dress."

Amelia felt he wasn't ready to let go of what happened in the past and sensed that he blamed himself. She reached over to him and put her hand on his arm. "It wasn't your fault either. You did all you could have done." She had seen still-born births while helping her father and recalled telling other parents the same thing.

Patrick felt her touch his arm. A welcomed touch, a touch he thought he wouldn't want to feel again. "That isn't what her parents thought. They blamed me. They said that I could have prevented it." He stopped talking and thought about how they had treated him. As they mourned the death of their daughter, they told him he shouldn't have listened to her when she begged him not to leave. They told him she would still be with them if he would have done the right thing. He wiped his eyes for a final time and decided not to dwell on bad memories. It was time to change the subject. "What are you doing out in the rain, anyway?"

Knowing he didn't wish to talk about it anymore, Amelia dropped it and answered his question. "I was out doing an errand for my father."

A puzzled look came to his face. "Your father didn't let you use a carriage on a day like this?" He must have known it would rain sooner or later.

Just then Amelia laughed as she realized that getting soaked in the rain was her fault. "Oh no, he told me to take the carriage, but I insisted on walking. I was such a fool for not listening." She continued to tell him about the way she preferred to walk and why she was out near his house to begin with.

Patrick prepared tea for the two of them. Amelia never had a man serve her anything before; it was strange to her. He laughed and told her he was only being respectful to his company. Together they sipped tea and spent the next couple of hours talking. Patrick had many questions about Millersport and Amelia was glad to answer them. She also asked questions about him but was careful not to bring up anything that might have been painful. She found out he was from the Rochester area and moved to make a new life for himself.

Patrick told her he planned on growing an apple orchard and that is why he was out in the fields that previous time she had seen him. She thought it would be delightful to purchase home grown apples to make pies and fritters. Amelia never knew that she could have such a delightful conversation with a man before. He made her so comfortable and she wondered how she made him feel? Before they knew it, the sun was shining again outside and the fierce rain had gone away. Deciding that her clothes were dry enough, Amelia went back to his bedroom and changed. When she came out, she told him she should get home before her family wondered what happened to her. Patrick agreed and walked her out.

They were only a few steps away from his door when he remembered her flowers. "Your flowers, don't you want them?"

Amelia smiled and thought that his house could use them more than hers. She had placed them on his table while

42

they drank their tea and thought they cheered the room up. "No, you keep them. It's the least I can do for all your kindness."

She turned and walked towards the village. He stood and watched her go. At that moment he wished that she were staying. She was almost out of sight when he ran after her, "Amelia, wait." He was just about out of breath by the time he caught up with her. "I wanted to tell you I enjoyed your company today and I wondered if we can do it again sometime." He couldn't believe what he was saying to her, knowing it wouldn't be right. Still, he had to ask.

Amelia blushed. Why couldn't she feel this comfortable around Thomas? Why couldn't her fiancé be so kind? She despised Thomas Van Martin but admired Patrick. She knew her father wouldn't approve if he knew what she was thinking but she couldn't help but be happy that Patrick wanted to see her again. "How is tomorrow? I planned to go pick berries but then I can stop by."

It thrilled Patrick that it didn't offend her. He meant no harm, and he was sure she understood. "Can I pick with you? I know a place where the berries are plentiful."

"Okay. Then I will see you tomorrow." She smiled and then continued to walk home. Mud clung to the bottom of her dress but she was thankful for it. If it weren't for the rain, she wouldn't have been able to spend the day with Patrick Buchanan.

Chapter Six

The floor was wearing out as Anna paced back and forth, wondering where Amelia was. Never returning after running the errand for their father, Anna assumed that Amelia had spent the day with Emma. The clock on the mantel neared the dinner hour, and she knew that she would have to start the meal without Amelia.

Anna dreaded to cook and clean and wished that her older sister were not getting married. Housework wasn't her cup of tea; she'd rather be out playing stick-ball with the boys. Her father's decision to make Amelia marry was forcing Anna to learn how to manage a kitchen. "It isn't fair," she said out loud to herself, glancing out the window as she looked for Amelia. It was time to cook and she would have to do it alone.

A few minutes later the front door opened. She looked out of the kitchen to see who it was. "Finally," she sneered as Amelia walked in. "What on Earth happened to you?" Amelia was a mess from her river soaked shoes to her wet and wind- blown hair. She apologized for being late and promised to help out as soon as she cleaned herself and changed her clothes. Anna sighed and wondered which one of them was the tomboy.

After a while, the family sat around the table to eat. They were all quiet but Anna wanted to find out what kept her sister away so long. "So Amelia," she started, "You never told me why your dress was full of mud when you came home."

Henry's eyes moved from left to right, looking at the two girls sitting on opposite sides of the table. Wondering if his morning intuition was correct, he asked, "What's this?"

Amelia slide down her chair and blushed. "Oh Father, I should have listened to you and taken the carriage. I was on my way home this afternoon when the rain started and I had no place to hide."

The boys, who loved to play with mud and get dirty, laughed. "You were outside when it rained?" Little Charles' excitement brought a grin to his face.

Amelia wiped her mouth and looked to her father. She was afraid that he would yell at her for her behavior. "I'm sorry, Father."

Henry burst into laughter and the rest of the family then laughed with him. She was too defiant to listen to him. "That serves you right for not listening to your father."

She blushed again. "You are not upset with me?"

Henry reached over and touched her hand. He had missed the closeness between them. For the subject of her marriage, he knew that she wanted nothing to do with him. When the subject was about anything else, she was still his loving daughter. "Of course I'm not upset. I hope you found some kind of shelter, it was coming down hard."

They all looked at her, wondering what she did to protect herself from the rain. She didn't know what to say. Telling them she had spent the day with Patrick would have horrified them and her father would see to a punishment. Before speaking, she glanced at Anna who had seen that her dress wasn't wet. "I found a tree large enough to stand under. I could still feel the wind and rain but not as bad as being directly in it." She never thought she could lie to them and was surprised how easy it came out of her mouth.

The next morning brought another lie, and she didn't know what was coming over her. She had always been so obedient and honest now felt as if the truth would hurt her family. Before leaving the breakfast table, her father had asked her what her plans were for the day. She started off being honest and told him she planned on picking berries. "With Emma, I assume," he said to her. She nodded and told him he was correct. She tried to make herself feel better by telling herself that she didn't direct fib to him, she agreed with what he had said, but it didn't work. A lie was a lie, and she wondered just how many she would tell before she married Thomas.

A while later she grabbed her basket and was ready to leave. She opened the door and stood face to face with Thomas and her head ached. She should have known having a nice day was too good to be true. "Thomas, what are you doing here?"

Ignoring her question, Thomas took a seat on the top step of the porch and motioned for her to join him. She refused and tried to walk away. Thomas felt that her behavior was inappropriate but decided that he wouldn't allow it anymore. He flew down the porch steps, grabbed her waist, and pulled her close to him. She smelt sweet and her skin was so soft. Very inviting, he thought to himself. She tried to wiggle away, but he tightened his arms around her and then put his mouth right on her lips. He could hear her sounds of disgust but didn't care. When he stopped kissing her, he loosened his grip and said, "I've come here to see you."

Amelia wiped her mouth as hard as she could to rid herself of his wet kiss and moved away from him as fast as she could. "Why, don't you have a job to go to?"

Thomas laughed; he was enjoying seeing her squirm and decided not to let her get away so easy. He pulled her next to him again and rubbed her arm as he talked to her. "I was thinking," He explained, "We've been engaged for almost a week and you haven't yet shown an interest in me. How can we marry if we don't get to know one another?"

She shrugged. He had a good point and thought she should make more of an effort to avoid him. "You're right, Thomas. We can't marry if we don't get to know each other. So why don't you go away, never come near me again, and then we won't have to wed."

He didn't like the way she talked to him and didn't expect his prize to be so headstrong. "Oh Amelia, you think you are so funny, don't you?" It was time for him to put his foot down and demand they spend time together.

"Tomorrow is Saturday and I won't be working at the brickyard. You and I will go on a private picnic."

The thought of being alone with him made her insides quiver. "No, I don't want to be alone with you."

Thomas grew angry. She didn't have a choice; all he had to do was go to her father. He explained his intention of getting Henry involved until she lowered her head and mumbled her agreement. "That a girl," he said and pulled her closer again. "I'll be here to pick you up at noon. Be ready." He kissed her again and walked away but then remembered, "Oh yeah, prepare a nice meal."

Amelia felt dirty. She wondered how she could ever get him to stop kissing her but knew that there wasn't anything she could do. After he was her husband, he would have the right any time he wanted. The thought made her shiver, but she forced herself to think of other things; or the rest of her day would be ruined.

The ax in Patrick's strong arm had landed in the middle of a log when he spotted Amelia walking in his direction. He grinned and bit his bottom lip as unexplainable butterflies developed in his stomach. Patrick wasn't able to stop thinking about her since she left the day before and he realized just how lonely he had become since losing his wife. Patrick knew that it wasn't right to think of her the way he did and he also knew that it wasn't right to ask to see her. He didn't want to cause any trouble but yet, at the same time, he didn't want to stop seeing her either.

"Am I interrupting anything?" Amelia asked as she walked up to Patrick.

Patrick put the ax down and wiped his forehead. The previous day's rain had brought humidity to the summer air. After adjusting his eyes from the blinding sun, he noticed the basket she carried and knew she wanted to pick berries. "Ready to go?" he asked.

Amelia's circled mouth and wide eyes had told Patrick that she liked the spot he'd chosen. He watched as she filled her basket with black raspberries. She would comment on the size as she picked one but then grow more excited when she found one larger. Patrick remained close as he held the basket for her. "Are they plentiful in the village?"

"Mmm, no," she answered after popping a berry into her mouth. The patches she knew of couldn't compare. "I never thought of coming out this far but wished I knew."

Patrick also put a black cap into his mouth and savored its taste as she continued to pick. When the basket was full, Amelia ate another. Patrick couldn't help notice the smudge left near her lip from the berry. She was standing close to him and the heat was bringing out her sweet scent. Being tempted beyond reason, he leaned forward and rubbed his thumb along her lower lip to remove the spec. Her eyes looked up and silently told him she wasn't afraid. Amelia laughed and then ran away. At first, Patrick thought she was trying to run from him but when she stopped a rod away and smiled again, he knew she was being playful. Dropping the basket, he raced to catch up with her. She would pause, allowing him to catch up, but then take off again just before he reached her. After a few attempts he gained ground and caught up. Being behind her, Patrick grabbed Amelia's waist, spun her around and then embraced her.

Amelia's laughter was contagious as she fell into his arms. She didn't know what she was experiencing but knew she preferred the feelings over the way she felt around Thomas.

"Come with me," Patrick said as he placed her gentle hand into his. "There is a creek nearby. Let's go sit by it." Leading her the short distance, he picked up her basket as they passed the berry patch.

Again, Amelia's eyes gave away her amazement. The water glistened from the sun as she threw herself down on the grassy bank. Patrick stretched out beside her and stared up at the blue sky. "This is nothing like the creek near my home," she informed him.

"I believe they call that a river, Miss Samuels," Patrick joked. He listened as she told him about a creek north of her father's house and compared the two.

They remained by the creek for the better part of the afternoon. It amazed both of them how easy they conversed and how many likes they shared in common. He watched her mouth move with every word she said and glanced into her eyes every time she paused. He wished that she had something else on her face he could wipe off.

"I better head back home," she said though she would rather stay with him for the rest of the day. They stood up at the same time and their faces become unexpectedly close. Knowing his lips were close to hers made her hope he would lean in and take advantage of the moment. She remembered the way Thomas stole kisses from her but knew that receiving one from Patrick would be completely different. Time stood still as they remained in that position.

Patrick sensed what she wanted, and he wanted nothing more than to give it to her but her being someone else's pained his heart. Her life was complicated enough, and he didn't want to cause any more trouble. As much as it tore him to break away from her, Patrick turned his head and took a step back. "I'll walk with you a way."

They were silent for a few minutes as they walked. Amelia was disappointed but understood why he hadn't kissed her. She was positive he was just as much attracted to her as she was to him. His resistance and honor made her admire him even more than she already had. The silence was too awkward, so she spoke, "So, will I see you in church on Sunday?"

He reached over and squeezed her hand and then let go. "I say my prayers at home."

She wasn't surprised with what he said and knew of others who chose not to attend the services. "Can't you come just once?" She asked in hopes to see him again. "You should get to know the community. I feel I'm being selfish; hogging you to myself."

He knew that she was right and should have told her his reasons for not attending church. He had only been to one service since losing his wife. The people gathered around him to give condolences and it had been too much on him. He decided not to mention it to her. "I have no problem with your selfishness." They laughed and continued walking until they were close to the village. "I will let you go alone now," he told her. "I think people would talk if they saw you walking with the stranger."

"Will you ever not be the stranger?" Amelia didn't want to leave his side but understood what he was saying.

"Yes, in time." Patrick placed her basket in her hand and then lifted it to his lips. Her skin melted beneath them and Patrick yearned for more. "Are you free tomorrow?"

Amelia's happy face soured as she told him. "I'm sorry. I have to go on a picnic with Thomas. I'd much rather be with you but it'll please my father."

"I understand," he told her without letting her know how it upset him. He knew he was becoming far too attached to someone who he could never be with. "Then, I'm sure we'll see each other soon. Take care."

She said farewell as he kissed the back of her hand again. He watched her as she continued walking home and then smiled as he turned and began his journey back to his house.

That night the family all sat in the sitting-room. The boys were playing a game of chess, Henry was reading, and Amelia was teaching Anna to knit. She was proud of her younger sister who had grown a lot since her engagement almost a week before. She thought she would be an old lady before Anna would show an interest in knitting. It was a peaceful night at home until Henry took a break from reading. He put his book down and said to Amelia, "I saw Thomas today and he told me that the two of you are going on a special picnic tomorrow. It's good of you to spend time with him."

The boys stopped playing and Anna nervously played with the yarn. Everyone in the room knew that Amelia still hated being with Thomas, except for their father. Again, she stood her ground. "I don't want to go."

Henry asked the others to leave them alone. The three siblings had done what they were told and filtered out of the room. When he knew that they were no longer around he prepared himself for another battle with Amelia. "What do you mean? Get to know him. You'll be married to him in the spring."

She grew as mad as a March hare. They had yet to discuss a date, and she wondered if this was just another thing he would force upon her. "What do you mean, Father? We have not set a date."

"Daniel and I think the spring will be best." Henry stated though what he really wanted to say was that Daniel thought it was best. Truthfully, he didn't have a say in the matter.

"You and Mr. Van Martin are setting our wedding date? That isn't fair. I don't even get a choice who I marry. Now you're telling me I don't get a choice when I will marry?" She hated how he was treating her. What was next? Would he tell her when she would have her first child too?

Henry knew that he shouldn't have brought her marriage up but he couldn't keep avoiding the subject with her. "For Heaven's sake Amelia," he hollered, "If I leave it up to you, there will never be a set date and you know that as well as I do."

She didn't know where the courage was coming from or what would happen to her for fighting for what she believed in but she would not lie down and take it anymore. "There would be a set date if you allow me to marry who I want."

Henry shook his head, she would never hang up the fiddle, he thought. "You will marry him, young lady, so drop it." It was quiet for a few minutes and Henry could see how upset she was as she fought back tears. He never thought that the two of them could have such heated discussions. Henry wasn't happy with the way he was treating her but he believed it was for the good. He brought the subject back to where it began. "Please tell me the real reason you don't want to go tomorrow."

Amelia took a deep breath. She wondered how her father would react to the way Thomas made her feel. It was best to be honest with him, she thought. "Father, I'm afraid that Thomas would make a pass on me he shouldn't be taking yet."

He straightened in his chair. He still had certain morals and not losing one's virginity before she wed was one of them. "Has he tried to touch you?"

Amelia blushed. She had wished that she could have talked about what was bothering her with someone else, Beth or even her aunt, but she talked to her father and knew that she had to continue. "No, Father, not in that way."

Henry felt relief. He wanted nothing like that to happen to his daughter. That was the worst thing he could ever imagine. "See, I told you that Thomas Van Martin is a good fellow."

"But he isn't," she insisted. "He has forced kisses upon me and he even told me he wouldn't wait until we were married." She hoped that telling her father what Thomas was like would help her cause.

Henry didn't believe what she was saying. Thomas was a model citizen of Millersport and Henry knew there was no way that the boy would behave that way. "Amelia, don't lie." The Van Martins might have been forcing this marriage but Henry still thought that Thomas would never do the things she said.

"I'm not lying." She felt a lump in her throat as she thought of Emma and the tree she said she found shelter under. Still she was dumbfounded by his remarks because this time she was telling the absolute truth.

He knew she was gumming to get out of her engagement. Henry had a good mind to box her ears for behaving that way but he thought they had been through enough already. He tried to comfort her. He knew that Thomas would not try anything but wanted to set Amelia's mind to rest. "I'll tell you what," he started. "David told me he was concerned about you. I'll ask him to follow the two of you and if the boy should try anything, then your brother will protect you."

Amelia could finally relax again. She knew that her father loved her and knew that he would always protect her. "Thank you, Father." She yawned and told him she wanted to retire to bed. He hugged her as he said good night. For the first time in days, she was feeling better about their relationship, a feeling that wouldn't last.

Chapter Seven

The next afternoon brought Thomas to the Samuels house as planned to pick up Amelia. She showed no interest to be going with him but yet felt a sense of security knowing that David would be there. He'd be hiding somewhere and ready to protect her if needed. Her father had left the house earlier to speak to her brother. Amelia thought for sure that everything was set. Thomas met her at the door to escort her to the carriage. Anna stood to see them off. As she waved goodbye, she asked if Amelia would be home in time to help with the evening meal. Amelia knew that her sister was just trying to get the young man to return her in a timely manner. Thomas assured Anna that they would be gone for only two hours and as they drove away, Amelia mouthed, "Thank you," to Anna.

It seemed like an eternity before they reached their destination. Amelia was eager to get off of the carriage so they could get the picnic over and done with. Thomas came around to her side and helped her down. He put his arms around her. She wiggled herself free and reached for the basket in the back of the carriage. "I'll set everything up," she mumbled.

Moments later the two of them sat down on the blanket she had laid out. To Amelia's surprise, Thomas sat a couple of feet away from her. He leaned backwards and used his arms to support him. Thomas talked to her, he wanted to be friendly so she would open to him. He would make his move when she relaxed and had her guard down. "I suppose you know all about Jacob asking Emma to court him. They are going to the social dance together."

"Oh bully for her! I know that she admires Jacob." Amelia didn't bother to tell Thomas that she had heard that straight from Emma's mouth. She allowed him to think he was informing her of what was going on around the village. It gave him a false sense of importance and the thought made her smile.

"Then why can't you admire me? Jacob and I are best chums."

All she could do was shake her head. True, they might have been the best of friends but they were as different as night and day. She told him that, hoping that maybe she could change him. "You, Mr. Van Martin, are nothing like your friend. Perhaps if you were," she wanted to continue, but he didn't let her.

"What if I were?" Thomas interrupted. Jacob was too kind, too gentle, and Thomas knew that being like him would get him nowhere in life.

Amelia prepared their plates as she said, "You are arrogant and rude and selfish. If you were kind, like Jacob, and if you cared about anyone other than yourself, then maybe you would be a better mate for me."

Thomas sat up straight and moved closer to Amelia. "I need not be, now do I? We're already betrothed so why should I change?" He leaned closer to kiss her, but she backed up and he fell flat onto the ground. She tried so hard to get away from him and that only made him angry. She would give into him, he thought, and it would start today. After she received his magical touch, she would never turn his kisses down again.

"Don't you care about making anyone happy?"

"I'm trying to make you happy but you keep moving away." She put his plate in his hand and told him to eat. "Fine, we'll continue this after our meal," he said so low she couldn't hear him.

As Amelia ate, she wondered where David was hiding. He was doing a good job at not being seen and was being silent. She was looking around when she heard Thomas ask her what she was looking for and she told him she was just watching for birds. Believing her, he continued to eat. When they finished, Amelia wanted to go back to the village but Thomas insisted that they should relax before heading back home. He knew what he was doing by bringing her out this far for the picnic. They were completely alone and he could do what he wanted to her. He glanced over at her. She was almost as beautiful as he was. He licked his lips and could still taste her from when he kissed her the day before. He longed to taste her lips again, and he gave into his temptation. Before she got away from him, he leaned over and forced her onto her back and then straddled on top of her.

"Get off of me," she insisted but Thomas put his disgusting mouth on her lips. She squirmed to get free and wondered how long it would take her brother to rescue her. He must have been hiding several yards away and was why it was taking so long to reach her.

"Relax," Thomas said to her when taking a breath from kissing her. "We're engaged, we're not doing anything wrong." As she struggled to get away from him, he became curious why she acted the way she did. He knew other girls would love to be in her position. "Why won't you let me love you?" He asked in anger.

Tears filled her eyes. "What do you know about love?" She snapped at him as she used all her might to shove him off of her. It was doing no good though because he wasn't budging. "You said yourself that you don't love me. You know this marriage is nothing more than a business deal between our fathers and I will get out of it. So take your hands off of me, now!" She was afraid of what he would try while they were in a secluded area. She wanted to cry out for David, he had to be almost there to help her, but she couldn't because again Thomas' lips covered hers. He took his hand and placed it on her jaw, opening her mouth. She tried to turn her head but his hand was too strong. With his mouth still on hers, he slid his tongue inside. She could feel his wetness as he choked her and she wanted to throw up. She tried to get out from underneath him but it was doing no good. The harder she tried to free herself, the tighter he held her close. She would have never guessed his strength, but she was learning what he hid for so long. She was alarmed when

56

he took his free hand and rubbed her breast and she shook her body to get him to stop but it wasn't working. Where was her brother?

Thomas was enjoying himself all to pieces. He would finally have his way with her. She was protesting, he could feel her fighting but the more she tried to escape, the more excited he became. Her breast overflowed his hand, but he greedily tried to grab as much as he could. It wouldn't be long now, he decided, for he couldn't wait to take her.

Tears streamed down her face as she realized that David would not help her. It was no wonder why she couldn't see him when she searched for him; he hadn't come. Now she was in trouble and she didn't know what to do. She could feel Thomas' tongue gushing around as his lips pressed hard into hers and she felt his other hand squeezing her breast. He let go of her breast and took his hand and placed it under her dress. Rubbing his hand up her inner thigh, she knew that his hands were moving towards for her most treasured private spot. She didn't know what to do but knew that she had to do something quick to stop him. She gagged as she felt his tongue exploring the inner most part of her mouth and then thought of a way out of the horrible experience. Before he could defend himself, she bit down as hard as she could on his slimy tongue.

Thomas jolted off of Amelia in pain. Anger came over him like a hurricane and he wanted nothing more than to punish her. "You little quim," he yelled but then realized that she was running away.

Amelia jumped up the minute she felt the pressure of him off of her. She didn't hesitate to run to get as far away from him as she could. It wasn't long before she heard his footsteps behind her so she picked up her pace and ran faster. She could feel his blood in her mouth and knew that she must have bit him hard. Amelia wiped it as she ran and noticed that she no longer heard him behind her. She stopped to check and sure enough he was gone. Fear came over her again though because she knew he must have gone back for the carriage and there was no way she could out run a horse.

She came to a split in the road and turned. It wouldn't be long before she reached residential houses and if he caught up with her, she would only have to scream and someone would be around to help her. Still she didn't stop running.

Thomas grabbed the blanket and basket and threw them in the back of the carriage. He prepared the horse as fast as he could and then climbed aboard the carriage to chase Amelia. He needed to make sure she didn't get far, needed to keep her away from the residential area.

Thomas was no longer in the mood to enjoy her body but wanted to punish her instead. He whipped the horse and started after her but couldn't find her right away. She was faster than he gave her credit for. Finally he spotted her but it was too late, she was too close to someone's house and he knew that he couldn't lay a hand on her there. Thomas had no choice but to settle this some other time. He stopped the horse and turned the carriage around and continued to go home the way he had come. He knew that she wouldn't remain quiet about what just happened and thought of things to say to her father to cover up his behavior.

Amelia glanced back and saw Thomas on the carriage. She was afraid of what he would do if he caught her. Then she noticed him turning around and giving up. She didn't trust him and thought he was up to something. She slowed down, relieved to see him leave the area, and walked. She wiped her eyes and the rest of Thomas' blood from her mouth as her thoughts returned to David. It hurt her to think that her big brother couldn't be there to protect her like their father asked. She went straight to his house and ask him what was going on.

Still shaking when she arrived at David's house, she could barely knock on the door but knocked hard enough for someone to hear her. Beth answered the door and asked her to come in. Once inside Amelia realized that she shouldn't say anything in front of his wife but her anger was overwhelming. "David," she exclaimed with fresh tears in her eyes, "Why didn't you do as Father had asked you this morning?"

David looked over at Beth who also seemed concerned about Amelia then he went up to his sister and placed his hand on her shoulder. "Amelia, what is wrong?"

"Father said that you would be there, David," she explained but was to upset. She needed to catch her breath.

He shook his head in confusion and guided his sister to a chair to have a seat. "I don't know what you mean. I haven't seen Father at all today."

Amelia looked stunned. She remembered her father saying he was going straight to David's asking for his protection. Then it hit her; her father had lied. She cried as hard as she could and she felt her brother wrap his arms around her.

"Drink this, Amelia," Beth said to her as she handed her a glass of water. She knew that everyone wanted her to leave the room when something was wrong but now she saw her sister-in-law shaking and in tears, there was no way she was going anywhere. She glanced over at her husband who knew not to argue with her about it and urged him to sort this out.

David understood what his wife was motioning. "Tell me what happened."

Amelia now knew that none of this was David's fault and decided that she needed someone to talk to. Nothing like this had ever happened to her before but who better to talk to than her older brother.

Amelia explained everything and David was dumbfounded and furious. What was his father thinking to let her go with Thomas even after she explained that the boy had forced kisses on her before? Why would he tell her he would have her brother's protection when he didn't plan on that? He wondered what was going on with his father to make him disregard his daughter the way he had been. "I'm so sorry for you. Please know that I would have been there if I knew."

Beth sat on the other side of Amelia and rubbed her back to comfort her. "He is telling the truth. Your father hasn't been here at all today." She cared for Amelia and wanted what was best for her. She knew, the best thing was to help get her sister-in-law calm.

Amelia looked over at the two of them and smiled. None of this was their fault. Her problems were with her father and the man he was making her marry. She embraced David and Beth and thanked them for their concern. Then she stood and told them she would take care of everything though she didn't know where to even begin.

David offered to talk to their father and tell him all that had happened to her but Amelia asked him not to. She felt it would only make things worse. She said goodbye to them and then left their house. Standing out in the street, she thought about her father lying to her. Breaking promises was something he would never have done to her before. There had to be a reason he was treating her this way. She ran all the way home and then up into her room where she landed on her bed and cried again. She heard Anna rush into the room and ask her what was wrong. She told her young sister to leave her alone and then she fell asleep; tired from running and tired from crying.

After returning the carriage to his father's stall in the stable, Thomas decided not to wait until Henry came to him for an explanation. He knew that Amelia was angry for the way he behaved with her but also knew that she would be too ashamed to tell her father. He wanted to make sure she was punished for biting him and knew who he needed to talk to. He walked up the street and went into her father's store and hoped that he would be there. He was in luck as he saw the older man talking to his employee.

Henry looked across the room and noticed that Thomas had walked in. The boy looked a mess, and he wondered where his daughter was. He let his employee go home and waited until he left before greeting Thomas. "Where is Amelia?"

Thomas took a deep breath and thought of the right words to say. He knew from Henry's question he hadn't seen Amelia. He was glad, now he could say whatever it took to get Amelia in trouble. "That is what I'm here to talk to you about; I didn't think she would be so difficult. Perhaps we should change our plans." Thomas knew that Henry would rather see his daughter unhappy than be reported. He knew that the elder would make sure everything turned out fine. There would either be a wedding or a necktie social; Henry was too smart for that.

Henry wasn't happy with what the boy had just said. If Amelia had made Thomas change his mind about the marriage, Daniel would tell the authorities everything he knew. "Tell me, what is going on?"

Thomas thought for a second to make what he was about to say sound real. "We were having a nice time, but she still said that she didn't want to marry me. She said that she wanted to find someone else to marry."

"That doesn't surprise me any, my daughter has been clear about her thoughts on marriage." Henry knew that in time she would come around but was a little concerned about her hurting the boy by being so blunt with him. "Don't worry; she will do as I tell her, she'll be your wife."

Thomas shook his head and continued to tell lies. "I'm not too sure. I asked her if I could kiss her. I wanted to show her a little of my affection. That is when she took me off guard."

Henry tilted his head to the side and wondered what the boy meant. Amelia had told him that Thomas had tried kissing her before; still he couldn't figure out what was wrong. "What do you mean about her taking you off guard?"

Thomas grinned on the inside. On his way over to the store he had forced himself to bite his own lip enough to make it bleed. He wanted to tell her father about her biting him but didn't want to tell him exactly what he was doing. "Well, she surprised me and said that I could kiss her but when I leaned in she bit my lip and ran away."

Henry didn't know whether to believe Thomas but as he moved closer, he could see a little fresh blood around Thomas' lip. "Thomas, I'm very sorry for my daughter's behavior." He was now angry and upset with the lengths she would get out of their marriage. He wouldn't let her behave that way and planned to take care of the problem right away. "Don't worry either, she will marry you."

Henry hurried home and called for Amelia as soon as he stepped inside. Anna told him where she was and he flew up the stairs. "I'm calling you girl," he growled as he barged through her bedroom door.

Amelia's back was towards him when she jumped up off the bed. She heard him call out to her and was about to go downstairs but waited until she wiped all the tears from her eyes. She was surprised to see him come to her. "I'm sorry Father; I was just on my way down."

Henry could see her bloodshot eyes but decided it best to not let her soften him. "I saw Thomas," he started. "Give me one good reason why you would bite him."

"He was being improper," Amelia snapped.

Henry mistook her statement as a confession but didn't believe her reasoning. "Don't lie. I know that he asked for your permission."

It was then that Amelia knew that Thomas had embellished the story in his favor. "I haven't lied, that is what you do best."

Without a thought, Henry reached over and back-handed her across the cheek. Right away she held her hand over the sore spot he struck. "You'll make no more attempts to get out of your engagement, do you understand?"

Amelia's heart broke from his behavior towards her. She wanted to cry but at the moment was too angry to let him see how she felt on the inside., and she knew that he was the reason behind it all. "No, I don't understand," she squealed. "I don't understand how you can turn your back on your daughter. I don't even know you anymore."

"You will marry Thomas and you're just going to have to adjust." Henry left his reply unanswered as he stormed out of her room and entered his own. Sitting on the bed, he could feel his body shake from guilt. He stretched his hand out in front of him and could see her face still embossed on it. Henry placed his hand over his heart and leaned back onto the bed. She'd forgive him if she knew, he thought, but he was too shameful to admit what he'd done.

Chapter Eight

After the church service, David wanted to speak to Amelia to see how she was doing but he noticed that she took off as soon as the service ended. He thought it was odd she didn't stay to talk to anyone. She was a social person. He found Anna and asked where Amelia was off to in such a rush.

"I don't know," Anna answered. "But I bet she is going back to her bedroom to cry again. Father hit her last evening." She had snuck up the stairs to see what the yelling was all about but ran back down after her father had struck Amelia, in fear of being punished herself. It sent an uneasy feeling through Anna to think that her father could do such a thing to one of his children.

David was beside himself. He knew that Amelia was upset as it was and wondered why she deserved punishment. "Why?"

"I don't know that either." She lied. Anna heard the entire conversation until the slap and knew Amelia had mouthed off. She knew better than to tell David that though because she knew eavesdropping wasn't tolerated.

David was determined to get to the bottom of the problem. Something was going on and David would find out what, somehow. He spotted Henry talking to someone and thanked Anna for updating him. Then he stormed off towards his father in search for the answers he wanted.

Henry was discussing the sermon with a couple of friends when he saw his son approach him. "Excuse me, fellows," he said as he walked towards David.

David was in no mood to be polite to his father. He didn't let his father say a word before he demanded, "Father, I want to know what is going on with Amelia. Why on Earth would you strap her?"

Surprised by David's behavior, Henry stated, "David, this is none of your concern."

"Well, it concerns me now you brought me into it." He still couldn't get over the way his father lied to his sister.

Henry chuckled. He had no idea what David was talking about. "How did I bring you into the situation?"

David shook his head. His father would stand there and pretend that everything was okay. He knew that his father just wanted him to back down, but he refused. "You told Amelia that you would ask me to watch over her. You never came but she did and she was very upset."

Henry didn't think there was a reason to have David protect her and never intended to ask. He only said that to Amelia so she would calm down and go on the picnic. He didn't think that she would even remember. "She went with Thomas and I know that he would never do anything to hurt her. I meant to ask you," he lied again, "Just to make her feel better, but I got sidetracked. Besides, it's no big deal. Thomas is the one who needs protection."

David couldn't believe the way his father talked of Amelia and sided with Thomas instead of his own daughter. He wanted to tell him what Thomas had tried with Amelia but he promised her he wouldn't. "Don't be foolish, Father." He said. "I hope you are more concerned about your own flesh and blood in the future." Then he turned away without saying goodbye and walked home. He knew that Amelia would take care of herself.

Ruth had seen Henry talking to David. They didn't look like they were having a friendly father and son conversation and she wondered what could cause tension between the two men. She told her boys they could go play with Henry's younger sons and then she waited around for her turn to speak to him. Finally, David stormed off and Ruth walked over to Henry. As she got closer to him she thought he must have been discussing Amelia. He didn't look happy, and she knew better than anyone else that letting Amelia down was the only thing that could make him unhappy. "Is everything all right, Henry?"

He looked over at Ruth and could smile. Ruth had that effect on him. She took all troubles away. "Yes, everything is fine. Care to walk with me?" He asked her.

Ruth walked close to Henry and wished that he could offer her his arm to hold onto but knew that they would be seen. He had told her many times that their love for each other had to be a secret. She didn't agree with him. With Henry, it seemed, everything had to be a secret. Only she knew the real reason he was forcing Amelia into a loveless marriage, only she knew what illegal activities he was up to, and she was the only one who knew that he loved her far more than he led others to believe. If anyone could get through to him, it would be her. "Henry, are things okay between you and Amelia? I sense that things are still bad."

"She refuses to talk." Ruth looked confused so Henry continued and told her about the feud he had with Amelia and the slap that resulted from the argument.

Ruth second-guessed being the voice of reason but she knew that someone had to be. "Henry, you can stop this nonsense." Henry objected, but she continued, "You know you can. Amelia doesn't love Thomas, but she loves you and I'm sure she will forgive you for hitting her if you let her marry for love."

Henry laughed. How could Amelia marry for love when Daniel Van Martin held so much over his head? Ruth was the only person who he had told, the only person who knew how he felt about Amelia's marriage. "You know why I'm doing this, besides whom would she marry? There is nobody around here that she is interested in."

Ruth was getting frustrated. Henry claimed that forcing Amelia into a marriage was damaging his relationship with the girl but yet he still refused to let her marry on her own. "Oh, you know that isn't really the point. You are doing this for your own good. It's selfish of you."

"Don't speak like that." Henry admitted many things in his lifetime but he would never admit when he was wrong. Though he knew that those weren't her exact words, he knew what she meant.

She continued to plea, "Henry, please. Stop what you are doing and then turn yourself in. Perhaps the government will go easy on you if you come forward on your own. Yes, there will be consequences to pay but not the sake of Amelia."

Henry thought she was vulnerable to believe that the authorities would be so gentle. They would kill him whether someone blew the whistle on him or if he stepped forward and admitted his crimes. He also knew that she was looking out for Amelia's best interest and for that he loved her even more. He had to convince her that everything would be fine. For the sake of keeping up his front; he had to convince her he was in favor of the marriage. "Look, I have given my promise to the Van Martins. And, Thomas is a good young man and I know he will provide a nice home for her. Amelia will love him once she gives him the chance."

Ruth slowed her pace down. He glanced back and wondered why she was straggling behind. "Don't you remember what it was like?" She questioned him.

"That was different and you know it." He didn't want to bring up the past. Henry stood still and waited for her to catch up to him.

"How was it different? Was it because you were not the father?" She didn't mean to bring up a subject they haven't discussed in years, it happened naturally.

Henry was getting emotional and was afraid that someone would see the way he looked or overhear what he or she was saying. "No," he said in a near whisper. "It's different because that happened to a couple that was in love. Amelia has nobody to love. I'm giving her Thomas and she must accept that."

She wanted to give up. Poor Amelia, she thought, nobody could help her. "Henry Samuels, you are so tenacious." After arriving at his house, Ruth clarified she was going home. Henry had asked if she would like to come in for tea but she turned him down. "You need to patch things up with Amelia. Don't let this come between you. Whatever you need to do to fix it, do it." She continued walking home as Henry stepped inside his house.

Chapter Nine

   Patrick walked through Millersport on his way to the loading docks to make purchases from the merchants. This was his first time since he arrived in the village but knew that Amelia often made purchases there and he wondered if he would run into her. He wondered how the picnic went with her fiancé. Perhaps she needed to spend time with the young man so she could come to terms with marrying him. She was special to him though, a fondness he wouldn't tell her. As much as Patrick disagreed with prearranged marriages, he also knew it was right to be respectful of her father's wishes. The right thing for her to do was to listen. She had told him she would fight it every step of the way hoping someday soon her father would stop the wedding. If that day ever came, he told himself, then maybe he would open to her about his feelings.

   He was thinking about her so much that he didn't realize that he was only feet away from the loading dock. Patrick looked around at the turn out of shoppers. Along the side the docks, the merchants set up their booths. They were selling everything from spices to furniture, and he didn't know where to look for what he was after. He wished that he knew someone other than Amelia, someone that could show him the way around but knew no one. Patrick decided that the only way to learn was to walk around and watch the others.

   He was being friendly to all the people who turned their necks to look at him. He smiled and nodded his head to all who passed his way. Being the stranger made him feel uneasy. Perhaps he should have gone to church and introduced himself to some of the other men in the village. He remembered his conversation with Amelia about not going to church. He thought he should have explained to her his reasons. He didn't want her or anyone else to think that he didn't believe in God because he did. He also wanted no one to think that he blamed God for losing his wife and son because he knew the blame was his own. Patrick continued these thoughts as he received blank stare after blank stare and decided that the following week he would attend the service.

Again, he let his thoughts carry him away and he didn't realize that he must have walked into a private area. Patrick saw two men with their backs turned towards him. He wanted to introduce himself and ask for a little help but then he realized that they were having a serious conversation and didn't want to interrupt. He didn't intend to eavesdrop but he couldn't help but overhear the conversation.

Henry stood by the merchant and pulled an envelope out of his jacket. He knew they were away from all the other merchants and shoppers but still felt the urge to be careful. As he pulled it out, he said to the merchant, "We have to be more careful than usual. I'm afraid that someone has found out what I've been doing."

The merchant looked frightened. He made a lot of money for the secret job he was doing, more money than he could ever make selling coffee and tea, but not enough to end his life. If the authorities ever caught him that is exactly what would have happened to him. "What do you mean? Someone knows?"

"Yes, and trust me, I'm paying for it." Henry remembered the day that Daniel Van Martin discovered his secret and blackmailed him. He knew that he shouldn't continue but had promised the funds and he wasn't a man to break a promise. "My daughter would hate me if she found out.

"Are there authorities around?" the concerned merchant asked. Henry shook his head. He didn't tell the merchant he was being blackmailed nor did he tell him who knew what was going on. Henry made sure that Daniel wasn't around the loading docks and thought of this new meeting place. He had to let Van Martin believe that he stopped the funding. "No," he answered, "We are safe as long as we stay away where nobody can see us."

70

Patrick stood behind a stack of crates and wondered what was going on. He knew that he could be in danger if one of those men spotted him. He turned around to walk back where he had come from but before he did, he heard a little more of the conversation that set off an alarm in his head.

The merchant put the envelope in his own jacket and patted his chest to confirm that it was safe inside. "All right then," he started. "I will see the Brit's soldier in about one week and then I'll be back this way in about two. Can I tell him to expect more from you?"

Patrick high tailed it out of there before he had the chance to hear the answer. He couldn't believe what he was hearing. He was so overwhelmed that he went straight home and didn't even bother with the other merchants. Patrick had heard that there were men in the northeast who were funding the British but he never imagined that there would be someone right there in Millersport. He had witnessed treason first hand and was shocked. He wondered what he should do and thought about it on his walk back to his house.

After Amelia cleaned her father's house she wondered what she should do with her free time. Mondays were merchant days but her father had made it quite clear she didn't need to go to the loading docks. She wondered if he ran short on coins because it he insisted that they needed nothing and he offered her no money. Amelia shook her head while she thought and realized that it had nothing to do with how much money he had. She remembered a couple of times he told her he would make the purchases himself. She thought he was planning on making all the family purchases once she was married to Thomas and then continued to think about what to do with her time. Amelia wouldn't be picking berries with Emma because she knew that her friend was preoccupied with her new beau. She didn't feel like calling on Minnie in fear that her sister would only ask about Thomas. Anna left for the day doing whatever Anna got herself into.

Then for a brief second she thought she should see how Beth was feeling but seeing Patrick suddenly filled her head.

Although she wasn't crazy about using the carriage, it was a long walk to his house and in her opinion; she had more than then enough exercise during the past few days. Amelia was feeling lazy and decided to ride out to Patrick's house instead. She walked up to the stables but just before she arrived, she noticed Thomas inside returning his families carriage and horse. There was no way she wanted to see him, not even to be friendly, after the way he had treated her. The thought of being his wife had disgusted her. If things went like she planned, she would spend little time with him before their wedding day. She leaned against the side of the building and did her best to stay out of his sight and waited for him to leave. It worked, and he left in the opposite direction. When he was out of sight she asked the stable boy for her father's carriage and then was off to visit the one person who she enjoyed spending time with.

Patrick wasn't home for over ten minutes when he heard a knock on his door. He was still feeling nervous and his mind played games with him and thought that the conversing men had spotted him traced him back to his house. He wondered if they were there to make sure that he kept quiet about what was going on. Patrick felt better seeing Amelia standing at the door when he opened it. "Oh, Amelia it's you."

Amelia could sense that something was wrong. "Patrick, you look as if you saw a ghost. What on Earth is wrong?"

He opened the door wider and gestured her to come inside then glanced around the outside to make sure nobody was watching him before he shut it. "Tell me, how do the people of Millersport feel about the war?"

"I don't think about the war as much as I should," Amelia started. "If President Madison says it's right then it must," She started but her male friend didn't seem to care how she felt.

Patrick cut her off because she wasn't telling him what he wanted to hear. "No, no," he exclaimed. "The others, what do the others think?"

She wanted to think about his question. From what she knew there were mixed feelings in the village. He was urging her to answer him. "I don't know, Patrick, why are you pushing me so?"

Patrick took a deep breath and realized that she was right. He was anxious but knew that he couldn't take it out on her. He took another deep breath and asked, "Okay, think about it if you have to. Are there men who oppose the war?"

Amelia was happy to see that Patrick calming down but still worried about him. "There are some who agree with the war but many who oppose it." She put her hands on his arm and encouraged him to sit down. "You're all a mess. If you would like, I will get you some water."

Patrick felt his heart rate slowing down. He had a great deal of pride for his country and supported Madison's war. Someone from the area was funding the British, and he felt obligated to let the government know. He looked over at Amelia and could see the concern on her face. He kept her out of it, knowing that things could get dangerous and he never wanted to see her hurt. "I'm fine," he told her and then changed the subject. "I'm glad to see you. What brings you by?"

She sat next to him, happy to see he was relaxing again. "Usually on Mondays I go to the merchants but my father didn't want me to today. I suppose we needed nothing. So anyway, I didn't know what to do with my spare time. I hope it's okay to call upon you."

Patrick smiled, "Of course it's okay. I came home from going to the merchants myself."

Suddenly she knew why he had so many questions about the war. He probably needed supplies that were not available. It must have been his first time down at the docks which would explain his frustrations. "Oh, what did you purchase?"

"I bought nothing," he told her as he remembered the crowds and his sense of being lost.

"It can be overwhelming. Perhaps next week we can go together and I'll show you around." Amelia was wishing she could spend more time with him in public places. She hoped that he would meet her father soon and then it would be socially all right for her to befriend him.

Patrick wasn't as optimistic as she was. He knew that she couldn't escort him. "I don't think that your father or fiancé would approve." He had hoped that she would tell him that her engagement was off but could tell by the look on her face she was still to be married soon.

Amelia didn't want to think of her engagement and all the bad things that had happened because of it. She stood up and said, "It's such a lovely day. Would you like to walk to that creek of yours?"

Patrick agreed, and they started their walk. Along the way he watched her pick a couple of berries and watched as she put them in her mouth. It reminded him of the past weekend and wondered how it went. "You never told me how the picnic went on Saturday. Are you and Thomas getting along better?"

They reached the creek and Amelia sat down in the grass. "I'd rather not talk about it." She avoided looking at him in fear he would see the light bruise left by her father's hand. Explaining that to him would lead to her explaining Thomas' lies and the way he treated her. It was something she never wanted Patrick to know about.

Patrick could tell that she didn't want to talk about Thomas. He felt ashamed of the emotions he felt when he was next to her. She became more beautiful every time he saw her and more knowledgeable every time she spoke. He wondered what it would be like if he could lean over and kiss her. He couldn't because he knew that once he tasted her lips, he would never have enough of their sweetness.

74

They spent the next two hours together and were both happy to relax and felt as if they were in their own world. Amelia knew that it was time to go back home. She hated leaving the creek where everything was so peaceful, to return home, where the tension grew stronger every day. She told Patrick that she must go and the two of them walked back to his house.

Along the way, Patrick realized that he couldn't just ignore what he had discovered earlier that day. Being the stranger in the village, he didn't know who he could or couldn't trust. He didn't even know the name of the man committing such serious crimes or point him out since he had only seen the man's back. He looked over at Amelia and spoke, "I'm going on a trip and will away for two or three days."

Alarmed by his sudden departure, she asked, "Where are you going? How will I know when you are back?"

"I need to speak to someone in Albany," he answered.

"But," she continued to ask, "What for?" She couldn't understand why it bothered her to know that he was leaving. Amelia wondered if the feelings that were growing inside her were sincere. She didn't need to second guess if she would miss him or not, she knew she would.

Patrick wanted to tell her everything. He didn't like to keep secrets from her but; he also wanted no harm to come by her way. "I can't tell you." He looked at her concerned face. "I will be okay. I have something I need to take care of. As far as when I come back, somehow I will let you know." When they reached his house, she told him to be careful and then headed back to her father's house.

"I will be," he whispered to himself and then packed up to leave.

That night after their dinner, the Samuels house was quiet like it had been for the past week. Henry said that he was off to visit a friend and told the girls not to wait up for him. By eight o'clock, Amelia had the boys tucked into their beds. It was just herself and Anna sitting alone in the sitting-room. As she worked on her needlepoint, she offered to show Anna how it to do it. As she sat there, she tried to take her mind off of Patrick but it was of no use. She wondered who he had to see in Albany and why he was leaving so soon. Her concern must have been obvious because she could hear her sister call her name several times. "Oh, I'm sorry Anna. What did you say?"

"I said nothing," Anna stated. "I just called your name. Your mind must be somewhere else. You look so distracted." Anna had looked at her older sister and noticed that she wasn't even looking at her needlepoint as she done it. Anna wondered if Amelia was feeling all right.

Amelia sighed and sat back on the sofa. She had never remembered a time in her life when she felt so much stress. These days it was all she knew. "I'm fine," she answered, "Just a little tired I suppose."

Anna didn't want her sister to think that she was meddling but also knew that her sister was running out of people whom she could talk to. She wanted to be there for her sibling. "Are you thinking about that man you were with today?"

Amelia's jaw dropped and at first didn't know what to say. She wondered how Anna knew of Patrick and how she knew that she was thinking of him. She decided it was in her best interest to deny everything. "I don't know what you mean."

"I saw you today; you were with that stranger by the creek just west of here." Anna knew that it wasn't proper for any girl to be alone with a man, especially since she was engaged to another, but had seen Amelia with this man long enough to know that her sister wasn't doing anything wrong. Anna wanted to prove she could trust her.

Still in disbelief, Amelia thought it best to avoid Patrick in their conversation. She decided not to deny that she was near the creek but hoped that they wouldn't discuss who she was with. She tried to change the conversation a little. "What were you doing by that creek, Anna? You should have been closer to home."

Anna lowered her head and blushed. In the past week she had learned to prepare meals, clean the house, and mend socks but she was still the same girl she always was. Amelia had asked her a question though, and she would not hide the truth. "Catching frogs," she answered.

"What was that? I hardly heard you." Amelia asked.

"I said I was catching frogs," Anna answered this time louder. She thought that her sister would lecture her about being lady- like and less of a tom boy, but to Anna's surprise, she didn't.

Amelia laughed out loud. "Oh Anna, you will never change will you? That still doesn't answer why you were so far from home. What about the creek up the road?"

It appeared to Anna that Amelia was interested in what she was doing. She liked the attention and was glad she could be herself. "Yuck," she started, "That water is so dirty."

"Well, I agree with you there. You wouldn't catch me dead at that creek." Amelia looked over at her sister who was open enough to tell her the truth about what she was doing. It occurred to her that her younger sister was trying to be a friend. "Will you tell Father that I was talking to Patrick?"

"So you were with someone today. I told you. Who is he, were is he come from?" Anna was full of questions about the strange man in the village.

"You didn't answer me, Anna." Amelia was feeling a little relieved that she could talk about Patrick but yet worried that her father would find out and punish her. "Are you going to tell Father?"

Anna could sense Amelia's anxiety. She recalled the past several days and knew how unhappy her sister was. She didn't in any way want to bring more unhappiness to her. "No, I promise. Now will you tell me about him?"

Feeling relieved, Amelia was glad to tell her sister about her friendship with Patrick. She told Anna how she met Patrick, about the day she walked so far and saw him; she even told her about how she was trapped in the rain and found warmth in his house.

"You lied to Father," Anna gasped. Her sister was changing and was no longer the perfect girl everyone thought she was.

"Please don't say a word about what I tell you. Father wouldn't understand and he would strap me again for sure." Amelia now wished that she said nothing.

"Oh Amelia, please believe me, I won't say a word to anyone. I want you to trust me." Anna reached over and hugged her sister. Amelia was opening to her and Anna didn't want to ruin that. She didn't want to be treated like a little girl that nobody could depend on.

Feeling her sister hug her, Amelia lost the tension building up inside her. She wrapped her arms around Anna, thrilled to have someone she could talk to. "I don't want to marry Thomas," she said with a cry in her voice. Then she told her sister about how her fiancé had been treating her.

Tears swelled up in Anna's eyes. A week ago she didn't want her sister to marry for her own selfish reasons but now she could tell how unloved Amelia felt. It was then she was bold to find out how Amelia felt. "You love him, don't you?"

Amelia couldn't believe what she was hearing. Love Thomas, she wondered how on Earth her sister could think such a thing after what she had just told her. "Oh Anna, don't you understand, I can't stand Thomas."

Anna shook her head; that wasn't what she meant. "Not Thomas. You love that stranger, don't you?" She saw her sister's expression when she talked of the man; it was the same way Minnie looked whenever she spoke of her husband Phillip.

Amelia blushed. She had never thought she loved Patrick. He was a friend, a friend she so desperately needed. He was a shoulder for her to cry on and vice versa. They needed each other. Hearing her sister ask if she loved him

78

made her think of him more. "First of all his name is Patrick, he isn't a stranger. Second," she was about to tell Anna how she felt about him but the sound of the front door stopped their conversation.

Within seconds Henry entered the sitting-room. It surprised him to see both of his daughters still awake. It had been dark for several hours and he had expected them to be in bed. "You two are still awake? I had thought you would have retired by now."

Amelia stood up. "We were just catching up." She looked over at her sister who had a look of agreement on her face. Amelia reluctantly gave her father a hug and said that she was heading for bed. Anna did the same and the two girls went up to the room they shared and changed into their night garments.

Anna lied on her bed and was thankful that Amelia confided in her. She wished that she could help her sister out of her troubles. She looked over toward Amelia, who had her back turned towards her. "You never told me. Do you love Patrick?" Her question would go unanswered because she could tell by Amelia's breathing she was fast asleep.

Chapter Ten

Anna just passed the window when she saw Thomas walking up to the house. Knowing what kind of man he was, she knew that her sister wouldn't be happy to know he was coming to call on her. "Amelia," she whispered to her sister sitting in an arm chair working on her needle point, "Thomas is coming. Go slip out the back door and I'll tell him you aren't home."

Amelia quickly jumped up and left her needle point where it fell. Thomas Van Martin sure had a nerve to call on her after how he behaved. "Thank you," she whispered back and then took off towards the kitchen and went out the back door. She tiptoed around the house and then leaned against the side to listen to what excuse he had to be there.

Anna opened the door almost immediately after he knocked. "My father isn't home," she said to him knowing that Thomas wasn't there to see him.

Thomas smiled at the young girl and took notice of how grown up she was becoming. "I know; he has sent me here to see Amelia. Where is she?" He tried to peek his head in the door to find his blushing bride-to-be but Anna shut it on him. He placed his foot down by the door so she couldn't close it.

"She isn't home," Anna stated. She didn't want to tell him where Amelia was because she knew that fibbing wasn't one of her strong suites. "I don't know, she said she would be back soon and then she left," Anna lied when she heard him ask where he could find Amelia.

Thomas felt that Anna was playing games with him. He didn't believe a thing the girl was saying. "Are you telling me she left and didn't tell you where she would be?"

"That is right," Anna fibbed as her body twitched. She hoped that he would believe her and then go away.

Amelia stood and listened to every word being said, unaware that a garter snake was just inches away from her shoe. She glanced down and saw it slivering towards her and let out a scream.

Thomas was about to buy into Anna's story when he heard the scream from the side of the house. Anna heard it too and the two of them ran outside to see what was wrong. Amelia, feeling foolish for blowing their cover, grabbed flowers to make it look as if she was picking them. The screech from her voice had made the snake squirm away; she only wished that Thomas would do the same.

"Amelia, what are you doing?" Anna asked. It came across as concern but inside she was furious that Amelia had ruined their cover.

Amelia looked at the others and said, "A snake," and at that moment she forgot if she was talking about the one in the garden or the six foot man in front of her. As soon as she said the words, she noticed her tomboyish sister bending over to pick up the snake that didn't get too far away. "Oh Anna, you put that dirty snake down right now."

Thomas was amused. He stood there watching the girls as if they were his entertainment. Anna held the snake and walked a few yards away to release it. She came back, wiping her hands off, when Thomas realized that he should be alone with Amelia. He turned to his fiancée and said, "Come, let's go inside. You can give me a drink, something sweet perhaps."

Amelia squeezed the flowers were in her hand. She knew it wasn't polite to have a gentleman caller in the house when her father wasn't around. "My father isn't home, Thomas. It wouldn't be appropriate." Anna nodded her head, agreeing with her sister.

Thomas was no fool and knew that they didn't want him around but their tactics wouldn't work with him. "On the contrary, your father is the one who sent me here to see you. He said given our soon to be marriage, it was fine to sit with you inside away from the sun." Thomas could tell that

Anna would stay by her sister's side and was positive that Amelia filled the girl's head about him. He didn't care; he had a way of making whatever she said into a lie. "Oh and Anna, he told me that if you were here that you should go call on a friend and leave us."

Anna gasped. She didn't want to leave Amelia alone with Thomas and could tell by the look on her sister's face she didn't want to be alone with him either. "I apologize to you Thomas but Amelia and I don't believe you."

Thomas was getting angry. He knew that Amelia had a stubborn streak but was seeing that the younger girl was just as stubborn if not more. He looked at the girl and said, "Do I need to go tell your father you are not listening to the message he sent?"

Amelia heard all she cared for. She couldn't understand why her father would allow Thomas in the house when he wasn't there. Amelia was glad that Anna was being supportive of her but didn't want her to get in trouble either. She already knew what Thomas was like and would have her guards up. "Go ahead, Anna. I don't want to see you get strapped by Father."

"Are you sure?" Anna asked.

Amelia was about to answer her but Thomas cut her off, "You know it only takes a few minutes to walk to his store. Shall I go tell him?"

Not wanting to get punished, Anna turned towards Amelia and said, "All right but I'll be back soon to help prepare dinner." She gave her sister a hug and then dashed off. She glanced back and saw that Amelia was showing Thomas into the house. Her first thought was to hide around the outside of the house, to be there for Amelia in case she needed her, but the thought of her father catching her made her continue walking away.

After shutting the door behind him, Thomas asked, "So what about that drink I asked for?" Though, he couldn't care less about the drink. All he cared about was being alone with her.

Amelia was disgusted and shocked about his visit and wished that she wasn't home when he called upon her. "I have nothing sweet. You know how things are with the tariffs on trade." She lied again knowing she had sugar locked away in the dining room.

"Then get me a drink of water and you will have to be my sweet," he said to her as he placed a kiss upon her lips.

Amelia pushed him away from her and wiped her mouth off. She was getting used to his behavior but still couldn't stand it. "I told you to never do that again," she pointed to the sitting-room and continued, "Go sit down and I'll be right back with your water."

Thomas decided that he should apologize to Amelia for the way their picnic turned out. He knew that he didn't think he was wrong but yet felt he should at least let her think that he respected her. He took a seat on the sofa and put his arm up on the back, leaving a spot for her to sit next to him. When she returned, he thanked her for the glass and motioned for her to sit, but she sat in the arm chair. Thomas was becoming very impatient and couldn't wait to marry her so she would have no choice but to get close to him.

Amelia would no sooner want to sit next to him on the sofa than she would a wild bear. "So what are you doing here?"

"I told you, your father sent me," he reminded her. It was all a lie. He saw Henry in his store but her father didn't ask for him to pay her an unsupervised visit. "And," he continued. "I want to tell you I'm sorry for what happened between us the other day."

"You are not," Amelia snipped at him. She was far too angry about his behavior, angry for her father's lie about protection, and she was angry that he allowed Thomas in the house.

Thomas thought she was correct and perhaps she already knew him well. He felt he had every right to behave the way he did. He was apologizing, so she learned to trust him again. He couldn't show her off to all the villagers if she never agreed to be around him. He started to lie. "I let my emotions for you carry me away and I'm sincere in my apology."

She couldn't believe a word out of his mouth. "You told me last week you didn't love me and that you were doing me a favor by marrying me. What emotions?"

"Okay, that is true but the more I thought about our union, the more smitten on you I became."

Amelia shook her head. She would never accept his apologies, no matter what his reasons were. She changed the subject and find out why he was calling on her. "Why did my father send you here?"

He had to think of something she would believe. Thomas knew that he was already stretching the truth and was afraid that she wouldn't buy anymore of his stories. He told her what her father told him not to say. "Oh yes, I almost forgot. Your father bought us a wedding gift."

Amelia's stomach turned. The thought receiving gifts to marry him made her sick. "What do you mean? I haven't heard about this."

Thomas chuckled; she hadn't heard yet. "He told me he would tell you more about it later but said it was fine for me to come over and share the excitement with you."

She groaned so low he couldn't hear her. What was her father up to? She wondered. Thomas looked at her with enthusiasm but she wouldn't give him the satisfaction of talking about it. As far as she was concerned, their visit was over. "Well thank you for telling me. I have to get our meal ready for this evening so if you don't mind," she left the rest unsaid hoping he would get the hint as she pointed towards the door.

Though he didn't want to leave yet, Thomas thought it was for the best. He didn't want Henry to arrive home and see him there.

Amelia walked towards the front door and he followed behind. Before she could open the door, Thomas grabbed her waist and pulled her next to him. Amelia tried to get free of him but he had her in an awkward position. He was embracing her when she demanded, "Thomas I told you no. Now let go of me." He let go but not before putting his disgusting mouth on hers and leaving it there for what seemed an eternity. As soon as he showed the slightest easement, she pushed him away and told him to get out.

Thomas was happy with himself. Every time he tasted her lips he wanted more, and he knew that soon he would have that opportunity. Once she was his wife, he'd taste her nonstop. "I'll be seeing you soon then," he said to her and didn't wait to hear her reply.

Amelia watched him walk down the street and prayed that he wouldn't return. When he was out of sight she cried. She wished that she could feel kisses from someone who loved her. Thanks to Thomas and her father that would never happen. She wiped the tears from her face and took a bath to rid the scent of him off of her.

Later that day while taking a walk, she passed the church and noticed that Reverend Mayer was inside. The front door was open and she could see him walking through the pews and it appeared as if he were placing something on the seats. She went inside and see what he was up to. "Hello," she said when she stepped inside. Reverend Mayer looked her way and was surprised to see he had company. "Amelia dear, hello," he answered. "What brings you by today?"

Amelia sat down in one pew and he sat next to her. She thought for a moment about what her father would think but then decided that she needed to tell someone how she felt and the Reverend was the only person, besides Patrick, told him everything. She told him how uncomfortable Thomas had made her feel and how everyone seemed to think that he was a charming man. The only part she failed to tell him was meeting Patrick and the times they've spent together. She told him, "I don't wish to marry him."

His reply surprised her. Mayer felt for her and her story and understood why she would feel that way but it was his job to teach the lessons in the bible so he said to her, "My child, you know the commandments, honor thy mother and father." She looked at him with a pout and he continued to explain to her, "You must obey your father. I'm sure he has your welfare in mind and only wants to see you settle down with the right man."

"I'm obeying him," she remarked. "But, I don't like it and feel so trapped."

The Reverend reached over and patted her on the shoulders. "Parents have been prearranging their children's marriages for many years. What your father is doing is nothing more than clearing your way to a bright future. Have patience young one; soon you'll see that everything will be fine." He then tapped her knee and told her he must return to work and saw her out.

Realizing that everyone saw things the way her father did, Amelia finished her walk and again went straight to her bedroom. She lied across the bed and took a deep breath. She was losing the war and was running out of soldiers to stand behind her. Feeling exhausted, she closed her eyes and went to sleep for an afternoon nap.

Chapter Eleven

Patrick returned home after being away on his trip to Albany. It had been a long four days, starting with the day he left Millersport. He was unprepared to take a journey and his decision to go came to him quickly. He didn't have the proper rest and was tired long before he reached his destination. He set up camp as soon as he arrived at the capital. Patrick knew of several inns he could have stayed in but he always preferred to save his coins and lay under the stars. The next day when he awoke he set out to seek the governor and tell him what he had heard at the docks. Patrick refused to discuss the funding with anyone other than Governor Tompkins. Unfortunately, Tompkins wasn't available until Wednesday afternoon. Patrick didn't enjoy hanging around an unknown city. He was very impatient, and he frequently checked in with the Governor's office to see if there had been an opening in which he could get into the office. By the time he had told the Governor what he had overheard, it was just about time for the sun to set again. Patrick had wanted to get home but wasn't about to travel in the dark.

He stopped thinking about his trip as his horse neared the land he owned. He was thrilled to know that his bed was waiting for him and his tired body but never would have imagined what else was waiting for him.

As he hurried into the house to relax, he heard the dog bark and then he heard the shuffling of a chair. His first thought was to grab a hold of the barking iron he carried with him for protection on his long trip. He thought that the men who he had heard on the loading docks had found out about him and that he traveled to turn them in. If a fight was what they wanted, a fight was what they would get. Patrick held on tight to his weapon and flung the door wide open. He put the weapon down though when he saw Amelia sitting there. He couldn't tell her but she was a sight for sore eyes. Her blue eyes reminded him of crystal waters in a lake which made him thirsty. It was a thirst he couldn't tell her about; a thirst for her. Her smile displayed her sparkling white teeth and her hair flowed down the curves of her breast. He shook his head to rid himself of the impure thoughts running through it and told himself that she wasn't that kind of girl. "Amelia," he said, "What are you doing here?"

Amelia blushed. She wasn't sure when he would return home and his sudden entrance had startled her. "I hope you don't mind," she explained. "The dog let me in." She laughed as she bent over to pet the animal that had barely moved the whole time she was there. "I needed to get away, and this was the only place I could think of where I wouldn't be found."

Patrick then slapped his hands onto his legs and said, "Here boy," and the dog ran and put his front paws up on his owner as fast as he could. He stuck his tongue out and panted as he smelled Patrick all over. He heard Amelia say she brought the dog water so he let the dog outside for relief. When the dog ran out, Patrick said, "That is fine, I told you that you are welcome here anytime you like."

"Thank you," Amelia replied. "How was your trip?"

"Long," Patrick replied the only answer he could give her. He wanted someone he could confide in but he didn't want to put her in dangers way if it should come looking for him. He took a seat across the table from her and the two of them caught up with what had been going on while he was away. She told him she would bake something for the dessert table for the social and he looked at her as if he hadn't a clue of what she was talking about. "A social, a dance," she explained. "Haven't you ever been to a dance before?"

"No, I don't recall ever going to any back home." Patrick stopped to think about his old home. He missed it very much, but he needed to get away from the memory of his wife and child. "Now, don't get me wrong. That doesn't mean I don't know how to dance," he teased her.

Amelia laughed and asked, "So does that mean you will ask me for a dance at the social?" She would gladly give up a night with Thomas to dance with Patrick.

Patrick grinned. He wanted nothing more but knew that being the new man in the village, it would cause a stir. "Who said I was going," he decided not to answer her question.

"You have to," she pleaded. Society says she must go with Thomas, given their so- called courtship but she would be overjoyed if he came out to meet some of the people of Millersport. "I'm inviting you."

Patrick thought about it for a minute or two before saying anything else. The governor had asked him to get a description on the traitor. All the authorities would need was a description of the man and they could take it from there. He would meet someone by the name of Major General Downy in New Baltimore on Monday. Going to the social would be the perfect opportunity to search for the unknown man and get a description of him. "When is this dance?"

"It's Saturday night, this Saturday. Oh say you can attend," she about begged. His arrival would give her something to look forward to and something to take her mind off of whatever tricks Thomas had up his sleeve. She saw him nod his head in agreement and she was more than happy. Without thought, she jumped out of her chair and embraced him. It was a friendly hug to thank him for saying yes, but the way the hug felt told her that the two of them were not destined to be friends. His skin was warm and had a masculine smell that had waken her nostrils. She took another deep breath while her arms were still around him and hoped that she could always remember the aroma. Beneath his shirt she could feel the strength of his muscles, both on his arms and in his upper body. This was how a man was supposed to feel, she thought to herself, not the skinny little shell that Thomas was. Though the embrace only lasted for two seconds, to Amelia it was the highlight of her day that lasted forever. When she felt his hands wrap around her backside to return the embrace, she tingled all over. It was as if every single hair on her body stood and was trying to get beneath his gentle hands. Nothing lasts forever, and she had to be polite and pull herself away from him; blushing while she did. Then she decided that he should get rest after his long trip and she told him she would go.

"So, I'll see you in two days," he said to her as she prepared to leave. It would be the longest two days of his life for she was getting to him.

"Two days," she agreed and turned and walked out the door.

She only took a few steps away from his house before she turned to look back. He was standing by the window waving to her and her heart skipped a beat.

That was the first night Amelia didn't return home for dinner. She wanted to test Anna and see if the younger girl could prepare the evening meal by herself. Amelia went to David and Beth's house to help out with their meal instead. It was nice to be around different company; to be around people who wouldn't remind her of her duties to marry Thomas. Besides, she thought to herself, it wouldn't be long before Beth needed more help around the house with her swollen stomach and sore back keeping her from her daily chores. It would be a practice for her.

It was a peaceful evening and Amelia was at ease. By the time she arrived at her brother's house, Beth had most of the meal already done. Amelia asked how she could help as soon as she got there but Beth said that she had it under control. She wasn't used to doing nothing at all so she set the table. Not long after her arrival, the three of them sat down to eat. To her surprise, Amelia ate more than usual. With all the stress she had been feeling at home, her appetite had diminished.

The conversation was pleasant too. There wasn't one word spoken that wasn't welcomed. They talked about the social for it was the talk of the village; something that everyone looked forward to. "I'm not too sure if I can still dance," Beth giggled.

Amelia knew that Beth was referring to her pregnancy. She realized that her sister-in-law might not make it through the whole night. "Sure you can," she replied.

David couldn't help join the conversation about his wife. He was looking forward to the social because after the baby arrived there would be less time to spend with her alone. "The question is," he put his thoughts into the discussion, "Am I going to reach her backside when we dance? Or will that midsection get in my way?" The three all laughed as they imagined the couple on the dance floor.

It wasn't long before it had turned dark and Amelia knew that she should head home to see how Anna made out. She wished that she didn't have to go. David's house was the only place where she could forget about her troubles. There was also Patrick's house but Amelia knew that there was a different kind of trouble there. She would fall head over heels for the handsome man and that would make for more trouble than she knew what to do with. She snapped her head to bring her out of her fantasy then gave her hosts their thanks and left to go home.

Once there, Amelia looked around the house. It was quiet and Amelia knew that all was fine. There was a note on the kitchen table from her father that said he wanted to meet her in her room at noon the next day. It said he had important work to finish at the office and that he wouldn't be there for breakfast. She moaned. She wondered what he was up to. After entering the bedroom she shared with Anna, she realized that her sister was sleeping. Hard work must have tired her out. Amelia tipped-toed over to her bed and pulled the blanket up to Anna's shoulders. As long as she could remember, Anna always kicked the blankets off and being the big sister she was, Amelia always tucked her back in before she too went to sleep. She bent over and placed a soft kiss on Anna's head and then turned to get ready to retire herself.

Chapter Twelve

Henry reached into his closet and pulled out a box that had been sitting in there since their arrival in Millersport. He turned and placed the box on his bed as he swallowed a lump in his throat, overwhelmed with guilt knowing that the owner of the box wouldn't want Amelia to wed the young Van Martin boy. He felt his eyes water because he too didn't want the union but he wiped the moisture away. His family was angry with him for what he was putting Amelia through but he had to stand strong. He knew that Daniel would run straight to the authorities if he backed out of the arrangement. He straightened himself out and took the box down to the girls' room where he had instructed Amelia to meet him.

The door was open, and he walked in unheard. She was sitting with her back to him and had not realized that he was there. She looked so unhappy and his heart wanted to reach out to her. He knew that she had to marry Thomas, for his sake, but also knew that with the right words she might understand. Again he cleared his throat, and she turned and looked at him.

"Father, I didn't hear you come in," Amelia said as she jumped up from her bed and turned to face him. Immediately she saw the box in his hands and wondered what was going on. "What is in the box?"

Henry placed the box down onto her bed and brushed the dust off of his hands. What was in the box had been in there for years and he had been instructed for it to be never opened until Amelia wed. Although the wedding was still not for some time, he knew it was the best way to break the ice with his daughter. "This is for you," he said to her as he pulled his wife's wedding dress out of the box. "It was your mother's."

Amelia gasped. Never in her life had she seen such a beautiful dress. Her father held it up and its beauty flowed down to the floor. Ivory lace covered white satin from top to bottom. The sleeves, though short, were also made of ivory lace. Looking at the dress, Amelia saw purity and an endless love. Until now the dress had represented honest and continued commitment. She couldn't uphold the standards that came with it. "Oh, it's so beautiful," she said as she reached out to touch the fabric that once touched her mother's skin.

"You should fit into it fine," Henry proudly stated. His daughter resembled his late wife so much: he knew that she would look outstanding in it.

As Amelia pulled the dress close to her own body she asked, "But if this is Mother's, why didn't Minnie wear it?"

"She insisted, before you were even born, that you wear it." Henry was silent for a moment as he remembered the day she gave him the instructions. It was the day they moved into their first house together. She had put it in the box and told him she wanted her first daughter to wear the dress. Now looking at Amelia, he smiled as he thought about how much his wife had loved her. "You are her eldest daughter, the one she dreamt would wear this," Henry explained. "I couldn't have let Minnie wear it."

The emotions, that Amelia was feeling, overflowed. She sat on the bed as she held the dress over her lap and cried. Amelia didn't look in his direction but felt Henry sit on the bed next to her. She thought maybe this emotional moment would make him realize how unhappy she was. "I wish Mother was still here," she sobbed. "She wouldn't let you force me into this marriage. She would understand me, she would understand," she wanted to tell him that her mother would understand that she loved someone else but knew that she would have to reveal those feelings to Patrick before she could to her father.

Henry tried to comfort her. He placed his arm around her shoulders but she pulled herself away. Bringing the dress

93

out wasn't helping him at all like he thought it would. "Your mother might object, you are right," he started. "But, she would have told you to obey me and Amelia, I can't believe that you have to be reminded about respect."

Amelia wiped the tears from her eyes. She wondered what he knew about respect when he treated her like one of his business deals; signed and sealed. He never once asked her how she felt. "I respect you. Oh but Father," she tried once again to get him to see things her way, "She would have wanted me to marry someone I love. She would remind you how important that is to a marriage."

Henry couldn't take it anymore. What Amelia said was wrong, and she didn't even know it. It was time to make her understand. "Our marriage was prearranged too," he blurted out. He never thought he would tell his children this, but it seemed to be the only way to get her to accept her union. Besides, perhaps it was for the best because in time he would want to tell his children about his love for Ruth.

Amelia held the dress tight in her hands and was shocked to hear him say such a thing. "No, that isn't true. Mother told me how much she loved you."

Henry knew that telling her about his own marriage would be very difficult but it was something he had to do. He had turned towards her and pulled her shoulders until she faced him. "In time, she loved me and I her, but it wasn't always the case."

Amelia was in disbelief. She remembered how they used to look at each other, the way they were always so happy to be together. She knew that he was just telling her this to make her think that her marriage to Thomas would be nice too. "That isn't true," she cried and wondered why he would go to such extremes.

"It's true," Henry said as he recalled the days when his own world was turned upside down. He thought he would never forgive his parents for what they've done to him but in time he loved his wife and she did the same. "Amelia, I was in love with someone else," he searched for the right thing to

94

say and continued, "But our parents split us up. They thought it was better their way and the one I loved with all my heart was given to someone else and I never thought I would recover."

She didn't know what to think. She realized that it wouldn't matter if she told him about Patrick. He claimed to be proof that love didn't always win. He would still keep his promise to the Van Martins'. She felt helpless. The two of them were silent for a while until curiosity came over Amelia and she questioned, "Who were you in love with?"

"It doesn't matter anymore," he said to her and noticed the hurt in her blue eyes. Henry had been using the silent moment to recall the days when he was split from Ruth for good. Henry didn't want to tell her though. He had revealed enough for one day, telling her about his love for Ruth would set her over the edge. He needed to get his point through to her though so he went on. "And your mother, oh now that is a different story. You look like her but the child named after her holds her personality." Amelia cocked her head to the side as he continued. "She wasn't interested in marriage at all. She was a spitfire and defiant. Your mother fought tooth and nail and even on our wedding day she was out climbing trees instead of preparing herself for the ceremony." He took his fingers and wiped the rest of her tears away. He loved his daughter so much and hoped that she would come around and forgive him. "So things have a way of working themselves out. I know for a fact that Thomas is already becoming fond of you and in time you will love him too."

When she was told that he wanted to meet her, she thought he would punish her for something. Now, she knew it was true. Telling her all those awful things about her parents was the biggest punishment she could think of. She didn't know what else to do but lay her head on his shoulders and cry. She felt his arms wrap around her but she became too numb to return the embrace.

Chapter Thirteen

Saturday came and Amelia decided that it would be the day that her life would change. Throughout the night she had tossed and turned; her mind was too consumed to sleep. Thoughts of Patrick flooded her mind. She recalled how her younger sister, of all people, had asked her if she loved Patrick. It was a question that was never answered but Anna would get the answer she had been waiting to hear. She thought about all the times she had been in Patrick's presence and how she felt like she was floating on clouds just to be near him. Whenever she was close enough to feel his skin, whether it be his hands or arms, she was overcome with tingling sensations that made her skin produce thousands of goose bumps. It might have taken her a while to realize how she felt, but she loved him and would tell him. Amelia prayed that he loved her too.

She sat in front of her mirror and brushed her hair and then tied it up into a bun above her neck. There was something in the reflection that caught her eye. She turned around and looked at the wedding dress that hung on the other side of the room. Amelia wanted to wear her mother's dress but not to marry Thomas Van Martin. She would first wait to hear how Patrick felt and if he returned her affection, then she would tell her father she wouldn't, under any circumstances, marry Thomas. She wasn't sure how she would call the marriage off or what she would do to make her father change his mind but she knew that she would think of something. Until then she had to handle the situation like she had been doing, defiant like her mother had.

Henry sat at the breakfast table and noticed a change in Amelia. There was something different about her he couldn't put his finger on. She must have had a good night of rest. She refused to come out of her bedroom after he had given her the wedding dress. He remembered how he tried telling her it was still many hours of daylight left, too early to retire, but she wouldn't budge. She was stubborn, he already knew that, but remaining in her room for the better of the day was beyond any reasoning he could understand. He smiled at her. It occurred to him she might have come to her senses, at last, and accepted her new life. It was about time, he thought. He looked up and secretly thanked his beloved wife for saving the wedding dress. Telling her about their marriage was just what she needed to brighten her spirits. He waited until she looked at him and then asked, "Are you excited about the social tonight?" He knew he was. It was his opportunity to be with Ruth, dancing close to her, with no one suspecting anything.

Amelia swallowed her food and then wiped her mouth with the clothe napkin she held over her lap. "It's going to be wonderful," she exclaimed. It wasn't a direct answer to his question, but it was the reply he was looking for. "In fact, right after we're done here I have to bake for the dessert table. Should I bake a cake or a pie?"

"Cookies, cookies," Henry Jr. and Charles said in unison. They were not shy at all about saying what they wanted. Amelia always made the best cookies.

She laughed at their enthusiasm and nodded her head in agreement. "All right then, the youngsters get their way," she expressed and the two boys cheered with joy. Even Henry and Anna chuckled over their excitement.

"I'll help," Anna had tuned into the conversation. "If you would like me too," she questioned Amelia. She couldn't figure out why her sister looked so thrilled to go to the dance. All she knew was that she didn't want to attend because she would have to behave ladylike and Anna was tiring of proper behavior.

"That would be perfect," Amelia answered. "There is something I want to talk to you about," she began but was cut off.

"You want to talk about the dance?" Henry quizzed. He heard her say yes, but he hoped that she would say they would talk about her wedding. After breakfast was over, he left the girls to clean up the kitchen and to get on with their baking. He hurried the boys along and told them he would take them to visit their cousins for the day. They never turned down the opportunity to go play, and they both jumped up and raced outside.

"What did you want to talk about," Anna asked with flour splattered all over her arms and face. She was learning how to cook and clean the house but she was yet to master baking without getting the ingredients all over herself.

Amelia couldn't help but giggle at her sister. She looked ridiculous with all the flour plastered to her face. She took a hand towel and wiped Anna up. "I'm in love with Patrick Buchanan," she straight out stated. It felt great to say it out loud. She longed to say it again.

Anna dropped an egg on the floor and shrugged knowing she could always clean it up after she was finished helping Amelia. "What?" Amelia's announcement was out of the blue and it took her off guard.

Amelia thought she was clear but maybe she needed to clarify what she had said. "You asked me once before if I loved Patrick and now I'm telling you. I do."

Anna was delighted for her sister and she gave her a giant hug to prove it. "I'm so happy for you," she shouted. Amelia had returned the embrace but then pushed Anna away in a joking manner.

"You're a mess," Amelia joked. "Get off of me." The two girls laughed and threw food at each other. They continued to bake the cookies as Amelia told her sister about the way she came to realize that she loved him. Anna had asked what she would tell their father and what she would do to get Thomas away from her but Amelia couldn't give any of those answers yet. She still had to figure them out for herself. Anna was enjoying herself throwing eggs shells and flour at Amelia but when she stuck her hands in the sugar jar, Amelia objected, "Oh no Anna. Not the sugar, it's very expensive." Anna removed her hand from the jar and apologized.

Amelia's forehead leaned on Anna's as she whispered, "It's okay," then kissed Anna's nose.

They took several hours to finish the baking and clean up the kitchen. Afterward Amelia sat in the parlor and worked on her needlepoint and was happy to have Anna join her. Her little sister had grown up so much during the last couple of weeks and Amelia thought of her as a good friend. Amelia asked Anna if she would help her keep Thomas away once they were at the dance and Anna was honored to help. They plotted until it was time for them to continue with their chores.

Amelia prepared an early dinner so the family could get ready for the social dance. She didn't make too much food because there would be food and drink at the dance. Her family had come into the kitchen to eat their evening meal and it was all Amelia could do to keep her younger brothers away from the delicious treats she had baked earlier with Anna. After they ate, everyone cleaned up and dressed for the event. Amelia wore the same dress she wore to both Minnie and David's weddings. She had spent so much time making the dress and even though she would be escorted by Thomas, she felt that the social was a good event to wear it to. Besides, she thought, Patrick would be there, and she wanted to look her best for him. It was the same color blue as her eyes and it flowed down to her ankles. The sleeves were long and formed along the back side of her hands but Amelia was fine with the length since the nights had been getting cooler. When she was finished preparing, Amelia glanced in the mirror and was pleased with her appearance and hoped that the man she loved would be too. Amelia helped Henry Jr. and Charles put on their little bow ties. They didn't wear them that often, not even to church, but they both wanted to look nice for the dance.

Soon it was time for them to leave and head down to the Meeting house where the social was held. "I'll take the boys with me," Henry told Amelia who would wait for

Thomas to pick her up. Then he turned towards Anna and asked, "Do you want to ride in the carriage with us?"

Anna looked over at Amelia. She said nothing but Anna could tell that Amelia didn't want to be left alone. "No thank you, Father," she turned him down. "I would rather walk if you don't mind." She wanted to wait and leave after Thomas picked up Amelia.

Henry smirked; he knew that she would want to be independent. "Suit your-self," he replied. Then he put a hand on each of the boys' shoulders and told them it was time to go.

A few minutes later, Thomas had shown up to escort his fiancée to the dance. He was looking forward to the evening since he had yet to be seen in public with Amelia. Many people questioned whether he was courting the girl. He would show them all at the dance and he couldn't wait. They would be the most handsome couple there and all the single men attending would be jealous that he was the one holding her arm as they entered. He stopped his carriage in front of Henry's house and walked up to the door. Amelia didn't give him the chance to knock. She had opened the door and was standing there with a platter of cookies in her hands. "Aren't you going to invite me in for a drink before we leave," he questioned as he moved closer to her wishing she didn't have her hands full.

"Not a chance," she answered. She ignored what her father had told Thomas about entering the house and insisted that they remain proper.

Anna stepped out of the door just seconds after Amelia and Thomas groaned upon seeing her. He thought she would have ridden to the Meeting house with her father. It didn't matter, he thought, he would not offer to take her. He had planned an enchanting evening with his betrothed and wouldn't let a pesky younger sister interfere. He didn't want Amelia to get upset with him from the start so he said, "Anna, I'm afraid that my carriage only carries two people."

Anna shook her head. She had planned to walk and wouldn't accept a ride from him even if he offered but she knew that he was lying. She had seen Thomas ride around with his friends and there were always three or four people in the carriage. "Don't worry any," she scorned. "I'm walking."

Amelia stepped closer to Anna and kissed her on the cheek. "You'll be coming along soon, won't you?" Anna nodded and Amelia looked at Thomas as if to say she was ready to go. She headed towards the carriage when Thomas stopped her. "Where are you going with those?" He quizzed while looking at the platter.

Amelia wondered where his head was. Many women had prepared dishes and desserts to pass at past socials and he must've known she would too. "To the social," she answered.

Thomas smirked. She was going to the dance in his carriage and he wouldn't be seen walking into the Meeting house with a platter of pathetic cookies. He wanted her hands free to hold onto him and show her love to all who watched them enter. "No, no. Anna, you take them."

"Anna is walking, Thomas," Amelia reminded him. "Here, I'll put them in the back," she said as she moved closer to his carriage.

Thomas stepped in front of her and insisted that the platter wouldn't go with them. "She is more than capable to take some measly treats with her." He took the platter and shoved them into Anna's hands.

"My cookies are not measly treats," Amelia argued. He had a nerve to say such a thing to her. She reached over to retrieve the platter from Anna's hands as she said, "I have one of the best cookie recipes in all of Millersport."

Anna sensed Thomas' anger as he and Amelia argued over who would take the cookies to the dance. She didn't want to cause trouble for her sister and even though she wasn't keen on carrying the platter, she had agreed to take them. "It's fine, Amelia," she assured her sister. "I hope that the frogs don't jump onto them when I stop along the way to go catch them."

Amelia laughed but Thomas didn't look amused. She knew that her sister wasn't serious and that the cookies were in good hands. "Okay then," she told Anna. "Then take them to the back door of the Meeting house. You'll see where to place them from there." Amelia thanked her again and then turned to climb up into Thomas' carriage. She knew that if she took her time he would rush over to her to help so she did it as fast as she could. She didn't want his hands anywhere near her. Thomas gave her a look of disapproval and then got himself into the carriage.

People were coming from all directions, making their way to the dance so Thomas knew that he couldn't take Amelia for an extra-long ride. Tonight there would be dancing but he wished that he could dance privately with her before displaying her in front of everyone else. They arrived at the Meeting house and Thomas pulled the carriage over. He turned to Amelia and warned her not to get down on her own. She didn't look thrilled to have him help her down, but she listened.

The night had only just begun but already Amelia was embarrassed to be there with him. She noticed the men and women outside of the building looking over at her and Thomas. He looked as proud as a peacock. Amelia was glad that Patrick hadn't yet arrived because she didn't want him to see Thomas making such a spectacle over her. "Thomas really," she hissed, "I can get down myself."

"But why would you when you have the most attractive man in the village willing to help you?"

"Oh," Amelia couldn't help but correct him. "Where? I don't see him." Again, Thomas wasn't amused.

Even though Henry had left the house before Amelia, he arrived at the same time because he also picked up Ruth. He wished that he could hold her close as they walked in but for now they had to play the part of in-laws joining each other for the night. Nobody was surprised to see them together, they were family. Henry even thought of surprising them all by planting a huge kiss on her lips but knew that it would cause talk and he didn't want to take away from the coming out of Amelia and Thomas. People have heard that the two were courting but until now, nobody had seen them together. He looked over to his daughter who was being helped down from the carriage by Thomas. She didn't look happy, which had surprised him because he thought she had come to terms. He hoped that the other attendants wouldn't notice how she looked. The boys took off as soon as their feet touched the ground and Henry was left standing there with Ruth. He glanced at her and then the two of them walked over to Amelia and Thomas. "Shall we all walk in together?"

Thomas didn't like the idea but he could tell that it put Amelia at ease. He didn't want to chance upsetting her so he pretended that it was a grand idea. "That would be delightful," he sarcastically said. "Wouldn't it, sweetheart?"

Amelia felt like getting sick. He didn't need to call her such pet names; she wouldn't be calling him anything special. Nothing nice at least, she laughed at the thought. She smiled. It was directed at her father and Aunt but, like usual; Thomas assumed it was guided towards him. She felt him reach over to hold her hand as the four of them made their way towards the main entrance. It felt like a parent holding onto a child's hand while walking through a crowd. In no way did it feel tender and sweet like she had always hoped to feel. As they walked in the door, she could feel hundreds of eyes staring at them.

The decorating committee had the Meeting house looking very charming. The social was held in the dance hall on the second floor but there were chairs in the hallway on the main floor for villagers to rest and feel fresh air coming through the open doors. Streamers were twined through the railings of the staircase going up as if the attendants would have to be reminded that the event was upstairs. Up in the dance hall, there were more chairs lined up against the longer walls for anyone who preferred to sit instead of dance. The girls who had not been asked to dance sat on one side, bashfully looking across the room. Shy boys stood on the other side until they got the nerve to ask one girl to dance. There was a quartet of musicians in the far right corner that had already played a beautiful melody with their instruments though there weren't many couples out on the dance floor. The opposite corner displayed a table with a lace covering and on that table sat a large bowl of punch and fragile cups for anyone who desired a drink. Amelia knew from experiences that later on in the evening someone would bring out fresh coffee and hot tea along with delicious scones. The wall in between the dessert table and the quartet held a buffet of food like salads, fresh meats, baked rolls, and cheeses. There was no reason for anyone to leave the festivities with an empty stomach. The biggest attraction to the room was the direct middle, the dancing area. Ribbons and streamers were strung from corner to corner and confetti sized paper dusted on the floor just ready for dancers to step on them as they swirled from one side of the room to the other.

Soon after their arrival, the room filled up, and the music became more festive which invited more people to display their dancing abilities. Amelia stood awkwardly next to Thomas. She knew at any moment he would ask her for a waltz and she dreaded having to agree with him. When he asked, she wanted to laugh at him and tell him never but she knew that she had to present herself as the respectful girl that her father raised. From a distance she spotted Emma and Jacob and wanted to be social. She would've preferred to leave Thomas behind but since he was chums with Jacob, she grabbed his arm and walked over to the other couple. "Good evening," she said to them when they noticed her approach. She watched Thomas shake hands with Jacob and then bowed to Emma. Amelia wondered why he only behaved so well when there were others around. Amelia and Emma moved away from the men, just far enough were their conversation wasn't heard. "Emma, you look absolutely beautiful tonight," Amelia confessed to her friend.

Emma had worn a peach colored dress that was just the right color to bring out blushing of her cheeks. Her hair was gathered down by her neck into a ribbon that matched her dress. The hair that hung down curled. Amelia could tell that it wasn't just the dress that made her look beautiful. "I can see how happy Jacob is making you and I'm glad for you," she said and meant every word.

Emma smiled at her friend and then gave her a hug. "It has been way too long, Miss Samuels. I've missed you." She was happy to see that Thomas was behaving himself around Amelia and in return Amelia didn't seem to be bothered by his presence.

"And I've missed you too," Amelia returned the feeling. "I have so much to tell you," she said but couldn't finish due to Jacob, who had cut her off.

"Shall we dance?" He asked Emma while holding her hand and pulling her closer to him. She jumped to the opportunity as if she had been waiting all of her life for him to ask that one question. They walked out to the middle of the dance floor and then swayed to the music.

Thomas didn't ask Amelia for a dance, he grabbed her hand and led her to a spot on the floor where everyone could see him hold her. Amelia knew that his good manners would not last once there was nobody left to show them to. She tried to squirm to get away as he pulled her close. She thought it was unacceptable behavior, but he showed her other couples who were dancing just as close to one another. Amelia thought she should make the best of it and made small talk with him. "What do you think of the decorations?"

He didn't answer because he was too busy looking around the room to see who was looking at him. It was the longest song Amelia had ever heard and was relieved when it was over. The audience applauded and dwindled off the dance floor until the next melody began. Amelia noticed Patrick walking in and was reminded of the anxiousness she felt. She had to get rid of Thomas because she wanted to tell Patrick how she felt about him. "Thomas, can you get me some punch?"

Thomas had seen other men get the drinks but felt he didn't have to behave like they did. They were wooing their dates, but he had his girl and she didn't have a choice. He decided that if she was that thirsty then she could get her own drink. "No," he simple answered.

She wasn't surprised at his rudeness at all. She feared that he wanted another dance, so she thought that asking again would delay him from pulling her out on the floor. "But I'm very thirsty."

"Then get it yourself," Thomas snorted.

She didn't mind getting away from him. "Fine," she told him, "But I'm not bringing one back for you." She stormed off towards the punch table but as soon as she mingled into the crowd and was unseen by him, she bolted off to find Patrick.

Patrick felt uncomfortable walking into the Meeting house. People close to the entrance had turned to look at him. Though their stares were not as obvious as the day he went to the loading docks, he could still feel their eyes on him as he passed by. He saw Amelia standing near Thomas. It was hard not to see her, he thought, her natural beauty made her stand out from the crowd. Patrick continued to walk through the crowd. He noticed that Amelia was walking away from Thomas and he wasn't ready for her to find him. She had a spell on him he couldn't explain and knew that being around her would blur his vision. Patrick had to be on his toes until he found the man who funded the British. He zigzagged through the crowd trying to both avoid Amelia and find a spot where men might stand trying to get away from their wives. He thought that the man he was searching for would want to talk business and thought he wouldn't do that in front of female witnesses. It was just a hunch but one he had been correct about. Several minutes later, he had edged his way into a room was on the lower level of the Meeting house.

He could smell cigar smoke and wondered if there was still someone there. There were no candles burning inside but the lights from the festivities filtered in just enough for him to spot two men inside the room talking. They didn't hear him enter. He stayed in the shadows so that his arrival would remain unannounced. He recognized one voice, it was the man he had been looking for but he didn't recognize the other man. As luck would have him, he could get a good look at the man and could now point him out if he could get the authorities to agree to travel down to Millersport. It was enough for him and he was about to head back towards the dance but realized that there were other men standing just outside of the door. He was stuck there for a moment. As he stood waiting for the men in the hallway to leave, his luck grew. The men inside the room talked about funding the British and Patrick was surprised to hear that the other man was also against it.

He remained still to listen to them. The man who wasn't at the docks talked, "So Henry, you are telling me you had stopped the funding completely."

"Yes," Henry had said to Daniel, "Can't you see, I have already got myself in boiling water? You are holding something dear over my head but I'm getting off easy. If anyone else found out then," he stopped. He thought he had heard something but then realized it was just passing people outside the room.

Daniel finished the sentence for him, "Then you would be number one on the state's execution list!"

Patrick didn't feel the need to stay there any longer. He now had a name, though not a last name, it was at least a great help. It was more than he set out to find. He slid out of the room as quietly as he had entered and then looked for Amelia.

Amelia couldn't find Patrick anywhere. Her search was constantly interrupted by villagers she hadn't spoken to in weeks. One by one, they stopped her and asked about her relationship with Thomas. She hated to put on a charade but yet still didn't have it in her to tell them how cruel her father was being. She couldn't wait to get away from all the nosey women. There was something more urgent that she had to do, she had to find Patrick and be able to speak with him before Thomas would realize how long she had been gone and would come to find her. As she made her way past the food table, she wondered if perhaps Patrick wasn't able to find her and went home instead. Amelia had hoped not because she couldn't wait to see him again.

She rushed down to the entrance to see if he was anywhere near the building. She walked out the main door and stepped out into the dark night. Amelia turned towards the side of the building and jumped when someone tapped her on the shoulder.

"I didn't mean to scare you," Patrick said when he found Amelia. He was relieved to have his business done for the night and was looking forward to seeing her.

Though she was initially scared, Amelia smiled when she realized that it was Patrick. She was nervous about Thomas trying to find her and decided it was best to tell Patrick about her feelings somewhere else. "Let's go for a walk," she flirted with him.

"Okay, but I thought you wanted me to meet your father," Patrick replied to her. He loved getting away with just her but knew the real reason she wanted him to attend the social. She wanted him to meet others in the village.

"I want to tell you something," she answered. Amelia grabbed his hand and ran behind the Meeting house and entered a wooded area. It was an area that Amelia knew well and wasn't afraid of, even in the dark. The moonlight guided their way. She stopped in an area of the woods clear of trees and shrubbery but yet far enough into the woods were nobody would see them or even think to look for them.

"Where are we," Patrick queried. Leaving the social was unexpected and Patrick wasn't sure what to think of her behavior.

Amelia blushed but didn't know whether he had noticed. "It's just a clearing I discovered when I was younger. We won't be spotted here, don't worry."

Patrick wasn't nervous about being caught with her but found it a little uncomfortable. The people in the village wouldn't trust him since they didn't know him and they would accuse him of taking her there instead of the other way around. "Amelia, maybe we should head back out," he said out of nervousness. "What do you suppose people would think if they caught us here?"

Amelia laughed though she knew he was very serious. "Trust me, they won't even look here." She had no doubts that Thomas would eventually wonder where she was and look for her but she knew that he would never expect her to be in the woods. "Besides, when I was looking for you earlier I saw my sister, Anna, and told her if anyone should question where I was then she should tell them I felt a headache coming on and I went home to bed."

Still a little uneasy, Patrick could see the glitter in her eyes. "So, it's okay?" The smile across her face told him she knew what she was talking about. "Well then, young lady, what is it you want to tell me?"

Amelia wasn't as nervous as she thought she would be. She had been thinking about this moment all night long and now it was about to happen, she knew that the timing was perfect and so was their surroundings. She stood tall and said it with no hesitations, "I realized that I'm in love."

Patrick was quiet for a minute. He hadn't expected her to say that. It was apparent that she was coming around to her marriage. He was afraid that she wouldn't want to be his friend now she was settling down. Though, she seemed happy about her decision and he didn't want to ruin it for her. "Congratulations," he started with an choppy voice. "When are you and Thomas going to get married?"

Amelia gagged on the thought but realized that she was unclear. "I can't stand Thomas Van Martin. I refuse to marry him whether my father approves or not."

"Oh, I thought," Patrick explained, but he didn't need to finish.

"No Patrick," she couldn't take it anymore and needed him to know that she was calling off the marriage so she could be with him. "Don't you see?" She thought for a moment and then continued, "I love you. I wasn't sure what I was feeling, but I knew it was something I've never felt before." After her words were spoken, Amelia felt another lump in her throat and butterflies in her stomach. She hadn't thought of what she would do if he didn't return the feelings. The moment became awkward, and she wondered what would happen.

Patrick was overwhelmed with emotions. Hearing her say she loved him was more than he could have ever hoped for. He too had feelings for her but had denied them because of her commitment with her fiancé. He couldn't believe that she was telling him she loved him. "But," he asked to make sure he wasn't dreaming, "What about your marriage?"

She shed tears she hoped he wouldn't see. It wasn't the way she thought it would be. She wondered how she could have been so wrong. "I don't love him and my father can't force me to take vows. I refuse to marry him."

Patrick noticed that she was crying and reached over to wipe the tears off of her face, "Don't cry. This is a happy moment, right?"

He pulled her close to him and said, "I love you too."

Amelia was overjoyed for the first time in her life. She thought she would never experience the emotions that ran inside of her; the tingly feelings and the skip of her heartbeat. For the first time in weeks things were looking up. Patrick was holding her close to him and she embraced him while looking into his eyes. They sparkled in the moonlight. The hands that rested on her back were tender the way she had always thought hands should be.

He stood there holding Amelia close to his chest and wondered if she could feel his heartbeat. It was beating fast, but he knew it wouldn't be broken again. He brought one hand up to the back of her head and held it back at an angle. The whole time she kept her eyes locked with his. They were close enough for him to feel her breathe on his face; it was warm and inviting. He leaned in closer and placed his lips onto hers. When he discovered that she didn't pull away, he pressed them harder until he felt her lips respond. They were sweeter than anything he could imagine and had a taste he couldn't get enough of. For every pucker he gave her, she returned to him.

Amelia closed her eyes as Patrick kissed her. She never knew that a kiss could be so delightful. She pressed her lips in line with Patrick's. They paused for a brief second but neither one of them wanted to stop. She opened her eyes and saw him moisten his lips and she knew that he would award her with another. She never knew that it could be so beautiful and felt she could go on that way forever.

The moonlight was shining down on them and a breeze had blown by but they were too involved to notice. Several minutes later their kiss had ended, but he still held her close to him as he told her he loved her again. He moved his hands over her face and traced her lips with his finger and then rubbed her cheeks. She never felt so happy before and promised herself that she would do whatever it took to guarantee she remained that happy.

Thomas walked around the room and shook hands with some of the men he knew from the village. They had made comments about the girl he had escorted to the dance and he smiled in pride. He knew that they were all jealous of him for there wasn't a man in Millersport who could deny that she was beautiful. With her in mind, he pulled out his pocket watch and noted the time. Amelia had left him quite a while before getting herself a drink. He assumed that she would return right away. From where he stood he looked over toward the punch bowl and she was nowhere in sight. He growled and excused himself from the group of men he was talking with. He scanned the room for his prize but she was nowhere to be seen. She wasn't preparing a meal for him nor was she fetching a drink for him either. His first thought was that she must have been making herself more beautiful in the powder room. Being with him would make any girl want to apply more powder. He marched right up to the entrance of the room and asked a young lady if Amelia Samuels was in there. She had told him she wasn't and Thomas smirked. If she was dancing with someone else, it had better of been her father or one of her brothers if she knew what was good for her. He walked on the dance floor and squeezed his way past all the couples waltzing.

Thomas didn't see her on the dance floor either and he got very annoyed. He walked up to Jacob and Emma and interrupted their conversation, "Have you seen Amelia?"

The couple looked annoyed that he disturbed them. Jacob had looked at Emma and she at him but neither of them knew of the girl's where- a- bouts. "No, not since before you danced with her," Jacob told Thomas before continuing his conversation with Emma. She nodded her head in agreement with him.

Displeased with their answer, Thomas marched off determined to find out where she had been hiding. He called her name out loud and noticed the looks on the faces that heard him but he didn't care. All he cared about was locating his fiancée who was supposed to be making him look good. He was fuming in frustration. He noticed Anna standing against the wall, waiting for a dance, and he walked straight up to her. If anyone knew where Amelia was, perhaps it would be her. "Where is Amelia?" he demanded to know.

"She went home," Anna stated as she looked around the room and not at him. Like her sister, she wasn't impressed by his demeanor and didn't want to give him any of her attention. She could sense him still standing there getting angry over what she had just told him. She wasn't

112

afraid to tell him exactly what Amelia told her to tell him. Others might have been, knowing it would upset him but Anna was one of those few people who couldn't care less if Thomas was angry.

Thomas' face became red with anger. He held his fists to his side and felt them tighten up. She must have lied to him about going to get a drink when all along she was just trying to get away from him. "What on blazes for," he asked.

Anna laughed at his behavior. She might have been young and immature but she could tell that he couldn't care less what the reasons were. "She had a headache, and I'm understanding why," Anna defiantly answered him.

Thomas was now steaming. He could feel his hot breath exhaling in places he hadn't even realized could breathe. Headache or not, she would come back to the social with him and put on the best show coins could pay for. He didn't bother to excuse himself from Anna; he felt he didn't need to. She was just the pesky little soon-to-be-sister-in-law. He left her standing where he found her and rushed off to the main entrance to go retrieve his possession. As he was trying to squeeze past the crowd of people, he overheard a group of men talking about the stranger in the village.

"He didn't stay long. You would think that he would want to meet people," one man had said. Then another man answered, "Or maybe he met the one person he was hoping to meet. I thought I saw him strolling with that pretty Samuels girl."

Thomas' blood was boiling. Anna had lied to him and he had half a mind to go back to where she was standing and box her ears but he had more important things to do. Thomas had to get his bride away from that stranger before he hurt her more than Thomas planned on doing once he had her in private.

He pushed his way past the crowd and out the front door. He looked around to see if he could spot her out there. It wasn't long before he realized that she wasn't around. He paused for a moment and noted the places she could have taken the stranger to be alone. He remembered a time when he would follow her around the village in secret. It wasn't long before he thought of the wooded area that wasn't far from the Meeting house. She would be an absolute fool to take a stranger there, especially since the sun had gone down and darkness had set. It wasn't long before he had come to the clearing and spotted her. As much as he wanted to storm into the clearing and punish her, he remained hidden behind a tree.

He was outraged by what he saw; Amelia was with the stranger in an embrace. The stranger didn't appear to be hurting her but just the opposite; he was cuddling with her. Thomas watched as Amelia pressed her red lips against the man's and right away he was overcome with jealousy. He couldn't care less if Amelia gave her heart to that man or not, she was his fiancée and there was no way she could stop what was meant to be. He thought about the kiss he witnessed. She had pushed him away many times when he kissed her yet she lovingly kissed the stranger. "Little tramp," he whispered. Thomas was too far away to hear what the couple was saying, but he didn't dare to inch closer in fear he would be heard. He felt furious when he noticed the way Amelia laughed with the man. He was nothing in Millersport but a stranger. Nobody knew of him but Thomas now had his own thoughts. He was a woman stealing son-of- a-bitch who would pay for making moves on Thomas' girl. Thomas vowed that the man would never be near Amelia again. He pondered how he would do that. If he were to announce to the public that the stranger was kissing his girl, the people would ridicule the stranger and drive him out of the village. Although, he thought, doing so would also let the people know that he couldn't control his bride-to-be and in return he would be the one ridiculed. Seeing enough of his devious fiancée, he returned to the Meeting house where he would continue to mingle among the villagers and carry on as if Amelia went home to tend to her headache. He would think of something to split Amelia and the stranger, and a way to discipline her, as the night went on.

Chapter Fourteen

Sunday morning brought most of the villagers to church like every other Sunday. The congregation gathered in the pews and listened to Reverend Mayer give his sermon. It was a warm morning and most of the people were eager to leave the building and step foot outdoors. They stood and sang the final song in unison as women fanned themselves to keep cool. When they finished, they took their seats and waited for the Reverend to tell them that the service was over. Except, Reverend Mayer stood at the front of the church and said, "Before you leave, Thomas Van Martin has an announcement he wants to make," then moved to the side to make room for Thomas.

Amelia glanced over at her father. She wondered if he knew what was going on; knowing that if he did, he wouldn't tell her about it. Then put her eyes back on Thomas. She tried to guess what he was up to and tried to read his face to figure out what he would say. She couldn't believe it when he said to the congregation, "I know it's warm in here but this will only take a moment. First, it was nice to see all of you at the social last night. My mother appreciated that her hard work paid off." Amelia shook her head at his words; Catherine Van Martin wasn't the only person who made the social a success. She kept her eyes on Thomas as he went on, "Now to my announcement. As some of you may have already known, Amelia Samuels, and I have been courting since the start this month. I'm honored to tell all of you I have asked for her hand in marriage and she has accepted."

Amelia's jaw dropped into her chest. She could hear the congregation clap and cheer and could hear him thanking everyone. His proud face was held high as he walked down the aisle towards the entrance and she glared at him the whole time. When her eyes made it to the door though, her heart sank. Patrick. She had been asking him to attend church since she met him and he picked that Sunday to attend, the one service she wished that he had not shown up. She wanted to scream and run to Patrick but as Thomas brushed past the new man in the village, Patrick took off. Her heart wanted to reach out to him. The hurt on his face broke her heart in a million pieces.

The villagers piled out of the church, all shaking Thomas' hand on their way out. Henry remained in the pew and looked over at Amelia. She was outraged at what just happened. "Father," she cried, "You said that we couldn't speak of this until after my birthday. Are you going to allow his show to go on?"

Henry knew that it would be of no use to fuss over Thomas' announcement. If the villagers were to think that he was happy about the marriage, he couldn't try to take back Thomas' announcement. If he were to say something to Thomas or Daniel, he would have a sharp reminder of his own mistakes. He decided to just let it go. "What is there to do, Amelia?" He answered. "There was no harm in it," he finished.

Amelia no longer knew what to think about her father. She inhaled and fumed as she exhaled her breath. "I'm so disappointed in you," she steamed as she shoved her body passed him in the pew to get out to the aisle. Then she stormed off to give Thomas a piece of her mind. When she stepped out of the church, the crowd of people that were still hanging around clapped their hands and cheered again. She heard them congratulating her and stretching their hands out to shake hers but she refused to touch anyone. They might have been happy, but she sure wasn't. Thomas was standing next to his parents and talking to several people who seemed interested in the upcoming wedding. Amelia didn't care what people thought anymore. She raced up to him, grabbed his arm and pulled him away from the others. "How dare you," she shouted at him.

Thomas continued to walk further away, squeezing Amelia's arm as he pulled her along. He knew what he was doing by announcing their engagement early. It would make everyone know just how serious their relationship was. It would let them know that under no circumstances should she be talking to the stranger. "Be quiet," he told her but with a smile remaining on his face so not to let the villagers know that they were arguing.

"You had no right to discuss our relationship," she yelled at him. "You know what my father told you."

"He won't mind," Thomas laughed. Henry Samuels could do nothing but smile at this point. "Besides, I know where you were last night and who you were with. I won't tolerate it."

Amelia looked stumped and wondered how he had found her but he wasn't about to explain it. She even wondered for a moment if he was being honest or not. She would not let this ruthless man ruin her life. "I won't marry you," she insisted as she stood tall and fought the water building up in her eyes.

"You will be my wife and I forbid you talking to that stranger." Thomas wanted to let her know that he was the one in charge and there was nothing either her or her father could do about it. "Say, you know what? I've just decided that we will wed next week. An August wedding how does that sound?"

"No," she screamed as her insides twisted up. There was no way she would be his bride. The thought of him being her husband made her insides tighten up. She couldn't help but to release the tears that swelled up in her eyes.

"Yes, I think your father would be pleased to marry you off sooner than expected," he snorted at her. He noticed that the crowd was looking their way, so he turned his attention to them and said, "She's just a little shy about having our personal life displayed like this."

The crowd dwindled and Thomas' parents and Henry walked over to them. "What is going on over here?" Daniel asked. He knew that Henry had given strict time lines about when their announcement would be made but yet he also knew that Henry would not say anything to them on the matter.

"I've just decided that there is no reason we should wait any longer. Amelia and I will wed one week from today." Thomas put his arm around Amelia and brought her close to him. She resisted, but he pulled her until her bosom flew onto his chest. "My darling here was just protesting because she would prefer it to be sooner," he said to the elders.

Amelia could hear Catherine burst with excitement as she went on about planning the event. She saw her father shake hands with Daniel and Thomas and knew that he wasn't objecting to the sudden change in plans. She lost her breath as her heart beat faster. In a few short minutes her heart went from joy knowing that Patrick loved her to total humiliation hearing Thomas tell the whole village they were getting married.

The four standing in front of her waited for her to say something but she was too angry to even attempt to be polite. She looked straight into her father's eyes and wailed, "I'll never forgive you." Then she grabbed a hold of her skirt and ran away from them and went straight to Patrick's house to make sure he was okay with what had happened.

Catherine thought she could catch up to Amelia and followed her, but stopped a few feet away when she realized that the young girl didn't want to talk. Changing her mind, Catherine saw group of her lady friends and went up to them to further share the good news.

Henry stood with Daniel and Thomas until Thomas to saw someone he could go talk to. When he was gone Daniel said, "Well, seems she is still not coming to terms with the marriage."

"No, I'm afraid that she isn't." Henry was too caught up in what she had said to him to even be bothered with what Daniel had to say. Within in a couple of weeks she had gone from the sweetest girl he had the pleasure of knowing to the most defiant child in the world. It pained him to hear her say she would never forgive him; though he remembered saying the same thing when he was split from Ruth. He said a prayer that what she would come around the same way he had. He prayed that what she said wasn't true.

Daniel stood tall and said, "Then I suppose you are feeling the punishment of your stupid mistakes."

"Save it," Henry snapped back. He knew what he was doing and didn't need to be reminded. "I paid the day I gave her hand to your son." Then he too turned and left the church. He knew that they would gather around again in a week for a wedding celebration and there was nothing he could do to stop it. He hung his head in shame as he walked home alone.

Patrick arrived back home quick since he had ridden his horse into the village to attend church. He was glad he had sat in the back because it gave him a better opportunity to dash out of the church when he heard Amelia's engagement announced. He was angry and took his frustrations out on some logs he had been meaning to chop up. As he mutilated the wood, he thought of Thomas and pictured him standing in front of the congregation. The kid was rather homely looking; though he didn't make a habit of noticing the appearance of other men. Patrick couldn't help notice how thin Thomas was, and he knew that he could snap the twerp in two if given the chance. Patrick lifted the ax above his head and brought it back down, slamming it on the log in front of him. For every stroke he took, he imagined Thomas' face on the log. He wanted to rip him apart for destroying Amelia's life. His own life, for his heart wanted her to be his wife. He was preoccupied in slicing Thomas' face beyond its core he didn't see Amelia running towards him.

She ran at the church and didn't stop once, not even to catch her breath, until she reached Patrick's land. Upon her arrival she saw him outside his house chopping wood. She was about to call out to him to let him know that she was there but noticed that he wasn't wearing a shirt. She couldn't help but stop and stare at the man she loved. His arms and chest were tanned golden brown, and she wondered how many times he had worked outside without a shirt on. The sun was bright and sweat was building up on his muscles and then rolling right off to dissolve into the already hot ground. Those muscles, she couldn't take her eyes off of those muscles. She felt herself drawn to them and wanted to touch them. Amelia desired him and imagined herself rubbing her hands all over his strong arms as she placed gentle kisses all over his hard chest. She wasn't sure how long she had been staring at him. He realized that she was standing there and must've known what she'd been thinking because the most seductive smile spread across his face. She shook her head to rid herself of those shameful thoughts and then ran to him and fell into his arms. "I'm so sorry that you had to hear that," she sobbed.

Patrick was glad to see Amelia but was saddened to see her tear-streaked face. He wrapped his arms around her and kissed the top of her head. "It isn't your fault." He let go of her and returned to his pile of wood. Patrick saw the way she looked at him as he glanced her way out of the corner of his eyes. He wanted to do so much more than cut logs and his frustration let out a horrific moan. "Damn it, why did he do that? Did you know he would make that announcement?"

"No," Amelia replied. Just when she was getting somewhere in her battle, Thomas messed things up again. "It gets worse." She told him how she had it out with Thomas and how he embarrassed her. "He decided that we would wed next week and, of course, my father thinks it's a wonderful idea."

Patrick was hurt to hear that the girl he loved so much would marry someone else that soon. He was tempted to find Van Martin and ring his little neck. "Amelia we can't let that happen. I love you too much."

"And I love you." She couldn't help but cry again. Patrick put his ax down and held her close to him. Between her hysterical sobs, she thought she heard him cry too. "Oh Patrick, you're the only one who can help me now. Is there something we can do?"

He looked over her shoulder as he held her tight. She had told him she ran from Thomas and her father and he was becoming concerned. They might search for her. "First thing we need to do is get inside in case we're seen." Amelia didn't fight him at all. They entered his house and as soon as the door shut, he pulled her in for a kiss. She responded like she had every time he kissed her. Right away he thought they should run away together but decided that it wasn't something he should bring up right then and there.

Amelia loved it when he kissed her and realized that every time he kissed her the kisses were more intense. She tilted her head back and enjoyed feeling his lips on her. Before she knew it he had left her face and was planting kisses on her neck and then back up to her ear. She tingled when she felt him open his mouth and brought her earlobe into it with his tongue. She didn't know what he was doing, but she knew that she liked it. Amelia could feel his warm breath inside her ear and his teeth nibbling on her lobe and it made her want to fall to her knees. She resisted her weak knees and held onto him as tight as she could. His shirt was still off and she couldn't help but to follow through with the desires she felt as she stared at him. She let her fingers glide through the small hairs on his chest and it was more magical than she could have ever imagined. Her instincts told her to explore the sweat filled area more, and she circled her finger around his nipple. He looked down when she did that and found her mouth once more. This was love, she told herself, and this is what she dreamt of having with someone.

Patrick pulled himself away from her. "We have to stop," he said. He could feel the effects that their moment was having on him and didn't want her to feel it too. He was afraid that he would get caught up in the moment. Patrick wouldn't take advantage of her innocence, he told himself.

Amelia backed up in shame. She knew that she should not have touched him in that manner and was afraid that she had offended him. "I'm sorry, did I do something wrong?"

"No, you are perfect," he answered her. How he wanted to continue kissing her! "It isn't right." He looked at her as she batted her hurt eyes and bit down onto her bottom lip. He could tell that she didn't want to stop but for her sake, he had to. "I want you to be my wife, not his, and then we can continue."

"I would like that," she said determined more than ever to make it happen. "I promise; I'll find a way." The thought of her unwanted marriage made her cry again. "What am I going to do?"

Patrick reached his hands over to hers and held them tight. He wasn't sure how to go about their situation. Patrick only knew that he couldn't allow her to take vows with Thomas. He wanted to storm into her father's store and tell him he was in love with her but knew what the consequences would be. Patrick was a mere stranger that nobody knew except Amelia and his confession of love would look more suspicious than he cared to admit. The bottom line was that the times they had met in secret were not acceptable by respectable men such as her father. There would be no easy way for her engagement to be called off. Even then if it was, they would have to start over again from scratch with the supervision of her father. Patrick continued to listen to her talk as she told him that Thomas had seen them the night before. "Do you suppose that he saw us kiss?"

Amelia frowned. She couldn't even guess what was going through Thomas' sneaky mind. For all she knew, he might not have seen her at all but was trying to get her to admit something to him. "I don't know, but that would explain why he made that announcement."

"Yeah, you are right. He knows that you don't love him and the thought of you being with someone else has made him over jealous," Patrick guessed.

"He doesn't even love me, why should he be jealous?" Amelia would never figure Thomas out. They were quiet for a while before she said; "Now everyone in the village knows of my marriage and they know that I should not be seen with you."

Patrick lowered his head; those were his thoughts which were why he attacked the wood before she arrived. He could see the pain in her face which caused a pain in his heart. He didn't know how they would work things out but he knew that somehow, someway, she would be his bride and not Thomas'. Patrick sat there and recalled the social and what had happened afterward. Then he remembered the reason he went to the dance to begin with. He combed his fingers through his hair and without removing his hand; he placed his elbow onto the table. He was reminded that he would have to take another trip. Wondering how she would take the news he said to her, "Amelia, I have to take another trip tomorrow."

"What?" She questioned full of shock. Her bewildered face searched for answers as she wondered why he would leave that soon after their union. "I need you, please don't go."

"Not as long this time, I'll be back on Tuesday," he explained to her. She didn't like not being near him but nodded her head in understanding. Patrick couldn't wait until this whole thing with the government was over so he could concentrate on being with her.

Chapter Fifteen

Daniel hurried along to Henry's store to tell him what he had just heard. He was down at the loading docks where there were rumors of a regular merchant who had been caught with British funds and executed. The other merchants were spreading the word and Daniel was interested in hearing more information. He went up to one merchant and asked if the word was true. "What is this I hear about British funding?"

The merchant looked around to see if anyone else could hear his answer. He had been selling items in villages up and down the Hudson for several years and knew that the man who asked him questions was a reputable man and saw no harm in answering him. "Someone on another craft," he started, "Was caught red handed with an envelope addressed to the Brits'."

"I didn't think that a merchant could afford to fund the enemy," Daniel had said knowing that the merchant was just a man in the middle.

The merchant snickered, "Nah, it wasn't his. He was working for someone."

Henry Samuels, Daniel thought to himself. "Oh, so the plot thickens."

The merchant continued to make sure that nobody could hear him. It was obvious that this business man was looking for more answers. "They say that when he was caught, he refused to say who was responsible. I suppose we'll never know."

Daniel knew though and headed straight to Henry to make sure the responsible one learned what his dealings had done. He looked forward to throwing it in Henry's face. When he arrived at the store, he demanded that he see Henry right away and the employee waved his hand, given him the sign it would be all right. Daniel barged the door open and noticed Henry jumping up off of his seat. He shut the door behind him and said, "Have you heard the latest on your treason?"

"I don't know what you mean," Henry answered. He was trying to get work done though he could concentrate.

Daniel took a seat and watched his rival do the same. He then explained to him what he had heard on the docks. "So, are you responsible for this innocent man's life?"

Henry felt a sudden lump in his throat and pit in his stomach. The merchant was married and had two young children. His mistakes have now made them fatherless. "They executed him on the spot?" he asked instead of answering.

"Apparently," Daniel told him. "Did he work for you?" Henry leaned back in his chair and covered his face with his hands. The guilt was gaining control more every day. He dropped his hands to reveal a red frustrated face. "What is it you want from me, Van Martin? You already have my daughter marrying your son."

Daniel laughed. There wasn't anything else that he wanted to take from Henry. "Henry, I'm not such a wicked man," he said. He looked over at the other man who didn't seem to believe him so he went on, "Come now, this changes nothing and I don't want more from you. I'm not a fool. I can see that there is so much tension between you and your daughter. Your mistake has caused a wedge in your relationship and you may never get that back." Then he laughed at his next thought and couldn't help but let out his reasoning. "Maybe once she accepts her marriage, she'll prefer me over you."

Henry was steaming, and it took all of his strength not to knock Daniel out. He stood and pointed towards the door and yelled, "Enough, you've made your point now get out."

Pleased with the outcome of his meeting, Daniel stood to leave. "I'm going," he started, "I wanted to see if you understood all that happens when you mess with the government. That merchant's blood is on your hands,

Samuels." Then as quick as he arrived he turned and left. He had set out to throw salt in Henry's wound and as far as he was concerned, he was successful.

Again, Henry leaned back in his chair and covered his face. He couldn't help but think about all the lives he was ruining because of his decision to defy Madison's war. An innocent family was parted from a loved one on account of him. Then there was his daughter. She was more defiant than her mother ever was and that made him wonder if she would ever forgive him. His chances were slim; he knew that unless he changed things for her. He slammed his fist onto his desk, caring not of the ink that spilled because of the impact. Perhaps it was time to turn himself in like Ruth had told him to do so long ago. No, he decided. Ruth. Ruth would make him feel better. He wiped up the ink and then locked the door to his office. Walking past his employee he told him he had errands to run and that he would be back before the work day ended to lock up the building. Then he left the employee and marched straight to her house. He needed her now more than ever.

Ruth was in the spare room weaving a rug with her loom when Henry had barged in and asked where her boys were. She was surprised to see him but even more surprised to see the look upon his face. It was a look that scared her, something was wrong. "They're in school, like your own sons," she answered him. She wanted to ask him what the problem was but could tell that he wasn't there to talk, at least not right away.

Henry pulled her off of her stool and grabbed her waist to bring her closer to him. He pressed his lips hard against her mouth; harder than he usually done. There was no other way for him to take his frustrations out but to make fierce love to her. He took his foot and brought it to the back of her knees causing her to fall backwards. Still holding her tight, he fell down with her and continued to kiss her. He heard her ask, in between his kisses, what was wrong but he didn't care to answer. Henry needed to release some of the pressure building up inside of him and knew that she wouldn't object.

He pulled her dress up around her waist and tugged on her bloomers until they exposed her womanhood he longed for. Ruth was still crying out his name, but he now considered it a cry for pleasure and nothing else. With one hand he unfastened his belt and let his own unmentionables fall to his ankles. Climbing on top of her and between her knees, he entered her with one long thrust. He could hear her cry out and for a brief second he wondered if he was being too rough with her. Their love making was usually slow and tender but his anger had forced him to take her quick and hard right there on the wooden floor.

This wasn't a time for sweetness or even love, there was nothing this time but lust and an overbearing amount of guilt. He felt her hips move to meet his as he continued to push his body in and out of her. Several minutes later he felt his climax coming, and he fought it off as long as he could. He had wanted to wait until she too reached her climax but he could no longer hold back. Without a thought his bodily fluids shot up inside of Ruth as he let out a moan of delight.

Ruth held Henry as tight as she could. Henry remained in the same position when he finished and let out a soft cry. She reached up and kissed him and then pulled his head down onto her bosom. Both of them were breathing rather hard when she asked again, "Henry, please tell me what is wrong."

Realizing how he had just treated the woman he loved, Henry rolled over to his side. Shame on you, he thought. "I'm so sorry if I hurt you," was his reply to her.

"Something has upset you," she told him. He might not have been saying much, but she knew him well. They cleaned up, and she told him she would prepare tea. They entered the kitchen and Henry sat at the table while she put a pot of water onto the fireplace. As she retrieved two cups from the cupboard and placed them on the table, she spoke again. "What happened?"

Henry spoke. "The merchant that has been working for me was caught with my envelope and was executed straight away."

Ruth's hands shook, rattling the container of sugar she held. It was no wonder why he had to take her with such force. He wasn't in his right state of mind. If they killed the merchant, how long would it take for them to come for Henry? She couldn't bear the thought of losing him again. "They know about you?" She asked in a very scared voice.

"No," he assured her. "Apparently he died without exposing me. Or at least that is what Daniel said."

Ruth gasped. "What, he knows? What else can he keep over your head?"

"He claims he already has what he wanted, Amelia." Henry slammed his fist down again for the second time that day and was feeling the pain it had caused. "How could I have been such a fool? I've ruined so much," he continued to sob.

She sat beside him and put his head down on her shoulder. If only he had listened to her in the first place, she thought. She told him that funding the British was wrong. "Promise me you won't continue to give them money," she begged him.

Henry already knew that it would be too risky to continue. "I won't," he told her. "What about Amelia? What do I do about her?"

"Well," Ruth thought for a moment as she poured the hot tea into their cups. "You can't call off the wedding now. Daniel will report you and you'll be responsible for that merchant's life." Ruth watched him stir the hot beverage in front of him and knew that he wasn't interested in drinking it. "She'll come around. She'll love you again."

It had been too long, as far as Amelia was concerned, since she had spent time with Emma. Though she knew the only reason her friend could be bothered with her was because Jacob had to report to work. Still, she cherished the time they had. Together they went to the trail behind Emma's house and picked black raspberries like they have done so many times before her nightmare had started. The two were quiet, as if the weeks that had passed, had separated them. Amelia realized that Emma was the one person she could tell her deepest secrets too, and she wondered if that closeness was still there. "Emma," she talked to her friend, "Can I still tell you how I feel inside or will you be reporting everything to my father?"

Emma felt like crying when she heard Amelia's question. She knew that her friend was upset with all that was going on but to take it out of her was painful. She loved Amelia very much and wanted nothing more than to rebuild the friendship that had taken a beating. "Why do you say such hurtful things? None of this is my fault yet you act as if you no longer trust me."

Amelia felt bad and knew what Emma spoke was true. These days though, Amelia would take her frustrations out on anyone. "I'm sorry," she apologized. She hugged Emma and never wanted to let go.

Emma hugged right back; she had missed her friend. After they separated from the hug, Emma threw a berry at Amelia to clarify they could still have fun times together. Both girls laughed. "So, tell me what you wanted to tell me."

Amelia thought for a moment. She didn't want to hurt her friend anymore but still there was a part of her insides that said that she should not give her secrets away. She fought those thoughts and let her desire for someone to understand her win. "Remember the man we met the day I told you about my union with Thomas?" She looked at her friend who was nodding her head then continued, "I fell in love with him."

"The stranger," Emma exclaimed.

"No, his name is Patrick Buchanan, not a stranger," Amelia assured Emma.

Once again Emma felt fear for her friend. What was she doing falling in love with someone who she didn't even know? She wondered. "Still, he is a stranger; you name one person other than yourself who knows him. What about Thomas?" She felt herself panicking as the questions just rolled off of her tongue.

"You know I don't want to marry him," she answered without hesitation.

Emma's face turned scornful. "Amelia Samuels, you're not carrying on your wild idea of finding someone else to prove a point to your father, are you?"

Amelia laughed at what Emma was suggesting but it wasn't the case. She told herself from the start she wouldn't use Patrick in that manner. "No. Besides, I already asked my father what he would do if I fell in love with someone and he told me that even so I would have to marry Thomas."

"Then why would you allow yourself to fall in love?"

Amelia thought about the question. She didn't have an answer. "It happened on its own," she informed her friend.

Emma was quiet for a while as she thought about what was going on. She wished that she knew more about the stranger but as far as she knew; nobody knew anything about him. "You should stay away from him. Nobody knows anything about him," she told her friend. Her imagination painted horrifying pictures in her head. "What if he's an Indian and wants to kill you?"

Amelia giggled, "That is absurd, Emma."

"No it isn't," Emma insisted, "Haven't you heard of the Battle of Frenchtown and haven't you heard about the Raisin River Massacre? How could you say that Indians don't kill?"

Amelia tried to calm Emma down. She had heard of those events but it had nothing to do with Patrick. "Patrick isn't an Indian," she pleaded, "He's not going to kill me or anyone else."

Emma had nothing but concern on her face. Emma pondered even if he weren't an Indian, how could Amelia be in love with him when she would be marrying someone else in less than a week? "What are you going to do," Emma questioned but feared that she wouldn't receive any answers. Her overreaction had seemed to have scared Amelia off of the subject.

"I don't know," Amelia answered her. She knew that whatever she decided, she could no longer confide in Emma.

After the girls were done picking berries, Amelia excused herself from her friend's company and said that she would go home. She no longer found a need to be social. She said goodbye to Emma and then walked in the opposite direction to head back to her father's house. As she walked, she looked down to her basket now full with black raspberries and couldn't help but think they were small compared to the ones she had picked with Patrick. She thought of him and missed him while he was away on his day trip to New Baltimore. She didn't understand why but he took many business trips and wondered what that was all about.

Patrick paced back and forth while he waited to talk with the Major General he was told to report to. Over and over again he repeated the traitor's description in his mind so not to forget and he repeated the name he heard too. His trip to New Baltimore wasn't as bad as going to Albany. He had left his house before sunrise and had reached his destination by noon. Now he was waiting, as patient as he could, for the man named Major General Downy.

What seemed like an eternity later, Patrick noticed a distinguished looking man heading in his direction. He knew that he had to be the military man he would speak to. Downy, appearing to be in either his late forties or early fifties stood tall and looked Patrick in the eyes as he walked closer to introduce himself. He was wearing buff pantaloons, a white vest that covered his shirt, and a pair of high military boots that had gilt spurs attached to the side. This dress wasn't what Patrick had imagined when he heard word of the military changing the uniform for the war. However, he dared not question why the Major General looked so informal. As they stood face to face, Patrick noted the militia man's size. He stood a head taller than himself and though he wasn't considered overweight, Downy had wide shoulders, a solid torso, and strong arms. Patrick felt honored to speak to this man who was a highly respected officer in the war.

"Mr. Buchanan, I'm to presume?" Downy drilled as he shook Patrick's hand.

"Yes Sir," he answered. He almost wished that he didn't have to have this discussion with the Major General because he felt intimidated. He tried not to look too nervous.

Downy led Patrick towards his quarters where they could talk in private. After offering him a seat, Downy started, "I was informed of a man funding the Red Coats and hear that you have information that can lead me to him." Patrick nodded his head to let him know that he was correct and the Major General questioned, "What can you tell me about this fellow?" Patrick swallowed hard; he didn't want to mess this up. He explained what he had overheard on the loading docks, the same way he had reported it up in Albany. Downy scorned, "No, I already know about that. Don't waste my time here. Can you give me a description?"

Patrick spoke the right thing and explained that even though it was dark, he got a good look at the culprit. He gave the Major General as many details as possible and when he heard Downy ask if there was more, Patrick cheered, "Oh yes, I was also able to catch a first name. Henry."

"You only caught a first name?"

If Patrick didn't fear the government, he would have given the Major General a piece of his mind. He thought he had more than what was asked of him. No wonder this man was a Major General; he thought to himself, he was a definite hard ass. "I'm sorry Sir, but no I didn't have time to hear the last name."

Downy thought about what Buchanan said. He wanted to know more but knew that he had to get information in other places; he had to do his research. "You've been more than helpful, Buchanan. Thank you for your time."

"What will become of this man? This Henry that we speak of," Patrick asked. He didn't know why he even cared. The traitor had what was coming to him but yet something inside him felt there was more than met the eye.

"That is none of your concern now," Downy scowled. He knew what he would do; he would execute the man himself. The Major General felt as if Buchanan would continue to ask questions so he hurried him out of his quarters and again thanked him for coming.

There was nothing that Buchanan could do. "You're welcome," Patrick said to deaf ears as he walked away from the Major General's camp quarters. He was concerned about the devious look on the officer's face but didn't know him well enough to read him. He discarded the topic, wiped his hands, and put his mind back to where it should have been. Amelia. He decided that he wouldn't wait to head back home. He made sure he had all of his belongings and then jumped onto his horse and headed south.

Chapter Sixteen

Drops of cold sweat fell down Emma's neck as she knocked on Patrick Buchanan's door. Her decision to speak with the stranger had happened before she had the time to stop and think about what she was doing. She knew Amelia was busy back in the village and used the time she had to her advantage. She thought it was absurd for her friend to be in love with someone she hardly knew. Emma needed to break the connection between him and her friend before Amelia wound up hurt somehow. She paused on the thought and realized that her actions would also cause pain but Emma was convinced it was for the best. She held her breath as she knocked again and hoped that Amelia would never find out.

As she waited for the door to open, she thought about Thomas. Emma hated him marrying Amelia almost as much as Amelia did but she thought he would at least protect her from any harm. Once she was successful at turning Patrick away from Amelia, Emma hoped that her friend would respect her fiancé.

"Can I help you with something," a voice said. Patrick stood behind the girl who jumped high into the air when he called to her, "Its Emma, right? Emma Cooper?"

Emma was at a loss for words and hadn't expected him to be outdoors when she arrived. It threw her approach off a little, but she had to regain her courage. She cleared her throat and said, "That's right."

Patrick stood back and looked at the girl he had met the day he met Amelia. He didn't know why she was there. He stood there with his arms crossed over his chest waiting for her to say something but she was silent. She was looking around as if she was afraid to look him in the eyes. "Well?"

Emma realized that she had to do this and get it over with. She only hoped that her best friend would forgive her someday. "I meant no disrespect by showing up here, but we need to talk."

Patrick knew that she wouldn't accept his invitation into the house so he gestured for her to follow him. He walked several feet away from the house and pointed to two logs he was preparing to chop up. He motioned for her to take a seat as he took one himself. "So tell me what is troubling you, Emma."

Emma bit on her lip thinking of how to start the conversation. She decided that she couldn't beat around the bush, so she came right out and said, "I know that you have been together with Amelia. She told me all about you."

Patrick wasn't surprised. He knew how close the girls were. She was still working on her father to allow them to be together and she must have asked her friend for help.

"Listen, it's not what you might think. I would ask nothing improper from her. We like to," but he was cut off.

"It's all a lie and you need to know that," Emma poured out. She knew this would hurt Amelia's feelings, but in the end it would make everything all right again. Emma started at the beginning. "Has she told you about her engagement to Thomas Van Martin?"

"Yes, as a matter of fact she did. But she doesn't love him and she is convinced that her father will end the engagement before it goes too far." Patrick was intrigued about what this girl was trying to say.

Emma stood up from the excitement and paced back and forth before saying anything. She knew that she would twist things around, but she had to be convincing. "That is only part of it. I'm here to stop her before she gets you all caught up in this whole mess."

"What do you mean?"

"She is using you, don't you see that?" Emma told him about Amelia's plan to get out of her union with Thomas. She told him that Amelia wanted to make her father believe that she loved someone else, anyone else so he would call of the marriage.

136

Patrick listened to what Emma was saying but didn't think that it had anything to do with him. He had met Amelia, spent time with her, and they fell in love. It wasn't a scheme. "Maybe she said that, but that isn't what she is doing."

"Yes, she is, Mr. Buchanan," Emma stated.

Patrick laughed; he wasn't used to formalities. "Please, call me Patrick."

Emma was impatient; there was no time to argue about the proper way to address someone so she agreed, "Okay, Patrick." She stopped for a moment to pull her-self together. "Don't you think it's kind of ironic the way after just meeting you, she suddenly finds a reason to see you more? Then even though you have only known her for a few weeks, she is in love with you? How can you not think that she isn't carrying out her plan to change her father's mind?"

"She hasn't told him. So there goes your theory." Patrick didn't know what to think at the moment. Emma was part right and their relationship happened fast. He remembered how sweet Amelia was to him and how they had shared special moments together and how they opened to each other. No she was wrong, Amelia loved him. He went on, "And if she tells him, I mean when she tells him, she'll tell him how much she wants to be with me."

Emma shook her head. He wasn't seeing the whole picture the way she was trying to paint it. "Okay, you're right. She will tell her father about you and she'll give you the fluttering eyes when he is around and I'm telling you, once he goes to the Van Martins and tells them that the engagement is off, she'll want nothing to do with you."

He was having a hard time believing what the girl was saying to him. "How do you know this," he asked. He had to figure out whether it was true or not because as much as he didn't want to admit it, what Emma was saying was making sense.

Emma paced for a while then stopped to look him square in the eyes, "Because she is my best friend and we share everything. She told me you were the key to getting Thomas out of her life." Emma couldn't believe how well she had done. She wanted the stranger to keep his distance from Amelia and she was sure that her plan would work fine. She noticed how his face changed and how upset he looked. For a second she felt bad, perhaps he was a nice man with no intentions on hurting her friend. Maybe they were in love but Emma couldn't take that chance. She had to make sure he understood and believed her. "See, what you don't know about her is that she always gets what she wants. She doesn't want to marry Thomas and will use you to break the engagement."

Patrick was saddened. He had shared his most intimate thoughts with Amelia and the thought of it going in one ear and out the other upset him. He knew that Emma thought of him as nothing more than the stranger in the village so he wondered why she would bother to spare him the heartache. His voice got dry as he asked, "So why would you tell me all of this?"

Emma had to think of something fast. She didn't have a reason that would satisfy him. Because of her reaction to Amelia's feelings, Amelia didn't tell her anything about Patrick. She knew that if she didn't sound like she was sincere than he wouldn't believe her. Emma made something up. "She told me what happened to you before you moved here and I didn't want to see you get hurt."

Patrick was shocked. Amelia must have told Emma about his wife and child. He didn't want to hear anymore. "I have things to do," he tipped his hat off and said, "Good day, Miss Cooper."

Emma, surprised that her excuse worked, watched him storm into his house before she too stood to leave. As she walked away curiosity grabbed her insides, and she wondered what happened to him before moving to Millersport. She had come to see he never interfered with Amelia's affairs again and she was positive it worked. It was time to see to the other half of her plan.

Jacob looked over at Emma and put his arm around her shoulders. He could see that something was bothering her, but she was silent. Jacob wanted to find out what her troubles were, but expected it had something to do with Amelia. He knew that she missed her friend though they lived only a half mile apart it felt as if they were hundreds of miles away from each other. "What is bothering you," he asked her hoping she would open with him.

Emma swore to Amelia that she wouldn't tell a soul about her sudden feelings for the stranger but Emma couldn't help but worry about the situation. Still, she feared that something terrible would happen if she kept quiet. "It's Amelia," she explained but before she could continue, Thomas had appeared out of nowhere.

"What about Amelia," he demanded. He was still furious over seeing his fiancée with that stranger and wondered if perhaps Emma knew something too.

Jacob jumped up from the bench he and Emma were sitting on and faced Thomas. He wondered where his friend came from; he hadn't seen him coming. Chances are if he had known that Thomas was around then he would've never of asked Emma what was wrong to begin with. Jacob knew how touchy the subject of Amelia has been for Thomas since he announced their engagement. Something had made him mad but whatever it was; he wasn't telling Jacob about it. He stood between Emma and Thomas. "Thomas, you should stop sneaking up on us like that. Where did you come from, anyway?"

Thomas grinned. He didn't sneak up on anyone but he knew that he had soft steps that often were unheard. "I didn't sneak, I need not sneak around either," he arrogantly said. He looked past Jacob to see the girl still sitting on the bench. "What were you about to say about Amelia?"

"She doesn't have to tell you anything," Jacob snapped in defense of his new girlfriend. Thomas might have been his best chum, but that didn't give him the right to treat Emma the way he did.

Emma stood and interrupted the brief argument between the two men. "It's okay, Jacob," she started. "Maybe it's best I talk to Thomas." She looked at them and paused. She would never tell him but she knew that Thomas was nearby, and that is why she brought up her best friend's name. Jacob didn't seem to understand, so she said, "Alone." Jacob looked confused and concerned but he honored her with a little time with Thomas. He told her he would go inside the general store for a minute but he would be right back. When Jacob was out of ear shot, Thomas sat down on the bench next to Emma. "Now are you going to tell me what I want to hear?"

Emma swallowed hard. This was all happening so fast and she no longer knew if what she was doing was right or not. All she knew was that her best friend was becoming dangerously close to the stranger and someone had to stop it. "I don't know how to say this," she started.

"Well then just tell me," Thomas snorted. She was trying to beat around the bush, and he didn't have time for such foolishness.

Emma growled at his interference. Poor Amelia, she thought, she could never talk for the rest of her life once she marries this man. "She claims she has fallen in love with someone," she stopped to swallow the lump enlarging in her throat. "It's not you, either."

Thomas was more enraged than he thought he would be. It wasn't a shock for him to hear that she had fallen in love but his pride had been telling himself that he was wrong about the situation he saw. "She's in love with the stranger, right?"

Emma was surprised to hear him say that. She had no idea he suspected Amelia. "You know about him?" She quizzed.

"I had a bad feeling about the guy since the day you two first ran into him near the docks," he admitted to her.

140

Looking back to that day, he found it strange that Emma was scared but yet Amelia remained calm. There must have been an instant attraction for Amelia and the unknown man. He didn't want Emma to know how angry he was though so he tried his best to be polite. "What makes you think that she loves him?"

"She came straight out and told me," Emma stated and then continued to tell him all that Amelia had said.

Thomas rubbed his boney chin with his forefingers. He was trying to figure out why she couldn't love him. Why couldn't she give him a chance? His family was the richest in Millersport which meant he could give her whatever she desired, including him. After all, he was the most handsome man around, not just in the village but in all the United States, he thought. "What about me?" He furthered his questioning. "Doesn't she look forward to our marriage?"

Emma laughed. Thomas was trying to be so sincere, but she knew that he meant none of it. "You know she despises you," she chuckled. "What makes you think that she wants to be with you?" Noticing that Jacob was heading back towards them, Emma wanted to make sure that Thomas would protect her friend. "I only told you this because I worry about her. It's not safe or proper to hang around with strange men. Are you going to make sure she is taken care of?"

Thomas had plans to take care of Amelia all right but they might not be what Emma had in mind. He couldn't wait to make her his wife, now more than ever so he could punish her for being unfaithful to him. "Yes," he lied to her face. Before they could continue to discuss it any further, Jacob came back from the general store and insisted that they wanted to be alone. Thomas took the hint and tipped his hat to Emma and thanked her for giving him the heads up and then walked away as quietly as he had arrived.

"What was that all about," Jacob asked Emma.

"Nothing," she told him. "It's all taken care of now."

141

Chapter Seventeen

Wednesday, August 25, 1813

The day started off like any other day since the dreadful announcement of Amelia and Thomas' engagement. Amelia still hadn't talked to her father. As far as she was concerned, he could have stood up for her when Thomas insisted that they marry sooner than expected. After all, he was her father and has said from the start they wouldn't marry until after her twenty-first birthday. When the Van Martins defied his only request, he stood there and went along with them. Coward; was the only thing she could think of to describe him. He had tried to communicate with her but she ignored him and no longer cared if he would punish her for it or not. When he left for work Amelia mocked, "Don't you damage my reputation, Amelia. Do what I tell you to do, Amelia." Anna had glanced at her but said nothing. She helped clean up and then went up to her bedroom to straighten herself out. Her mood changed as she brushed her hair knowing she was off to spend the day with Patrick.

Walking the dusty road to his house, Amelia's imagination toyed with her mind. Patrick told her he would let her know, somehow, when he was back from his trip. He hadn't. She wondered if she was traveling for nothing, perhaps she wouldn't find him there. She hoped that nothing bad happened to him on the way. As she neared his home, she could see smoke circling out of his chimney and she felt relief. Maybe his attempts to contact her were useless, she pondered. Right away, she knocked on his door.

After several knocks, Patrick opened the door. "What do you want," his sour voice had said and then he shut the door in her face.

Amelia didn't know what had come over him. He was acting completely different than she had known him to be.

Even when they didn't know each other well, he didn't behave that way. He was displeased with her, but she wondered why. "Patrick," she cried out. "What is the matter?"

Patrick stood on the other side of the door with so many mixed emotions going through him. Part of him wanted to pull her inside his house so he could kiss her again the way he had done before his trip. He loved her and just wanted to hold her but the more sensible side of him wanted her to go away and never to return. "I'm not your toy," he said and tried to shut the door again.

She pushed the door and forced it to remain open. If she didn't know better, she would think that she was at the wrong house. "Patrick, please," she now begged. "Tell me what this is all about."

He realized she would not leave without an explanation but then again, he thought, he was the one who deserved an explanation. He allowed her into his house so they could talk. He waved his hand, motioning for her to enter, and she brushed passed him. She stood there with her hands on her hips as if he had done something wrong and she would scorn him. "Why don't you start," he snipped at her. He could see she didn't know what he was talking about. "Why don't you tell me about your plan to find someone to love so you could talk your father out of your marriage to Van Martin?"

"That was before I met you," she told him not realizing that her statement made her look guilty.

"So you admit it," he snarled. He couldn't believe that Emma was right. How he wished that Amelia would have said that she didn't know what he was talking about. "You were just trying to use me," he reminded her.

"No," she replied. Amelia was baffled. She refused to use him in that silly plan of hers. The feelings she felt for him were very much real. At the moment she couldn't remember if she told him what she originally wanted to do or not but she didn't think that she had. "Where did you hear that from," she questioned him.

Patrick smirked. He wondered how she would feel to know that her best friend had betrayed her. "Your friend Emma cared enough to prevent me from getting hurt by you. Something you couldn't care less," he was saying to her when she interrupted him.

"Emma?" She thought back to the conversation she had with Emma about her feelings for Patrick. Her friend was convinced that Patrick would hurt her but Amelia never would've thought that Emma could do anything as harsh as to confront Patrick and make him believe that she was out to break his heart. Why would she do it? She wondered. Amelia realized that she had to make him understand that her stupid plan had nothing to do with him and she disregarded it as fast as she had thought of it. If she didn't prove to him how much she loved him, she would lose him. "Patrick, what did she tell you? I stopped that conception as soon as I realized how immature it was. It had nothing to do with you."

"And my wife, you told her about my wife," he shouted at her. How dare her to spread his intimate thoughts to her friends?

Still confused, Amelia stated, "No I didn't. She must've manipulated you to think I did. You have to believe me."

Patrick was skeptical. He wanted to believe her but since her engagement wasn't yet called off, he was still afraid that she wanted him back into her clutches until it was. The tears in her eyes made him feel the pain she was in at this sudden change. He didn't want her to be hurt more than she already was with her life. He leaned in to kiss her but before his lips reached hers he had to ask again, "Are you sure?"

She stood there and shook. At last she found true love, and it was being torn apart by her best friend of all people. She cried for all she has lost; her father and now Emma. The thought of losing Patrick too was more than she could handle and she couldn't control her bottom lip as it trembled. She knew that she had to assure him she loved him enough to be with him forever. "Honestly; it had nothing to do with you. I love you so much. Please don't disregard me the way they do. If I behaved that way, don't you think that I would have told my father about you already?"

With his lips less than an inch away from her mouth he whispered, "How do I know you haven't told him?"

"Oh for goodness sake," she cried as she pulled herself away from him. "For starters I haven't introduced the two of you yet. If I was up to no good like you claim, he wouldn't call off my engagement with just my word. I would have to bring you to him so he knew you weren't just my imagination."

He stood there and thought about what she was trying to say. She had a point, a good point, she could have taken him back into the Meeting house the night of the social to introduce him, but she didn't. Amelia stood in front of him with tears rolling down the side of her nose and her body shivered. She didn't look like a girl who was playing head games. All he wanted to do was to hold her and feel her heartbeat. Her heart couldn't lie to him. He gave in to his temptation and wrapped his arms around her by the waist. She hesitated moving closer to him at first but once she felt his embrace she too leaned in to feel him next to her. He felt her heartbeat; it was pounding fast and hard and as he rubbed his hand up to the small of her back, he could have sworn that it skipped a beat. "Don't break my heart," he said just before he kissed her lips. "I love you too much."

Amelia was relieved that he was holding her close and not accusing her of awful things. She closed her eyes as she rested her head and listened to him say he loved her. Nothing else mattered at that point; not Thomas or her father, not even Emma. All she cared about was being with him and any cost. She tilted her head up as he kissed her. Amelia took her hands and cupped his face. She wanted to let him know that she was more than eager to respond to his kisses.

It occurred to Amelia that neither her words nor her kisses were enough to prove her love to him. There was just one other way that would confirm her love and devotion; she would make love with him. She said a silent prayer to ask for forgiveness for the acts she had in mind. "Patrick," she said to him, "Make love to me, right here and now."

Patrick was breathless and had no idea how to respond to her request. He wanted her, that was a fact he couldn't deny, but he hesitated. "Just because we love each other doesn't give us the right," he informed her. "We're not married."

Amelia pulled away but still held onto his hand. If she has learned anything it was that the proper way of doing things wasn't necessary the right way. "It's my commitment to you. I'm your wife, if not by law by the heart."

Unable and unwilling to let go of the grip she had on him, Patrick followed her to where she was leading. Amelia stepped into his bedroom and closed the door behind him. Her heart fluttered and her head felt as if it were spinning as nervousness overcame her. This is what she wanted, what she needed, to feel his loving arms around her and know that she was returning his love. She wrapped her left arm around his neck and kissed him more passionately than she ever had before. Her right hand fumbled for the buttons on his shirt and then slid inside to feel his warm skin. She wouldn't let him stop the desires she knew they both felt. Copying everything he had done to her, Amelia left his lips and brushed her mouth over the lobes of his ear and down his neck while the hand wrapped around him combed the back of his hair. "Take me," she whispered.

Patrick lost control of his senses and gave her what she asked for. He knew her heart was with him and somehow, someway, she would be his bride. He flexed his head backwards as she kissed his neck and now bare shoulders. For every breath of hers he felt on him, he felt more excitement building up inside. Amelia had undressed him and without second thought, he reached over and helped her disrobe. Looking over at her naked body, he couldn't get over how beautiful she was. Patrick pulled her close to his cloth-less body and slid his hand under the heaviness of her breast. He looked her in the eyes as he caressed every inch of her upper body. When she reached up and unpinned her hair, allowing it to flow down her backside, he knew that he could hold off no longer. He picked her up and laid her across his bed and without hesitation, he entered her inviting body.

For a few moments, as Patrick made love to her, Amelia didn't give a second thought to Thomas, her father, or Emma. They were all problems that disappeared and she hoped that it would remain that way forever. Perfect. She felt Patrick move her hands up towards the headboard and then move his hands back down their long lengths, stopping at the curves over her midsection. She felt his release inside of her and knew that their first act of love was over.

Patrick kissed her again and then rolled to his side. "I love you," he told her as Amelia's heart burst with joy.

They remained in Patrick's bed for hours, talking about their dreams and loving each other more. Patrick knew that she wouldn't want to discuss the real problems in their lives but it had to be talked about. "I know what we have to do," he started.

Amelia frowned. She would like to forget everything and remained in the perfect world they created but knew that she couldn't ignore the situation either. "Tell me," she answered.

"We can run away and get married and nobody can stop us."

"Elope?" Amelia questioned. There had to be another way. As much as she felt a strain from her father, she still couldn't imagine getting married without him. Amelia noticed Patrick nodding his head, and she cried. "Oh no Patrick, I want my family with me when I become your wife."

Patrick leaned over and wiped the tears off of her face. "Don't cry. You know your father doesn't want that for you. If we don't elope than he will make you Van Martin's wife."

Amelia knew he was right. Her father had destroyed so many of her dreams but she refused to let him interfere in this one. She took a deep breath and agreed.

They put their clothes back on and discussed what they needed to do. They wanted to leave right away and head up to Albany but both of them had something on their minds. For Amelia, it was her mother's dress. She wanted to wear it more than ever. Hearing Patrick say what he was thinking, made her realize that she would get that chance.

"It isn't a good idea for us to leave this late," he begun. "The sun will go down soon." He explained that it would be best if she returned home and pretended that nothing has changed. They would meet in the morning and would ride out of Millersport then. "Come," he said to her, "I will walk you as far as I can without us being seen together."

They were strolling in a secluded area outside of the village when they heard unexpected voices. Amelia just about threw herself down to the ground and hid behind a bush. She pulled on Patrick's hand and motioned for him to do the same. "Who is it," he whispered.

Her heart raced. She thought they would be alone this far away from the village but then when she least expected it; she heard the voices of her father and her aunt. "It's my father and Aunt Ruth," she answered him. "I don't think they know we are here." Her eyes focused on the couple she saw through the branches and she wondered what they were doing out there. She was there with Patrick because they didn't want to be seen by others and wondered if that was the case for the older couple. It wasn't long before her thoughts were answered as she saw her father kiss her aunt with more passion than she'd ever seen him give her mother. She gasped and couldn't believe what she was seeing.

Patrick had seen the couple that Amelia referred to but wasn't bothered by their coupling. What bothered him was the identity of the man. "That is your father?" He quizzed her. The sun was shining bright, but he still recognized him as the man he had overheard on the loading docks. This couldn't be, he insisted to himself.

"Yes," she whispered, "But this isn't a good time to meet him." She hung her head down and thought that she was just like him, sneaking around. As she watched her father's display of affection for her aunt, she realized that Ruth was the one he was torn away from years ago. How painful it must have been for him to see her marry his own brother. For a moment her heart reached out for him. She wished that he would have told her instead of hiding his relationship with her. Did he think that she wouldn't understand?

"Oh my God," Patrick gasped and Amelia looked at him. "There is something I must tell you."

Still peeking through the bush, Amelia questioned what Patrick was talking about. "What do you mean? Did you know they were lovers?"

Grabbing her arm, he told her they had to get out of there but she had shown him that there was no other way to go without being seen by her father. She urged him to talk to her right there. "Is his name Henry?" He whispered and Amelia nodded her head as he continued, "I saw him one day, the day I went to see the merchants. How can I tell you this?" He cleared his throat, but she was looking very impatient so he finished, knowing that what he was about to say would hurt her. "Your father has been funding the British."

Amelia was speechless for a few seconds. She didn't know why Patrick was turning on her. "That is absurd, why are you telling me such horrible things?"

"I'm sorry. It's true," Patrick said to her, but she was persistent to argue back.

"How dare you," she snipped. Her father had been doing things that she wished that he hadn't but a crime such as Patrick spoke of was just unheard of. "You are only saying this to get back at me for what Emma had told you."

Patrick knelt with his head in his hand. He knew that she would be upset but didn't know that she would be so defiant. "Please," he whispered so not to be heard by the unexpected couple, "Amelia, listen to me."

They both became extra quiet as they heard Henry say he heard something and walked their way. He was only inches away from the bush they hid behind when Ruth suggested that someone was watching them. Amelia's heart raced again but to her surprise Henry had agreed with Ruth and they split before being caught together. As soon as they were out of sight, Amelia jumped up and shouted, "I can't believe you are doing this. Even after I assured you I loved you. Why?"

Patrick stood and tried to put his arm around her but she wouldn't allow him to. He wasn't trying to hurt her the way she accused him and he needed to make her understand. "I know you love me, it's not about us." She still looked skeptical as he went on, "It's about what I saw at the loading docks. Don't you remember the day you came to my house, and I was upset?"

Amelia recalled that day he talked about and remembered how upset he was. She knew that something was bothering him and if what he said now was true, it had to be someone else and not her father. She calmed down, but it was hard to do with seeing with her own eyes the intimacy between the elders and what he was telling her. "Are you sure it was him?"

Patrick knew there was no easy way to discuss this with her. "Yes," he started but then became very distraught. He thought of his trip to Albany but didn't want to upset her more than she was.

She turned towards him and grilled him for more information. "Why did you ask me his name? Did the man you saw on the docks say his name?" She knew her father well enough to know that if he was involved in some heinous crime, he wouldn't be stupid enough to use his real name. This all had to be a misunderstanding.

Patrick recalled how he knew the man's name, "No, I spotted him at the social and I heard him talking to someone else. They were discussing the funding but the other man didn't approve either. The other man called him by his name and that is why I asked you if his name was Henry." She was still quiet, and he added, "Amelia, I know that the man who funded the Red Coats was named Henry." He took her by the hand and was glad to see she wasn't so quick to pull it away.

Amelia became even more concerned to think that if what Patrick had claimed was true and if someone else knew about it, her father could be in a lot of trouble. Patrick described the man that Henry was speaking with at the dance and almost immediately she spoke the name of the one person who matched the description, "Daniel Van Martin?"

"Van Martin?" Patrick inquired. "Isn't that the father of," he began but then other memories came flooding back to him. He paced back and forth trying to put the pieces together when it all made sense to him. Amelia looked concerned about what was going on in his head. "The first day I overheard the man on the dock giving an envelope to the merchant, he said that someone knew and that they had to be careful." Amelia listened. "Oh no," he said but wasn't sure if he should tell her what he heard next but he went on after seeing her face searching for more answers. "The guy I know now as Henry said that his daughter would hate him if she found out."

Amelia shook her head, "Well I found out, if what you say is true, and I don't hate him. It's not like that is the reason he is forcing me into," she choked as the thought entered her head. It was as if they were both putting the puzzle together.

"Into marriage?" Patrick suggested.

Tears filled her eyes as she discovered why her life had been turned upside down. She could never imagine her father committing such crimes and wanted it all to be just a lie. It was a definite explanation why he sided with Thomas. It explained why he would never listen to her pleas and why he said nothing when Thomas had announced the engagement. That was why he behaved, in her mind, so cowardly. After seeing her father with Ruth, it made sense why he wouldn't want her to think that love won in time. She thought, after all this time, that her initial thought was correct. She was his pawn, he had to choose whether to marry her off to Thomas or be turned in to the authorities. He used her.

"I'm sorry," Patrick told her. "But now you know why he is forcing you into this marriage. All you have to do is tell him what you know and he must let you out of your engagement."

Amelia thought for a while. Her father had let her down in the worst way but her true spirit had showed. She was a very compassionate person and wasn't about to let anything happen to her father. She looked at Patrick, the man she fell in love with on her own, the man she wanted to spend the rest of her life with but couldn't. The last thing she wanted to do was hurt him but the need to protect her father was over powering. "No, I'm the one who should apologize. You will always be the man I love but I need to marry Thomas, with no more arguing."

Patrick felt as if Amelia just ripped his heart out with her bare hands. She couldn't have meant what she said but seeing the look of sincerity on her face confirmed her statement. Hurt and jealousy made him angry. "No, you won't," he screamed. "You will marry me. You've already given yourself."

Guilt flooded her mind. She should have known better to rush into pre-marital sex but dwelling on it wasn't helping her right now. She prayed that Thomas wouldn't find out she lost her virginity before their wedding night. "Patrick, I have to. It's the only way to protect my father." He didn't respond to her right away but instead grabbed her arm and pulled her in for a kiss. It wasn't the loving kisses he always gave her, this time his lips pressed hard on hers until she felt a tingle of blood spill from her bottom lip. In that one instance he reminded her of Thomas. Amelia moved her mouth away from his but Patrick still had his grip on her arm.

"Your father has wronged you. Why do you care?"

Tears rolled down her face as Amelia tried her hardest to control her emotions. It didn't matter to her what her father had done, she needed to be there for him. If he would have been honest with her from the beginning, this whole mess could have been avoided. She pulled herself away from him and answered, "If I don't marry Thomas, they'll turn him in to the government."

Anger exploded inside of Patrick. He loved her too much to lose her but if he didn't bring her back to her senses, losing her was what he would do. With his hands to his sides, he formed tight fists and shouted, "I already done that."

"No," she screamed in devastation as she fell to her knees. "Why would you do that?"

"I think Madison's war is just and am disturbed to think that our own citizens are supporting the enemy," he tried to explain to her but he could tell that she didn't want to hear that. "I had no idea he was your father." He told her about both of his trips and their purposes. She knelt on the ground and sobbed as he told her, "Amelia I will correct it. I will tell them I was wrong if you will stay with me. Be my wife, I love you."

Amelia jumped up and ran. She realized that it no longer mattered if she married Thomas since both the Van Martins and Patrick knew of the funding. She wanted to tell him she loved him too, and that he was the one she wanted to marry but she was still to upset with him to let him know that. Amelia could only focus on finding her father to warn him. She would go to Patrick in the morning, like they planned, she told herself as she rushed away.

"Amelia, get back here," Patrick yelled as she hurried away from him. "We need to talk about this," he hollered. She didn't respond, but he knew that she could hear him. When she was out of sight, he turned to return to his house.

She would be his, he assured himself, and there was no way he would let the Van Martins win.

Emma and Jacob were walking towards the Coopers' house when they spotted Amelia rushing their way. "She looks different," Emma had stated to Jacob but she couldn't figure out what had changed. Amelia had a face of satisfaction and content, yet, she was sending out signals of anger. Anger that seemed to grow as the three stepped closer to each other. Emma looked over at Jacob who also had a puzzled look about him. She wondered what the urgency was and decided to find out. Facing Amelia, she asked, "Amelia, what is going on?"

Amelia replied to Emma's question with one hard open-handed slap across Emma's face. She had slapped so hard that the echo could be heard several houses away and her own ears where ringing from the sound of the impact. Removing her fingers, Amelia could feel them tingle from the sudden rush of blood that raced through them on their way to their destination. Amelia looked and could instantly see her hand print on the cheek of her betrayer.

Emma felt a stinging sensation after receiving the uncalled for slap. She put both of her hands over the area which she felt swelling and tears raced down her face. The tears came so fast that the angry girl standing in front of her became a blur. Her face hurt but not as much as her heart. She didn't know what had come over her best friend and her mind couldn't think of one thing she had done to deserve such treatment. She was about to ask Amelia what she had done but before she could get the words out, she could see Amelia's hand coming at her through her blurry eyes. Without hesitation, Emma cried and hid her face in Jacob's chest.

"Stop," Jacob insisted as his one arm wrapped around Emma to protect her and his other hand reached out to grab Amelia's hand that was coming back for another whack.

"What has come over you? You're leaving me no choice but to tell Thomas about your behavior."

Through with being polite, Amelia snapped back, "Go right ahead and while you are there, tell him it's over. I know what is going on and I don't have to marry him." She felt horrible for speaking in such a tone to Jacob but she wasn't about to back down. This little incident had nothing to do with him at all, it was all aimed at Emma; she was the one who had tried to ruin her life more than it already was.

Amelia realized that Jacob would not allow her to hit his little girlfriend so Amelia stepped closer until she was just inches away from Emma. She could see how scared Emma looked but she no longer cared. Amelia thought she couldn't get away with what she had said to Patrick to split them apart. "I thought you were my friend. How could you do that to me?"

Still hanging onto Jacob with all her might, Emma didn't know what Amelia was taking about. She had talked to both of the men in Amelia's life but didn't think that those conversations would have thrown Amelia over the edge as she appeared to be at the moment. She thought she did nothing wrong and wasn't ready to apologize. Amelia must have been talking about something else. "I don't know what you mean," she spoke between sobs.

Amelia stood with one hand on her hip and the other hand holding onto her forehead. She didn't have time to play these games with Emma. "You know exactly what you've done," she screamed in rage.

"Stop it now, Amelia," Jacob demanded. He wished that there was someone else around that could grab the girl and take her away from them. He thought for sure she would attack Emma again. "You two are best friends. What is this all about?"

Amelia laughed. True, they used to be best friends. They used to be closer than sisters but that all changed when Emma accepted Amelia's marriage to Thomas. They hadn't been close in weeks. "Oh no," she corrected him, "She isn't a friend of mine, not now, never."

Emma cried even harder. Her heart was broke by Amelia's harsh words. If she was referring to the talks that Emma had with the two men, didn't Amelia know that she only did it for her sake and protection? To have a quarrel was one thing but to hear Amelia say they would never be friends again was more than Emma could tolerate. "Amelia, we are best of friends. Why are you so upset with me?"

"You tried to come between me and the man I love. How could you?" Amelia asked; hurt herself that her friend could do such a thing to her.

Jacob thought about how suspicious the conversation that Emma had with Thomas was to him. He didn't know what they said to each other but knew it had to do with Amelia. Then he was confused because he knew that she didn't love Thomas. He listened to the two girls argue and then Amelia mentioned someone named Patrick. The stranger, he wondered? Then it made more sense to him; Amelia was in love with this stranger and Emma must have stood in between. "Emma," he looked at her "What have you said to this Patrick guy?"

Still feeling the sting on her face, she answered. "Nothing wrong, but protect Amelia from him."

Amelia's hands were aching to strike Emma again. Protection from Patrick was the last thing she needed. Emma had no right to intervene the way she had done. Then she heard Emma explain to Jacob that she had also told Thomas about what was going on and fear came over her. He would soon hear that their so called engagement was over but the thought of him hearing about Patrick before- hand was enough to make Amelia panic. Who knew what Thomas would do knowing that his fiancée was sneaking around to be with someone else. She no longer cared about Emma's explanation, though she still wanted it clear that their friendship was over. "I don't even care anymore, Emma. Keep your distance from me because you and I are no longer friends," she warned just before taking off. Not only did she have to find her father to warn him that the authorities knew of his treason but she also had to do her best to avoid a run in with Thomas.

Emma could barely stand. Everything she had done for Amelia's sake had backfired onto her and now Amelia wanted nothing to do with her. She almost fell over but Jacob caught her and held her in his arms. "You told Thomas about all of this?" Emma nodded her throbbing head in agreement and Jacob finished, "Well don't fret, she'll get over this and you two will be the best of friends again."

When Patrick returned home, he realized that he wasn't alone. As he stepped closer to his home, he knew that his visitor was Major General Downy. Knowing that Amelia had run off to be with Thomas, he had a good mind to keep his mouth shut. However, no matter what she chose to do, he loved Amelia with all of his heart and would risk lying to the Major General to save Henry for her sake. "Major General Downy," he greeted his visitor, "I'm surprised to see you but am glad you're here. I need to talk to you."

Downy couldn't understand why Buchanan was surprised. He must've known that sooner or later he would come to Millersport to investigate the British funding. That wasn't the only business he set out to do though. That is why he located Buchanan's house; there was something he needed to speak to him about. "I think you know why I'm in Millersport."

Patrick was nervous. Downy still intimidated him and to tell him lies made his stomach twist in knots. He decided to just come out and say it, "I've made a horrible mistake. I was wrong, there was nobody here funding the Red Coats."

The Major General chuckled; did Buchanan take him as a fool? Patrick had given him too much information for it all to be a mistake. "On the contrary, Mr. Buchanan; Henry Samuels is the culprit we are looking for."

"Samuels? I never gave you a last name."

Again Downy laughed. "Come on, did you think that I wouldn't look into this myself? His name is Henry Samuels, he has six children, his wife is deceased, and he is the village apothecary. I'm very thorough."

Patrick lowered his head and took a deep breath. He wanted to avoid an execution for Amelia's father but he thought it was too late. "Well yes that is Henry Samuels, but I was wrong about him. I over heard him say something about the Indians but that was for his remedies."

"Bull shit," Downy snapped. He wondered what had got into Buchanan to have him change his story but didn't dwell on it. Henry Samuels would pay for his treason, he'd see to that. Shaking his head, he returned his thoughts to why he was there. "Never mind that," he said. "Can we go inside? There is something I would like to speak to you about."

Patrick agreed. He wanted no one to see him converse with the Major General because when Henry was caught, he didn't want people to know he was the one who turned him in. They sat down at the table. "What could you possibly want to talk about?" He quizzed.

"The war," Downy answered. He could see how devoted the man was to his country and now the country needed him. "I'm asking you to help defend America. Come with me and be a soldier."

Patrick was speechless. What did he know about fighting in the war? "You want me to join the militia?"

"My thoughts exactly," the Major General replied.

"But I know nothing about fighting in a war. I'm an apple farmer for goodness sake."

Downy interrupted him. He knew of what Buchanan did for a living but Madison needed more men. "That is fine, providing you will commit to the cause. Besides, there are many like you, untrained."

Patrick looked around the room as he thought about what to say. He had been pro war but he had never even considered joining the military. Besides, he continued to think, there was just too much going on right in Millersport.

If there was the slightest chance that Amelia would return to him, he would want to be there. He finally answered, "No, I'm very sorry but I can't help you. I have matters here that I have to tend to."

The Major General was sorry to hear the refusal, but he hadn't given up. He knew what matters Buchanan wanted to tend to, clearing Samuels. The treason culprit would be apprehended and then Buchanan might join the militia. "I think that you might change your mind. I'll give you some time to think it over but I'll be back this way soon. You can answer me then."

Patrick didn't think that he would change his mind, but he nodded in agreement, anyway. He saw his visitor out and then put his mind back to where it was, on Amelia. He then left his house and set out to find her.

Amelia kept running towards her father's house to confront him. She didn't want the thought of Emma's lies to get in the way of what she had to do. She entered the front door to the house and there was nobody home. Amelia wondered where Anna and her brothers were but knew that her father was at Ruth's. Maybe they were all there, she thought as she walked through the house searching for someone. Making her way back towards the front door, she paused for a moment at her father's desk. Perhaps she should leave him a note explaining that she was looking for him. Then she decided against it and left the house still looking for the man who would rid her of her unwanted fiancé.

Amelia ran about a half of a mile before she found herself near Minnie's house. She intended to just keep going, not having time to chit chat with her sister who hadn't bothered to visit her for weeks. She passed the house and was several feet away when she heard someone calling her name. It was Minnie. Feeling frustrated to have to stop and be polite, Amelia turned around and greeted her sister.

"Where are you going in such a hurry?" Minnie wanted to know. She was just about to sit on her front porch and work on a blanket she had been knitting for her soon- to-be nephew or niece when she saw Amelia rush past the house.

Taking a deep breath, Amelia answered, "I'm searching for Father, have you seen him?"

Minnie wasn't in a hurry to answer her sister. Instead she preferred to sit down and think about the question. She gestured for Amelia to join her and although she didn't look like she wanted to, Amelia sat beside her. Minnie ignored the question and asked her own. "Why are you looking for him? Isn't he home?"

"Minnie," she shrieked more than just a little annoyed. "I need to find him. Do you know where he is?"

"Haven't seen him," she replied with her head hung low. Minnie had missed her sister and hadn't seen her in a while, not even at the social. All she wanted right now was for Amelia to sit and talk. She wondered why everything with Amelia was always more important than anyone's feelings.

Seeing the way her sister's face had frowned, Amelia felt bad for disregarding her. Not that she didn't love her or want to be with her, it was just that she felt everyone was against her and she didn't stop to think about who was sincere with their friendly conversation and who wasn't. "I'm sorry," she stated. "I was just in such a hurry I; well there is no excuse for my behavior."

Minnie lifted her head to look at Amelia who was still very distracted by something. She wished that her sister would come to her with her problems; she would love to talk to her. Minnie wasn't sure what to say in fear she would upset the older girl. "I heard that Father gave you Mother's wedding dress," she started but then realized that it was a topic related to her wedding.

Amelia surprised Minnie by not being angry by what she had just said. It was, after all, her mother's dress and she still hoped to wear it when she married Patrick. Thinking back on when he gave her that dress, she remembered what he said about his first true love, Ruth. Amelia wondered if

Minnie also knew of his relationship with their Aunt. "Minnie," she began, "Did you know about our parent's marriage?"

"Yes," Minnie answered. She had overheard her father speaking with Ruth once before; talking about how they were separated as lovers. It was a shock to Minnie at the time but since then she had learned to accept that they were once in love and if they were to rekindle that love, it would all be the same to her. She didn't wish to reveal that to her sister who didn't seem to be so sympathetic. She heard Amelia asking her how she knew and thought of something to cover up, "Mother told me once."

Amelia cocked her head to the side. "You were only ten when she passed away. Why would she talk about marriage to someone so young?"

Minnie couldn't look her sister in the eyes and she bit her bottom lip as she thought of something else to say. "I was a very curious child, you know that," she continued making things up. "One day I was asking tons of questions and I think she told me that to keep me from asking anymore."

"Then how did you know it was true," Amelia quizzed her sister. She thought it was comical the way Minnie was squirming in her seat.

"Oh Amelia," Minnie shouted. "Does that really matter?"

Amelia supposed that it didn't. She knew the truth, saw it with her own two eyes. She wanted to see how much her sister knew but it sounded to her she was innocent of the whole situation and Amelia thought that was how she should be. "Anyway, I should get going. It will be dark soon and I want to find Father. I have to tell him something rather important."

"Does it concern your engagement? You know it upsets Father when you argue with him on the matter."

Amelia didn't know what to say. In her mind the engagement was over but knew by telling that to her sister, Minnie would be full of questions. "Indirectly," she answered.

Minnie looked up at the sky and could tell that it had to be near eight o'clock and it would get dark soon. "Then why don't you go home?" She more or less told her than asked her. "He is bound to be there sooner or later."

Her sister had a superb point. She was tiring of running all over the village trying to find him. She was better off going home where she could confront him the minute he arrived. "You are right," she said and then hugged her sister as she finished, "Good night."

She stormed off before Minnie could ask her to calm down. The whole time that Amelia sat on her porch she seemed impatient and upset about something. Minnie sat and picked up the blanket she intended to work on and told herself that whatever her sister was huffing and puffing about, it would soon pass.

As Amelia passed the general store she saw two ladies walking in the same direction as her. She had known them well and hadn't talked to them in quite a while. They noticed her walking behind them and they slowed down for her to catch up. Her conversation with Minnie eased her mind a little, and she was no longer in such an angry mood. Conversing with these ladies would do her some good, she thought to herself. "Hello," she said to them as she met them in the street. They were being friendly to her even though they had many questions about her marriage to Thomas. Amelia wanted to laugh and tell them that the wedding wouldn't take place but she knew that they were not the ones who should know first. They would find out in due time. Until then, she humored them and told them whatever they wanted to hear. The sun had set and darkness fell. They were turning onto another road but Amelia still had a good twenty rods to go before she reached her destination.

"Goodness," one of them remarked. "It's getting dark already. Are you sure you'll be all right?"

Amelia smiled. She could see her father's house in the distance. She saw no reason she couldn't walk herself home.

"Oh of course," she told them. "I can see the house from here." Then she continued on and the little old ladies went their own way. Amelia walked only about ten or fifteen feet before she turned to look at the ladies behind her. She was young and full of life but they were up in age and she wondered if perhaps she should have walked them home. She spun back around to continue home when out of nowhere she felt a hand covering her mouth. Amelia tried to scream but someone was blocking the sound. She tried to run but whoever it was who had her mouth, had a hold of her upper body too and she couldn't get free. "Let me go," she muffled but there was no answer. She turned to see who it was and then tried to break away but was unsuccessful. The more she attempted to wiggle free, the tighter the perpetrator squeezed her. It was then she realized that she was in trouble and she tried to scream again but with no avail. The offender dragged her and as much as she tried to dig her feet into the ground to stay put, it was of no use. Before anyone could see what was going on, she was out of sight and in dangers way.

Part Two
Chapter Eighteen

Anna hurried down to the kitchen to prepare the morning meal. She knew that breakfast was late and didn't want to upset her father. Amelia was nowhere to be seen and Anna was more than a little aggravated by her sister's apparent decision to spend the night away from home. The night before, Anna had tossed and turned, waiting for Amelia to retire to their bedroom. Every time she thought she heard someone coming, she would get excited only to find out it wasn't her sister but some other noise instead. Nervousness became her as the night got later and Amelia still had not returned. In the wee hours of the morning Anna realized that her sister must have spent the night at David's house to be with Beth. If she would have informed her then at least she wouldn't have worried and she would've been able to sleep; which would've prevented her from over sleeping and the morning meal wouldn't have been late. As she rushed around the kitchen, she prepared something easy and fast; oatmeal. She had just finished pulling bread out of the brick oven when she heard the boys and her father enter the kitchen. "Good morning Father." She said to him hoping he wouldn't notice the mess she had made in her rush. "I'll pour you some coffee."

Henry couldn't help but notice the messy kitchen. He could tell that that his younger daughter was on her own and from the looks of things, he wondered if she would ever be ready to take over caring for the family. "Where is your sister? I didn't know that she would have you cook by yourself."

Anna was surprised that he didn't know where Amelia was. Her sister had been spiteful but she would never stay away without telling someone where she'd be. "She must have spent the night with David and Beth last night. She didn't come to our room," she explained as she fixed plates for her brothers. Henry rubbed his chin. He had seen David the day before and his son made no mention of Amelia preparing for the baby's birth as yet. He thought it odd but yet didn't dwell on it. Amelia would do anything to avoid him and he thought she must've wanted to get away. He took a mental note to tell her that he would appreciate a notice. He took a sip of his coffee and looked up at Anna with puckered lips and wide eyes as he swallowed. She tried, he would say that much, but she still needed a little help preparing the morning brew.

Just as he put his cup back onto the table there was a knock on the front door and he glanced over at Anna who looked right back at him with concern.

After knocking, David entered the house. He knew it was breakfast time and didn't want to disturb them. "Pardon me Father; hope you don't mind the intrusion."

Henry jumped up from his seat the minute he heard David's voice. His son was making his way towards the kitchen and because Amelia slept at his house; there could only be one explanation why David was there so early in the morning. "David, is everything all right with the baby?"

David had entered the kitchen and patted his young brothers each on their heads and kissed Anna on her cheek. "The baby is doing fine," he answered, "A couple more months and you'll be a grandfather." He took a seat at the table and looked at their concerned faces and wondered what the fuss was all about. "Actually, with all the excitement of the soon to be arrival, Beth forgot to purchase coffee, and that is why I'm here. I wanted to ask Amelia if she had any she could spare until the merchants come back this way."

Henry looked to Anna, Anna looked to Henry, and David continued to look at both of them. Something was going on, but he wasn't sure what. "She isn't here," Henry stated. "We thought something happened with the baby and she made a last minute choice to sleep at your house." When he saw his eldest son shake his head in disagreement, Henry got worried. It wasn't Amelia's way of doing things; she had never stayed away at night unless it was an emergency.

"Perhaps then maybe she slept at Minnie's house?" Anna questioned with hope. The pit in her stomach she was feeling the night before was reappearing. She could think of no reason Amelia would sleep at Minnie's house, but it was the only thing she could think of.

Henry decided that he would not wait around. He stood up and took one last sip of his extra strong brew and then said, "Then, I'm going over there to see for myself."

"I'll come along with you," David told his father. He knew of the tension between the two of them and if she was there, he didn't want either one of them to get upset with each other. Anna had given him a small sack of coffee grinds and he turned to her and thanked her.

Henry looked to the boys and then to Anna. "Stay here and clean this place up and keep an eye on the boys." Anna had blushed as she lowered her head towards the floor and told him she would do as he said. Then he motioned for David to follow him and the two men were out the door. As they passed the neighbors' house, he politely nodded toward the elderly man.

"Some wind we had last night, wasn't it? Darn near sounded like an animal in a trap," the old man mumbled as the Samuels men passed. Henry thought about what he said. It was windy when he returned home from Ruth's house the evening before but from where he was, it didn't sound like an animal. Old age, Henry thought and continued walking with his son.

Minnie was busy cleaning up her kitchen when she heard a knock on her front door. She wiped her hands on her apron as she walked towards the main entrance. She opened it and saw a grim look on her father and David's face. "Father," she said, "What brings you by so early?"

Henry embraced his daughter and watched as David did the same. "Actually, we're here to see Amelia. She is here isn't she?"

Minnie was confused. She didn't know what he had meant. Amelia seldom visited her and when she did, it was never early in the morning. "Amelia? No, haven't seen her since last night."

Henry had the sudden urge to sit down and David paced back and forth. Phillip had come out of the parlor and greeted his wife's family but could tell that something was bothering them. "I didn't know that Amelia was here last night but she didn't sleep here if that is what you are asking."

"She didn't come home last night," Henry explained. "Anna claims she never retired to their room, and she wasn't around for the morning meal. We thought she stayed with Beth,"

"But obviously she didn't stay at our house," David chimed in. "You saw her last night? Where did she say she was going?"

Minnie recalled the conversation she had with her sister. "She seemed very distressed, but I thought nothing of it. Seems these days Amelia has been that way all the time. She said she was looking for you, Father, said something about important information she had for you." Minnie looked at three men; David and Phillip looked to her father as if wondering what Amelia had to tell him and her father looked confused. "She was running all over the place but I stopped her to talk to her. I told her it made more sense for her to go home and wait for you to show up than to run all over the village. She said that's where she was going."

More than just a little concerned, Henry was feeling his heart rate jump. Something was wrong, he told himself. He didn't know what information Amelia had for him and why she felt she had to run to find him but he hoped that whatever the information was, it didn't put her in danger. "Minnie, do me a favor. Go to my house and help Anna with the boys. This news will alarm her too and I don't want her to be alone. You two," he said to his son and to his son-in-law, "Search for her and if need be, get all the help you can. Phillip, call upon Emma and see if she is there. David, it's a long shot but see if she is at the Van Martins with Thomas." Henry knew that she wasn't there but it was worth a try. "If

167

you have no luck, ask for as much help as possible. I'm going to the constable's office, just to play it safe. Tell anyone willing to help find her to meet at my house and we'll put our heads together then."

They all agreed, and each went their separate ways to search for the one girl they all thought was too responsible to let anyone worry over her. Each of them was positive about finding her. An hour later Anna, Minnie, and Beth, who had caught wind of Amelia's disappearance, sat in the parlor anxiously waiting for news. Minnie sat and twiddled her thumbs together as Beth rubbed her pregnant stomach for comfort. Anna had prepared some hot tea, the one thing she was good at, and was placing it on the table in front of them when they heard someone rushing towards the house.

"Amelia's home," Anna shouted with excitement. She didn't care where Amelia had been or what their father would do to punish her for worrying them all. She was glad that her sister was home and that everything would be fine. The three ladies made a quick dash towards the door just to be let down by their aunts arrival with her sons. "Oh, Aunt Ruth; we thought you were Amelia."

Ruth had seen Phillip knocking on all the doors on her street and knew that something wasn't right. When she stopped him and questioned him, he explained what was going on but didn't go into details. He told her they were searching for Amelia and that a search party was being planned at the Samuels house. She had grabbed her boys and arrived at the house as soon as she could. Ruth explained all of that to the other girls and asked for more information. They each told her all they knew and then the four of them sat down and tried to figure out where the eldest daughter could've been. "Nobody has even an idea of where she is?" She asked.

Anna sat and thought about all the possible places and how they were so obvious that someone must've gone to each place looking for her already. Then she thought of one person who nobody knew, where no one would think to look. Relieved, she jumped up and put her shawl on. "I think I know where she might be. I'm almost certain," she explained to the others. She heard them asking her where but she didn't want to reveal Amelia's private secrets to them. "Just tell Father to hold off on the search until I return. I'm sure I'll find her and I'll ask her to come home." Then she ran out the door and headed up the hills to the west. Anna should have thought of Patrick Buchanan right from the start.

Patrick paced back and forth inside of his home. Was this his wedding day or was it not, he wasn't even sure himself. Their plan was that Amelia would meet him there soon after dawn and they would go to Albany together. He remembered how things impeded their plan and how she ran off to marry Thomas to save her father. It hurt him very much, and he even tried to find her, to bring her back to her senses but was unsuccessful. All he could do was hope she would show up. It was later than dawn but fine with him as long as she made it there soon. He glanced out his window and saw a girl running towards his house but it wasn't Amelia. Patrick opened his front door as the girl ran closer and he recognized her as the girl who had been sitting next to Amelia in church. "Anna?" He questioned as she fell at his door step.

She ran to his house without taking a break to catch her breath. All she could think of was getting to her sister and convincing her that hiding from their father would cause more serious consequences. Panting and sweating, she insisted on seeing Amelia. "I need to see Amelia. I need to talk to her."

"What are you talking about girl? Amelia isn't here."

"What?" Anna quizzed. She thought he didn't know that she knew the true feelings that Amelia had for him and that she was on their side. "I know how she feels about you. She isn't anywhere else either so she has to be here with you. Tell her it's all right and that she can speak with me."

Patrick's heart broke even more than it was before. He thought for sure she would come to him and not go to

Thomas but she must've run off with the Van Martin boy. "She must be with Thomas Van Martin; she told me yesterday she would marry him."

Anna wanted too bad to believe that her sister was there that it pained her to hear that she wasn't. She wondered why Amelia had agreed to marry Thomas but she knew it couldn't have been true. That wasn't where her sister was at. "No," she started. "I know she loves you and she wouldn't marry him."

"Things have changed and you don't understand," Patrick tried to explain to her.

"No, I said," Anna pleaded. "Even if that was true, which it's not because it's so insane, she wouldn't just run off with him. She would have let my father know she gave him what he wanted and became Thomas' bride. There was no word from her."

Though he still had doubts, Patrick worried too. For a second his heart rejoiced in knowing she hadn't married Thomas but then hurt again when he realized that she was missing. Knowing he'd never met Henry Samuels before, Patrick decided it was time. "Take me to your father. I want to help." Anna agreed and Patrick saddled his horse. He told her it would be faster to return to the village and she didn't hesitate. A gentle kick to the horse and they were off to help in the search.

Chapter Nineteen

Henry grew very impatient as he waited outside of his house along with at least twenty other men from the village. So far nobody had seen Amelia, not even the people closest to her. Others have gathered around too to see what was going on; her friends and neighbors, and of course the Van Martins. David had asked them if they had seen the girl and they were quick to assume that she ran away to get out of the marriage. Arriving at the house to form a search party, Ruth had explained that Anna had run off and said that they should wait for her to return and that she knew where Amelia was.

God, he had hoped Anna was correct. Moments later he spotted a horse charging towards the house, ready and eager to join the search. He didn't recognize the man but Anna was also seated on the mare. "Anna, what is this all about?"

Thomas knew too well who the stranger was that was riding into the village with Anna in tow. Patrick Buchanan, the man who thought he could take his prize away from him. He was angered from the moment he heard Amelia was missing. Seeing her lover ride in like a knight in shining armor made him fury even more. "What are you doing here?" He demanded as Patrick stepped off of his horse. "You have no right; go back to where ever it was you came from."

Henry could see the tension between the two men but he wasn't about to let Thomas think that he was running the search. It was time to take a stand and neither one of the Van Martins would stop him. He didn't know who the stranger was, although Amelia mentioned him once before, but he knew that it was another person willing and able to help out. "Thomas," he shouted. "I'll call the shots here. Now the constable is out of the area," he said loud enough for everyone to hear him. "I have sent word to tell him that there is an emergency here in Millersport. Until then, this is my house, my daughter, and you all will report to me." He tried not to show his emotion in his little speech but was finding it hard to fight back the tears. For this many people to be here to help meant that nobody knew where she was and the thought of something happening to her tore him up inside.

"But, I'm her fiancé," Thomas shouted right back though it was guided towards Patrick more than it was to Henry. If anyone was a victim here, it was him and everyone should comfort him in this time of need.

Patrick wasn't about to let Thomas speak to him in that way. Maybe the rest of the villagers were afraid of the young man but he wasn't. "That might be, Mr. Van Martin, but let me tell you this. Whether you like it or not, Amelia has been spending her time with me so if she isn't with me; and none of you have seen her, then there must be something seriously wrong. You can't stop me from helping in this search."

"Enough," Henry screamed, and the crowd shushed. He pointed to all the men and told them which direction to search and who they should search with. He took a look at Patrick and his instincts told him he should remain by his side. "Mr. Buchanan, you're with me, David, and Phillip." He heard Thomas object, but he ignored him. Then just before everyone dispersed he had a horrifying thought of someone out there hurting innocent women. "I'm sure the constable would agree with me if he was here but I must insist that all women and children be kept inside until we figure out what is going on. It's for their safety."

Everyone seemed to agree, except Anna. "But Father, I want to help," Anna interrupted. There was no way she would be able to just sit around and wait for good news, she would go insane. She had to be out fanning the area herself and at the moment felt as if she was the only one who would find Amelia.

"I said you will remain in the house," Henry snipped. The last thing he wanted was for something to happen to her, or anyone else. He continued to instruct the other men to make sure their wives and children were safe in their homes and then gave the go ahead for everyone to look for his daughter. Several hours have passed and there had been no word of Amelia's whereabouts.

Thomas looked to Jacob and shrugged his shoulders as if this whole search was a waste of his valuable time. "She ran to get away from me."

Jacob pulled Thomas away from the other men that so they couldn't over hear their conversation. "Come on, you know that isn't true."

Thomas was annoyed and getting tired but kept up with the search because once they found his fiancée, he would make sure she received her punishment. "You saw her last night, you know of her anger towards me. How can you possibly think that she wouldn't have run from me?"

"Because of Buchanan," Jacob explained what he thought. "If she would run off with someone it would be him. He's searching for her and I don't believe she would just run away by herself."

That was it, just then things made sense, and he thought for sure he knew where to find her. "You're right my friend." Then he turned to the others in his group and told them they were heading in a different direction. He wasn't positive where they were going but he had a good idea. Within minutes they were outside of Patrick's house and Thomas' insides gleamed, thinking he would be the one who found Amelia's hiding spot. "She's in there, I know it." He continued to tell the others what he suspected about Amelia and the stranger. Without hesitation, they barged into the house.

Henry's little group were silent most of the time, all of them trying to figure out where Amelia could be. They were about two miles away from his house and he feared that she couldn't have been too much further away. Along their ride out in that direction he also thought about what Buchanan meant by saying that Amelia had spent time with him. He was about to question him but his thoughts were interrupted by Patrick's outburst.

"What are they doing going into my house?" Patrick was furious for he knew that the group entering his private domain was none other than Thomas'. He looked over at the others and could see they didn't approve of the behavior of the other group. They rode faster and as they reached the house, Patrick jumped off his horse to see what was going on.

"Thomas," Henry shouted. "What is this all about?"

Thomas was angry to think that Henry was taking sides with Buchanan. "I'm searching for Amelia. What else would we be doing?"

"In my house," Patrick steamed.

Playing dumb Thomas answered, "Oh, is this your house? We had no idea; all we were thinking about was searching for Amelia." The others in his group all nodded their heads to confirm what he'd said.

"That's bull shit," Patrick snapped. "You weren't given directions to search this part of Millersport. You're here for other reasons?"

"No," Thomas continued to make a fool of the stranger. "We searched the area you told us to," he said as he looked at Henry, "and decided since there was no word yet that we should go on. Just happens that we ended up here but since we are, what is the harm? Got something to hide, Buchanan?"

Patrick growled and wanted to knock the idiot's lights out but felt David's hand on his shoulder. "Let him look," he whispered into Patrick's ear. "They will not find her here, right?" Patrick knew that he was correct and just nodded his head to allow the others search the insides.

Henry's group had waited outside of the home, giving Thomas his moment of glory. Henry was convinced that the stranger wouldn't harm his daughter. He could sense the way the stranger cared about her and thought they might have something in common. But, that feeling changed within a few minutes and Henry himself became skeptical for the matters of Patrick Buchanan.

"Well, well, well," Thomas smirked as he came out of the house. He didn't find Amelia inside but knew that she was there at one point. It might not have been much to go on but if he were lucky, it could have been just what they needed to pin the blame onto Buchanan. As he stepped closer to Henry, Thomas again played the concerned fiancé and looked Amelia's father in the eyes. "Isn't this her hair ribbon?"

Henry was astonished. He knew that ribbon all too well because he was the one who had bought it for her on her eighteenth birthday. She had worn it many times since then and he even remembered her wearing it the last time he saw her. He turned to Patrick for answers. "Where is she?"

Patrick could sense the tension building up as all eyes stared at him; even the eyes that were on his side just a few minutes ago. "I told you, her and I have spent time together. She must have left it here the last time she was visiting."

"It was in your bed chambers," Thomas snarled. His intuition about the couple must have been correct and his blood boiled. Buchanan stood up and got in his face and Thomas became nervous when he realized how much smaller he was than the stranger.

"Stop," Henry insisted. Then turned towards Patrick and demanded to know more. "I asked you where she was."

Patrick, who looked right into the eyes of Thomas, answered, "I told you, I don't know. I said she must have forgotten that ribbon the last time she was here and I'm standing firm on that." He felt Thomas backing away from him and if the situation was different, he would have laughed.

Everyone from both groups looked concerned. Nobody knew what had gone on between Amelia and Patrick but their fear of the unknown, Patrick Buchanan, forced them to suspect him. "She isn't here and all we have is her hair ribbon," one man stated as he urged the group to continue their search. They left Patrick's house but this time they were all one large group instead of the two smaller ones

175

they began with. Everyone was silent as they searched; the only sounds were of men calling out Amelia's name in hope of her answering. Everyone had one eye looking for Amelia and their other eye glued on Patrick; just waiting for him to mess up somehow.

Chapter Twenty

By the end of the day the search party had grown from twenty men to every available man in the village. Businesses shut down so that the owners and workers could join the search, even the brickyard and shipyard. Daniel took full advantage of the situation and made it clear to everyone that if they couldn't communicate with Henry, then they were to report to him. Henry wasn't thrilled of Van Martin taking over but he felt his body drain its energy and figured he could use all the support he could get. Patrick continued in the search even after the other men had practically accused him of foul play. Thomas insisted on searching by Patrick's side, confident that the stranger was bound to lead the group to Amelia. When that happened he wanted to be the one who took all the glory and make them all believe that he loved her.

By the time that darkness fell upon the sky, the Samuels family learned more about what happened the night before. Emma had explained that she had seen the missing girl, and that she was very much distressed. She showed them the bruise that was forming on her cheek bone and told them how Amelia had slapped her for no apparent reason. All were shocked that Amelia would behave that way, and it built more concern among them. Later they discovered that the last known people who had seen her were the two elderly ladies she had walked with for a while before they turned to walk down a different street. They both said that they felt bad and they should've followed their instincts and not allow her to continue her walk alone. Henry assured them that none of this was their fault. That conversation confused him, knowing she was last seen just rods away from their home. Where did she go? He wondered.

It became too dark to search any longer and the search party called it a night. Henry and his family weren't happy about the situation but they all fully knew that there was nothing they could do that late at night. Patrick also objected to the break, but he was out numbered. He would have continued by himself if it weren't for Thomas and his father getting in the way. "I don't think he should be alone until Amelia is found. He had her ribbon, for all we know he could have her somewhere too. It's too risky to leave him be." The others agreed, and they locked him in the ice house and had two men guarding the door throughout the night.

"You can't do this," Patrick demanded, but it fell to deaf ears. Nobody trusted him.

Henry paced back and forth in his parlor, too eager to just sit and wait for Amelia's return. He glanced around the room and looked at all the worried faces. Knowing they were all looking to him for strength, he told them they should eat something and to take a drink to calm their nerves. The entire Samuels family was there, deciding that they didn't want to leave the house in case they received any news. Even Ruth and her sons stayed. She got all the younger boys to bed but it wasn't an easy task to do since they all knew something was wrong. Charles has asked for Amelia, saying she was the only one who could comfort him in bad times. She prayed that he would come to understand what was going on.

"Father," David spoke after a long silence. "Do you think that Buchanan has anything to do with her disappearance?" He hadn't known Patrick but there was something in the man's eyes that told David to trust him.

"I'm sure of it," Henry spoke but was interrupted by his youngest daughter.

"No," Anna shouted. "Father, you can't. Trust me when I say I know that he couldn't have done anything to harm Amelia."

Henry thought Anna was foolish, and that she knew nothing. Truth was he didn't give her enough credit. "We found Amelia's hair ribbon in his house and I know for a fact she was wearing it when she served me my morning meal yesterday."

"But that doesn't mean he hurt her in any way," Anna continued to plead. She had heard from the others they had locked Patrick up and wished that she could free him. If

178

anyone could find her sister, it was him but the villagers wouldn't allow it.

Henry heard enough from her and directed his conversation to David. "I will see that the man is hung if he has done something to her."

Anna could hold off no longer, she cried. "No Father, no," was all she could say, but it did her no good. She was the only one left who had any faith in Patrick Buchanan.

The next day the searching started again. Though Thomas would like to see Patrick locked until this whole thing was over, the constable had returned and said that they had no cause to hold him any longer. Henry remained in charge of the search party because the constable made rounds around the village to assure that nobody else was missing or hurt in any way. The women of Millersport were panicking and feared leaving their homes even though the constable said they could if needed.

The Samuels home became the headquarters for the searchers and men had come and gone all day long. Anna, Ruth, Minnie, and Beth did all they could to keep their minds off of the situation. They didn't need to occupy their time in the kitchen since many women had sent over dishes of food; casseroles, stew, smoked meat, and plenty of fresh baked bread. They encouraged any of the searchers, who stopped by to update the family of what was going on, to eat to keep up their strength. They were good at convincing the men to eat but not good at convincing each other. None of them had an appetite. They fussed over Beth and told her to get rest but the pregnant one wouldn't have it. She didn't know it was possible to have motherly instincts before her child was born but something was telling her that something serious was wrong with her sister-in-law.

Outside of the home the men furthered their look for Amelia. Some were in groups like the day before but others were alone to spread out and gain more ground. Henry had asked, with a broken heart, if they could also search in areas like wooded lands, in cellars, along the river, and the creeks.

That is when things looked bleak. A group of men that included Henry and David had walked to the creek just north of the Samuels house. They discovered that a plank to the bridge had been removed and blood splatter covered the grass nearby. Fear devoured them to think of what it could have meant.

Their search was again unsuccessful and not one trace of Amelia was found. They rowed a boat over the water but to no avail. Once again the villagers were questioned but nobody had any information. The constable asked several men to travel to the next town which was only five miles away from the village line. They visited all the businesses to see if anyone had seen a girl of Amelia's description but nobody had. They stopped people out on the streets and asked the same question over and over. It was apparent that she wasn't there either. Then one grocer said that there was one man who entered his store on the evening of Wednesday who looked a little odd. He said that man seemed to be nervous about something. His shirt was torn, and he had scratches on his face. When asked for a description of the man, the grocer could not give details. He said it was after dark and the man had been wearing a hat. He couldn't describe his hair or eye color and said he didn't note the size of the man. The searchers thanked him for the little information that the grocer gave but it wasn't enough to help in their search. It was possible that the mysterious man had nothing to do with Amelia's case at all. They kept the information in their minds and then returned to Millersport.

Once again, darkness came and still no hope in finding the girl. If calling it a night again wasn't bad enough, it also rained. Thunder and lightning were driving all the searchers into their homes, even the ones determined to continue the search.

Henry and his family were frustrated and scared. They gathered in the family sitting-room and prayed that they would find Amelia. It started off as an out loud prayer lead by Henry but none of them could find the strength to end the prayer. In different sections of the house, each one of them talked to the Lord as strength to get through the night.

Chapter Twenty-One

The Van Martins sat in their dining room on Saturday morning. Catherine bowed her head and prayed for Amelia's return but Daniel and Thomas had sipped on their coffee as if there was nothing wrong. Seeing the pained look on his mother's face and not caring at all, Thomas said to his father, "Do you suppose this is all just a hoax? Think they are just trying to get out of the marriage?"

Catherine had enough of her son's selfishness but wouldn't dare say anything to him. She gathered up the dishes and took them into the kitchen to wash. As she left, Daniel swallowed his coffee and answered his son. "No, I don't this time."

Thomas wasn't happy to hear that his father disagreed with him. To him, there was no other explanation why she was gone. Searchers have looked everywhere for her and the one thing they found was a hair ribbon. "Oh come on," he shouted. "We've looked everywhere. She's probably half way back to Connecticut by now and Henry is the one who has made all the arrangements for her."

Daniel knew that his son was thinking of himself but he didn't think that the boy could be so blunt as to blame an innocent girl's disappearance as a hoax. He slammed his fist onto the table and shouted back, "I've seen the faces of that family and don't believe that anyone can pretend that well. They don't know where she is either."

Thomas growled, "Then fine, she's gone and she won't be my wife like you promised me she would be. So what are we going to do about the information we have on Henry?"

"Nothing."

Thomas was more than a little disgusted with his father. "What do you mean? We have something big on him and you think we will not use it."

Daniel was getting angry with his son and angry at himself for allowing his child to grow up to be so self-centered. If he didn't spoil Thomas as much as he did, he might've grown to be respectable. "Henry has bigger problems right now than worrying about whether we report him or not. And as far as you're concerned, I refuse to use that information to get anything else for you."

Feeling betrayed by his father, Thomas growled, "Then just sit and do nothing. I don't need you to turn him in, I'll do it myself."

Daniel jumped up and grabbed Thomas by the collar of his shirt. He had been a harsh man in the past and admitted that he would still be one but for now he at least had a heart. Never in his plan to blackmail Henry did he want Amelia to be hurt and now with the thought of something horrible happening to her, he wasn't about to let his good-for-nothing son make things worse. "I said we will do nothing right now. The man is searching for his daughter who hasn't been seen since Wednesday night. Have a heart, you damned boy. Besides, you don't have proof. They won't believe you without evidence and I'll be darned if I will testify for you. Keep your mouth shut, do I make myself clear?"

Thomas pulled himself backward to free himself from his father's grip and straightened his shirt to be prim and proper. For once he did as he was told and kept quiet. Henry had nothing else that he wanted, not now at least. He decided that he would hold onto the information just in case he needed to use it soon. He took one last sip from his cup and left to play the concerned fiancé once again.

Patrick's heart broke as searchers tore through his property. Henry had insisted that they do a thorough look closer to Patrick's house. Henry stated that because Patrick had the hair ribbon and because there wasn't a trace of Amelia anywhere else, she had to be somewhere close to his home. The thought of her being hurt somewhere had pained him but it was three days later, the thought of losing her completely reeled him close to insanity. He had spent two nights locked up, the first in the ice house and the second in the jail after the constable returned. He had nothing but a wool blanket to keep him warm and a mere piece of bread to fill his stomach. Being on his own property warmed him. When someone opened the door to his house, the dog ran out and relieved himself. Poor animal, he thought to himself. Right after the dog ran up to him and just about jumped into his arms. "I missed you too," he said to the hound. Then the dog ran off to find something to eat, leaving Patrick alone still wondering where Amelia was.

Phillip had walked up to Patrick in hopes to end the nightmare. "Why don't you tell us where she is?"

Angered by how the villagers assumed that he had something to do with her disappearance, Patrick stated, "We've been through this. Your family has had me locked up when I could have been helping and even when we're on my land, you still hold me down as if I had no rights. I have no idea where she is but I damn well wish I knew where I could find her."

Phillip frowned. It was apparent that the stranger would not talk. "You're not locked up now, so then search." It was a pleasant voice but in no way did Phillip mean it to be nice. He was certain they would hang Buchanan for his wrong doing but they all knew that they had to find her first.

Anna looked out the window and noticed the puddles in the wet street. She wondered if her sister was some place shielded from the rain or was she huddled somewhere just trying to keep warm. Anna wrapped her arms around herself as if to warm up from a sudden chill in the air. The thought of her sister being cold somewhere bothered her a great deal.

Ruth looked over to the troubled girl by the window then glanced at the other two who couldn't resist rest any longer. Nobody slept much since Amelia had been gone. Whenever the opportunity arose, they would get caught up in thoughts of her possible whereabouts and would again be wide awake. Now Minnie and Beth slept practically sitting up on the sofa. Ruth wished that she could take them to a bed and let them get comfortable but she knew that would just wake them and their sleepless cycle would start all over again. Returning her direction to Anna, she spoke, "You should get rest too."

Anna turned, "How do I do that? I'm worried sick as we all are."

"I know," Ruth answered. She wished that she could give everyone more encouraging words but yet couldn't think of any. "Then why don't you at least eat something to keep your strength?"

"I'm not hungry or thirsty."

Ruth could hear the boys upstairs; they had been behaving well over the past few days. They seemed to be more content because they didn't know too much about what was going on and Ruth wondered if Anna could be more content herself if she tried to go on as if nothing happened. It was worth a shot, she thought to herself. "Anna, what would you be doing now if things were normal? What would you be doing on a rainy day such as this?"

Anna was confused for a moment and didn't understand what her aunt was asking. She decided to just go with the conversation, anyway. "Well, when the weather gets this way during the summer it brings out the frogs. I suppose I would be out to catch them but," she wanted to continue but got choked up.

"But what?"

Tears rolled down the young girl's face as she finished her sentence. "But Amelia doesn't like it when I catch frogs. She doesn't think its lady like."

Ruth too shed tears. It was then she realized that there were so many simple things in life that would be a constant reminder of Amelia. Still she knew that coming face to face with certain reminders would be the best way for the family to heal. "Then why don't you? Go ahead, if there is any news we promise to come find you."

Anna straightened herself up. Catching frogs, though it was the perfect day for the activity, was the last thing on her mind. "No," she answered, "I need to be here for Amelia."

Ruth frowned but knew she must convince her niece to occupy her mind. "Nonsense, I said we would find you if we hear anything. Now go, it's all right Anna, go."

Anna was quiet for a while but then agreed. She opened the door saying she wouldn't be long but before she left, Ruth told her. "Please don't go too far. Your father wouldn't approve."

Anna turned towards her aunt and glanced over at the sleeping girls and then back at her aunt. She knew that if something happened to her too, they could never rest. "Okay," she answered. "I'll go to the creek up the road and nowhere else. You can find me there if you hear anything but I won't be long." Then she turned and for the first time since Thursday, she set foot outdoors.

A few minutes later Anna had arrived at the murky creek. Along her walk there she was on high alert. She was convinced that she could see her sister somewhere and that the men had just overlooked her. She also knew that there could be danger out there too and for that she made sure she stayed in plain sight. When she reached the creek, the first thing she noticed was the missing link from the bridge. She had heard her father speak of it and how it didn't seem to have anything to do with Amelia. Still as Anna looked at the bridge, she wondered. It gave her uneasy thoughts, and she decided not to stand on the bridge when she looked for the green amphibians. She glanced out to the water and noticed how high it flowed. The creek wasn't one of her favorite places and she recalled the conversation she had with Amelia about it. "I don't blame you for not coming here," she said out loud as if her sister could hear her. "I shouldn't even be here myself."

She wiped her eyes that tore up again and then decided that the sooner she caught a frog, the sooner she

186

could go back home where she knew she was safe. Anna pulled her dress up and slowly walked closer the shoreline. Weeds grew taller as she neared to the water and she used one hand to push them out of the way. Frogs would be down in that area, she knew it, and she wanted to be as quiet as possible. Her eyes scanned the area, and she was caught off guard when she saw something in the distance. Anna couldn't tell, from where she stood, what it was for sure with all the weeds surrounding the object so she edged closer to get a better look. That was when she realized that it was her sister mangled in the weeds, face down in the water. For a brief second she was silent as if she was imaging the body but reality set in and Anna let out a horrific scream.

No longer caring about the frogs, she wanted to rush over to her sister but was too shocked to move. Amelia's body was brushing up against the creek's bank and then out into the deeper water, back and forth like an old log that fell in. Anna stood there for what seemed an eternity; traumatized and scared. Then she let out the scream of all screams; a scream of fear, a scream of pain, and a scream for help.

Henry, David, Phillip, and the rest of the men were in their group were headed towards the village. After their search had ended on Patrick's property unsuccessful, they went on but Henry couldn't stand to have Buchanan in his sights any longer. Every time he looked at the man he wanted to wring his neck and demand answers but the stranger still denied having anything to do with Amelia's disappearance. He figured he'd give a little punishment to Buchanan by forcing him to search with Thomas and his group. It started a pit in Henry's stomach and as the hours passed away without a word from his daughter, the pit grew. They were just north of his house where he thought they would stop by to see if anyone had returned there with news. Then out of the blue he heard a terrifying scream with a constant holler. The voice was screeching, "Oh my God," as they ran toward the voice. He knew that voice, it was his voice in a female's body, and it was his flesh and blood, it sounded like Anna. The pit he had in his stomach enlarged and he knew that the search for his daughter was coming to an unexpected end.

Moments later they arrived at the bank of the creek they had searched before. Henry saw Anna standing knee deep in the water, her body was shaking uncontrollable and her screams haven't led up. He was too afraid to look but knew that he must. He first looked at Anna who didn't seem to realize that there was a crowd of people around and then he turned his head to see his lifeless daughter floating in the water. Henry too let out a scream. "No," he yelled as he ran into the water. He kept repeating the word he screamed as he made his way through the murky water to Amelia's body, "No, no, no." Without hesitation, the instant he reached her, he turned her body over and then scooped her up into his arms and held her close to him. "Please God, bring her back to us. Don't let this happen to my precious girl. Oh please help her, make her breath again." He continued to plead as he headed back towards land with Amelia in his arms.

David was stunned and broken hearted but he knew that he had to remain strong for his family since it was apparent that his father wouldn't be. He ran into the water to help Anna out. His youngest sister looked as though she froze. She didn't move at all and the only reason he knew that she was alive was by the petrified scream being released from deep inside of her. He ran to the shore and wrapped his arms around her but it did no good. She showed no awareness he was there with her. David leaned over and with one scoop, lifted her up and brought her up the bank where Phillip stood with a blanket to place over her shoulders. The screaming still had not stopped, but she managed to lay her head in David's shoulder and cried.

Men had rushed to Henry's side as he emerged from the creek but he wouldn't allow them to touch Amelia. She would be all right; she took in a little too much water but God would make her breath again, he thought to himself. He inspected her body. Her face was bruised and her arms. As he placed his hand on the back of her head, he could feel a

188

swollen bump and was sure that at one point it must have been bleeding hard. Her dress was torn in several spots and her stockings had many tears in them. It tore Henry up to see her in such condition, so bad he couldn't face reality. She would need care when she came through, he thought to himself, and he demanded that someone get his apothecary bag but nobody moved. He yelled at the stunned crowd, "For goodness sake, she is all bruised up, something bad has happened. Now I beg of you, someone, get my bag and employee. She will need help." Still nobody moved and Henry knew that they would not attempt to save his daughter. He lowered his head onto her chest and sobbed as hard as he could, not caring who was watching him.

Word was sent to the constable and to the other searchers. It didn't take long for the crowd to grow, not only from men who searched but also women who had heard the news or the scream. Knowing that the sight was an ugly one, the searchers formed a barricade so that the women couldn't see the terrifying scene. This wasn't something that had ever happened in Millersport before and almost everyone wanted to say they witnessed what had happened.

The searchers could still hear the screams from Anna and they glanced over their shoulders and could see Henry hovering over Amelia as if some miracle would bring her back. It saddened the hearts of everyone and they all knew that there was nothing left they could do except to be there for the Samuels family. Soon the constable barged his way through the crowd to examine the situation and everyone knew that it was time to heal.

Word of Amelia's recovery had spread to Thomas, Patrick, and their group and they charged down to the creek where the commotion was taking place. Until their arrival, they had no idea that the girl was deceased, and they hoped for the best. Whispers of death were overheard and Thomas demanded that their one suspect be locked away right away. Patrick objected, saying he wanted to be there with Amelia but the crowd wouldn't have it. Hearing of his presence, the constable followed his instincts and with the help of several other respectable men, grabbed a hold of Patrick. He instructed them to lock Buchanan up again, and the men carried him away yelling, "No, let me go. Let me see her." But his request went ignored. He struggled to break free but could not. He felt the pain of losing another woman he loved with all of his heart and the insanity he had been fighting off had temporarily set in. As they dragged his uncooperative body towards the jail, he repeatedly said, "Oh God, this is my fault." The men considered that a confession and because of it, Patrick wouldn't be allowed to say his goodbyes to Amelia down by the creek or could attend the funeral. This was by far, worse than losing his wife because he wouldn't get that chance to see for himself that she was gone. Within a few minutes he was locked away and told that he would be brought up on trial as soon as the family could bury their loved one.

Chapter Twenty-Two

The constable ran to Henry's side and ordered one searcher to control the forming crowd. Henry was in deep despair and the law enforcer wasn't surprised. The scene was an ugly one in which he had never witnessed before. He looked to the victim, and it was apparent that she had been under water the entire time the search party had looked for her. This wasn't the girl he remembered, the girl who would sometimes stop by the station to share some warm treats she had baked, or the girl that would go out of her way to help someone else. She was exquisite then and though he was considerably older than her, he would have loved the chance to court her. Now she lay helpless on the creek's bank. The constable was scared to see that even with swollen skin tissue; her body was full of bruises. Her hair clung to her body, full of dirt and weeds from the creek. And, her clothes seemed ripped right off of her body. He knew from the start that this wasn't an accident. Someone had deliberately murdered this innocent girl but for the life of him, he couldn't figure out why. He was the man in charge but he knew right away he would need outside help. Not just because of the seriousness of the crime committed but because the community was so close, this was personal.

Deciding that the best thing to do was to get the family, and gathering villagers, away from the scene, the constable put his hand on Henry's arm and said, "Henry, its best you leave her now."

Disgusted that the constable would even consider leaving his daughter to lay there alone, Henry pushed the constable's hand off of his arm. "No," he answered. "Leave me alone. I'm not going anywhere."

"Mr. Samuels," the constable said in a more professional manner, "Let me find out what happened to

Amelia." He again reached over to help Henry up but the girl's father wouldn't have it and he pushed him again.

Protecting Amelia from any more harm, Henry once again hovered over her lifeless body. What could they do to protect her? He thought to himself. If they couldn't help her when she needed them, what were they going to do now she was gone? "Go away," he snipped. "Go on, you get out of here."

The constable knew that trying to get Henry to leave would be impossible. The man needed more time. He looked around for someone to help get all the people out of there. The constable thought if just one family member left than perhaps the crowd would follow. He knew just who he needed to leave to calm the villagers. He turned his head toward that awful scream that hadn't let up and saw young Anna in the arms of her brother. They were standing not far away from him so he could communicate with David from where he knelt with Henry. As soon as David made direct eye contact with him, the constable said, "Take her home now. There is nothing that either of you can do here." David nodded, and the constable breathed a little easier, finally someone would listen to him. Standing beside Amelia's siblings, the constable noticed Phillip standing there. "I need you to get a few men who can help me get Henry out of here. Can you do that?" He pleaded with Henry's son-in-law. He could tell that the younger man was upset himself but trying to find someone in Millersport that wasn't upset was like finding a needle in a hay stack. Then he turned back towards Henry who was crying like a baby and told him, "We will help you through this, Henry. You're not alone." But Henry didn't respond at all.

"Come on," David said to his youngest sister and he held the blanket around her shoulders. "Shhh," he tried to calm her. Somehow as he got her to walk beyond the crowd, someone had offered a wagon. He picked her up the same way he had done in the creek just a short while ago and placed her in the back of the wagon.

David knew he couldn't leave her side without her panicking more than she already was. Then he noticed Jacob Miller standing a short distance away from the wagon with an emotional Emma by his side. She shouldn't be there either, he acknowledged. "Jacob," he hollered and then motioned for the couple to come to him when they looked his way. Emma wrapped her arms around his neck and in between sobs told him how sorry she was. David faced Jacob and asked him to drive the wagon back to his father's house. "I need to get Anna home but fear leaving her back here alone and for Emma's sake, you shouldn't allow her to go any further, anyway." Jacob agreed and a minute later the four of them were turning away from the terrible scene and headed to safety.

The motion of the wagon helped Anna a little but not completely. Knowing she was leaving the creek, she stopped the scream as they rode away but she still cried. She leaned against David's chest and closed her eyes. His heart beat so fast she thought he would have a heart attack. She reached up and placed a hand on her own heart that beat just as hard. It was then she knew that they would not die themselves, they were just heart broken. She felt another hand on her arm, looking to comfort her, and she was convinced that it was Amelia. She turned her head toward the girl besides her and deliriously thought Amelia was saying, "It's going to be all right, Anna. You must remain strong." Anna smiled but couldn't help but continue to cry.

Emma was in shock herself at the discovery of her best friend's dead body. They were so close and Emma didn't think she could go on without Amelia there with her. Who would help her through this, she thought to herself since Amelia was always the one who helped her through everything. She reached over and tried to calm Anna down, knowing that is what her best friend would've wanted her to do, but the look she received from Anna was more than just a little frightening. She looked up to David and asked, "Why is she looking at me like that?"

"Anna?" David called his sister's direction back to him. "We'll be home soon and we'll take good care of you." Feeling her head lean back onto his chest, David looked to Emma and told her that Anna must be very confused.

The women inside the Samuels house knew that something was wrong. They heard a scream in the distance and they knew it was Anna. It had wakened Minnie and Beth out of a sound sleep and kept all three of them pacing back and forth. Ruth could see more and more men rushing down the street in the direction that Anna had said she was going. They all knew that something horrible had happened but yet they were too afraid to leave the safety of the house. Even the boys had come down the stairs and tugged on her legs, afraid of what was going on. Minnie and Beth had got them to calm down by giving them milk and cookies but the boys refused to go back upstairs. None of the women could blame them either, nobody wanted to be alone. "Someone is coming," Ruth screeched as she looked out the front window. They all ran outside to see Jacob Miller pulling up with a wagon that had passengers in the back.

David jumped out of the wagon and then reached in and carried Anna out like a baby. He told Emma to stay where she was and then told Jacob to take her home. He walked towards the house, towards the anxious family waiting for answers, with Anna in his arms as the wagon pulled away. Their faces looked confused, and he then realized that they didn't yet receive the bad news. He heard them calling his name and could sense all of their questions in that one word. David walked towards Ruth and handed Anna over to his Aunt as if she was an infant.

Ruth helped him with the girl she sent away a while ago hoping she would calm down. Apparently she did just the opposite and Ruth wished that she left well enough alone. "David, we thought you had news."

David stood before the three women and the boys and had no idea what to tell them or how. He looked to his wife and hoped that she would understand why he felt a need to reach out to his sister before her. Tears streaked down his face as he pulled Minnie close to him and whispered loud enough for all to hear, "I'm sorry Minnie. Our sister is gone." Then he held onto her with all of his might as he felt her fall to the ground.

"God no," Minnie cried as she felt the earth pulling her down. She had been so hopeful all the while and couldn't believe that it would end that way. Minnie thought of the conversation she had with Amelia the last time she saw her. She blamed herself knowing that her sister was distressed; she should've never let Amelia leave her house. The guilt that took over her, she let the earth win, and she fell to the ground with David in her arms.

Beth looked to Ruth who was cradling Anna. The horrible scream they've heard made sense now. Anna wouldn't have screamed like that if she had found Amelia alive, she must have been there when they found her. Then Beth turned to her husband and her heart went out to him. He was embracing Minnie at the moment and Beth just stood back and watched. She needed him too but knew that the siblings would need each other more than anything and because of that didn't mind at all he hadn't yet come to her. Beth realized that she wasn't alone, and that someone needed her for comfort. She looked down to see Charles squeezing her leg with all of his strength. Through her own tears, Beth could see the little boy crying. She reached down and returned his embrace. Right after, the other boys who were looking for someone to help them too rushed over to her side and almost knocked her down. She didn't care, she loved that they felt safe with her. "I will take these little ones into the house," she informed the rest of the family. They didn't seem to notice her or hear what she said but she understood and knew that in time, they would come to her too. She decided that she would remain strong for their sakes.

Back at the creek, the constable had found another searcher and told him to grab a couple of willing men and leave for the county seat, straight away. They would need help and they would have to make arrangements for an autopsy. He knew that they couldn't send Amelia's body there until they were successful at removing her father first. The constable continued, "Send a couple of men to Albany to find a judge willing to travel down here for trial. Tell him about Buchanan, the ribbon found in his house, and that he is locked up. I think a judge would agree that we have enough on Buchanan to put him on trial and when he learns of the circumstances, I think he'll even agree to get this trial over and done with." Then as the searcher left, the constable grabbed him by the shoulder once again. He wished that they didn't have to travel so far to retrieve higher authority. The county had a District Attorney who handled any small case without the aid of a judge and though he would preside over this case for the offence, he wasn't qualified to control something as murder. Just the word murder sent chills down his spine and even a man of power like himself had felt a tear fall for Amelia. "I know it's a long trip up there but if you can, please come back as soon as you find help. We will need you here."

By now many of the villagers have left but a few remained for answers. One man still behind was Thomas Van Martin. Thomas had stood several rods away from the victim's body but had shown no signs of distress. The constable found that odd considering he had just announced his engagement to Amelia. Instead of shock on his face, Thomas looked more pleased than sad. The constable shook the thought off of his mind; there was no way that one of Millersport's most respectable citizens could've done something like this. Besides, he reminded himself, they already had the stranger in custody and everyone involved knew that he was the one responsible. Still, he couldn't seem to get Thomas' look off of his mind.

"Can I help you with anything?" Daniel Van Martin had asked the constable. Daniel was stricken with grief at the sight of his would have been daughter-in-law. Right away he prayed that what had happened had nothing to do with his blackmail to Henry. It couldn't have, he told himself. He realized that he hadn't been a friend to Henry since he discovered the man's dirty secret just a few weeks before. Seeing him behaving so insane over her body, Daniel knew that he had to be there to help Henry through this tragedy.

Snapping out of his instinctive thoughts of Thomas, the constable turned to the boy's father. "Oh Daniel," he breathed a sigh of relief; someone else to help out. He turned his head back toward Henry and noticed that Daniel had followed his eyes. "I need help with him. We can't find out what happened until he learns to let go."

Daniel was more than happy to help out but was skeptical about whether Henry would allow him, of all people, to help. He had noticed that most of the people who had been standing around just moments ago had scattered in separate ways. Going to their homes to grieve, he without a doubt told himself. He told the constable he would see that Henry gets home and then headed over to the man who he knew hated him.

It bothered Daniel to be so close to Amelia's body. Before he viewed it from afar but, he was just inches away and the sight was gruesome. The smell was enough to turn his stomach. Daniel did not understand how Henry could just stay there and not let it get to him. Henry didn't budge at all when Daniel put an arm around him; he thought for sure he would object. "I'm very sorry." Henry glanced at him and he continued, "We've haven't been good friends but you know that I'm your friend and I want to help you."

Henry looked up to Daniel and for the first time didn't see the blackmailing man he recently knew. He didn't know if it was confusion but out of nowhere, Henry knew that he needed Daniel more than he ever thought he would. "How did this happen?" Henry asked Daniel.

"I don't know," Daniel answered. "That is why we have to let the constable do his work. Come with me, let me take you home." Daniel couldn't remember a time in his life he had been so soft but supposed that Amelia had that effect on everyone she came in contact with. All he knew at the moment was that he liked the way he was behaving and hoped that he would remain that way.

"But what about Amelia?"

Daniel overheard the constable set up an autopsy and knew that once they could get Henry off of the victim, they would send her body away. He thought for a moment on how to tell this to Henry in fear that Henry would object once more and again throw himself to the body. "Henry," he said, knowing he must, "They will take her away for a while." Then he saw a look of fear in Henry's eyes and continued, "They'll bring her back, I promise. And while she is gone, the constable and some other men will go through this area and find out what happened."

For the first time since his departure from the water, Henry stood. He felt wobbly at first but knew that his weak legs had to at least walk him home to where he knew his family would wait for him. It killed him to leave her but knew it was for the good. Soon, he assured himself, they would have all the answers and his family could cope with all that has happened. He felt Daniel put an arm around him and was overwhelmed at his body's welcome to it. Everything spun but Daniel's grip had prevented him from falling down.

"Take a drink," Daniel instructed as he guided a canteen towards Henry's mouth. Daniel held on tight to keep Henry upright. Then he looked around to see who was still hanging around and spied Thomas a few rods away. His son gave him a look of disapproval but Daniel didn't care. He returned his attention to Henry and walked the grieving man home.

When Henry arrived home, his family flocked to him and gathered in a family embrace. Everyone was upset and full of disbelief but Henry and Anna were the worst. Though Anna's screaming stopped when she was in the wagon, she had shown little movement since she returned. Before Henry's arrival, David had explained to the others it was

Anna who had discovered the body and then they understood what the scream was about. He knew she was in shock and that something had to be done. Henry had a blank stare in his eyes and his body shook tremendously. He decided that the two of them needed help and wished that he had taken the time to learn about his father's business but he hadn't; Amelia did. He whispered, "I'll be right back," in Beth's ear and then snuck out the door.

He ran through the village to the house where he knew his father's employee lived in and then pounded on the door. It didn't take long for the young man to answer. "David," he started. "I wanted to give my condolences on your loss but thought I should give your family some time alone before I came to your house."

David shook the employee's hand. He appreciated the condolence and wondered how many people had said that to him when he was still at the creek. Everything happened so fast he didn't know. "We need you to come now," he instructed.

"What is wrong?"

David put his hand on his head, it was aching. Taking charge of family matters like this was unexpected, and it weighed on his shoulders. He thought for sure, no matter what the conditions, that his father would have kept it together but it was apparent that for the time being he wasn't. "I think Anna might be in shock and my father just stares and shakes. You are the only person in the village who has knowledge of how to help people besides my father. Is there something we can do?"

The employee shut the door behind him and told David that they first had to go to the store to retrieve supplies. The employee had the key in his pocket and thought about how Henry had given it to him while they searched for Amelia. He had told him he should have it in case they needed medical supplies and he wasn't around. They rushed inside and the employee grabbed a few things and threw them into a bag and then they left to return to the Samuels house.

When they arrived back at the house, Anna was still standing in the hallway. Beth was trying to get her to sit down, but it was if she was talking to an empty shell. She glanced at David and the employee when they walked into the house and then let out a sigh of relief.

Henry was sitting in the parlor with his head in his hands and when the employee called out his name, he looked up but the blankness was still in his eyes. Ruth, Beth, Minnie, and Phillip now gathered around the two men who had just walked. "I think they both need to get sleep. After they awake, we can see how they behave and go from there," he whispered to them.

"We've tried to get both of them to rest," Ruth answered. "And it doesn't help that neither of them rested while the search went on." The others agreed with her but the employee held up the bag in his hand, telling them they would sleep now.

"I have something that will help them sleep but first we have to get them into their beds." David and the employee had agreed to help Henry up to his bedroom. The elder resisted, but they had a strong hold on him and told him it was for his own good. Both of them hoped that once Henry was feeling better, he would understand what they were doing. It took time, but they got him into his bed. Phillip had picked Anna up and took her up to her room.

"What are you doing?" Henry demanded. It was the first thing he'd said since his employee arrived at his house. He wondered what the employee was doing there and why he had been carrying the medical bag. "I'm fine," he insisted as he realized they were putting him down in his bed. "Stop this nonsense, I need to get back out there and find Amelia."

David cocked his head and looked at the employee. The employee wasn't surprised by Henry's remark. Tragedies had a way of making people say crazy things. He looked back at David to assure him that everything would be all right and to play along with his father. "Yes, of course Sir. We thought you could take a quick nap so you keep up your strength."

Henry objected as the employee knew he would so he went on, "Okay than, have it your way. But at least drink this water before you head back out. It sure is a hot day out there."

David stood with his arms crossed over his chest, wondering if it would work and to his amazement, it did. His father had picked up the glass and put it up to his mouth. At first he only took one sip, but the employee continued to remind Henry how warm it was and how the drink would do him some good. Henry opened his mouth up wide and drank the rest of the water in one sip. Then David worried again as his father attempted to get out of bed but soon after realized that his father wasn't going anywhere. The employee had put a sleeping remedy into the water and it affected the elder man right away. When Henry showed signs of being dopey, the two younger men had swung his legs onto the bed and Ruth entered to tuck him in. Before he could say anything else, Henry was sound asleep.

Treating Anna was easier since she wasn't coherent. David had asked him how he would get her to sleep and was a little nervous when the employee showed him a needle he took out of the bag. "I have to," he assured all that were watching him. "She won't drink and has to rest," he continued as he prepped her arm for the shot. Anna didn't fight him at all and the family wondered if she even knew what was going on. Within seconds the needle was in and out of her arm and the employee was rubbing a swab over the sore area. When he was done, Minnie had laid Anna back onto her pillow and within minutes her eyes had shut.

The others had returned to the sitting-room and thanked the employee for his help. He said he was glad to be there and that they could depend on him for anything else if needed. "I'm leaving other remedies behind, more sleeping powder in case any of you need it. It's important that you all get proper rest tonight so it might be a good idea to use it. Also, some ailments for headaches since I could already tell that you have one," he said as he looked into David's eyes.

The family thanked him again, and he left feeling better knowing he had helped a family in need. "We all should get sleep," Ruth instructed the others as the door shut. She knew in tradition of deaths, friends and neighbors would stop by and she thought they should all be rested before they arrived. They all agreed with her and within a few minutes they were scattered throughout the house finding blankets, pillows, and a place to lie down. They only slept for a few hours but it was rest well needed.

Chapter Twenty-Three

The next three days were frustrating and nerve ending for the Samuels. They wanted answers that nobody seemed to have had at that point. Once Henry fell asleep on that dreary day, he didn't wake until the next morning and when he did; his mind was clear and ready to focus on the situation. Anna didn't have it so easy. The sleeping remedies she had received only worked for a little while and then she woke from nightmares of her sister's death. Ruth could comfort her enough to get her back to sleep but only until the image reappeared in her mind. By the next afternoon, she was fully awake but still upset about what was going on. Everyone was, but Anna took it harder than the rest and they were convinced it was because she was the one who found Amelia's body in the creek.

Friends and neighbors stopped by often and some of them, such as Emma and the Van Martins, stayed for as long as possible. Reverend Mayer had come often to pray with the family. He also sat with Henry to discuss funeral arrangements but the date would have to wait until her body returned. Henry was growing furious. He couldn't stand the wait any longer. He was making his way through the house towards the kitchen when he stopped and put his hand over his heart. It was breaking underneath his skin. He closed his eyes before opening the door that lead to the kitchen and tried to smell the food that Amelia had prepared. His senses had detected scents of food but it wasn't Amelia's and he knew that. He missed her so much and wondered if that empty feeling inside of him would ever go away. He entered the kitchen when he heard a knock on the door. Assuming it was just another neighbor, he continued to take a seat at the table. Then he recognized the constable's voice and knew that information was coming his way. He jumped up and raced to the sitting-room where the constable stood with the rest of the family. "Do you have news? Is she home?"

The constable turned towards Henry and smiled the best he could in the situation he was in. Yes, Amelia was home, but it wasn't her, it was just her body. As soon as he received word from the coroner, he rushed over to discuss what they knew with the family. "Mr. Samuels," he began, "Her remains are over at the church, ready for her service." He made a gesture as if to ask if he may sit down and without a direct answer, he sat and faced the entire family.

"What happened?" It was a question that wasn't asked by one particular person but all the adults in unison.

"Henry," he said to the elder of the house. "Perhaps we should talk in private."

Henry was about to agree with the constable but the others wanted to be a part of the conversation too. They all objected but David pleaded, "No Father. Please allow us to listen. We will ask you for every detail anyway if you don't let us listen now." Henry nodded and remained in his seat.

The constable understood and was glad to oblige. He figured it would have been too emotional for the others to hear. "The autopsy report states she had water in her lungs at the time of her death. Her cause of death is drowning."

"Can I see this report?" Henry asked. He trusted everything that the constable said but wanted to see for himself.

"I can get a copy but I have to warn you it's very hard to understand." The constable informed him. "In fact, it was explained to me so I could explain it to you." He saw Henry nod his head and then fumble with his fingers and knew that it was all right to go on. "It gets harder from here so if anyone wishes to leave, now would be a good time."

Henry looked to Ruth and then to the others, they weren't going anywhere. The younger boys were playing a game in the corner and they didn't seem to pay attention but, he didn't want them to hear. He asked for them to go upstairs and they listened. It wasn't until he heard the bedroom door shut behind them he allowed the constable to continue. "Go on," he instructed.

The constable looked down to his shoes. He had never done this with a family before and stumbled over his words. How he wished that he was there to report a stolen cow instead of an apparent murder. "You saw the bruises on her face and arms but those were not the only ones. She had larger bruises underneath her breast and two her ribs were broken."

The thought of some stranger seeing Amelia's naked body to perform the autopsy made David uneasy. "What could have caused that?" He asked.

"We're not sure yet but we'll find out. I promise you that." Then he continued. "She had several puncture wounds on her legs and back, as if she was dragged against rocks and sharp branches." He noticed the look of shock on their faces but went on anyway, "And there were more bruises," but he was interrupted before he could go on.

"Where?" Henry had asked. From the sounds of things, his daughter had been hit in every possible place by someone or something. The thought of where these other bruises were made him very uncomfortable.

The constable looked to the ladies of the house and wished that they would leave. Nobody knew for sure what happened as yet but Amelia had been abused. They waited for him to answer so he spoke as soft as he could, "On her upper and inner thighs. The bruises appear to resemble marks of hands, one large and then several smaller ones just inches above, on both sides of her legs."

Anna let out a cry as did Minnie at the thought of someone hurting their sister in that area. Henry looked to Ruth and demanded that they leave the room. Ruth stood and took them both by the hands and led them out of the room. The last statement by the constable was too much for them and they didn't even try to object. Beth could tell that she wouldn't like what was coming next, so she also stood to leave when the others did.

"Are you suggesting," Henry asked about the bruises but the constable didn't give him the chance to finish. He was nervous and picked at his hat he held in his hands. He didn't want to go on, but they had the right to know everything. "The report says there is evidence of an entry and we believe she was raped."

That was too much for the three men to hear. Phillip bent over and covered his mouth, but it was too late and he vomited on the floor. David took a candle holder and threw it which knocked over a lantern that wasn't lit. Henry was too upset to notice his son's behavior but wouldn't have cared if he noticed. He leaned back on the sofa and covered his face then let out a scream of disgust. "My little girl was raped?" The constable understood that they had to let out their frustrations. Henry continued, "I want that son of a bitch hung straight away." He wasn't the kind of man who used foul language but learning more of Amelia's fate had brought out the worst in him.

"A judge will be here this weekend and we're set to begin trial on Monday," he said to assure Henry that justice would be served.

"What do we need a trial for," Phillip shouted. A part of him wished that he'd never learned what happened to his sister-in-law. He realized that it had been easier to know that she was dead than to hear more details. He thought about Patrick Buchanan, friends had told him that the man just about confessed by saying it was his fault. "Buchanan admitted what he had done. Why can't we just hang him?"

"Trust me," the constable said in hopes to calm the men down. "I knew Amelia, and she was a big part of this community. I would like nothing else but to see him put to death but the judge doesn't feel the same way. He ordered for a trial and we must go with it. But don't worry; once Buchanan confesses in front of the judge, it will all be over."

Phillip had left to clean himself up as Henry and David continued talking to the constable. Henry asked about the large bump he felt on the back of her head and the constable confirmed that it was in the report but wasn't the direct cause of death. "It could be related though," he added. "If she was hit in the head and then fell into the water, she might've been unconscious. But we won't know that, until we hear from the only witness, her killer."

They wrapped up their conversation and though it hurt him to hear what had happened, Henry thanked the constable for stopping by and letting them know everything he knew. He told him about his plans for the funeral. The constable promised to spread the word to let the villagers know, and then was off to continue in his investigation.

The women had returned to the room and could tell by the odor of vomit and by the broken lantern that something serious had happened but none of the men had offered to fill them in on what they missed. They didn't push the issue either for each of them had a good idea and thought it best they didn't know for sure.

Chapter Twenty-Four

The church was filled with people mourning the loss of one of Millersport's finest citizens. Anna looked the overcrowded room. She knew that everyone, old and young, had come to lay Amelia in her final resting place and a tear rolled down her face. Her sister would have been proud to know that so many people cared enough to attend. Anna continued to look around and realized that she didn't know everyone in the room; she would later find out that people from nearby villages had also come to pay their respects.

The Van Martins sat in the front row on the other side of the room. As far as Anna was concerned, they didn't have that right and should have saved those seats for others who loved Amelia more. She knew how her sister felt about marrying Thomas and had faith that her sister would've talked her way out of that marriage if she had lived. To see them sit there as if they were the victims, made her stomach fill with disgust. Behind them she saw Emma and Jacob and seated by them were their families. She made eye contact with Emma and could feel how her sister's best friend felt. Lonely. Then Anna scanned the room and searched for Patrick but she hadn't seen him. She didn't know that he was the suspect in Amelia's death so she spent the entire service wondering where he was and if he was okay.

The service started and everyone held their eyes onto the closed casket laid before the churches alter. This was it, the time that the Samuels family had been waiting for. In a short time they could heal their broken hearts and return their lives to normalcy. Reverend Mayer stood in front of the congregation and said the traditional prayers and spoke of the deceased. The attendants sang a religious hymn in unison and that was finished with a final prayer. For Anna and the rest of her family, the service itself went by too fast for them to remember much about it. At the end of the service, six young men, led by Jacob Miller, stood and took a hold of handles along the casket and carried Amelia's body towards her final resting place. The Reverend and the Samuels family followed close behind with the rest of the mourners behind them. They walked her casket through the small village and entered the cemetery where her grave waited for her and the six young men lowered the casket into the ground. Amelia would now lie with her mother to the right of her and her uncle just a few feet away to the left.

The Reverend faced the crowd and spoke more personable than he did at the church. "Amelia Samuels was a friend to all of us. She helped others and rarely accepted help for herself. I ask all of you now; did we ever hear her ask for help? Perhaps we took for granted that she didn't need it. Is it possible she called out for help in her final hours but were we ignorant to the sound? Was it the wind we heard so harsh on Wednesday night or was it our loved one begging us to come to her rescue? We'll never know for sure but if your heart breaks at the thought of not being there for her, fret not because she has gone home to a place where no harm will ever happen to her again. I knew her well and know that Amelia Samuels wouldn't want anyone to feel guilty for not hearing her cries for help. We aren't to blame for losing our dear one. A monster has come and taken her precious life away from her. The devil disguised as a friend perhaps is the one who has taken the last breath from her. I know in my heart of hearts that the monster will have to come face to face with our Lord on his judgment day and will pay for what he has done."

Friends and family embraced each other looking for comfort. Anna looked around once more. She thought maybe Patrick had been there somewhere but she couldn't see his face among the crowd. She turned her head towards David and whispered, "Where is Patrick Buchanan?"

David lowered his head in sadness for the death of one sister and pity for the innocence of yet another sister.

Nobody had bothered to tell her about Buchanan's involvement in the murder and he had hoped that she wouldn't even ask. He glanced at her questioning eyes and wondered why she seemed to care so much about the monster that Reverend Mayer had just described. It tore him to be so blunt but she would have to learn the truth sooner or later. "He is locked up, Anna. Patrick Buchanan is the reason we are here today."

Anna was in disbelief. The cemetery spun around her and she felt her older brother wrap his arms around her to keep her from falling. She knew that Patrick was a stranger in the village but she didn't think that they would assume that he was the one responsible for Amelia's death. There had to a mistake, she insisted but David held onto her as tight as he could in hopes to calm her down. Anna looked around again and realized that everyone there had known who the Reverend was talking about. They're wrong, she told herself, they had to be. After the service was over, she would get to the bottom of what was going on, she determined.

At last the Reverend announced that the funeral was over and that the congregation should leave the family to say their final goodbyes. The villagers lined up and walked slow past the hole in the ground and each said a farewell to Amelia. Some tossed flowers on top of the casket as they passed, some put the sign of the cross over their chests in private prayers for the deceased, but all of them shed a tear as they walked past one last time. As they left, they each embraced the family and then went on their way. The Samuels were the last to leave. They stood hand in hand along the side of the grave and cried as they said goodbye to their loved one. The emotional scene broke up, and they turned to leave themselves. Henry couldn't find it in himself to go and he fell to his knees where he swore he would stay forever until they buried him right next to her. Ruth came over and wrapped her arms around Henry. "Come now," she told him.

"No," he answered in a cracked voice. "How can I? I let her down and I have to stay with her."

"But you can't dwell on that anymore. It's time to go home." Ruth understood what he was going through but wasn't sure if she would be successful enough to get him away from the grave. She looked around for David or Phillip but both of the younger men had gone to comfort the others.

Henry cleared his throat and wiped his eyes. He decided that there was no point in continuing to cry but still he didn't want to leave his daughter's side. "I won't leave her. I can't go on anymore. I will stay here until I die myself."

Ruth swallowed the lump she had felt in her throat. She couldn't let Henry wilt away to nothing. She had been holding onto a secret, waiting for the right time to tell Henry, and as much as she hated just blurting it out right then, she knew it might be the one thing to keep him from falling into the grave with Amelia. "You have to go on, Henry. For the sake of our child," she exclaimed as she ran a hand over her stomach.

Henry looked up to Ruth with surprise on his face. He couldn't say he was happy to hear her news, but it didn't anger him either. She stood in front of him, asking him to let Amelia rest, and for the first time he realized that she was right. He stood and faced Ruth, grabbed a hold of her and let out his sorrows. She was, after all, the only one who could ever get through to him. They walked away, but he had only taken a few steps before he turned around and looked again at the new tombstone that said 'Murdered,' above Amelia's name. Then Henry shed his final tear and turned once more and continued walking away with Ruth in his arm.

"I want to see him now," Anna insisted when she went to the jail to visit Patrick. There was a man there who had been asked by the constable to keep an eye on the suspect while he was away gathering information on the upcoming trial. He stood tall with his arms crossed over his chest and demanded that Anna should go home where she was safe. "I know him and he would never hurt me or my sister, please." She brought herself to tears and won the sympathy of the man.

He took the key off of the constable's desk and opened the door for Anna to enter. "Only for a few minutes though," he instructed. "He doesn't deserve visitors as kind as you."

She was sick to her stomach as soon as she walked into his small holding area. Patrick had lain sleeping on a worn thin cot that had no blankets or pillows. The room smelt stale from the lack of air. It had one small window but it was locked tight. Anna tried to open it but something from the outside was blocking it. She shrugged her shoulders as she looked around again. One pail stuck half way out from under the cot, full of urine. She covered her nose and mouth with one hand to avoid smelling the stench and picked it up with her other. After demanding that the man outside to empty it, she returned to her new friend. His boots were thrown into the corner and his belt had been removed. She couldn't locate it and wondered why they would take such a thing from him. Patrick himself was nothing but a mess. His hair that was usually pulled nice behind his neck was stringy and sticking up in many places. He'd grown facial hair that was in dire need of a trimming. Anna leaned closer to him to make sure he was still breathing. "Patrick," she called out to him.

The familiar sound awoke him to see the bright light shining in from the window. He could see a feminine figure standing before him; an angel sent to comfort him, he thought. "Amelia?" He questioned.

Anna shed a tear. "Patrick no, it's me, Anna. I'm her sister, do you remember me?"

Patrick sat up and rubbed his eyes. He'd been spending as much time as he could a sleep because in his dreams his love was still with him. Seeing Anna had forced him to remember everything that had happened to her and was happening to him. "Of course," he mumbled.

She sat next to him and pushed his hair out of his face. She wanted him to clean himself up and take care of himself. "Why aren't you taking care while you're in here?"

"What's the point?" He quizzed. He knew in his heart he hadn't touched Amelia in any wrong way and that the real killer was still out there but he was too depressed to fight for his freedom. As far as he was concerned the sooner they executed him, the sooner he would be with Amelia again.

Anna was getting disappointed in his attitude. "You need to clean yourself up for the trial. Patrick, you have to make them believe that you had nothing to do with this."

Patrick stood and looked out the window. He realized what kind of position he was in, being a strange man in a small village, the citizens wanted him away from them. He was a threat to their community, and he wasn't about to stand in their way. "Did you know that she and I argued the last time we saw each other?"

"No I didn't," Anna answered but didn't understand why he was talking about it. "Just because you argued doesn't make you a killer."

Patrick continued to stare into the sun as he responded, "No I'm not but if she told anyone about that argument before she went missing, they'll use it against me. There is nothing I can do."

"What about my father?" Anna tried to come up with solutions.

Patrick laughed, "Ha," and then sat back down on the cot. "You're father wants nothing more than to see me hung. I saw the hatred in his eyes when we were searching for her. I know he couldn't have changed his mind about me now she's gone." He looked at the young girl and could see the hurt in her eyes. "It's best we let Millersport do what they please."

Anna jumped to her feet and faced him. He was giving up, and she didn't want him to. "Patrick Buchanan, if you give up then we'll never know who did those horrible things to my sister. Please come to your senses." She waited for him to say something back but he'd just lied back across

the cot, closing his eyes to sleep again. "You can't give up."
Tears filled Anna's eyes once more, and she wondered where
they all came from. She must have run out of tears, she
thought. "I came to see how you are doing but now I worry
about you. My sister wouldn't want you acting this way.
Please snap out of it, Patrick." He remained silent and turned
to his side. Anna had tried to get him to say something, but
he ignored her. The man outside the door had yelled to her
and told her she had to leave. She walked towards the door
but before leaving she spoke one last time to him, "Then I
guess I'll see you on Monday. I hope you've come to your
senses by then."

Chapter Twenty-Five

Monday morning came and everyone in the village prepared themselves for the trial. Henry fumbled with the buttons on his shirt as he dressed. He was nervous about the events he was sure would take place. As much as he wanted to see Patrick Buchanan hung for his crime, he was afraid to hear the details. As far as he was concerned, he had heard more than enough. When he finished dressing, he walked down the stairs and found his entire family waiting to attend the trial. He had told Anna that he wanted her to stay home but she was stubborn like him and wouldn't see to it.

Once arriving, Henry was overwhelmed with the people that came to witness Buchanan's death penalty. There had to be as many people there as there was for Amelia's funeral. It was clear to Henry that this crime had affected the entire community. He led his family inside the building and they took their seats in the front row.

Looking ahead, he saw the judge that came from Albany and the District Attorney that the constable had told him would be there for the trial. There didn't appear to be an attorney for the defendant but he didn't care. No point in hiring one if you are guilty, he thought to himself. While they waited for the trial to begin, he looked to his family and told them all that things could get ugly and if they wanted to leave, they should do it then. Nobody moved.

Patrick had been brought into the room, cleaned up and in proper dress, and noticed how everyone was staring at him. They all thought he was guilty, but he knew that he wasn't. Everyone glared at him as if trying to kill him with their eyes, except for Anna. She was the only one in the room who seemed to care for him. Patrick looked to her as if to tell her he had thought about what she said to him but turned away when he made eye contact with Henry. He didn't want

Anna to get in trouble for befriending the enemy. He noticed the Van Martin men, Thomas and his father, and they looked back at him with satisfied faces, happy to see him being prosecuted for a crime he didn't commit. Though at the time he had no proof, he was sure that Thomas had something to do with Amelia's death and if fortunate enough to get out of the position he was in, he would prove it somehow. He glared right back at Thomas until the scrawny kid tore his eyes away from him. Then Patrick continued to look straight ahead so he couldn't see the faces that scowled him from behind.

Daniel and Thomas sat behind the Samuels. Still a changed man, Daniel reached up and placed a hand on Henry's shoulders. "How are you holding up?" He asked. Henry shrugged his shoulders and kept his eyes focused at the front of the room. Daniel noticed Thomas' glare at Buchanan and whispered to his son, "This trial won't last one full day. He'll pay for his acts soon."

A few minutes later the jury entered the room. All the men on the jury were from Albany since everyone in Millersport was bound to convict Buchanan before the trial even begun. After they took their seats, order was called, and the trial begun. Judge Harrison pounded his gavel onto his desk and asked the District Attorney to begin.

"Gentle man of the jury," Richard Young, the District Attorney, started. "I ask all of you to turn your attention to the man on the left of me. His name is Patrick Buchanan, and he is on trial for murdering an innocent girl, Amelia Samuels, on the night of August 25, 1813." Then the District Attorney took his eyes off of the jury and placed them on Patrick as he continued to speak. "This isn't a man we see here but a demon, a violent monster, and whom I will prove killed our victim in cold blood."

Hearing someone come straight out and say he killed her made Patrick angry. He realized that Anna had been right, and he needed to take a stand. "I did no such thing," he shouted as he rose from his chair.

The spectators whispered among themselves, and Thomas decided it was time to get the villagers' attention. He stood up and forced a face full of fake tears and cried out, "You did. You killed my wife-to-be and I can't wait until we hang you for it."

"Order in this court," Judge Harrison demanded. "Mr. Buchanan, sit down and keep your mouth shut. You'll get your chance." Then he turned towards the District Attorney and signaled for him to continue.

Young returned to the jury and finished his opening statement. When he was finished, the judge asked Patrick if he would like to say anything to the jury since he didn't have an attorney present. Patrick declined because he felt he said enough. The District Attorney laughed at the defendant's faith and then called his witnesses. During the morning hours of the trial, he first called the constable to the stand and questioned him about the search and about details of her body when found. Then he had called up Emma, Jacob, and Thomas and quizzed them about what they knew of the relationship between Patrick and Amelia. All of their testimonials lead the jury to believe that Amelia wouldn't give Patrick the time of day, not to mention building a friendship with him, making him look guilty.

Anna didn't like the way things were going. She knew that her sister didn't tell Jacob or Thomas anything about Patrick but she wasn't sure what she'd said to Emma. She wondered, since the girls were best friends, what she might have told her but knew that Emma was making Patrick sound worse than he was. Anna knew that she could help Patrick and desperately wanted to. "Father," she whispered, "Please let me tell them about what I know. I know Amelia was friends with him, she told me."

"No," Henry snapped at Anna. He knew that it wouldn't take long for Patrick to bury himself and he would not let anything stop that if he could help it. He ignored her and continued to listen to what was going on.

Young called Patrick up to the stand to testify for himself. He was sure he could get the defendant to admit his crimes to the jury. Patrick was sworn in and then given the right to sit down.

The District Attorney began, "Will you tell the jury how you knew Amelia Samuels?"

Patrick answered. Wanting them to know the truth, he answered. "She and I became friends after she told me she was being forced into a marriage she didn't want to be in." The spectators got loud as what Patrick had just said was a shock to them.

"Why did you say it was all your fault after Amelia's body was found and you were carried away to be locked up?"

"I lost it for a while; Amelia meant the world to me. Hearing she was gone made me think about my wife." Again the crowd got loud as the District Attorney asked him to explain. "A few years ago my wife and son both passed away in childbirth. It was another thing that Amelia and I bonded over. I felt it was my fault because I didn't get to the doctor in time but Amelia helped me to see it wasn't my fault. When I heard that she was also gone, I felt like I lost my wife all over again. I tried to explain that to the constable when I realized what I had said but he wouldn't listen."

"Is it true you had an argument with Amelia on the day of her disappearance?"

"How did you know about that?" Patrick asked in return.

Judge Harrison interfered, "Mr. Buchanan, you are the one answering the questions, not asking. I suggest that you remember that."

Anna felt horrible when she heard the question and wondered if someone had listened in to her conversation with him. She lowered herself in her seat and prayed that she didn't make things worse for Patrick.

Patrick knew that he had to answer the question. He didn't know how someone might've found that out, unless who ever had seen her last, her killer, had known about it.

218

Patrick didn't want to talk about it, knowing it would convince the jury he murdered her. He swallowed hard and wished that they never quarreled. "Yes, I had told her something about her father she didn't want to hear but I felt she needed to."

Henry was now the one squirming in his seat. He remembered Minnie saying something about Amelia needing to speak with him. His guilt made him wonder if Patrick had known about his British involvement and if he did, he furthered wondered if Buchanan had reported him.

"So you argued with her, then she ran from you and that made you angry. Didn't it?"

Patrick knew the District Attorney would back him into a corner with that question. "No," he answered. "I let her go. She said she needed to talk to her father and I wouldn't interfere with that." He glanced towards Henry who seemed to think the same things he was. He hoped that Henry would regret all of his own crimes.

"Where were you after she left then?"

"Home," Patrick testified. "I had a visitor."

Richard Young turned towards the jury and then towards the spectators and smiled as if they had the case wrapped up. He laughed as he furthered his questioning, "You know no one in Millersport. Who would have been visiting you?"

Patrick wasn't amused by the laughter in the room. They all must've thought he was a fool but Patrick knew who was there. He didn't wish to talk about Henry's treason at the moment so he tried to get by without giving a name of the visitor. "An old friend who was just passing by; he isn't from Millersport."

Just then the doors burst open as if someone had been waiting for a signal to enter. The room of spectators was silent as an Army officer walked up the aisle. The judge, the prosecutor, and the entire Samuels family looked shocked, not even Patrick had seen this arrival coming. Everyone stared in awe as he made his way closer to Harrison; even the

219

Van Martins were impressed by his composure. He wore the same pantaloons, vest, and boots that Patrick had seen before but this time those simple clothes were companioned with a single breasted blue coat that had ten buttons and corresponding holes that formed like a herringbone. The skirt of the coat extended down to the back of the knees and the collar had a distinguished design embroidered on it. Around the officer's waist was a belt that held a French sword and a chapeau bra fanned over his head with a gold eagle in the center. As he approached the judge, Major General Downy took his hat off, held it respectively in his hands and announced, "I'm a key witness for the defendant and have the right to speak on his behalf."

Judge Harrison allowed the Major General to testify. He turned towards Patrick and told him he was still under oath but to return to the seat until called back to the stand. He thought that the trial was coming to a fast end but now had no idea what would happen.

The Major General was sworn in and then took his seat on the stand. Young questioned him, "Please tell us who you are and how you know the defendant."

Major General Downy had heard of Buchanan's fate and used it to his advantage. He had returned to Millersport in the nick of time and just walked into the town hall when he heard Patrick say he had a visitor the night in question. "I'm Major General Downy of the United States Army Militia. Like Mr. Buchanan had told you, I'm an old friend of the defendants."

Henry was now real nervous and avoided making any eye contact with the Major General. Patrick had told Amelia something about himself and in the same night he was visited by a high official of the Army. It was all too much for him and he wished that he could sneak out of the room with no one seeing him.

"Then, how long were you with the defendant that night?" The Major General knew he was lying but was confident he wouldn't get caught. "I was there all night."

The crowd became loud again, and the questioning continued.

"What is someone of importance like you doing visiting Buchanan when there is a war going on?"

"That is exactly what's going on, a war. I remember Buchanan as being a man proud of his country and I felt we needed him to help the militia. Since we are camped not far from here, I talked him into joining the Army to fight in the war."

Patrick sat with an uneasy feeling in his stomach. He didn't know what the Major General was doing there or how it would help him. There was nothing else he could do but listen.

"Did you leave him or did he leave his house at all?"

"Not once," the Major General answered. "It took a lot of convincing to get him to agree and I was there all night long, like I said. I left his house when the sun came up and told him I would return to take him with me to the war front."

"Why didn't he leave with you?"

"He told me that there was someone he needed to talk to first, a goodbye I suppose."

"Well then, isn't it possible that when you left he killed our victim?"

The Major General just sat there and didn't seem bothered by the District Attorney. "No, from what I understand about this case, the girl was already missing by the time I left Buchanan's house."

The crowd roared. They were disappointed to hear such news. The Samuels family looked to be in disbelief themselves. The jury didn't know what to think and the District Attorney didn't know what to ask. He wasn't prepared for an eye witness on the defendant's behalf and felt as if his case was blown apart. Judge Harrison heard enough to know that Patrick Buchanan wasn't the killer the village had assumed him to be. Interruptions such as this were not usual in his court but given the intruder's rank, he believed everything that was said. He let the case go and pounded his gavel for attention. "In light of this news, something nobody bothered to find out, I declare this trial over." He turned and faced Patrick, "Mr. Buchanan, you are free to go." Then he pounded his gavel one final time, and the crowd left the room.

Henry looked over to his family and wished that things had not changed the way they did. It was apparent by their faces they were disappointed to not know who had committed the horrible crime.

Anna, however, was relieved. She wanted to run to Patrick and congratulate him but he was speaking with the Major General.

Patrick and Downy left the building, through the side door; right after Patrick was free to leave. Though Patrick was relieved to know he was no longer a suspect in Amelia's murder, he was also upset with the Major General's testimony. He never had intentions of fighting in the war and now with the demanding need to find the real killer, he wasn't going anywhere. As soon as he knew they couldn't be overheard, Patrick asked, "What is going on? I told you I wouldn't join the militia, and how did you know that I didn't kill the girl?"

Amused by Buchanan's ungrateful attitude, the Major General answered, "Personally, I don't care if you did or didn't. I've pulled you out of a tight spot and you owe me."

Patrick didn't know what Downy was up to or how he even knew of the murder. He hoped that he could return the favor another way. "In all seriousness, you don't expect me to leave with you?"

"On the contrary, if you don't then you can take your chances back in there," Downy stated as he pointed to the Meeting house.

Looking back at the building, Patrick saw the people still standing around gossiping about the unexpected end of the trial. He knew they would all love the chance to retry him and therefore knew that he couldn't outsmart Downy. "But, I need to be here to help find the real killer," he pleaded.

Downy reached over and put his hand on Patrick's shoulder as if they were old pals. He had done his research, like he has always done, and knew that the people of Millersport would rather see Buchanan hang than to find the real culprit. "I think it's in your best interest to leave for a while. There will still be a lot of hatred towards you, besides you don't have a choice."

Patrick knew that he was right but there was still so much he wanted to do before leaving. One thing was to visit Amelia's grave and pay respect to her. "Well then, can it wait? There are things I need to do."

"No time," Downy replied. "We are needed in the Buffalo area as soon as possible. You must pack a few belongings. I'll meet you at your house in one hour."

Patrick was discouraged. He knew that it would take him a half an hour just to get to his house. Then he would have to pack before the Major General arrived. He knew that there wouldn't be time to stop by the cemetery and hoped that Amelia's spirit would understand. He continued to wonder what Downy was up to and why he wasn't going to escort him home. Patrick thought it might have something to do with Henry Samuels. After the treatment he had received, he no longer cared about what happens to his love's father. He agreed to the Major General's commands and the two men walked in separate directions.

Anna raced to catch up with Patrick. She had seen him end a conversation with the Major General and then saw him walk away. She didn't know if he was in a hurry or not but she had a hard time catching up to his brisk footsteps. "Patrick," she called out when she got close enough.

He heard a voice behind him and stopped to see who it was. Anna was rushing towards him but appeared to be running out of steam. Patrick waited until she was closer and then said, "You shouldn't be talking to me, your family wouldn't understand."

Anna didn't care how her family felt about him. She knew that he wasn't guilty all along. She wanted him to know that she was still on his side. "Don't worry about them. I wanted to congratulate you. Are you going to help us seek the real villain now?"

Patrick's heart broke knowing he couldn't help. He hoped that it would all be solved by the time he returned from the war. "I'm sorry, Anna. I have to leave this afternoon."

Anna was surprised. She didn't think that he would leave so soon. "But I thought," she started before he interrupted.

"I have to," he said. "Can you keep a secret?" Anna nodded and crossed her heart so Patrick told her the truth. "So," he finished. "If I don't do what is asked of me, the Major General will throw me back to the pack of wolves waiting outside the Meeting house."

Anna shed a tear but was glad that someone had come along to help him, even if it was all untrue. "I'll miss you," she said, "Nobody else sees things the way that you do."

Patrick held his arms out and embraced her. "Don't worry. I promise I'll be back just as soon as I can. Keep your chin up, everything will turn out fine," he told her. The more he talked to her, he realized, the less time he would have to get ready. He took a moment to make sure she was all right and then said farewell to Anna.

She watched him walk away and prayed that he would be safe while he fought in the war. Then she too walked away to return to her family.

Henry asked his family to leave the Meeting house before he left. He'd told them there were a few things he needed to do before he went home but the truth was he was afraid that Major General Downy would confront him. He didn't want his family to be there if that happened. His instincts were correct. Henry was less than a block away from the building when he heard a man call out his name.

"Mr. Samuels," the Major General called out with a firm voice. He had known from Patrick Buchanan's description that the man in front of him was none other than Henry Samuels; the man who funded the British.

Henry turned and saw Downy walking towards him. He was sure the Major General knew of his treason, knew that Buchanan had reported him. It was a moment he'd hoped never came but now he had lost Amelia, it didn't bother him as much as he thought it would. He remained calm as he asked, "Major General Downy. What can I do for you?" As if he didn't know.

Downy grinned as he looked Henry in the eyes and held out his hand for him to shake. Downy sensed Henry's nervousness. "Henry Samuels?" He questioned. When Henry nodded, the Major General continued. "I wanted to tell you how sorry I'm to hear about your daughter." He could see the hurt in Henry's eyes from the loss of his loved one and wanted to sympathize with him. He remembered a time in his life when he'd lost someone dear to him. If Samuels was anyone else, Downy would have felt sorry for him but considering the treason placed by Henry Samuels, the man in front of him might as well have killed the girl himself. Throughout his investigation, Downy learned of Samuels blackmail and what he was putting his daughter through and realized that the girl was just another victim caused by British funding. Downy saw no reason to believe that Henry would continue since the funding had stopped after the death of the merchant who worked for him. Major General decided not to carry through with any charges. Henry Samuels had already paid his price for the crimes he committed and Downy was satisfied leaving the matter alone.

"My daughter," Henry was surprised to hear that coming from the Major General.

"Yes," Downy explained, "Violent crimes like your daughter's case don't happen around these parts too often. The Governor sends his wishes as well."

Henry couldn't believe it, he thought for sure he was about to be arrested. He glanced over Downy's shoulder and could see Daniel and Thomas in the distance. He knew that they would speak to the Major General if given the chance. Henry didn't want them to have that opportunity since it was apparent that Downy knew nothing of his crimes. He appreciated the man's kindness but wanted to get the Major General to leave Millersport as soon as possible to avoid a run in with the Van Martins. "Thank you," Henry replied as he quickly shook Downy's hand, "My family is still grieving and I must get home to them straight away."

Downy chuckled to himself, knowing that Samuels was trying to avoid the topic of his treason. He smiled and let the traitor believe that he had won. "All right then, just wanted to give my regards." He placed his hands behind his back, turned and walked towards Buchanan's house.

Henry watched him walk away and realized that the Van Martins must have traveled in a different direction because they were out of sight. Relieved on how the situation turned out, he thought it best to never bring up the topic to anyone ever again.

Downy walked away from Samuels and made his journey to Buchanan's house. He didn't get very far when he was approached by a tall, yet scrawny looking young man. "Can I help you with something?"

"Yes you can," Thomas replied. He'd been determined to make Henry pay for his crimes even if his father told him not to. As far as he was concerned, Henry interfered with his marriage to Amelia. He was still convinced that her death was just caused to separate him from her. There was nothing else he wanted from Henry so he decided to report him to the Major General. "I should have said something sooner. I know for a fact that someone in Millersport has been funding the enemy and demand that justice is served." He wanted to tell the Major General who the criminal was but he was interrupted.

"Oh yes, I know already and is one reason I came to Millersport." Downy knew who the man acting all high and mighty was. He played with the lad. "The culprit is a man named Thomas Van Martin," he said as he looked around pretending to look for someone. He knew that Thomas would try to clear his name right away so Downy spoke fast to avoid giving Van Martin the chance. "He'll be executed the instant I find him, no questions asked. Could you lead me to him?"

Thomas didn't know what to think. He certainly didn't commit such crimes but yet believed if he tried to tell the Major General who he was, he would be killed before giving the chance. Thomas noticed how the Major General held a hand on his sword and for the first time, Thomas felt speechless and intimidated. He assumed that Patrick Buchanan had lied to the officer, in jealousy of his relationship with Amelia, and he sweat as he thought of the authorities having the wrong identity. He wouldn't be able to defend himself. He swallowed a lump he felt in his dry throat and shook his head to answer. This sudden change of events angered him but he believed what Downy said and couldn't think of a way to clear himself without being killed on the spot. "No Sir," the answer came from his dry voice, "I don't know the man personally."

Downy almost laughed out loud to see how much of a coward the Van Martin man was. He felt a chuckle deep inside of him, begging to be let out, but kept it inside. The lad looked as if he would wet himself but Downy didn't have time to torture the young man any further. "Well then if you see him, inform me at once!" He told Thomas to have a good day then continued toward Buchanan's house. When he was out of ear shot, Major General Downy let out the laugh that had been building up. He had no reason to lie to the young man but was glad he had. He thought it served him right for blackmailing another man the way he and his father had.

With accusing Van Martin the way he had, Downy was sure that nobody from Millersport would ever speak of British funding again.

Part Three
Chapter Twenty-Six

The spring of 1815 had brought an end to the war and by that time, Millersport had returned to a normal lifestyle. The Samuels family could face the days knowing that their beloved Amelia was no longer with them. They never forgot her or what happened but could smile when speaking about her, instead of crying like they had spent so long doing.

Beth had giving birth to her first child just months after Amelia's death. Her labor was harder than it should've been because along with the physical pain, she felt the emotional strain of a lost loved one. Henry had delivered his first granddaughter in which David and Beth named Amelia. They called the child Millie for short and everyone else followed suit. By the spring of 1815, they also welcomed a son, David Jr., into the family.

Henry and Ruth wed after being in love almost all of their lives. The family wasn't surprised at all and was happy for the couple. Seven months later, Ruth gave birth to Mary, the daughter she'd always wanted. Henry had shown no emotions towards Mary. By March, when the baby was eleven months old, Henry hadn't held her even once. He had a low tolerance of her night time cries and was annoyed by her laughter during the day. Some thought he was jealous of the attention Mary received from her mother but that wasn't the case. From the moment he found out Ruth was pregnant, Henry thought this child was someone to fill the void left by Amelia. He wouldn't have it and wouldn't share the love he had for his eldest daughter with anyone; although his relationship with Anna had grown. He had noticed how grown up she had become and vowed to right with his last unwed daughter. Mary, through his eyes, was Ruth's child.

Besides the occasional nightmares of her sister's death, Anna's life had changed the most. She no longer behaved like a tomboy and had become feminine. Because Ruth had moved into the house and has resumed all the chores, Anna was encouraged to socialize and begin courtships. After she learned to fix her hair and apply perfume and lipstick, Anna was one of the most beautiful girls in the village. Though she liked the attention she received, Anna didn't take courtships too serious. She could never settle until she learned what happened to Amelia. It was a topic that nobody wanted to talk about but everybody wanted answers to. Then one day all the recollection and emotions came rushing back when one man returned to Millersport. As soon as Anna had heard the news, she raced to see if the rumors were true.

Patrick sat on top of his horse as the mare slowly galloped through the village streets. People gathered to greet him. A year and a half earlier those same people considered him an outcast, a killer, but were now extending a welcome to him. He knew why. During the war he'd used his anger to fight the enemy. In doing so, several battles were won and Patrick Buchanan had become a war hero. It wasn't his intention, he only wanted the war to end so he could return to Millersport to seek Amelia's killer.

Emma stood on the side of the street, waiting for Patrick to pass her. She needed to get his attention so she could speak with him. Since Amelia's death, Emma had slipped in and out of depression. She couldn't get over the guilt she felt for interfering with Amelia's relationship with him. Every time she read about Patrick in the newspaper, she recalled the argument she had with her best friend the night she died. The same argument that gave Emma a bruise on her face that lasted for weeks. She couldn't stand the thought of Amelia never forgiving her. As the horse moved in her direction, she called out, "Patrick, please stop. I need to talk to you." She hoped that if he would forgive her for her lies, then Amelia's soul would too.

Patrick slowed his horse down when he heard Emma call out to him. He remembered her too well, and the trouble she caused, and had half of mind to just ignore her. It wasn't his nature to disrespect anyone though. He stopped the mare next to her but stayed on top as if to tell her he wouldn't stop for long. "What is it?"

She became nervous as she noticed Jacob and Thomas stepping closer to her. Emma had hoped that her conversation would've been private but she could tell that it wouldn't. Patrick looked to her and she could tell that he was becoming very impatient with her delay in speaking. She didn't want Thomas to hear what she had to say, knowing he became sore whenever anyone spoke of Amelia, and her unexpected audience made her change her mind about what she would say to him. "Only that I'm glad you are back," she said.

Tapping the horse on its side, Patrick continued to move through the village. As he passed he noticed that Thomas Van Martin had been next to her and the boy he remembered to be her beau. Maybe her sudden silence had to do with Thomas being there. He turned to take a second look at the girl and noticed the beau putting his arm around her waist in a loving manner but he saw something else and wondered if anyone else had noticed it too. Thomas had been glaring at the couple and the young man he knew as Jacob was returning the angered look. As he moved forward, Patrick wondered what that was all about. The last time he was in Millersport, the two lads were good friends.

As much as he wanted to go home and relax, there was one place Patrick was determined to stop. After a few turns through the small village, he entered Mount Hope Cemetery and searched for his love's grave. It took a while but once he found it, he stopped his horse, fell to his knees, and put his hands over his heart as he felt it break all over again. "Oh Amelia," he spoke out loud, "I miss you so much."

"I'm sure she misses you too," a soft voice spoke behind him.

Patrick whipped his head around to see who had spoken to him. She stood in the sunlight, and again Patrick thought there was an angel in front of him. He shielded his eyes and could see a young and exquisite girl standing there. After letting his eyes adjust, he inspected the girl. Patrick saw the remarkable resemblance of the love he had lost and realized that little Anna had been busy growing up while he was away. "Dear Anna," he said, "How grown up you've become." He stood and embraced her. She was softer than he remembered as if she had gained some much needed weight. He held her out for him to see again. "You look wonderful."

Anna blushed. There had been several beaus in the past year but none had ever made her feel so embarrassed. She glanced into his deep eyes and could see why her sister had fell in love with him so fast. He let go of her hands and she shook the thoughts from her head. This man, she told herself, would always be Amelia's and as attractive as she thought he was, he was off limits. Anna felt safe with him, unaware that was how her sister once felt. "I knew you would come here," she said to him.

Patrick looked down at the grave and wiped a tear that fell from his eyes. He'd been so lonely since Amelia had left him. Though he had become a war hero, he knew that nobody else in the village would befriend him how Amelia had; except Anna. Patrick was convinced that when the young girl talked to him she spoke her sister's words. She also seemed to know him well for knowing how to find him so fast. "It's all I've wanted to do since that awful day."

Anna thought about the things that had gone through her mind since he had left. The newspaper had run a story on him and his efforts to fight in the Battle of Lake Erie. That was almost right after he left. Then the newspaper reported the British had burnt the city of Buffalo and Anna had heard nothing about him since then. There had been rumors he was also in New Orleans but the newspapers didn't confirm that. All she could do was pray for his safe return. "I've worried about you and am so glad to see you are fine."

Patrick worried about her while he was gone. He knew that the monster was still out there and worried that innocent girls, such as Anna, were targets. "I'm glad to see you are safe too. Tell me Anna, did they ever found out who had taken her away from us?" He rubbed her tombstone as he waited for Anna's answer.

She looked down to the ground. There had been no witnesses and little evidence. As much as she hated the idea, the residents of Millersport healed from their pain fast and nobody seemed interested in finding the real killer. Everyone she knew, wanted to know who had done it, but nobody would go out of their way to try to find out who had. "I'm sorry Patrick," she replied with regret, "They're not even looking."

"Not even looking?" Patrick was upset with her answer but he knew why. When he left, though freed from the trial, everyone still believed that he was the guilty one. When he left town, they still believed that and it wouldn't surprise him if they stopped their thoughts when word broke out about his acts in the war. "Hypocrites," he stated but then felt the need to apologize to Anna.

"Oh, don't apologize," she answered. "I feel the same way, so does my family."

He once had a hatred for Henry Samuels and felt as though he was to blame for pointing the finger at him. Time had worn that down too, knowing that Amelia meant the world to her father and vice versa. "How is your father?"

Anna told him about his marriage to Ruth, her new sister Mary, and his never healing broken heart. "He has depended on the constable to find the answers we are looking for but I'm afraid that the constable has let it go. We need someone like you to help us."

"I'm honored to help, I want to find out who has done this too," Patrick told her. "But, I'm afraid that your father won't want my help."

"Does that mean you won't?" Anna questioned.

Patrick reached out and placed her hand in his. She still displayed her faith in him and he wouldn't let her down. "Anna, I won't stop searching for the answers. If your father doesn't want my help, then I'll do it on my own." She smiled at him and he knew that his words had made her happy. It was a promise not just to her but to Amelia's soul too. One way or the other, he would give Anna the answers she needed. He embraced her one more time, and they said goodbye to each other. Anna had walked away as Patrick climbed up on his horse. He turned his head one last time and looked down on the grave. "I promise," he said hoping Amelia could hear him, "I'll find out who had done this to you."

Chapter Twenty-Seven

Henry was in his store selling a remedy to one villager when he had first heard that Patrick Buchanan had return to Millersport. The villager had told him that many people were standing along the street clapping and welcoming him back with laughter and smiles. Henry kept his comments to himself but didn't see the big deal with Patrick's return. To him, no matter how much publicity Buchanan had received about being a war hero, Patrick was still a threat to society. He had come to terms that Patrick didn't kill his beloved daughter but thought there would be no way for the two men to be friendly towards each other. At least, he didn't want to try. A part of Henry was jealous of the love Buchanan received from Amelia before she died; in those days when she loved him less.

After the villager left, Henry wasn't happy to see his next visitor, none other than Buchanan. For a long minute he stared at the man he despised so much but then asked, "Are you ailing from something? What is it you need?"

Patrick knew that coming to Henry's store, things could be awkward, but he was out to do what he had promised and that was to find a killer; even if that meant making amends with Henry Samuels. "I'm not ailing from anything but a broken heart and I'm sure you can't do anything about that," he informed the apothecary. "I came here to ask you what you've been doing to solve Amelia's case."

"That isn't any of your concern," Henry spoke back. He felt guilty because he knew that he had done nothing but leave it to the authorities and didn't want to admit it to the man. "If you must know, perhaps you should go see the constable."

"From what I've heard, he's given up long ago," Patrick said. The way he figured, too much time had gone by and the sooner he began his own investigation the better.

Henry lowered his head, knowing that what Patrick had said was true. He had too much faith in the local constable. "Well, he'll solve it in time," he said to avoid getting into it with Patrick. The man didn't seem happy with his answers and Henry didn't like having him there so he continued; "Now again, do you need anything because I'm very busy here and have to get back to work?"

"What I need is your help," Patrick answered. He had learned to let go of the treatment he received after the death but still had resentment towards Henry. He wasn't thrilled to go to him for help in the first place but he could feel Amelia telling him it was the right thing to do. She seemed to have a lot of confidence in her father and Patrick thought that maybe he should too.

Annoyed with Patrick's presence, Henry responded, "Look, you made a mockery of my daughter's death by first saying it was your fault and then a fool of us all at your trial. What makes you think that we could help each other?"

"First of all, it was temporary insanity which made me say it was my fault. Wasn't it yours too? Wasn't it everyone's fault for not protecting her enough?" Patrick was losing his patience and felt anger fill his face with the lack of response from Henry. "Did you really know her?" He asked.

"What?" Henry asked in return as he slammed his fist down on the counter.

Patrick grinned, knowing he could get through to Henry one way or the other. "Well I did. True, we met weeks before her death. But I think it might be safe enough to say I knew her better than you did in those final days."

Henry had heard enough and turned around to walk into his private office. Why did Buchanan have to return to dig up hurtful memories? He thought to himself. "Good day, Mr. Buchanan."

Deciding that the conversation wasn't yet over, Patrick raced behind Henry and grabbed his shoulder to turn him back around. "Oh, she definitely knew you!"

Henry pushed Patrick off of him and was ready to throw punches if it came to it. He knew what Buchanan was saying, another thing he hadn't thought of since then, and that was that Amelia knew of his crimes before she died. "Get the hell out of here," he snorted.

Patrick wasn't done tormenting the older man. There was too much at stake in the situation and he wanted to be heard. "She knew something about you I'm sure you still don't want the rest of your family to know about."

"Are you threatening me, Mr. Buchanan?"

"Not at all," Patrick replied. "I'm just making a point. Listen, I know that General Downy was easy on you and I don't want to tell anyone else but would if I need to."

"So you are threatening me," Henry said but Patrick wouldn't give him the chance to take a stand.

"That isn't what I intended to do," Patrick shouted. "But since you mentioned it, maybe I am." He could see that Henry didn't seem to care, so he continued with a quieter tone, "Henry, whether you like it or not, she loved us both. And believe me; I still love her with all my heart. I know that she wouldn't want us to fight over this. I'm asking you to work with me so we can figure out what happened. Please."

Henry was quiet for a while and didn't answer. Instead he thought back to those days and how she hated the thought of marrying Thomas Van Martin. He also remembered the times she tried to convince him to let her find a true love of her own. Perhaps, he wondered, she was trying to warm up to him and tried to tell him about her feelings for Patrick. He wondered what he would have thought back then. He found it within himself to answer, "I might not be too fond of you, and I'm not fond of knowing that my daughter loved you and yet couldn't even tell me about it, but you are right and maybe we could be cooperative and work together." Patrick reached over and extended his hand for Henry to shake, in which he did. There was still the never dying thought inside of him of what her final thoughts were. "Tell me something," he said before letting go of the hand shake. "When she was last seen, she was searching for me, but was there something else that might have been upsetting her?"

"We argued when I told her what I knew of you. She didn't believe me until she realized that was why you were making her marry Van Martin. But then she changed, I thought she would be angry with you but she wasn't. In fact, the argument continued because she decided that she would wed without a fight, just to save you." Patrick paused and held back the tears building up as he recalled his last moments with her. "Even after I told her I already told the government, she insisted that she would do whatever it took to get you off the hook. She ran from me and as far as I know, she was convinced that marrying Thomas was for the best. I had no idea I would never see her again so when Downy arrived at my door, I did whatever it took to clear your name."

Henry could see the pain in Patrick's eyes and as much as he hated to admit it, he was feeling bad for the man. Thomas had said many times he loved Amelia yet he had never seen these expressions from that lad. "Why would you still do that after she said she would marry someone else?"

"Because she cared for nobody more than she had for you," Patrick answered. "So I figured even if she had married Thomas, it would please her enough to keep her friendship."

Henry reached over and placed a hand on Patrick's upper back "Then maybe by working together, we can each learn a little more about her."

"Then work together, we will," Patrick responded. He wasn't sure if he could ever get Henry to agree but was thrilled to know that he had. "Where should we start?"

Thomas was striding through the streets with glee in his eyes. He had denied himself of what he wanted for long enough and now his life was getting back on track. He'd played the mourning fiancé for as long as he could and then searched for the next Mrs. Van Martin. There were no girls in the village that wanted to be with him. They must have been intimidated by his gorgeous looks, he thought to himself. He was determined to have a soft body to lie next to at night, even if that meant that he had to threaten someone else. Anna Samuels had grown to be quite the eye catch, but he dared not try to force Henry into anything else, fearing that Samuels had lead the government to believe he was the one committing treason. Anna was off limits to him, but he found someone worth threatening, someone worth ending a long friendship with; Emma Cooper. He laughed at the thought of his pal Jacob objecting but there was nothing he could do to stop this new plan of his.

Jacob and Emma sat on the bench outside of the general store. As Jacob held onto her hand, he thought about how much he had wanted to make her his wife. The couple had talked of marriage but Emma wasn't yet ready to take that step due to the tragic loss of Amelia. Jacob had understood, knowing she feared marriage because when Amelia got engaged she was killed. Many times he tried to assure her she didn't hold the same fate as her late friend but it fell to deaf ears. He knew in time she would agree to making their love official. Emma had rested her head on his shoulder as Jacob noticed Thomas walking towards them. The relationship with his best friend hadn't been the same since Amelia's death either. He wondered if maybe Thomas was resentful of him because he had Emma where Thomas again had nobody. Emma had lifted her head and saw Thomas too and groaned. "I wonder what he wants now," he said to her.

Thomas saw his new love and the friend she would soon call her ex sitting on the bench. Some might say this should be tender moment but not Thomas, he was eager to torture the couple as much as he could. They sat close to each other, the sickening way that couples do, but it wasn't close enough where he couldn't interfere.

Without second thought, Thomas forced his skinny body right between them and sat down. "Isn't this cozy?" he asked.

Emma couldn't stand to be close to him so she jumped up and moved to the other side of Jacob, leaving Thomas on the end. Jacob was also annoyed and pushed Thomas to move. "What is wrong with you," he hollered.

Laughing out loud as if the soon-to-be-splitting couple amused him, Thomas demanded, "Oh no, Emma. I insist that you sit on this side of me."

"She doesn't have to listen to you," Jacob reminded his not so good friend. Thomas had been acting strange for a while now and his sudden orders to Emma were going too far.

Thomas would not lighten up to make them feel better. He would try harder to displease them. He reached over to Emma and pulled her hand until she was back on the other side of him. She shrugged and tried to get him off of her but he won and she sat down. "Now, I came here to tell you something very important and you aren't making me feel unwelcomed." Emma had moved enough so that her dress wasn't touching him but she didn't try to sit next to Jacob again. Jacob just glared at Thomas, added fuel to Thomas' fire. "Now listen carefully," he started. "I've decided to get married again."

Emma laughed and couldn't help but let it out. She knew all the girls in the village and none of them would even consider Thomas, not even for his money. Then her face turned sour when she realized that he must have been forcing someone else. "Who are you forcing now?"

She knew him too well, another reason he chose her to be his bride. Beating around the bush was just not his style, so he blurted out, "You, Emma Cooper. You will be my bride."

240

Both Emma and Jacob jumped up and faced Thomas with shock. Jacob was angered by Thomas' attitude. Nobody had the right to take his girl away from him, not even the Van Martins. "Over my dead body," he screamed as he formed a fist and held it close to his side.

"There is nothing you can do to make me marry you, Thomas," Emma insisted. She wondered what made him think that he could win her heart.

Now in full laughter, Thomas continued. "Oh beautiful girl," he said as he stood facing her and ignoring that Jacob was there. "Your father works for me and I told him that if he didn't make you marry me, then he would be unemployed."

No longer able to control his anger, Jacob reached over and grabbed Thomas by the collar. "You son- of- a- bitch," he spit in his face. "What gives you the right to treat people the way you do?"

"I don't believe you," Emma cried. She wished that her father had never taken that job at the brickyard but realized that was his way of feeding the family and keeping a roof over their heads. "He knows I love Jacob and wouldn't agree to your threats."

Thomas was proud of himself; he without doubt upset the happy couple. Emma was his for the taken and nobody could stop him. Grinning from ear to ear, he showed his desires to her right in front of the love of her life. He pulled her close and planted a wet long kiss on her sweet lips. He knew he had an audience, and he loved the attention; until he felt a cold hard fist slug him on the side of the head.

"Get your hands and awful mouth off of her," Jacob demanded. It was a demand that was followed through because Thomas' weak body fell right to the ground. Jacob glared down on the man that used to be his friend and added, "I don't care what you think you've said or done, Emma won't marry you and that is final." He grabbed her by her hand and the two of them ran to her father. They were convinced that they could talk the elder out of his decision.

Henry and Patrick stood inside his store waiting for the constable to arrive so they could once again reopen Amelia's case. Henry was updating Buchanan on the details he knew, details that were failed to be given to Patrick because of his immediate lock up. Their conversation was cut short and put on hold when George Cooper walked in. He asked for an ointment to comfort his aching back and Henry got busy preparing it. Cooper looked to Patrick and welcomed him back and made small talk with him. Henry was just finishing up and Cooper was just about to leave when his daughter and Jacob Miller had rushed in.

"Father,"

"Mr. Cooper," the two youngsters cried out at the same time. George Cooper knew what was bothering them. They must have received the marriage message from Thomas and it was apparent that they didn't like what they've heard. He knew that the apothecary store wasn't the place to discuss this so he said, "We should go somewhere else to talk. This isn't the time or the place."

Henry and Patrick just looked at each other as the scene unfolded before their eyes. The constable they had been expecting had also walked in right behind the couple and was just in time for the confrontation.

Jacob looked around and as far as he was concerned, this was the perfect place to talk about Thomas. He knew that the others in the room would back him up. "No, right here is good enough." He glanced over to Henry and calmed down as he spoke, "I'm sorry Mr. Samuels but feel as if you might side with Emma and me on this one."

Emma stood with tears streaking down her face. This was happening too fast for her and she remembered too clear how desperate Amelia was to get out of her engagement. "Oh Father. Why are you forcing me to marry Thomas Van Martin when you know I love Jacob?"

Henry's head spun as he heard Emma speak. He wondered what Thomas had over George but knew that if he kept quiet, he would soon find out.

George Cooper faced his daughter and put his hands on her shoulders as if he was trying to make her understand something. "His father is soon to retire so Thomas is taking over the brickyard. He said he would fire me if I didn't break the two of you up," he told her as he looked at Jacob.

Henry had enough and felt he had to speak up. Too many lives had been changed by Van Martin threats and it was time to put an end to it. "George, pardon me but you can't let him get away with this. You can't let him win."

Emma cried even harder knowing that what her father had said was true; she heard it right from Thomas' mouth. "I won't marry him. The last girl who was forced into a marriage with him was murdered," she cried but didn't mean to upset Mr. Samuels or Patrick who she had just noticed was there. She looked to Henry as if to apologize but he didn't seem bothered by what she had said.

George Cooper felt that his daughter was out of place and right away thought he should correct her. "Emma, you can't just blame Thomas for what happened to Amelia."

Jacob lowered his head like he was ashamed of something but then snapped it back up. There was no way he would allow his girlfriend to marry anyone other than himself. He would do whatever it took, and it appeared that now was the time to take a stand. "I'm sorry that I said nothing sooner," he said as he looked over at Henry, "But Thomas is Amelia's killer. I know that for a fact."

The constable who had just been a bystander until this point pulled Jacob aside and asked Henry if he could talk to the young man in Henry's office. Given the situation and what Jacob had just said, Henry was glad to be of service. The remaining four stood and waited for the other two to come out. It was only a few minutes but seemed like an eternity to all of them. George Cooper felt horrible to have put his daughter in that position but hoped that his decision provoked Jacob's long silence. Emma stood and didn't look to be in any shock at all. Jacob had never told her anything like that before but once she realized that Patrick Buchanan wasn't the guilty one, she knew that Thomas must have been.

Patrick paced back and forth, from day one he knew that Thomas was involved somehow and now he hoped that they would have the answers he needed. Henry put his head down on the counter and cried. Nothing had been said about Amelia's death until now out of nowhere, it seemed they had another suspect. Something wasn't right with this accusation, he told himself. Thomas would marry his daughter and Henry knew that there could be no way he would do anything to stop the marriage he looked forward to. He looked to the others and tried to read their minds. Part of him wanted this all to be over but another part of him couldn't accept that his daughter was killed by her own fiancé.

Twenty minutes later the constable and Jacob had returned from the private office. Both of their faces were grim at the news that needed to be shared with the others. This wouldn't be news that would go over well with the citizens of Millersport but everything that Jacob had told the constable had made sense. It was just one man's testimony but for now, it was enough. "Henry, Patrick, I'll need your help. George, take Emma home and stay with her."

"What is going on," Patrick spoke up. His patience was running thin, and he wanted answers. "Jacob has given me enough testimony to put Thomas Van Martin on trial. He said too many things that the public didn't know. I will arrest Van Martin and will need your help in apprehending him." Everyone else was silent; this was a shock, but they all did as they were told and within seconds were out to confront the monster that the village had been living with for over a year and a half.

Chapter Twenty-Eight

David had just put Millie down for a nap, as Beth nursed the baby, when he heard commotion going on outside. Beth heard it too, and the two gave each other a puzzled look. David crossed the room and took a look out the window. He saw a group of men, one of them his father and another he recognized as Patrick Buchanan. They were with the constable and people had gathered on the street to find out what was going on.

"What's going on out there," Beth questioned him. She decided that David Jr. had enough to eat and placed the sleepy baby in his cradle.

David turned to her and answered, "I don't know but my father is out there with Patrick Buchanan. I didn't even know he was back in town." He walked towards the front door and grabbed his jacket. "I will go find out," he told her. He heard her tell him to be careful, and he nodded in agreement then left.

David ran to catch up to Henry who was already a block away. As soon as he arrived, Henry looked his way and acknowledged that he was there. "Father," he started as he caught his breath. "What's going on?"

Henry didn't have time to stop to talk. He pulled David's elbow and gave him a signal to follow. He knew the news would be a surprise to his son, but he also thought it was a good idea to have him there to help. Bringing Thomas to lock up wouldn't be an easy task. The small group continued walking until they were outside of the Van Martin house. "We have a new eye witness," he explained but kept his voice down. "Thomas is the one who murdered your sister," he explained.

"What," David just about shouted. He assumed that Amelia's case would never be solved and now out of the blue,

245

someone came forward. "I wasn't aware that there was an investigation."

"There was going to be," Patrick cut in to the conversation. "Your father and I had agreed to work with each other but before we did anything, the witness came and told the constable details that weren't made public." He glanced at Henry and hoped that he hadn't said too much. He failed to tell David who the witness was but his common sense told him to protect Jacob.

David was stunned. He remembered Amelia running to his house the day she went on a picnic with Thomas and complained about how the man had treated her. He shook his head wondering why he hadn't thought of that after she died, it might've had Thomas paying for his crimes earlier. Like his father, he thought it was odd that her own fiancé would kill her when he wanted nothing more than to have her. "Are you sure it's him?"

There was no time for Henry or Patrick to answer. The constable had broken up their conversation and told them it was time to knock on the door and find Thomas.

Daniel Van Martin had changed his ways after Amelia's disappearance and even more after she was found dead but the soft side of him didn't last long. His high-almighty attitude had returned and his friendship with Henry Samuels had ended before it began. He sat in his parlor reading the newspaper when he heard a group of people outside of his house. At first he ignored the sound, thinking it was just people passing by, but curiosity caught a hold of him and he peeked out the window. Though he saw the crowd outside of his house, he didn't give it a second thought and returned to his seat and continued reading the paper. Then Daniel heard a knock at the door, and the commotion of the men still outside. "Catherine, answer the door," he demanded his wife. The knocks continued and Daniel's frustrations grew until he heard Catherine hollering she was coming.

Catherine raced down the stairs to see who was pounding on the door so hard. As she landed on the bottom step, she looked into the parlor and wished she could tell Daniel to answer the door himself but didn't want to cause an argument. Whoever was at the door wasn't there for a personal visit, she could tell by the banging that something was wrong. Once the door was opened, and she saw the constable standing there with a group of men behind him, she asked, "Constable, can I help you with something?"

The constable removed his hat and held it in front of him to show his respects to the lady. He'd hoped that she wasn't home because he felt she differed from her husband and son and felt she didn't deserve to see her only child being taken away the way he would be. "Ma'am," he started as he looked past her to see if there was anyone else home. "We need to speak to Thomas. Is he home?"

Daniel wondered what was going on. He jumped out of his seat and raced towards the door so that his wife wouldn't say anything. "What do you need Thomas for," he questioned.

The constable was glad that Daniel had been there and hoped that he would send his wife away but after a moment of silence, he realized that wouldn't be the case. "Its business, is he around?"

"No," Daniel lied. He had no idea what they wanted with Thomas or why they felt they couldn't discuss it with him. Unfortunate for him, as he denied that his son was home, Thomas descended from the stairs. "Oh," he covered up for himself, "Thomas I didn't realize that you've returned."

Thomas saw the group of men outside and wanted to know what was going on. If he would have realized that they were there to see him, he would have stayed up in his bedroom and let his father continue to lie for him. He had been lying down trying to rid himself of the pain that Jacob had caused and wanted nothing more than to go back up the stairs and put an ice pack on his head. Thomas had an uneasy feeling in the pit of his stomach as soon as he realized the

Samuels men were there along with Patrick Buchanan. "What is this all about," Thomas insisted.

"I'm afraid that you must come with us," the law enforcer told him. "We've just received word from an eye witness that puts you at the creek. You're under arrest for the murder of Amelia Samuels."

Catherine almost passed out and needed to have a seat. She excused herself and entered the parlor where she could regain her strength. Daniel instructed Thomas not to say a word and then he yelled, "What is this all about? Who is your witness?"

Ignoring his father's advice, Thomas defiantly snapped, "It's a lie. I know nothing of what you're talking about."

Patrick had looked to Henry and David and both men expressed confused looks. He wasn't sure if they were convinced that Thomas was the guilty one or not but he knew for sure. It was in his gut all the time and he would find out how. "You know exactly what he is talking about," he shouted. "Now constable, he demanded that I be locked up when Amelia's body was found and now I demand he gets his turn."

Knowing that Buchanan would only start trouble, Henry rushed towards Patrick and pulled him aside. "Let the constable do his job," he told him and the two watched from the side.

"Thomas," the constable said again, "You can either come with us on your own or we can drag you through the village streets. Do you want all of Millersport to see you that way?"

Thomas shook his head. He didn't know what to think and wondered who was telling horrible lies about him and his whereabouts the night Amelia disappeared. He didn't have to say anything because his father had stepped up and spoke.

"Thomas," Daniel instructed. "Don't let the villagers think something is wrong. You'll damage our name if you don't go with the constable right now."

"But, I did nothing," Thomas argued. He found this to be a nuisance and decided that the group of men was wasting his time. "I'm not going anywhere. If you have something to say, say it right here."

The men looked at each other. They all knew that it wouldn't be easy and knew that Thomas would put up a fight. They were all correct. It didn't help any to have Daniel acting so domineering, but the law was the law and not even a Van Martin could run from it. The constable looked to the other three as if to give the sign and within seconds they reached in and grabbed Thomas and pulled him outside. The only one who didn't have his hands on the young man was Henry.

"Let go of my son," Daniel demanded as he tried to grab Thomas himself to keep him in the house. When he realized that he was out numbered he took his anger out on the one man left who wasn't holding on to Thomas. He jumped in front of Henry and placed his nose inches from Henry's, clinched his fists and yelled, "You can't blame a Van Martin for your jezebel's death."

David and Patrick almost let go of Thomas when they heard Daniel speak so wrong against Amelia but the constable insisted that they held on. David looked to the elder Van Martin and wished that he could go tear the man into pieces. Henry pushed Daniel into the wall, grabbed his throat, and squeezed. He could hear him gasp for air and could feel Daniel's hands trying to break free but Henry would not let go so quick. "Don't you ever," he started with a cry in his voice, "Say things like that about my daughter if you wish to live yourself."

"Let him go," the constable had commanded. The whole scene was getting out of hand. He didn't know that Daniel would put up such a fuss. Henry wasn't obeying him so he asked the others to make sure Thomas couldn't get away as he rushed to the fighting pair and pulled Henry off of Daniel. "I said to let him go," he reminded.

Henry listened and walked outside to cover his face; he was angry and scared at the same time. Daniel straightened himself out as the constable stepped out to be with the others. Thomas struggled to get away from the men but could not; the longer they held onto him the more frustrated he became. The constable pointed towards the main street and the others walked toward the station.

Daniel watched them take his son away but wanted to put fear into them and assure Thomas that everything would be fine. "I'll see you in court and we'll have the best attorney money can buy." His words didn't appear to bother the group as they continued walking away. He reentered his house and could hear his wife crying in the parlor. Deciding that she could deal with the news on her own, he walked straight to his home office to look up the address of a lawyer he knew.

Thomas was forced to sit on the same cot that Patrick had slept on when he was arrested for Amelia's murder. It felt cold and lumpy and Thomas knew that he wouldn't be able to sleep there. The place was beneath him, and not where he belonged for sure. The constable had thrown him in there and then left, shutting the door behind him.

Deciding that he would not stay there, he jumped off the cot and ran to the door. It was locked and Thomas would've broken his foot if he kept kicking it to get someone's attention. "Let me out of here," he screamed but nobody had replied. They wouldn't get away with this, he told himself; then returned to the other side of the room.

Henry gathered his family together at his house and told them all the news. He had invited Patrick over as thanks for his help bringing Thomas in. The family couldn't believe what they've heard and Henry understood. He didn't believe it earlier either but seeing both Thomas' and Daniel's behavior had made him realize that Jacob Miller had said the truth. They were waiting to hear from the constable who was making arrangements to get the trial underway.

Anna was glad to see Patrick and her father getting along so well. She knew that in time her father would come to accept the man that Amelia loved. She sat beside him and whispered, "I'm happy that you're here. You shouldn't have to be going through this alone."

Patrick reached over and touched her arm and was grateful of her kindness. He wondered if anyone else had realized that young Anna had inherited her sister's heart. "I promised you I would help," he began. "Didn't I?"

The other adults in the room had asked many questions about Thomas. They still had their doubts about a man so high in society and even though the victim was their beloved, they still wondered if the constable had done the right thing.

Several hours later, the constable had returned to their house. He stood in the sitting-room, put his hands in his pockets, and told them what he knew. "We'll be able to have the same judge and District Attorney since they already know of the case. They'll provide a jury also. They don't want this trial to be as inadequate as the last one." He looked to Patrick as to apologize but Patrick wasn't offended. "They've asked," The constable continued, "That if we could do anything, find evidence or any cause that Thomas might've had to do this," he was cut off.

"What do you mean, might?" David shouted in fear they too didn't believe that Thomas could've done such a thing. He looked to Henry and apologized, "I didn't think of this until earlier today when we retrieved Thomas but I remember something that happened before Amelia was killed." The constable was intrigued by this sudden memory so he urged David to go on. "She went on a picnic with him but was told that I was watching, nearby to protect her if needed. Thomas tried to force himself on her and when she got away, she ran straight to my house and told me all about it." He looked at his father who had his head lowered. It was a lie he told Amelia and David had caught him in it long ago.

Henry snapped his head back up. He had felt a rush of guilt come over him but he felt then that Thomas wouldn't hurt her and therefore still held onto those feelings. "No," he spoke up. "Thomas confronted me about the whole thing himself. He had asked for a kiss and she agreed but then bit his lip. I saw the blood myself."

"How could you believe that," David shouted.

"Father, he's right," Anna spoke up. She had remembered the same conversation with her sister. "She also told me about that day. But she didn't bit his lip; she said she bit his tongue he'd put in her mouth."

Henry was upset that everyone else knew a different story than he did. He thought back to the way he argued with her for treating her fiancé so bad and how he never questioned her about her side of the story. Then he turned to Patrick to see if he knew too. "What about you, did she tell you this?"

Patrick realized that everyone was looking to him as a conformation of what was being said but he had no answers for them. "No Sir," he replied. "I remember her going on the picnic. She said she didn't want to go. But she and I had just become friends at that point. A few days later I asked her but she refused to talk about it."

The constable had heard enough. As far as he was concerned, two people spoke the same story, so it must've been true. "Don't speak of this to anyone," he told them. "We might be able to use it if you're willing to testify," he said as he faced David. The young man nodded in agreement as the constable continued to ask, "Is there anything else that Thomas has done to her?" Nobody seemed to have anything to say, so he decided that he should be going. "All right then," he added before leaving, "The trial is set to start two weeks from Monday. If you think of anything else, please let me know." He tilted his hat towards them and then left the family facing another turbulent time.

Chapter Twenty-Nine

The following two weeks had the citizens of Millersport preparing for a new trial. Thomas fought to be let out of the station but his demands went unheard from everyone except his parents. Daniel had paid him a visit the day after his arrest to let him know that he was leaving to find a suitable attorney. Daniel encouraged his son to keep his head up and assured him that nobody had the right to lock a Van Martin up the way they had with Thomas. He didn't think for one moment that his son could commit such a heinous crime and was determined to do whatever it took to help set Thomas free. He traveled to New York City to look for a lawyer willing to take on the case. Daniel planned on using as much money as it took to find someone respectable and powerful. Once he found the right man for the job, he had brought him back to Millersport where the attorney could learn about what was going on and to get as many details of the murder as possible. Daniel had brought him to see Thomas as soon as they arrived and though Thomas was relieved that someone would help, he shown no appreciation towards his father at all.

Catherine went to see her son every day and did all she could for him. He had complained about the bed he was forced to sleep in and she had rushed out to bring him comfortable blankets and pillows. He then complained about the food and insisted that she bring him something worth putting in his mouth. Again, she did as she was told and brought him all of his meals. Still Thomas scowled her to where she cried in front of him. She begged him to treat her like a mother instead of a maid but his only reply was, "What's the difference?" One day she woke and thought about not wasting her time to see him but then feared that he would be disappointed. It wasn't like Catherine to displease him and she knew that she held most of the blame for the way he turned out. Thomas was a spoiled rotten son, and she knew that all the years of given him everything his heart desired had caused his attitude.

There was nothing for the Samuels family to do throughout the two-week span but to wait. Wait to see what happened the night that Amelia disappeared; wait to see what Jacob had said to the constable to convince the authority that Thomas was the killer they've been waiting to find. Business slowed down for Henry as half of the village sided with the Van Martins. Some of the people who believed Thomas innocent did so because of family friendships but most of the people who acted as if they didn't believe he was guilty were families were employed at the brickyard. Nobody could ever confirm that they were threatened by Daniel but as time went by, it had become obvious. The only villagers who dared step foot into the apothecary store where true mourners of Amelia's and wanted to see the villain pay just as much as the family did.

For Jacob Miller, the two weeks were pure agony. First, they tried not to let anyone find out who was responsible for having Thomas put on trial but things of that nature were not kept quiet in a village as small as Millersport for long. Once people learned it was Jacob, they tormented him every chance they had to the point where he'd spent most of his time indoors and away from all the criticizing. He had his doubts about how he had handled things and even went as far as trying to convince the constable to forget what he had said. It was no good though and deep inside Jacob knew that the truth needed to come out. Emma had remained by his side and encouraged him to tell the public what happened that night. He had told her he didn't think she should go to the trial, given how close she was with the victim. Emma wouldn't listen though. She said that she needed to know what happened to Amelia and even hoped that something would be said to make her believe that Amelia forgave her before she died.

At last the opening day of the trail came. The village was sure that this time it would be longer than the last which was only hours long. Thomas awoke early and was eager to get the day going. He looked at himself in the damaged mirror that was provided for him. The clothes he wore had been on him since the day they brought him to the horrible jail. He thought even with dirty clothing he was the most handsome man around. He was rubbing his hands through his greasy hair when he heard someone being let in. "It's about time you arrived," he shouted at Catherine when she poked her head through the slight opening of the door. "I hope you have a wash tub for me and clean clothes, Catherine." He hadn't called her 'mother' since he was old enough to attend school.

"Thomas please," she pleaded once again as she stepped into the room. She didn't need him to tell her what to bring on such an important date. Placing the small basin of hot water down on the only table in the room, she reminded him how much trouble she had gone through just to get there. "You know Thomas, that it isn't easy for me to bring you these things. Everyone is stopping me on the streets looking for the latest information."

"You should just ignore them," Thomas shouted at her for her ignorance. Catherine looked down at her shoes. She would have liked to put him in his place but knew that would get her in trouble. Truth was, she couldn't let herself fall out of the social circle and wanted to talk to all the women who met her along the way to the constable's station. She took a clean towel and hand clothe out of the bag she carried along, hung his suit up so it wouldn't wrinkle, and then told him to wash up as she stepped outside the door.

"Where is the soap?" Thomas snapped. He had his hands in the water searching for the bar, not caring how much water he was spilling. He heard his mother answer, telling him she must've forgotten to take it out of the bag. "Next time, don't be so stupid," he yelled at her. He cleaned himself up and put on his suit before telling her she could reenter the room.

"You'll find your socks and shoes in this other bag," she informed him. "I can't stay. I'll see you in a few hours at the town hall."

"No, I don't want you there," Thomas instructed her. He knew she was too emotional and the last thing he needed was for his mother to embarrass him. "There's no need, the last trial was over before it began and so will this one."

Catherine said nothing to him but she would not stay home as her only son stood trial for murder. Instead she hurried herself off but before leaving, she leaned over to kiss him on the forehead.

Thomas felt he was too old for a mother's kiss and moved away just seconds before her lips reached his head. Catherine stopped and thought for a moment about what she should say to him but knew that nothing would bring him closer to her. She stood and walked out the door.

Once again, Henry had gathered his family to attend the trial together. This time Beth had stayed at the Samuels house to care for Millie, David Jr., and for little Mary. She had made an agreement with Ruth and the two ladies would take turns so they each could hear what was going on. As soon as he saw she had the children settled, Henry led his family off towards the Meeting house.

When they arrived, they noticed Patrick waiting for them by the entrance of the building. Anna rushed up to him and they embraced each other. Henry noticed but said nothing. His mind was still wondering what Jacob had said that brought everyone together to try another man. With Patrick joining them as if he were part of the family, they entered the building and took their seats in the first row. Minutes later they noticed the District Attorney walk in the room and move towards them. They all knew him from the first trial and hoped that this time he would make the jury believe that Thomas was guilty. The District Attorney looked at Patrick but made no comments about being surprised to see him there.

The crowd behind them had got excited as Thomas Van Martin was escorted by his fancy attorney. He glanced over to the family and showed a sarcastic smile. By the end of the day, he told himself, he would be set free and would then let them know what he thought of them. Thomas took his seat and looked around the room. He waved at all the people he knew like he was away for a long trip and returned just in time for church service. He wasn't nervous at all about how the day would go since he was convinced that it was all a waste of time.

Soon after Daniel and Catherine Van Martin entered the room and everyone grew silent. They eyed the parents' every move as if they were the ones who should've been convicted. The two sat behind Thomas and Catherine reached up to rub her son's shoulder. He brushed her off and reminded her he didn't want her there.

Catherine sat back in her seat and waited for the trial to begin. Daniel then leaned up and whispered back and forth to the defending attorney. He sat back, glanced at his wife and then to everyone else and too smiled. Like his son, he wasn't the least bit nervous. This trial would prove his son innocent and then everyone else who didn't side with him would have to be punished somehow.

Anna sat away from her father this time and sat on the end of the row with Patrick. She looked at him as his face focused on the front of the room where the judge would sit. He was edgy because he knew that when he sat in the defendant's seat, he was innocent. He hoped that it wasn't the case for Thomas and that they would learn the truth. Anna kept her eye on him until he turned her way and said, "I'm wondering if you should be here, Anna. I know you've grown up since then but I still am not sure if you should hear what will be said."

"I'll be fine," she whispered to him. She knew that hearing all the details would be the hardest thing she would ever have to do, but it was something she needed; and she needed to hear it first hand and not sugar coated by her father.

Before long Judge Harrison had made his now second entrance into the Millersport Meeting house and looked at all the familiar faces he had seen the last time he was there for the same murder. He was skeptical about taking on the case a second time but was assured that this time the local authorities had the right man. Before pounding his gavel, he looked at the two attorneys out on the floor. He knew the District Attorney since they had worked together for the previous trail but he worried when he saw the defendant's attorney. His name was Joseph Maxwell and had been in Albany a few times to help out. From what Harrison knew Maxwell had only lost a few cases and won hundreds in his career. It was an impressive number for anyone on his side but intimidating for anyone who wasn't. Continuing his look around the room, the judge made eye contact with the man he swore was the defendant the last time he presided over this murder. He wasn't surprised to see the man in attendance, recalling how the man had said he was a friend of the victim, but more surprised to see him sit with the immediate family. Things sure seemed strange in this small village. Moments later he raised his gavel and then dropped it hard on the desk to make the onlookers aware that court had begun.

Chapter Thirty

     Judge Harrison turned toward the jury and told them that the opening statements would begin and then turned towards the District Attorney and gave the sign to start. Richard Young had known this case like the back of his hand. He had spent two weeks refreshing his memory of what had happened in this small village when the innocent girl was killed. He remembered the family's distraught faces as the then accused was found not guilty and set free. They had hoped to settle the case, then and there, but it didn't turn out like they had planned. Before speaking, he once again glanced at Patrick Buchanan and pondered about the man's relations with the family. Something must have changed for them to allow the man to sit so close to them. He decided that if this current trial lasted like most did and he was forced to spend time in Millersport, he would question the family and find out what had changed. Then he looked straight at the jury who were waiting for him to begin, and realized that he had a job to do. He began his opening speech. "Gentlemen of the jury," he started, "Let me update you on what is going on here. On August 25, in the year 1813, Amelia Samuels was said to have argued with a friend, and then talked to her sister, and was last seen by two elderly ladies who regret to this day letting the girl leave their sight. She was within twenty rods of her father's house when those two ladies turned leaving Amelia to walk the rest of the way by herself. Twenty rods," he reminded them, "Isn't that far but someone had stopped her from reaching her destination. Through-out this trial I will prove to you that the defendant here, Thomas Van Martin, abducted and pre-meditated the murder. With the help of witnesses who can vouch for the way Mr. Van Martin treated Amelia before she died and with an eye witness who had come forward to tell the authorities everything he saw, I will leave no doubt in your minds we have the right man on trial. I know that when all is said and done, you will find him guilty and the Samuels will finally be able to see their beloved's killer receive the proper punishment." He paused from looking straight at them and turned towards the residents sitting on the edge of their seats waiting to see how the events would unfold. "And I think it's safe to assume," he added without looking at the jury, "That it's not only the family of the victim who want answers but all the citizens of Millersport. This is a small village where crimes of this nature never happen and they've been affected. It's time to put their minds to ease as well. Thank you."

"Gentlemen," Maxwell stood up as soon as Young had taken his seat. "If you know anything of this case at all, you would know that the last time someone was on trial for this same murder the local authorities didn't do their homework. They put the blame on the first man they found convenient and now they're doing the same. To be honest with you, I do not know who committed this crime but it wasn't my client. What the District Attorney has failed to tell you was that Thomas Van Martin was engaged to marry Amelia Samuels. He couldn't wait for their wedding day and couldn't have been more proud to have a wife such as the young girl. You'll find out throughout the course of this trial she didn't want to marry him but as far as Thomas is concerned, he wasn't the one forcing her into marriage, her father was." The silent room of onlookers turned their heads towards Henry in shock.

"Your Honor," Young yelled out. "Mr. Samuels is not the one on trial."

Judge Harrison agreed with the District Attorney and advised the defending attorney to not make such comments against the family. Then Harrison told him to continue.

"I'm sorry," he apologized more to the judge than to Henry. Joseph Maxwell was the perfect match for the Van Martins, considering he presented himself like them. Even before becoming a successful attorney, he had come from a rich family and never failed to show his arrogance. "Furthermore," he continued talking to the jury, "Another thing the authorities failed to check was where my client was on the night in question. He had been in Kaatskill and one grocer in that town even confirmed that when they searched for Amelia."

Henry glanced towards the constable who was looking back. They had a group of men find out if the neighboring town had seen anything but none of the information that the men came home with could help them. The grocer they spoke to had said it was too dark to even describe the man. Henry leaned forward and whispered what he knew into Young's ear. The District Attorney turned and thanked Henry and told him they could use such information as the trial continued.

"And in conclusion," Maxwell finished his opening statement to the jury. "I will prove to you that Thomas Van Martin is just as much a victim in this case. The testimony that Mr. Young claims he will present to you is false and once again by someone who just wants this case closed once and for all. You will find Thomas not guilty, thank you." Then he took his seat and knew that the fun would continue.

They took a brief, ten minute recess, and when they returned, the prosecution called witnesses to the stand. The first person called up was Emma. Many people had snickered about a woman testifying at the last trial, and most of the same people let out an uproar again this time but the judge allowed her to speak. He knew that they were now fighting time and anyone who remembered anything would be a help to the case. She stood and placed her hand on the bible and was sworn in before taking her seat. Emma seemed to be very nervous and the defending attorney noted her behavior. Young began, "Please tell the jury who you are and how you knew the victim."

"My name is Emma Cooper," Emma explained. She never thought she would be in this position but was glad to help. She hoped that everything she had to say would convince the jury that Thomas was the guilty one. "Amelia and I were best friends."

"Did you know the defendant?"

Emma answered her questions without hesitation. "Yes Sir, I've known him all of my life."

Young updated the jury on the relationship between the girls and stated that Amelia had often told Emma that she felt uncomfortable around Thomas and when asked to confirm it, Emma agreed. "Now can you tell us about the last time you saw her?"

Emma looked down. It was still a subject she didn't want to talk about and hoped that too much information wouldn't be forced out of her. She felt comfortable talking to the District Attorney but was uneasy about Maxwell. "She was angry," she answered.

"Was she angry with you?"

"Not just myself," Emma furthered her answer. "But I felt she had a lot of resentments towards me. She slapped me across the face which is behavior that Amelia had never shown before. I knew then that something was wrong with her."

"Did she say anything to you that would make you think that it's possible for Mr. Van Martin to kill her?"

Emma looked towards Thomas but continued to tell the truth. "She said that she knew what was going on and that she didn't have to marry him."

Young paused and looked at Thomas. "Why would he want to kill her over such a statement?"

"Because he was obsessive of her," Emma responded.

Young asked Emma to explain to the jury how Thomas would have known about what Amelia had said to Emma. "After she took off, Jacob, and I went to find him. At the time I thought nothing of it. I thought I would help her. I hesitated on telling him what she had said but Jacob thought it was for the best."

"And how did Thomas react?"

"He was upset," she cried out. "He took off straight away and said he had to find her. I don't know what happened after that."

Richard Young then turned his direction back to the jury and told them that information was never given to the local constable before. The searchers had no idea that Thomas had been looking for Amelia the night she disappeared. They would've questioned him about it. Then he looked at Emma and the judge and said he had no further questions.

Harrison asked Maxwell if he had questions for the witness and he did. He stood from his chair and walked towards the girl who looked scared. He wasn't about to beat around the bush, he wanted to go straight to the girl's weak spot. "Miss Cooper," he started unsympathetic. "Tell me why Amelia was angry with you."

"We argued," Emma answered knowing that the two had never exchanged bad words to each other.

"That's a lie, isn't it?" Maxwell shouted loud enough to be heard outside of the building. "Is it true she was angry with you for interfering with her deceitful relationship with Patrick Buchanan?"

"What is your point?" Judge Harrison questioned.

"Your Honor," he continued. "And gentlemen of the jury, I'm trying to prove that Thomas didn't run off to search for Amelia because he was afraid she wouldn't marry him. Instead, he ran off looking for her to make sure she was safe from Buchanan." Again he turned towards Emma and asked her to answer the original question.

Emma burst in tears. They were still trying to pin the blame on Patrick even though she, and many others, agree that he didn't hurt Amelia at all. She was shameful of her behavior and now would have to admit what she had done in front of everyone. "Yes," she answered. "She was upset because I told Mr. Buchanan that she was just using him to get out of her marriage to Thomas. I thought I was protecting her but now I know that she didn't need protection from

Patrick." She looked over to where he sat and again hoped that he would forgive her.

"No further questions," the attorney stated and then took a seat. Harrison looked to Young as the District Attorney again stood and called his next witness. He called David to the stand and when the brother was sworn in, he began his questioning. "How are you related to Amelia?"

David answered, "I'm her older brother."

"You recently told the constable a story about your sister you hadn't thought of when she disappeared. Can you share it with us now?"

"Yes Sir," David responded. Once again he told the story of Amelia's behavior after her picnic with Thomas. He seemed to get upset as the story went on but could remain calm.

"Did you believe what she'd told you," Young quizzed. He knew that David's testimony would make the jury realize how violent Thomas Van Martin was.

David had no problem answering the question. "She had never told me lies. I had no reason not to believe her."

"Did she ever speak to you about Thomas in that manner again?"

"No Sir, not to my recollection."

The District Attorney had set out what he wanted, and that was to inform the jury of Van Martin's temper. He was finished with David and hoped that the defendant's attorney wouldn't be so tough.

Maxwell stood and then paced back and forth for a few minutes before asking his first question. He needed a moment to make sure he had David's story straight. "Were you there at the picnic, Mr. Samuels?"

"No, I was home, and she came afterwards."

"Then how do you know she bit his tongue when my client told your father it was his lip?" Thomas was afraid that the picnic incident might come up so he had already told his side of the story to his attorney.

264

David wasn't afraid of Maxwell or the Van Martins, he was just telling the story as he heard it. "Because," he answered, "Amelia, and I were close and I know that she would never tell me a fib. David knew that it would help to tell the jury that Amelia had also told the same story to Anna but didn't want them to call Anna to the stand. He knew that she wouldn't be strong enough to stand up to this man. David must have said enough to satisfy the attorney because Maxwell had too said he was done with questioning him. David could step down. He wasn't sure if his story was convincing or not to the jury but he hoped that he helped. He took his seat with the family and prepared for more testimony but the judge had informed the court they would take a two hour recess.

Chapter Thirty-One

After the break, Richard Young got right to the eye witness. He would prefer to have Jacob Miller testify the following day but changed his mind when he remembered how fast the previous trail had ended. Thomas Van Martin claimed that he wasn't in the village on the night in question and Young was afraid that the jury would buy the story. He knew to convince them; he would have to bring Jacob in early. After everyone took their seats, and the judge informed him it was time to resume, Young called Jacob to the stand.

Jacob stood and could feel a hundred or more eyes on him. He had wished that he could stay as calm as Emma and David but knew that he couldn't. His hands sweat, and he rubbed them against his pants as he walked to the stand. When asked, he placed his hands on the Bible and vowed to tell the truth and nothing but the truth. He was told to be seated and when he faced out to the crowd, his nervousness grew. Jacob looked over to Thomas who was snarling at him. He took a deep breath and let the District Attorney see he was ready to begin. It would be a long afternoon, he told himself.

"Mr. Miller," Young started. "Thomas Van Martin was your friend. Am I correct?"

"He was," Jacob gave a hesitant answer. He'd wished that they remained friends but there was a wedge between them after Amelia had been killed.

"And the two of you haven't been as kind towards each other as you used to be ever since the death of our victim?"

Jacob nodded his head and heard the judge tell him he would need to speak all of his answers. "That is correct," he answered out loud.

Young paced back and forth as he asked the rest of his questions. He knew that whatever Jacob said would affect everyone in the room. "Let us start with the confrontation you and Emma received from Amelia before she disappeared. Did you think something was wrong with her at the time?"

"Yes, she was in a hurry to go somewhere and then when she slapped Emma, I knew something was wrong."

"What did you do next?"

Jacob looked to Emma and then to Thomas. She had already told the jury they went to Thomas and like Emma, Jacob regretted that too. He looked around but could see that the judge wanted him to say it. "We went to Thomas and told him about her behavior."

"Why?"

Jacob hadn't expected this kind of questioning. He thought he was only there to tell the court what Thomas had done to Amelia. He continued to look around as he became confused. "I'm not sure I know what you mean, Sir."

Young paused from pacing. He was trying to lead up to the murder, but it was apparent that the witness didn't know. "I'm trying to establish why you felt it was important to tell him what was going on. I'm trying to understand what would make him want to kill an innocent girl."

"It was my idea to go to him," Jacob answered. "Neither of us thought he would want to hurt her. I figured that he should know that his fiancée slapped my girlfriend."

"Did you want to see Amelia punished?"

"Not the way he did," Jacob insisted. "I had nothing against the girl but I didn't think she should get away with the way she treated Emma. I thought Thomas would say something to Amelia to correct her."

"What happened after Thomas ran off to find her?" Young wanted the jury and the family to hear what had happened, the things they never heard before.

"I took Emma home and then took off to find Thomas," Jacob again answered. He knew that he was getting closer to the murder and sweat even more. He also knew that he would be asked why he went searching for Thomas so he continued before giving the District Attorney the opportunity. "Emma was concerned about her friend and was uneasy about us telling Thomas. When he ran off, it made her worry even more. I went to find him to make sure he would not do anything he would be sorry for."

Henry and his family sat in their seats waiting to hear what was coming up. It had been a long time for them and the pieces of the puzzle were going to finally come together. Henry glanced down the row of seats to Patrick and wondered how he felt. He learned, since his alliance with the man, that Patrick was disappointed in himself for not being able to protect Amelia.

While Henry thought of Patrick's feelings, Young continued his questioning. "Did you find Thomas?"

"Yes," Jacob answered. "I found him before he found Amelia."

"And what happened?"

Jacob thought about the question. He was so afraid of how his words sounded and didn't want to mess up. "I asked him what he was doing and he said he would punish Amelia for her behavior. He also said he would punish her for spending private time with a strange man."

Young shook his head in confusion as if to let the jury know that he missed something. "Did you tell him about Emma's interference?"

"No, we didn't tell him about Mr. Buchanan and I don't know how he knew."

The District Attorney stopped pacing in front of the jury members and put his hands on the rail that divided them from the rest of the room. He didn't take his eyes off of them when he asked Jacob Miller to tell them what had happened that fatal night. "Mr. Miller, please tell us what happened next and continue until you are done."

Jacob felt an uneasy pit growing in his stomach. He knew the time had come that he'd been waiting two weeks for. He licked his lips which had become parched and swallowed a lump that had gathered in his throat. Then he began. "We were close to her house when Thomas saw her walking in our direction. He asked me to hide so she couldn't see me and that he would do the same. I didn't understand why he felt the need to sneak upon her but didn't have the time to question him. As she walked past, Thomas grabbed her and covered her mouth. She tried to break free of him but Thomas is stronger than most people give him credit for. Amelia tried to cry out for help but his hand was too tight over her mouth and allowed no sounds out. Amelia turned her head and she saw him. She fought harder to be freed. She didn't see me and when I attempted to move, Thomas had warned me to stay still. At that point she didn't know that I was there. Thomas lifted her and carried her away. I followed but remained hidden so she didn't see me.

He carried her almost to the creek north of her house but made the mistake of putting her down for a rest. She took advantage of his hands being off of her and she took off. Thomas was mad and chased her. Amelia would have headed back towards the village and he didn't want that. I wasn't there when she ran from him, I was still trying to catch up myself, but I arrived just as Thomas grabbed a loose plank from the creek's bridge and hit her in the back of the head. I was shocked. I didn't think he would go that far to punish her for her behavior. I was believing that he was taking it too far and for Emma's sake, and Amelia's, I screamed at him and told him to stop. I said she didn't deserve what Thomas had just done to her. That is when she realized that I was there but I'm still not sure if she knew it was me or not, she seemed very dazed after he hit her.

The strike on her head had forced her to the ground and Thomas knelt over her and punched her in the face and upper arms. When Amelia cried out, Thomas thought that her sounds were bound to be heard by someone so he jumped on her chest to muffle her cries. It worked, though I insisted that he was going beyond punishment and that he should stop. She was still crying and calling out for help but she could barely speak not to mention scream. Thomas turned and told me he was just putting her inline so she didn't misbehave anymore. I thought he was too harsh, but he assured me he was doing what was right. He said a woman had to be beat once in a while or they would talk back the way Amelia had.

While he was arguing with me about whether he was treating her right or not, she crawled away. By the time he noticed, her dress had become torn and her leg was bleeding from scrapping against some rocks. I felt bad for her and decided it was time to stop him but he threatened me to stay out of it. I was afraid of him by that point, I've never seen him act that way before and I couldn't believe what he was doing, so I took a few steps back but for her sake I didn't leave. Thomas must have thought I was gone because his torture continued. He kept one hand on her to hold her down and used the other to take his belt off. I thought he would use it to hit her but instead he tied her wrists together."

Jacob took a deep breath before continuing. He could already see the alarm on her family's face and knew that the rest of the story would upset them even more. He was being urged by both the judge and Young to go on so Jacob continued. "Thomas tied her wrist together and then placed them over her head. The next thing I knew, Thomas was on top of her and raping her. I ran to him and tried to pull him off of her but he insisted that I leave the area. She was crying and her face begged me to help her but I couldn't. I should have but I was too afraid and didn't know what to do. Thomas warned me I should never say a word to anyone about what I saw and assured me that everything would be fine and that even Amelia would respect him more from that moment on. I did what I was told and ran home. When Amelia was reported missing, I knew that he killed her but her body wasn't found in the creek when it was searched. He told me I should've had more faith in him and once again I believed that he wasn't responsible for her disappearance. He

270

said that she ran away after the way he punished her and I thought that made sense."

The entire room was crying or tear-streaked except Thomas. Jacob wasn't happy that he had to tell the entire village what he had seen but a part of him was glad it was over, for now at least. He knew that soon Maxwell would question him more. Jacob looked at Henry and finished speaking to him more than to anyone else, "I wouldn't have left her if I would have realized he would kill her. I'm sorry."

Even Young was choked up to hear Jacob's story, but he swallowed the sadness he felt and said, "No further questions."

Judge Harrison took a moment before allowing Maxwell to take his turn. He looked around the room and saw the hurt in the citizens' faces. Harrison knew that they believed everything that Miller had said but was more concerned about whether the jury did. He turned to Maxwell and asked him to continue.

Joseph Maxwell whispered into his client's ear and then faced the judge. "Your Honor," he started. "I request the right to question this witness later." The room filled with surprise and Harrison had to call for order before they quieted. The defending attorney continued, "I'd like to prove to the jury what kind of man Thomas Van Martin is, his credentials so to speak, before asking Miller to clarify some of his answers."

The judge was surprised just as much as the crowd but agreed to let Maxwell question Jacob later in the trial. He turned to the witness and reminded him he was still under oath and not to speak a word to anyone about the case. Then he decided that the family had heard enough for one day and recessed for the night. "In that case, court is adjured until tomorrow morning at nine." Then he again struck his gavel against the desk and stood to leave the building.

Outside Patrick paced back and forth, waiting for his chance to speak to the District Attorney. The women were sent home and Young was with Henry, David, and Phillip, discussing what would happen next. Patrick wanted to be part of that conversation but was skeptical about how the District Attorney would feel about having the ex-suspect joining forces with him. He had hoped that Henry would speak for him and explain why he was there but he was too emotional from the testimony. Patrick heard Young tell the immediate family that there was still no motive in the murder and that he was afraid of how Maxwell would twist Jacob's words in their favor. Patrick couldn't stand the wait any longer, he had the missing piece to the puzzle and though it might jeopardize his new friendship with Henry; it had to be told. "Excuse me, Mr. Young, but I think I know what his motive was," Patrick exclaimed as he moved closer to the others.

"What are you doing here in the first place?" He quizzed. Before Patrick could answer for himself, Young heard the others tell him they had made amends and that Patrick will help in any way he could. "All right then, what is it you think you know?"

Patrick decided that he shouldn't say anything in front of Amelia's family and asked to speak to the District Attorney alone. The truth would hurt these men more than they were already and Patrick didn't want to tell them to their faces. He pulled Young to the side and the two men talked.

Henry was astonished. He wanted to know why Patrick was being secretive when he thought they had discussed everything together. He gave the other two a puzzled look, wondering if they had any ideas what was going on, but they shrugged their shoulders back at him.

"Put me on the stand tomorrow," Patrick insisted to the District Attorney. If he learned anything about Thomas Van Martin, he knew that what he had to say could well be a motive to kill.

Young looked around to make sure nobody could hear what they were talking about. He knew why Patrick didn't want to say this in front of the victim's family. "He appears to have anger problems and this could well be what

272

we need, but," Young explained. "You're not on my list of witnesses and I'm not sure if Maxwell would agree to let you testify."

"You have to," Patrick chimed in. He knew that what Jacob had told the court was strong but yet it wasn't strong enough for a defense attorney with Maxwell's reputation. "I'm needed more in this case than you give me credit for. I'm not proud of what happened but I'm glad it did. And, I know that Thomas Van Martin knew and his temper must have flared."

"Fine," Young reluctantly agreed. He would have to convince both the judge and Maxwell but it shouldn't be too much of a task. "I don't foresee Maxwell giving me too hard of a time, considering they still think that you are the guilty one." He shook Buchanan's hand and then turned back toward Henry and the others; then said his goodbyes to them.

When Young stepped away, Patrick rejoined the other men who were very interested in what he had to say and why he couldn't say it in front of them. He assured them that everything would be fine. Both David and Phillip said that they were headed home; leaving Henry alone with Patrick. "Tell me, what did you say to him?" Henry pleaded for an answer.

Putting his hands in his pockets and lowering his head, Patrick found it hard to look into Henry's eyes. He felt as though he was betraying a new friendship and breaking Henry's trust but this wasn't something he could tell him face to face. Still, he didn't want the elder man to hate him again after hearing his testimony so he tried to make an agreement before he even said a word on the stand. "Henry," he started. "You and I have put our differences behind us and I want nothing to interfere but I'm afraid what I told Young would do just that. I will testify tomorrow, if the judge allows it, and you will not like what you hear."

"How do you know? Test me," Henry interrogated Patrick. If Patrick knew something about his daughter's case then he demanded that he knew too.

"No," Patrick shouted. "You'll hear it in court tomorrow but I want you to remember that I loved your daughter very much and will do anything it takes to see the bastard who killed her pay for his crimes; even if that means you detest me again." He waited for Henry to speak to him but no words were spoken until he spoke up again. "I hope you'll take the time to understand and that it doesn't come to hatred. We're not so different, you and I."

Henry's curiosity was more than he could stand. He wanted to know what was going on but Patrick wasn't speaking a word of it. He wondered what the man could say that would cause hatred and how they weren't so different. "All right," he replied. "I'll keep that in mind." They shook hands and then parted their ways agreeing that they would meet up at the town hall the next morning.

Chapter Thirty-Two

When court was called back to order the following morning, Judge Harrison looked to Richard Young and asked, "You've called your last witness yesterday. Am I to presume that is correct?"

The District Attorney looked towards the defendant and then up to the judge. He wasn't sure how this turn of events would go over with them. "No Sir Your Honor," he stated. "I would like to call Patrick Buchanan to the stand."

Uproar arose in the crowd and, like the day before, Harrison had to demand order by banging his gavel. He wasn't sure what Young was up to but had no time for interruptions such as this. "Mr. Young, he isn't on your list of witnesses. What is the meaning to all of this?"

"Your Honor, I object," Maxwell shouted. If anyone would have tricks up his sleeve, it would be him and not Young. "My client has never met Buchanan before she disappeared and I don't believe that Buchanan has anything to say that could leave the jury to believe my client is guilty."

By now the judge was disturbed and wasn't in the mood to play with the two fighting attorneys. He pointed his finger at both of them and demanded that they come forward to speak with him. At the sidebar, Harrison questioned the District Attorney, "What's this all about?"

"I feel that Buchanan has sufficient testimony to prove a motive."

"That is crap, Your Honor, and you know it," Maxwell insisted. Young was stalling in the trial, perhaps he didn't want his key witness to be cross examined just yet.

"If it's crap, Maxwell," Young almost shouted, "Then you would have no problem with him speaking his word. What do you have to lose besides this case?"

Again the judge had enough. Maxwell wasn't happy about the change in the witness list but it wasn't his court. "Fine," he decided. "I'll let him testify but I hope for your sake he comes through with a motive."

The men turned back to their places though the defendant's attorney wasn't pleased. Young glanced at Patrick to let him know that it was all right for him to come forward. As Patrick passed him, Young whispered, "You realize that he will come back and fight everything you tell me." Patrick continued up to the stand, was sworn in, and took his seat waiting for the questions to begin. Young looked around the room and could see everyone sitting on the edge of their seats. He began, "Mr. Buchanan, did you know the defendant before Miss Samuels was killed?"

"No, Sir," Patrick answered but continued on to explain himself. "I've never met him before but knew of his demeanor from Amelia."

"Can you please tell the jury why you think you know what Van Martin's motive was?" Young wasn't convinced that this would help his case or not but maybe there would be some kind of reaction from the defendant's face to make the jury believe what Buchanan was saying.

Patrick took a deep breath and looked out to the Samuels family. He had forgotten that Anna would sit there anxiously waiting to hear what he had to say. At that moment he wished that he could yell out to her and tell her to go home. Everyone was staring at him, waiting for him to speak. "Between Miller's testimony and the autopsy report, we know that Amelia was raped by her killer."

"And how does a motive fit into that statement, Mr. Buchanan?"

He swallowed and licked his dry mouth before continuing. Many of the villagers accepted him for who he was but admitting what he shared with Amelia was bound to tear them away again. "When Thomas Van Martin raped her, he found out she wasn't a virgin."

The crowd was outraged and made more noise than ever. Henry was sick to his stomach and couldn't even look to his family to see how they were reacting. He wanted to scream but couldn't find the strength in him. It was no wonder why Patrick had asked him to understand the day before.

Anna glared her eyes ahead at Patrick and couldn't believe that he dared corrupt her sister's reputation the way he did. For a moment in time, he wasn't the man she thought him to be but in time she too would come around to forgive him. Thomas had heard more than he wanted to and decided, once again, to play the innocent victim and mournful fiancé. "You son-of-a-bitch," he screamed as he jumped from his seat. "She was my fiancée, not yours."

Harrison used all of his might to bang his gavel that seemed to be unheard. "Order, I said order in this court," he demanded. It took several minutes for Maxwell to calm his client and for the rest of the room to return their attention to the testimony.

When all was quiet again, Young continued. "Are you suggesting that Thomas Van Martin killed Amelia because his fiancée wasn't pure?"

"Exactly," was all that Patrick could say. He had let them all down but worst of all, he had let Amelia down by revealing their secret. He heard Young announce that he didn't have more questions and knew that Maxwell was coming to take his shots.

"Mr. Buchanan, you were once on trial for the same murder; were you not?" Maxwell was determined to bring Patrick down and clear his client.

"Yes."

"And by some miracle that an Army General appeared and cleared your name, you were freed. Isn't that the truth?"

Patrick nodded but received the same advice that Jacob had received from the judge. Making himself heard, Patrick answered. "Yes that is true."

277

Maxwell paused from questioning Patrick and turned his direction to the jury. "Gentleman, this man here was found not guilty by chance but many still believed he was the killer even after he was declared innocent. Now he tells us that the victim has had sexual relations and we can only assume he meant with himself. He says his word is proving my client had a motive to kill but perhaps it was his own motive he is speaking of." He paced back and forth for a minute before turning back to Patrick to continue pressuring him for answers. "Did you force yourself onto her?"

"No way," Patrick insisted. "Amelia and I were in love. She was devastated by her best friend's ploy to separate us and decided that she would not allow others to determine her fate for her. She wanted me to make love to her."

"So you gave the lady what she wanted?"

"Not right away, I told her it wasn't right," Patrick explained. Hoping it was helping the family understand more than it did the jury. "She said she would rather marry me than Thomas and then seduced me." He looked out to the audience who were giving him evil looks as if he was the devil. "I'm only man," he remarked in defense.

Maxwell chuckled at the situation. Buchanan was putting himself into a grave and didn't even realize it. "Mr. Buchanan, it's my understanding that after your premarital intimacy the two of you argued and she ran from you. Could it be because she became remorseful for giving herself to you?"

If Patrick could have, he would've jumped over the stand and strangled the defense attorney. The man knew nothing of his love for Amelia or hers for him. "No, we argued because she found out why her father was making her marry Thomas. She didn't like what she heard, but I knew that her anger wasn't guided at me."

"Oh that is right, Mr. Buchanan," Maxwell stated as if he didn't know what happened that night. "She ran off to marry my client as soon as she could."

"As far as I know," Patrick replied, "Yes."

"And as far as you are concerned, that was enough to chase after her and murder her in cold blood."

Anna was upset with what Patrick admitted but still knew that he wasn't the one who had taken her sister away. She had listened to all she cared for and would not let them back Patrick into the corner. "No," she stood and shouted. "He didn't kill her."

Phillip, who sat right next to her, stood and grabbed a hold of her but, Anna fought him to be let go. The judge was calling for order again and she could hear her father demanding that she be taken out of the building. She struggled, wanted to be there for her sister's sake, but was too weak to get away from her strong brother-in-law. He took her outside and stayed with her until she calmed down.

Back inside the building, things were settling down. Harrison instructed Maxwell to go on. He was satisfied even though Buchanan never had the chance to reply to his last statement. As far as he was concerned, it had put doubt in the jury. "Your Honor, I have no further questions."

Patrick could step down and Harrison declared a recess. As the crowd dwindled out of the building, Patrick looked towards Henry. He would not run from the family over what was said so he walked right up to them.

"You're a bastard," Henry snapped when Patrick approached. All that Patrick had done was confuse the jury of who was the killer and that made Henry angry. He didn't know what he would do if Thomas was found not guilty.

There were women standing in the group who had heard more than enough of unladylike talk and Patrick didn't want to make things worse. He thought of the best words to use. "Say what you like, Henry but I told you, you and I were not that different. Your daughter loved me enough to want to give herself to me and we promised each other we would wed as soon as we could. Did you promise your brother's wife you would marry her before the two of you engaged in premarital sex?"

Henry was glad that Ruth hadn't been at the trial that day and didn't hear what Patrick had just said in front of his entire family. He glared into Patrick's eyes but could see that the man would not back down. He was right he told himself, and his relationship with Amelia wasn't any different. Henry turned towards his family and asked them not to mention any of this Ruth and that they shouldn't turn their backs onto Patrick for speaking the truth. "If I weren't so stupid to begin with," he said to Patrick, "She would've been able to tell me about you and by now you would've wed." The two men shook hands, and the others returned to their seats.

Phillip had returned with Anna right after the commotion with Patrick had ended. He glanced around and whispered into Minnie's ear. She returned the whisper, and he sat down next to her without saying another word.

Anna saw that her family was seated and were all silent so she sat in her seat saying nothing to them. She leaned her head towards Patrick and spoke. "Why couldn't you have told me that before?"

"It was between your sister and me," Patrick answered. "The only reason I asked to testify is because I'm convinced that after Thomas raped her, he was angered even more by what he had discovered." He looked towards the young girl and then wiped a single tear that had formed in the corner of her eye. "Besides," he added. "I told you yesterday you shouldn't be at the trial, remember?"

Anna nodded her head but didn't have the chance to respond. Several bangs from the gavel were heard, and the room became quiet once again. It was time to hear more.

It was then time for Maxwell to take over the trial since Young had no more witnesses he wanted to call up. The defense attorney wasted the rest of the day by calling up men employed at the brickyard, neighbors, and friends. They all spoke of Thomas as if he were the most caring man of all of Millersport. There wasn't doubt in anyone's mind that all of those witnesses were threatened by the Van Martins. One by one they all said that Thomas never lied, and that he was

280

always there for them when they needed help with something. The men said that their daughters would've cherished the chance of courting him and that made the few families were against him to chuckle amongst them. Everything that was said in Thomas' defense was believed by the jurors. They were men that weren't from Millersport and some believed that was the only reason they could believe Thomas was a good man.

The testimonials made things look bad for the prosecution. Young knew that his only key witness was Jacob Miller but Maxwell was out to prove Jacob a liar. It worried Richard Young and the victim's family could see it on his face. He turned back to Henry and whispered, "Don't worry. We have a fifty-fifty chance right about now."

Looking down at his notes and glancing at his pocket watch, Harrison knew that it was getting late. The last witness he knew Maxwell would call up would be Jacob Miller, and he had a feeling that testimonial would take awhile to wrap up. He adjourned court once again until the next morning. He lifted his gavel, dropped it onto the desk, and then stood to leave. This trial was more interesting that the last but Harrison was afraid that it was one person's word against another's and that nothing would be solved. As he left the Meeting house and walked towards the inn he was staying at, the judge hoped for the best.

Chapter Thirty-Three

The third day of the trial was the most talked about in the village. Everyone who was able was planning on attending. They had a feeling that something would break the case. It was the day that Jacob would have to testify for Thomas' attorney. Everyone believed what he had said about Thomas and Amelia but yet there were still many people who had mixed thoughts on whether he was guilty or not.

Emma had walked to the Meeting house with Jacob and was very nervous about the day's events. After hearing all the brickyard workers lie about how great Thomas was, she was skeptical to whether the jury believed what he admitted. "I'm scared, Jacob," she confessed to her beau. "What if they don't believe you now and when Maxwell gets in your face, what if they straight out think you are lying?"

"You can't think that way," Jacob responded to Emma. He had the same thoughts but prayed that things would work out. He had to have faith that his prayers would be answered or else he wouldn't have the strength to go on. "I hear people whispering, Emma," he explained. "They realize now he's the one who done all those horrible things to Amelia. How can the jury not believe me?"

They both continued on to the Meeting house and were greeted by others who were also waiting for the trial to resume. Henry walked up to them and pulled Jacob aside. "I wanted to thank you for all of your help," he told the young man. Jacob wasn't so sure he helped at all. He nodded his head to acknowledge that he understood what the elder was saying before Henry turned and walked inside the building with his family. Jacob and Emma looked at each other with hope and went inside.

Before he knew it, Jacob was called back to the stand and reminded about his oath he had previously taken. As he lowered himself to sit, he couldn't help notice the look on

Thomas' face. It was polite which scared Jacob. He knew the Van Martin man better than anyone else and knew that the only time Thomas ever acted nice is when he was up to something. Here, it was Thomas' lawyer up to something and Jacob could feel it coming a mile away.

Maxwell reminded the jury of what Jacob had already testified as Jacob sat impatient waiting for his questions. Maxwell said, "So let me get this straight. You saw Thomas carry Miss Samuels away and all you've done was follow?"

"That's right," Jacob answered. So far, not so bad, he thought. "Like I said before, I thought he was just going to strap her for her behavior."

"And you thought it was appropriate to watch?"

Jacob frowned; already Maxwell was making his words seem different. "I watched because Emma was concerned and because I was alarmed myself in his behavior. I wanted to be there for Amelia."

Both Maxwell and his client laughed. The judge looked at Thomas and he stopped but the attorney didn't. "If you wanted to be there for her so badly, then why is she dead?"

"Strike that question," Harrison instructed. "Mr. Maxwell, the witness isn't on trial here."

"Sorry Sir," Joseph Maxwell replied. He lowered his head, put his fingers on his chin, and walked back and forth for a few minutes. Then he stopped in front of the jury and continued to question Jacob. "Mr. Miller," he quizzed. "You said that my client attacked the victim, beat her senseless, and you claim he raped her. Did you see Thomas Van Martin kill Amelia Samuels with your own eyes?"

Jacob looked to the District Attorney and couldn't remember if this was talked about when he was questioned. "I have placed him at the murder scene, Sir."

"It's a simple question," Maxwell snapped at the witness. "Did you, or did you not, see my client kill her?"

It pained him to admit it but he hadn't. When he ran away that awful night, she was still breathing and as far as he knew; she was just beaten and raped. "No," he answered as low as he could.

Maxwell's enthusiasm grew. "A little louder please," he exclaimed.

"No!" Jacob wasn't a man who cried in public but felt a sting of tears escaping his eyes. There was no other explanation of Amelia's death and since he knew what he saw; Jacob had spent the last year, and a half convinced that his so-called friend was the killer.

There was an unexpected hush in the room as everyone listened to the rest of the testimony. The defending attorney went on to not only clear his client's name but also to show the court why Jacob pinned the blame on Thomas. He was calm for a few minutes as if satisfied by what Jacob had admitted. "Now," he went on. "Let us ponder about the past few weeks. Is it true that just before you went to the local authorities on my client, Thomas had said something to you and Emma Cooper that you didn't like?"

Jacob nodded his head but revealed no information. Again, the judge told him to speak up but Maxwell said that it was all right and answered his own question. "Mr. Miller, isn't it true that the only reason you pinned the blame on Thomas is because he told you he would marry Emma?" The room filled up with noise because just a handful of people knew of Thomas' plan to marry Amelia's best friend. "Admit it, Mr. Miller," Maxwell pressed on. "The only reason we're here today is because you would do anything to keep Thomas away from your girlfriend!"

A bolt of anger ripped through Jacob. Without caring of the consequences, he jumped off his seat and shouted, "Nobody has the right to treat people the way you do," he said looking straight at Thomas. He looked to Emma who looked scared to death. He wanted no one else to be with her but it was also true what he testified; yet he felt that at this point he couldn't win.

"Gentlemen," Joseph Maxwell said to the jury. "This witness didn't see my client murder the victim and he would do anything to keep my client away from Emma Cooper." He turned his direction back towards Young and gave him a smug smile. He knew that he would win yet another case and his smile was thanks for a good fight. "Your Honor; I'm finished with this witness."

"Mr. Young," Harrison acknowledged the District Attorney. Even the District Attorney was blown away by what was just said in court. Nobody told him about Thomas marrying Miller's girl. He could see why Jacob would want to protect her and keep him away but if he would've known in advance, he would've been prepared to speak now. Instead, he was left standing dumbfounded. "No, Sir. I have no questions." From behind he could feel the eyes staring at him.

The family wasn't happy that he was finished but at that moment he wasn't pleased with them either. Nothing bothered him more than when important pieces of a trial aren't told. He stood and with the best of his ability tried one last time to convince the jury that Thomas Van Martin was guilty. He gave it his all though he knew that his all would not be good enough.

After him, Maxwell closed his case to the jurors too. It had been three long days but this part of the trial was over.

The jury was instructed on what to do and they left the room to discuss the case. Everyone exited the building but all the key witnesses and the family were all quiet. They didn't know what to say to each other. Patrick joined the Samuels and tried to assure them that Thomas would be found guilty. He knew that was true. Some people left the building to return home but most stayed feeling it wouldn't take long for the jury to come to their conclusion.

The village was filled with anxiety while the jury stayed behind closed doors. More people had left the area to return to their normal daily life but still many had remained. They whispered about jurors being out sometimes for days but yet none of them felt that would be the case. Some villagers were convinced that Thomas would be sentenced to death while others still argued that he would be set free. All of them knew that one verdict, or the other, was coming soon but nobody could prepare themselves for the moment it arrived.

It had only been two hours but word that the verdict was in spread fast. Villagers dropped what they were doing in their homes, or workplaces, and ran to the Meeting house. Catherine Van Martin wrung her hands over and over again. Although she was his mother, she was still unsure. She feared that her son would be executed and cried at the thought.

"Stop it now, Catherine," Daniel insisted. He knew their case was wrapped up, and they would win. Still his wife was making a fool of herself. "It's bad enough that people are talking bad of us now. We don't need you acting like something was wrong." Just after speaking to her, Maxwell had stepped up to them and informed them it was time to go inside the town hall to hear what the jury had to say. He smiled at Daniel as he led Thomas' father into the room.

Several minutes later, they all sat in silence waiting for the word. It was the moment that Henry and his family had waited a long time to hear but now he wasn't too excited to hear the news. His insides were telling him that something wasn't right, and that things would change.

"Gentlemen of the jury," Harrison stated. "Do you have a verdict?"

One man of the jury stood up, walked to the judge and handed him a piece of paper, then walked back to his spot in the juror's box. He made no eye contact with anyone, not the District Attorney, not Henry, not even Thomas. Harrison gave the signal to continue and the lead juror stated the outcome. "We find the defendant, Thomas Van Martin, not guilty."

The room was out of control; half with excitement and half with disappointment. Catherine was so relieved that she wanted to embrace her husband but Daniel was too busy shaking hands with Maxwell. Then she tried to reach out to her son but Thomas wouldn't allow her to embrace him in public. As happy as she was, Catherine sat in her seat and said nothing to anyone. On the other side of the room, the Samuels hung their heads. They believed that they had the right man this time and weren't convinced that Thomas didn't commit the crime.

Anna lost control and cried. Patrick had opened his arms to her, and she fell into his chest and sobbed. He'd promised Amelia that he would find her killer and though the courts dismissed him, he knew that her killer sat in the front row with a satisfied look on his face.

Judge Harrison struck his gavel against the desk until the crowd quieted down and paid attention to him. They thought it was over but it wasn't. He pointed to Maxwell, Young, and to the constable and asked them all to come forward. Moments later the men returned to their spots, but the constable walked down the center of the room with a grime look on his face. The judge spoke again. "This trial is over and unless there is any physical evidence, the murder of Miss Samuels will never have another trial as long as I'm a judge. This investigation has led us to two separate but uncalled for trials. It has been a waste of the state's funds and of my time. But I have one more notice to make. The jury and I believe that we have sufficient enough evidence for a case of false swearing. Jacob Miller, you will be apprehended and tried in private for perjury."

The constable reached out and grabbed Jacob but wished that he didn't have to do it. He wasn't a follower of the Van Martins but it was the judge who was making him do this. A judge, he thought to himself, who was no doubt paid off by Daniel Van Martin and Joseph Maxwell. He knew already that Jacob wouldn't stand a chance to get out of this conviction. "Come with me, son," he said to Jacob in a tone to assure the young lad that everything would be fine.

"No, please no," Emma begged as the judge declared the trial over. She had thrown herself onto Jacob and held onto him as she cried out for someone to help him. "He isn't the one who lied," she shouted. "All those men who said Thomas was good, those were the men who should be convicted." It hurt her any to hear Jacob pleading his innocence. Soon his parents rushed to his side, but the constable had told them they could see him down at the station.

The somber villagers left the building. The judge and District Attorney were already gone and the Van Martins were taking Joseph Maxwell back to their house for a celebration. Henry had sent his family home but remained for the sake of the Miller family. Patrick had stayed by his side and both men were overwhelmed with the outcome of the court. "She's right," Henry said to Patrick. "Jacob doesn't deserve what is happening to him."

Patrick agreed with Henry but didn't know what to say at the moment. His head was full of terrible thoughts of what he should do next. Amelia's murder wasn't over and he was determined to make Thomas pay.

Chapter Thirty-Four

A little over a week after the trial ended, Patrick stood and talked to Henry in his store. They had formed a bond and were both surprised how courteous they were towards each other. They were allies but still had differences. Henry couldn't emotionally continue investigating Amelia's death and had accepted what the judge had said at the end of the trial. Patrick, though, had a promise to keep and was determined to stick to his word. Thomas Van Martin was freed but Patrick knew he wasn't innocent.

It didn't take long for Thomas to strut around the village to show everyone he wasn't to be messed with. The other villagers might have feared him but Patrick knew that he could still break the younger twerp in two if given the chance. He had to give credit to Thomas for staying clear of himself and of the Samuels family. Returning his thoughts to the conversation he was having with Henry, Patrick stated, "We can't just let him get away with it."

Henry frowned; he knew there was no point in proving that Thomas was the culprit since none of the authorities would hear of it. "We have to go on, Buchanan." He looked around and when Patrick didn't respond to him, Henry added, "You know that she'll forgive you of a broken promise."

A loud bang rang through the room as Patrick slammed his fist onto the counter. He couldn't rest knowing he hadn't come through with his word. He was running out of support in his decision to keep searching. The Samuels family wanted to heal their wounds and face life again, and the constable would do nothing else until there was evidence. It was grim because everyone knew that any evidence left by the monster was long gone, even before her body was found.

"And what about Anna," he remarked. "I promised her too. She wants to know who took her sister away from her."

"Damn it," Henry snapped. "We all do. We all want answers and I believe we have those answers," he went on. "Everything Jacob had testified was true, all the bruises and cuts on her body matched what he said Thomas did to her. I know that he's responsible but there is nothing I can do about it." He was silent as Patrick stood by the window and looked out to the streets. It seemed like a long time before Patrick replied to him.

"Then why should he be allowed to continue to walk these streets?" Patrick turned but kept his eyes out the clearing on the wall. "Should we allow him to do it again?"

Henry was just about to answer Patrick but was alarmed by screaming out on the street. He ran to the door and stepped out to see what was going on as Patrick followed him. George Cooper was riding his covered wagon and Henry knew right away that something was wrong. The screams weren't his though; they were coming from inside the wagon. Emma, he realized. The wagon paused in front of the apothecary store as Henry and his companion rushed out to see what was happening. "What is going on?"

George turned his head towards the back of the wagon and tried to comfort his daughter. Her mother was also back there but nothing helped the young girl. George turned towards the men and almost cried himself when he said, "They found Jacob Miller guilty of perjury."

"Oh my God," Patrick stated. He imagined Amelia crying for him if roles were different and wondered if Emma had felt the same way that Amelia once did.

Henry didn't ask permission to put one foot on the wagon and push himself up so he could see Emma inside. "Will you come out here, Emma, and talk to me?"

"No," George answered. As far as he was concerned he never wanted his daughter to step foot on Millersport ground again. Henry looked confused and George continued to explain. "They took Jacob straight to the state prison and without him here to protect Emma, I don't want her here. I'm moving the family far away from the Van Martins."

Patrick walked around to the back of the wagon and poked his head through the canvas. He saw Mrs. Cooper trying to comfort her daughter and noticed how Emma was just about rolled up in a ball. She saw him and turned her tear-streaked face towards him. "I can help protect her, Mr. Cooper," Patrick insisted. He couldn't get over how scared the girl looked. His offer would be denied as George said it was best for them to start a new life. "Where will you go?"

"We want to help," Henry added and thought Patrick was being brave to offer such responsibilities. He glanced back in the wagon and could see Emma reach her hand out to Patrick and could see for the first time why his daughter fell in love with him. Henry would've been proud to call him a son-in-law but Thomas took that away before it even became an option. George just looked ahead and shook his head. Henry could tell that he had no plans, only to leave town to protect his family. "George, I know this might sound like a long shot but my cousin moved out west. He said that Indiana was beautiful. I can get in touch with him; ask him to help you out if you would like?" He looked at Emma again and knowing she was leaving town was like learning that his daughter had died all over again. Until Amelia's death, the two girls were never apart and Emma was like a daughter to him. He'd miss her and wanted to make sure she would be well cared for.

George thought about Henry's offer for a few minutes and agreed to head out towards Indiana. He didn't know where they would go or what he would do for a living but knew that he had to take Emma away from Thomas Van Martin, who after all he had gone through still wanted to marry her. He motioned for Patrick to get away from the wagon and when he saw Emma let go of the man's hand, he moved his carriage towards the road that left the village.

Standing together again, Patrick kicked the ground below him. As the dust flew up in the air, he looked to Henry and asked, "You still think we shouldn't do anything about Thomas?"

"It's a tragedy, I know, to see them leave this way but perhaps it's for the best. Thomas will know that he can't control everybody."

Henry tried to be optimistic in the situation but the truth was he couldn't take the law into his own hands. "Where are you going?" He asked as he noticed Patrick walking away.

"To cool off," Patrick replied. He needed to go home and clear his mind of what he witnessed. If he thought too much about Thomas, or the pain he has caused for Emma and her family, or that an innocent man was now on his way to prison because of him, Patrick would go insane. He needed time; time to be alone before he could face the citizens of Millersport.

Turning the other direction, Henry headed back towards his store where he hoped he could escape from the curious people who would want to know what was going on. He watched Patrick walk up the street and hoped that he calmed down. Then Henry went inside to finish his normal business day.

By the next afternoon, everyone had heard the news about Jacob and the Cooper family. Once again, the village was stunned and somber. Many people had gathered at the general store to catch up on the latest information; including Thomas. He wasn't afraid of what they would say to him nor did he care what they thought. He admitted to himself that it was weird not to have Jacob next to him but brushed the thought off his mind. Jacob back stabbed him because of jealousness over a girl and now had what was coming to him. It didn't matter to Thomas that they were once best chums; it was just another button off of his shirt as far as Thomas was concerned.

Anna was inside the store when she noticed Thomas walk in as if he had just as much of a right as everyone else.

She wanted to slap him but realized that he didn't care how his actions affected others. She knew the best thing to do was to leave the store but yet was caught up in the action and didn't want to miss a thing. He was bound to make a fool of himself and Anna thought she could use the humor.

"Jacob deserves all he's going through," Thomas arrogantly shouted to all who were snickering behind his back. They continued to call him names and insult him but it didn't bother him. They were all just jealous of his money, he thought to himself.

"Mr. Van Martin," the grocer said. "Perhaps you should leave."

Thomas was angered by the grocer's comment but wasn't going anywhere. He talked to a group of people and when they turned their backs on him, he went to someone else to talk. Everyone looked away from him and ignored him. He noticed Anna standing by herself watching every move he made. Thomas hadn't bothered going near any of the Samuels since his fiancée died and even more since they tried to pin the murder on him but this time she looked too nice to ignore. He walked straight up to her and noticed how charming she looked and how sweet she smelled. "Well, well, Anna," he spoke to the pretty girl. "It seems like you've grown up into a fine looking woman."

Anna was disgusted with Thomas' appearance and attitude. He had a lot of nerve to think he could befriend her. "Get away from me," Anna remarked with a growl in her voice, "Now!"

"You're still stubborn," he said to her, ignoring that she wanted him to go away. Anna turned her head and that flared a fire inside of him. He was reminded of all the times her sister had turned from him. He was just about to touch her face to bring it back towards him when out of the blue he felt a strong hand on his shoulders.

"She said to get away from her," Patrick yelled at Thomas. "Didn't you hear her?"

When Thomas turned and saw who had the guts to talk to him in that manner, he realized that he was messing with the wrong girl. He didn't know why but Patrick Buchanan was always there for the Samuels women and Thomas was getting sick of him trying to be a hero. "Mind your own funeral," he barked back. The next thing he knew he was being removed from the store by his collar and everyone inside and out were laughing hysterically. Thomas wasn't hurt but the surrounding laughter had angered him. He stood and straightened himself out and noticed that Buchanan's back was turned away from him. He shouted so all could hear, "Don't have the guts to face me, do you Buchanan?"

Anna had rushed outside when Patrick came to her rescue and stood by his side. She was glad he was there for her although she was convinced she would've taken care of herself if he weren't. She worried about him because Thomas was getting in his face and Anna knew Patrick would not take any more from him. "Patrick, let's leave. He isn't worth it," she tried to convince him. Patrick didn't listen to her but instead turned back towards Thomas and hovered over him as they argued with each other. Anna became alarmed when she spied a barking iron sticking out of Patrick's pants. She'd never known him to carry the weapon before and was concerned for his sake. She feared that he would do something stupid to revenge Amelia's death. Again she begged him to leave the store with her but Patrick wasn't listening.

Patrick took two steps and if he took anymore he would've stepped right on Thomas. He was contemplating squashing Van Martin like a bug caught under his boot but the thought passed him as he looked down. "I've had as much as I can stand from someone like you, Van Martin."

"And who are you to speak to me in such a tone?" Thomas was foolish for letting Patrick get so close to him but he had no fear.

"No," Patrick answered with his own line of questions. "Who are you to treat people the way you do?" As he breathed down the younger man's throat, Patrick thought of Henry and how he tried to convince him that there was nothing they could do to Thomas. He wanted to control himself but he knew the man in front of him was responsible for the death of his love and that alone made him want to kill.

Anna was getting nervous about the situation. She knew that if Patrick were to shoot Thomas, his family would make sure that Patrick was executed. She didn't want that for him but didn't know what to do. Out of the corner of her eyes she saw her father and brother walking towards the store. They must've had heard Patrick's and Thomas' voices screaming at each other. She ran to them and told them about the gun. "Oh Father, he will do something stupid if nobody stops him."

"You're going to pay for killing Amelia," Patrick continued screaming at Thomas. He was surprised that he hadn't strangled the puny jerk yet. "You son-of-a-bitch."

"Let me remind you I've been found not guilty by the court of law," Thomas spit back. He wasn't afraid of Patrick's threats and dared to step on his toes even more. "You are more likely the reason she is dead."

Henry and David raced up to the scene and interrupted the feuding men. David, as much as he would have liked to see Patrick rip Thomas' face off, grabbed a hold of Thomas' arms and pulled him away while Henry held Patrick back. "This isn't the way to take care of things," Henry reminded Patrick but could tell that he was already fueled by Thomas' behavior. He continued to talk to his friend to stop him from doing anything he would regret later.

Anna had stood by their side also told Patrick to stop his nonsense. He appeared to be listening to them. They let their guards down when they saw the calmness return in Patrick's face but soon after wished that they hadn't.

David felt a strong urge to wring Thomas' neck while he held him back. He thought that Patrick was correct in saying he should pay for his crimes yet David knew that going about it themselves wasn't right. "Why do you look for trouble, Thomas," David asked as he let go of him. Thomas dusted himself off as if he was preparing for another round and David warned him to stay away from Patrick. He didn't listen; Thomas pushed him aside and moved back into action. This caused David to face the direction of his father and just as he did, he saw Patrick reach for the barking iron that Anna had told them about. In a flash he saw Patrick aim the weapon at Thomas and knew that he would get his revenge. In an instant he thought that his sister wouldn't want Patrick to be hung or sent to prison for a crime such as this and the Van Martins would see to just that for sure. Without hesitation, for his beloved sister's sake and not for Thomas', David jumped in front of the flying bullet and took the hit and fell fast to the ground.

Screams sounded from all over the general store. Patrick lowered his gun as he realized that David had been hit instead of Thomas and ran to the injured man. He shook with nerves as he got closer and saw the blood escaping David's body. "Oh my God," he screamed out loud. Then he looked to Thomas who was still there but too stunned to move.

Henry and Anna had rushed over to David as well and all they could think of was helping the fallen man. They heard Patrick repeat over and over again that he didn't mean to shoot David and they didn't turn their backs on him. Instead, Henry glared up at Thomas and threatened, "You better get out of here or I'll let him get you." He returned to David who was bleeding from the wound that hit him in the chest. Then he spoke to Patrick, "Help me get him to my house," and when Patrick didn't appear to hear him, he shouted, "It was an accident, now help me." Several men who were watching the confrontation came over to lend a hand. "Anna, go get my employee as fast as you can and tell him to bring my surgical supplies."

Anna didn't hesitate to run. She ran faster than she had ever run in her life as her eyes stung with tears. She was so afraid that something would happen and now knew that her fears were trying to tell her something. Anna continued running and didn't stop until she had done what her father had told her to do.

Thomas took off and ran home. He knew from that moment on that he couldn't take on Buchanan or the Samuels. Even after Patrick had shot David, Henry had glared at him with hatred and not the man who shot his son. He decided that he would talk to his father about getting away for a while until the dust cleared. For once he was afraid of someone. There was no way he would bring charges up against Patrick. He knew it was time to leave the citizens of Millersport but vowed that he would someday return and when he did, he would have his portion of revenge.

The family, including Patrick, waited in the sitting room as Henry and his employee worked frantic in a bedroom to remove the bullet. Nobody spoke or cried. Everyone was as quiet as could be so they could hear what was going on upstairs. Beth was beside herself and attempted to run up the stairs just to be held back by Phillip. "Let them help him," he told her. "He'll allow you to go up as soon as he thinks its best."

Patrick shook as Anna rubbed his back to calm him. Every time he'd see Beth trying to get to her husband his heart broke more. The incident made him hate Thomas even more. The others had told him it wasn't his fault and they would've done the same thing if given the chance. He knew they meant well but thought they wouldn't have missed the target.

Up in the bedroom, Henry did all he could. The bullet sat on the night stand as he made his oldest son as comfortable as possible. David lost too much blood and Henry knew that he would lose him. He'd sent the employee down to wash up and to tell Beth that she could come see

David. While he waited, he prayed for the strength to get through the death of another one of his children.

David laid in agony but he wanted to spend his last moments alive with his family and not sleeping. "Father," he whispered. "Be strong this time."

Henry knew what his son was talking about. He decided not to let the pain engulf him again. Just as he was about to assure David, the door burst opened. Beth rushed in and went straight to her husband's side and the rest of the family followed. He'd given permission for her to come to the room but should've known that the rest would too. He stood and allowed room for her to sit next to David.

Beth cried at the sight of her husband. He smiled up at her which made her feel worse. Her hand became wet with perspiration as she wiped his hair out of his eyes. "You're going to be all right," she informed him and prayed that she was correct.

"Shh," he spoke to her as he held her hand. David looked around the melancholy faces and couldn't understand why they were somber. He was off to see Amelia and his mother again, and David couldn't have been happier. In the back of the room he noticed Ruth and Minnie, each holding onto one of his children. He knew Beth would survive and knew that the children would as well but wondered if they'd remember him when they were older. He never thought they would be fatherless as they grew up and the thought made him sad. Everyone spoke to him at the same time, but their words were becoming hard to hear. Their lips moved, but no sounds were coming out. "Where's Patrick?"

"He went out to the porch," Anna had said but David couldn't make out what she was saying.

"Please don't hold this against him," he breathed. "It was an accident. He was just revenging Amelia's death." His eyes became heavier than he'd ever known them to be and David couldn't hang on any longer. His hand slipped off of Beth's as David passed away.

The family had their moment to say goodbye and then gathered back downstairs. Patrick sat on the top step of the porch when he heard them emerging down the stairs. He needed no one to tell him he'd just killed a man. An uncontrolled sickness came about his stomach as he leaned over and threw up in the bushes. A hand touched his shoulder to help him up. He'd expected it to be Anna, who had been helping him through hard times since his return from the war, but was surprised to see Henry stand before him.

"This isn't your fault," Henry said to Patrick as he looked at him through blurry eyes. "I would've liked to shoot that bastard myself. Come inside, I need to have a talk with my family and you must realize by now, that includes you." He reached down and grabbed Patrick's arm to help him stand and the two of them leaned against each other as they entered the house.

The first thing Patrick noticed was Beth cradling her two young children. Right away he knelt beside her and apologized. She cried on his shoulder as he held her tight. As he wiped her eyes, Henry spoke.

"We can't continue to lose the ones we love because we're trying to find out what happened to Amelia." He paused as he recalled all the events that took place since the day he gave her hand to the Van Martins. "It's in God's hands now to punish her killer. We tried but its backfiring on us. It's time to let go of Amelia's murder," he looked to Patrick to assure that he was talking to him. "We have to."

The rest hung their heads at the reminder of what they've lost. Patrick looked up to Henry and nodded then to Anna to see her weak smile at him. Later when the group had broken up, he apologized to her for not keeping his promise. Anna understood; she wasn't the child she was the day Patrick Buchanan moved to Millersport. She was a woman now; one who understood him and cared for him like no one has ever before- except for her sister, Amelia Samuels.

Epilogue
August 25, 1813, retold

Blood trickled down Amelia's leg after she scraped it against a sharp rock. Her head throbbed from the blow she'd received from Thomas causing her the inability to stand. She could hear him approaching her but felt she was going nowhere. Keeping her eyes ahead of her to find a tree or something large enough to hide behind, she didn't realize that he caught up. A strong hand grabbed her ankle as she let out another cry. It was an effort just trying to make any kind of noise. When Thomas kicked and jumped on her chest earlier, she felt like her insides collapsed. As she opened her mouth to call out for help, her sore body couldn't manage the sound.

There was somebody in the distance. His presence was felt by her but he wasn't helping. Amelia begged, both for Thomas to stop tormenting her and for the mystery man to lend a hand. Her attempts were useless.

"Leave now," Thomas turned his head and shouted. "Never speak a word of this, ever. She will respect me from now on." He could hear Amelia trying to plea for help but it wasn't loud enough for anyone other than himself to hear. The rustling of tree branch let him know that his friend had left, and he was alone with Amelia at last.

He turned his attention back to his misbehaved fiancée. Thomas slid his belt off of his pants, pulled Amelia's hands behind her back, and tied them together. She groaned and Thomas swore that she was getting louder. The last thing he wanted was for someone to find him treating her the way he was and was afraid that she was gaining her strength back enough to scream. He pulled his shirt off and used it to gag her mouth. He'd waited a long time to take her and though he would rather have her be a willing participant, he knew that she would refuse him. "After tonight you'll desire me and the next time you beg me it'll be for me to make passionate

300

love to you." He could feel her panicking underneath him. His manhood pushed the insides of his pants as he used one hand to release himself from the confinement. Thomas straddled her as he pulled her dress up to her midsection. He guided himself towards her tender spot and the anticipation of taking her virginity made him laugh. Without regards to how it would feel for her, Thomas shoved himself inside of her. Right away his anger grew at the realization she wasn't a virgin. His fingers tightened around her neck as he scowled, "You little whore." Still inside of her, his erection became excited as he tried to choke her. Thomas thrust several times as he hung onto her uncooperative hips then released his climax deep inside of her.

Amelia became numb from all the pain she'd been experiencing. She thought about how sweet her love making had been with Patrick and how it was ruined because of Thomas. Amelia wondered if Patrick would still have her now she was tainted by the one man she'd despised for so long. She could feel the tears rolling down the side of her face. "I hate you, Thomas Van Martin," she spoke after he released the shirt from her mouth.

Thomas was disgusted with her and decided that she needed more of a punishment. "I'm calling a village meeting tomorrow. You'll be marked a jezebel and your father a trader."

Amelia's knees were pulled close to her chest as she sat rocking back and forth. As far as she was concerned there was nothing more humiliating that he could do to her after his unkind acts upon her. "How Thomas?" She quizzed. "To tell them I'm not a virgin you will have to tell them you raped me."

Thomas' hand came down hard as he struck her across the face. "I'm not as stupid as you think I am. I will tell them I spied you and that stranger in the act. You'll never find a man who'll give you a happy life, the stranger will be hung for sexually violating you because they won't believe you when you say you wanted it, and your father will be executed."

"What does my father have to do with it?"

"Treason, you're father betrayed our country and I'm going to the authorities."

The conversation she had with Patrick flooded her memory of her father's crimes. As far as she was concerned the authorities were most likely already on their way to Millersport. She had to think of a way to stop Thomas. "I'll be your wife with no more fight, just please don't do that."

Thomas looked down at the beaten girl. Amelia was shameful and marriage to her was now out of the question. He straightened his clothes out and kicked her one final time. "You're not worthy of being a Van Martin." He walked away and never looked back. Part of him was thrilled that he could have his way with her and part of him was angered by the outcome.

Major General Downy was making his journey out of Millersport when he heard faint screams in the distance. The dark hours were upon him and although the sounds alarmed him, he felt it was not of his concern. There was a war going, and he was already in a sour mood from Buchanan's rejection to join the militia. A few minutes later he spotted a young man running out of the woods then bending over and vomiting onto the ground. There were still noises coming from the direction the young man came from. Downy investigated.

He walked quietly into the area and saw in the distance another young man and a young girl who looked to be in trouble. His unheard footsteps, a skill he gained being in the military, brought him closer to the scene as he watched the rape go on before him. Immediately he thought to help the girl but then stopped in his tracts. If he stopped the crime being displayed before him, he'd have to take the man to the nearest law enforcer and state what he had witnessed. War was the only thing on his mind, no time to deal with locals. Still, he wanted to make sure the girl was all right.

Downy had inched closer to the scene and overheard the conversation. The man spoke of turning her father into the authorities, causing Downy to realize the girl was a Samuels. He wondered for a moment which daughter she was but was not concerned at the moment. Henry was not the only one who would be punished for his funding; his daughter was taking abuse as well. He ducked down into the brushes when he saw the man he now knew as Thomas headed in his direction.

When the coast was cleared Downy hurried over to the girl. "What's going on here?" He asked as though he caught his soldiers doing something they shouldn't have been. "What's your name?"

Amelia sat crying when she was approached by a large man in an Army uniform. She had no idea who he was or what rank he held but her instincts told her he was in the village to capture her father. "Why didn't you help me?" She quizzed instead of answering. "I called out for you, heard you out there." She assumed this was the same man that Thomas had sent away even though she begged for help.

Downy sat down next to her and handed her a hanky from his pocket to clean herself up. "I heard no such pleas. Who are you?"

"Amelia Samuels," she stated, but he cut her off from saying more.

"As in Henry Samuels' eldest daughter?" He looked to girl to see her nod her head. "Do you know who I am?"

For the first time since his arrival Amelia realized the importance of this man and fear again rose inside of her. She had tried so hard to find her father, to warn him that someone might look for him but Thomas' stunt had prevented that. She feared that the officer already reached her father, feared that he was in custody some place waiting to be tried, feared that he was already dead. "Not exactly," she cried, "but please tell me that my father is all right. I know what he has done, and I knew it was only a matter of time before you would come looking for him."

He couldn't get over her loyalty to Henry when all that unfolded before him, moments before, was caused by her father's treason. "You mean you don't know?" He knew leading her to think the worst was cruel, but he was good at it. Her already sad face became more stressed and Downy's heart softened just a little. He reached his hand over to her shoulder and said, "You're father will be taken care of in due time. As of this moment, he's fine."

After all that has happened to her, the engagement, the distance it put her with her loved ones, the abuse and rape, her father was still the most important person in her life. "Thank you," she spoke. Her body was in a lot of pain and even a simple act like talking had made her ache.

"For now," Downy stated. He knew Amelia was physically hurt and wanted to help her but he was a man of his word and would not sugar coat things to her to make her feel better. "Let me help you home then I can bring your father to the capital with me. Save me time and another trip to Millersport."

"What? No," she wanted to shout if her lungs would let her.

"Don't take it personal girl, I'm doing my job." Downy heard her ask him questions about what would happen to Henry; questions he felt she didn't need to know at the moment. He didn't expect her sudden pleas.

"Please don't take him," Amelia begged with fresh tears rolling down her face. "My father made mistakes, but he's a good man."

He chuckled at the thought. "How can you say that? Look what has happened to you tonight because of him." She looked confused, and he continued. "Don't you think I know everything that has happened because Henry Samuels interfered with the US government?"

Amelia frowned, everything that happened to her was her father's fault but still she could not stand by while they took him away from her and her family. "Please sir, I still love him and I forgive him for what he's done to me and to the country. There must be another way."

"If I don't take Henry Samuels for the crimes he committed, who would I," he started but let his words trail off as he thought about the situation for a moment. There was a time back when he was younger when a robber had slit the throats of his wife and young daughter. He remembered begging the robber to do the same to him but he was only stabbed in the stomach and left for dead. The authorities captured the robber, and he was rightfully sentenced to a life in prison. For Downy, every day he lived without his family was a punishment from God for not protecting them better. He brought his thoughts back to Henry Samuels and knew that if he loved Amelia half as much as Downy loved his, he would feel a painful punishment if Amelia's life was taken for his treason.

The girl was crying and the Major General felt bad for her. He second guessed his decision, but this was war and she'd only be a lost soldier and would not weigh on his conscience. Trying to make her feel better enough to be comfortable around him, he spoke at last. "You're right; your father is a good man. Let's get you cleaned up so you can get home and care for those wounds."

Amelia sensed softness in him as she asked, "My father?"

"Your father will be fine," he answered. It wasn't a lie as far as he was concerned. Henry Samuels would grieve and pray forgiveness of his sins but in the court of law, he'd be fine in the long run. Downy stood up and waited for Amelia to follow but could see the pain it was causing her.

"I think my leg is broken," she cried as she felt his hand grab onto her arm to help pull her up. The agony shot through her body and she let out a scream. The Major General swooped her up in his arms and walked towards the creek.

Her scream alarmed him though he knew she did it out of discomfort and not for her safety. Still, he couldn't chance someone else coming to her rescue. "Shhh," he comforted her. He knew that she was weak, and he'd have no struggle from her. "Amelia, you must wash up before you go back home or people would ask questions. Think you can stand in the water?"

He let her down into the cold wet bank as she nodded her head. It hurt her to stand on it but she knew he was right and that she couldn't go back into the village with all the mud and blood still covering her body. They'd question what happened to her leg and why she will have bruises but to protect her father; she'd lie and tell everyone she fell. Before bending over to clean up, she questioned more. "What about Thomas Van Martin? When I refuse to marry him, he'll report my father."

Downy grinned at her innocence. In walking towards her death, she was still concerned with Henry Samuels. "Don't worry; I'll take care of all of that." He saw her look of approval in the moonlight and encouraged her to continue washing. As she stepped into deeper water, Downy slipped on a pair of gloves that were tucked into his pocket. When she bent over to wash her face, the Major General acted on an act of war; grabbed hold of her fragile body with one hand and her head with the other as she struggled just below the surface of the water. It wasn't long before her body stopped moving and he let go of his grip. He stood knee deep in the water, waiting to see if there was any movement from Amelia, until she was dead.

Walking back to dry land, Downy wrung out his gloves and placed them back in his pocket. He turned towards the body he noticed floating out to deeper parts of the creek and declared the case against Henry Samuels to be over.

About C.P Murphy

C.P Murphy lives and writes in upstate New York. She has been writing stories since she learned how to pick up a pencil. In 2003, her first novella was published. Although it left much to be desired, it opened her eyes to the world of publishing. When she's not writing for herself, C.P. Murphy helps other authors. She has written reviews, shared their news on social media, and assisted with many behind the scenes activities such as manuscript setup, proofreading, and occasional ghost writing. She works in correctional healthcare.

"Amelia's Story" was inspired by actual events. C.P. Murphy's village, characters, and plot have all been fictional but what happens to Amelia, happened. Many readers have shown their dislike for the book, saying it was a waste of time. This book was written for all the new generations of C.P. Murphy's hometown. It's her way of telling the story that was told to her, and generations before her. In no way was this book meant to entertain readers, but the author hopes you did feel something for it. Thank you for reading.

Find more books by C.P. Murphy

Love Everlasting
Paperback: 146 pages
Publisher: CreateSpace Independent Publishing Platform
Language: English
ISBN-10: 1492992062
ISBN-13: 978-1492992066

Product Dimensions: 6 x 0.4 x 9 inches

What would you do if you were still very young and your spouse suddenly died? Would you remarry? What if you were the young spouse that died? Would you want your other half to live a life he/she deserves, to be happy, have kids? Love Everlasting is a story about two people faced with these questions.

Love Everlasting has been called a cute story and quick weekend read!

St. Matthew's House
Paperback: 168 pages
Publisher: CreateSpace Independent Publishing Platform
Language: English
ISBN-10: 1540372316
ISBN-13: 978-1540372314
Product Dimensions: 5 x .5 x 8 inches

Sophia Demitri moved to Greenville to escape her obsessive ex-boyfriend. After renting a house she found through an online classified, she learns that her new home used to be a church.

Frankie Everhart lives his life carelessly until visions of his deceased bride, and a mysterious engagement ring, sends Sophia straight into his arms.

Things are going bump-in-the-night in the St. Matthew's House and Sophia thinks she's going insane. Her and Frankie are falling in love....but the St. Matthew's House has a mind of its own.

To learn more about C.P. Murphy, or to sign up for her newsletter, please go to her website at www.cpmurphy.com

Other places to connect:
Facebook: www.facebook.com/cpmurphy73
Twitter: www.twitter.com/cpmurphy73
GoodReads: www.goodreads.com/Cpmurphy
Blog: http://randomthoughts.cpmurphy.com

Made in the USA
Las Vegas, NV
07 December 2020